ACCIDENTALLY WEDDED to a WEREWOLF

Isabelle Taylor writes sweet, steamy fantasy romance books for adults. She works in one of the largest independent bookstores in New Zealand and stops to pat dogs in the street. If your local bookstore allows dogs, please bring them in! You could make a bookseller's day.

isabelletaylorauthor.com

- @isabelletaylorauthor
- @isabelletaylorauthor

Also by Isabelle Taylor

Claw Haven series

Christmas with a Chimera
Only One for the Orc
Snowed In with an Incubus

Accidentally Wedded to a Werewolf

ISABELLE TAYLOR

HarperCollins*Publishers* Ltd
1 London Bridge Street
London SE1 9GF

www.harpercollins.co.uk

HarperCollins*Publishers*
Macken House, 39/40 Mayor Street Upper
Dublin 1, D01 C9W8, Ireland

First published by Isabelle Taylor 2024
This edition published with revised text by HarperCollins*Publishers* Ltd 2026

1

Copyright © Isabelle Taylor 2024
Revised text copyright © Isabelle Taylor 2025

Isabelle Taylor asserts the moral right to be identified as the author of this work.

A catalogue record for this book is available from the British Library.

ISBN: 978-0-00-879831-4

This novel is entirely a work of fiction.
The names, characters and incidents portrayed in it are
the work of the author's imagination. Any resemblance to
actual persons, living or dead, events or localities is
entirely coincidental.

Printed and bound in the UK using 100% Renewable
Electricity at CPI Group (UK) Ltd

All rights reserved. No part of this publication may be
reproduced, stored in a retrieval system, or transmitted,
in any form or by any means, electronic, mechanical,
photocopying, recording or otherwise, without the
prior written permission of the publishers.

Without limiting the exclusive rights of any author, contributor or the publisher of
this publication, any unauthorised use of this publication to train generative artificial
intelligence (AI) technologies is expressly prohibited. HarperCollins also exercise
their rights under Article 4(3) of the Digital Single Market Directive 2019/790 and
expressly reserve this publication from the text and data mining exception.

Accidentally Wedded to a Werewolf contains on-page sex, knotting, discussions of arson, an unwanted psychic bond, and family illness.

Chapter One

Luna glared out at the snow disdainfully.

"I'm going to drive off a cliff and die," she announced to her empty car. "Play something fun at my funeral."

Her phone's loudspeaker crackled from the passenger seat. She paid for the best phone coverage, but the mountains surrounding the road made her think they didn't actually mean *full* coverage.

"Luna Stack," her fiancé said. "Putting the *fun* in *funeral*."

There was an annoying slurping sound.

Luna narrowed her eyes. "Are you getting started without me?"

"Babe," Hector said. "I'm not even on the *plane* yet. I don't leave for another four hours. I'm still at the restaurant having drinks with your family. They say hi, by the way."

"Hi," Luna said sourly. "Is Dad having fun? I hope he's having fun. I'm at a conference in the middle of Nowhere, Alaska, for *his* company."

"You *insisted*," Hector reminded her. "He didn't even want you to go!"

Luna ignored him, wiping a stray streak of lip gloss off her chin in the rearview mirror. "I'm gonna get stuck out here with nothing but bikinis and skirts for warmth. I packed for the beach, not this winter wonderland bullshit. Can you pass me to Dad?"

There were sounds of a scuffle.

Luna frowned. "Hector?"

Her brother's voice echoed through the receiver. "Hi, Luna. Hector says you're stranded in monster country. Don't get eaten."

"Monster country," Luna repeated. "*Everywhere's* monster country, dipshit. Your best friend's a vampire, Clancy."

"I heard there are way more in those mountains," came Clancy's breathless voice. He sounded tipsy, which he shouldn't have been, since he was still nineteen.

"Are Mom and Dad letting you drink?" Luna asked.

Clancy snorted. "I'm in *college*, Lu. I've been drunk before."

"No, I know. I'm just surprised they let you after you puked in a potted plant at Mom's birthday party."

"I had food poisoning!"

"Yeah, from all the tequila," Luna groaned. "Hector, be a dear and take the phone away from my idiot brother."

"On it, Popsicle Princess," Hector called.

Luna rolled her eyes. "I'm not frozen yet!"

There were more scuffling noises and a whine of protest from Clancy.

Luna peered out at the road. The snow was definitely getting thicker, and she had another hour before she reached the airport. She had never driven in snow like this before, and every passing minute in this snowy hellscape only made her more convinced she was going to freeze to death in an icy wreck.

She poked at her phone, bringing up Google Maps. There was a town coming up, right? She wouldn't *actually* get stranded in her car, slowly freezing into an heiress popsicle.

Google Maps dropped in and out of service, her little dot appearing and disappearing on the long stretch of road.

"Still can't believe I'm the only one who had to go to this stupid conference," Luna mumbled as she tapped hopefully at her glitchy phone.

Her dad's voice echoed distantly through the crackling receiver. "You begged, honey. How was it? As boring as I told you?"

Luna sighed. It *had* been kind of boring. And the parts that hadn't been boring, she couldn't talk to her dad about.

Her dad let out a satisfied grunt. "What did I say? Stacks aren't made for work, hon."

"You're the CEO of a major company, Dad!"

"So I can get my employees to do the work for me," he replied. "I've done all the hard work in my youth. Now we can lie back and enjoy life."

Luna grumbled under her breath. It wasn't that she didn't *appreciate* the lavish lifestyle her dad provided her, all travel and parties and fun. She just wondered sometimes what it would be like to…*do* something. Hence begging to get sent to a boring company conference. She was technically her dad's employee, after all. She had the degrees to qualify her for it and everything.

"I did have some interesting chats with the marketing team," she said hopefully.

Her dad groaned. "Luna. Don't start."

"I'm not," she said hastily. "I just—"

"I know you got those fancy degrees," he continued patiently. "But let's face it, hon. You're not made to sit in an office and send emails about which logo makes people want to buy hand towels more. Stop bothering the marketing team with all your little social media ideas, alright?"

"Right," Luna said bitterly. She actually *had* been about to tell her dad about logos. She'd secretly been in touch with the marketing team for years. They *loved* it when she "bothered" them. They *asked* her to bother them at least once a month, cc'ing her on email chains as they discussed their latest projects.

Her dad was happy with her work when he thought it was someone else's, but every time she tried to bring it up, he told her to stick to what she was good at: having fun and throwing parties. Which, admittedly, she *was* pretty great at. But part of her longed to know what it would be like to do something else. Something that didn't end after one night or require cleanup in the morning. Not that Luna ever stuck around for the cleanup. The cleaning staff could take care of that.

She tweaked the windshield wiper controller desperately in the hope that there might be a secret faster setting if she held them at the right angle. No dice. The snow kept battering down, only allowing her glimpses of the white road in between gusts.

"Dad, I don't know if I'm going to make my flight. Can you book me a new one if I get stuck here overnight?"

"Send me the details when you get out of the snow," her dad said. "I have to go, your mother's calling. They did something horrible to our mai tais."

"A fate worse than death," Luna said flatly. "I'll just be here. Your only daughter. Suffering. Hope I don't get trapped and have to start eating local townsfolk, Donner-style."

Another burst of static. Luna cursed at the cliffs surrounding the roads.

"I hate Alaska," she yelled uselessly at the flurrying snow. "Why are you *like* this?"

"Definitely yell at it more," came Hector's voice down the crackling line. "That'll fix it. Hey, did you know Alaska's covered in snow for six months of the year?"

"That's ridiculous," Luna hissed, longing for their heated pool at home in sunny California as she stared out at the street, which was slowly but surely whiting out. "Six months out of a *year*? Who in their right mind would *live* here?"

"Eighty thousand people."

"Idiots," Luna declared.

The car swerved. Luna yelped, jerking the steering wheel as the car wobbled from side to side on the slippery road.

"Babe?" Another slurping sound. "Did you die?"

"I'm fine," Luna said, slowing down to a crawl. "I'm— Oh, thank god, there's a town."

"Does it say *abandon hope, all ye who enter, you're about to get eaten by an orc*?"

"Ha, ha," Luna said. "No. It says…"

She squinted through the snow. It was hard to see anything beyond her windshield, let alone the half-covered wooden sign on the side of the road. The font was almost too swirly to read. Like the person designing it had gotten too excited about being fancy and forgotten that the point of road signs was for people to read them quickly and clearly as they careened past ten miles over the speed limit.

"*Claw Haven*," Luna read out, "*for the monster who wants some peace and quiet.*"

Hector hummed. "Huh. Doesn't sound very murdery. Maybe you won't get eaten after all."

"Nobody's eating me," Luna protested.

Her car swerved again. Luna straightened out with an embarrassingly fearful squeak.

"Hey," Hector said, voice softening through the static. "Worse comes to worst, you stay overnight in some crappy little town, then get the next flight out. I'll meet you in the Bahamas. You, me, some meetings I'm going to blow off, and mai tais made by someone with more than two hours of bartending experience."

Luna laughed shakily. "That bad, huh?"

"*So* bad. I know your mom's a drama queen, but this time, she's right on the—"

The phone fuzzed out into static.

"Hector," Luna said. "Babe?"

Nothing. The static grew louder and louder until Luna winced and stabbed the End Call button.

"Ooookay," she said. "This is fine. Just gotta find a motel. Do they have motels in towns this tiny? They have to. Right?"

Her phone sat in the drink holder, silent and useless on the subject of tiny-town motels, or any motels for that matter. A quick inspection showed that she had absolutely zero cell service.

"Great," Luna muttered. She searched up *motels Claw Haven*. No hits. But there *was* a place not far away. *Musgrove Inn*. It had one four-star rating saying the service was good and they had a wide range of dietary options for the mer reviewer, who was used to eating human food when he traveled. But the inn needed some touch-ups. Apparently, the owners had remodeled it themselves, and they were *not* professional contractors.

"As long as it's got a roof, four walls and indoor heating, I'm down," Luna declared.

She attached her phone to her dashboard holder and set off. It was only a few minutes away, but she wasn't taking any chances in this weather.

She eyed the road as her glitchy dot crept closer and closer to the inn. Her wheels kept skidding, which was even more alarming now that she had things to crash into. She drove down a main road, catching glimpses of stores as she crawled past: a café, a bakery, a chocolate store, a florist and a cute little bookstore. Claw Haven would probably be picturesque in the morning: a quaint town covered with snow. But right now, it was a seething, hellish snowscape that Luna wanted nothing more than to escape. Hopefully, the roads would be clear enough to drive tomorrow. She didn't want to be here any longer than she had to.

"Cliff Street," Luna read aloud from her map. "Come on, Cliff Street."

"*In one hundred feet, turn right,*" Google Maps said.

A tiny road sign glinted through the snow: *Cliff Street*.

Luna made a triumphant noise and turned.

Her car swerved again. Luna tried forcing it back into its lane, but it was too late. Her wheels locked, sending the car skidding helplessly off the road.

Luna yelled, pumping the brakes. Nothing worked. Her car pointed straight at a signpost. *Welcome to Musgrove Inn.*

"Wait!" Luna yelled as she barreled toward the sign. "Shit, wait!"

No use. Her car cracked into the signpost, breaking the wood in half before coming to a shuddering stop in the snowy parking lot.

"*You have reached your destination*," Google Maps said calmly.

Chapter Two

"The roof's gonna cave in," Leo announced.

Oliver Musgrove sighed and looked up from the front desk. His six-year-old nephew was lying in the middle of the empty lobby, staring up at the ceiling.

"Nothing's going to cave in," Oliver told him, shuffling a stack of invoices. "Get out of the lobby. The guests don't want to step over a kid to get to the front desk."

"We don't have guests," Leo pointed out, not moving. He kicked his feet in the air, his light-up sneakers glinting. "Mr. Jackson says it's gonna cave in, and his *job* is roofs."

"His job isn't just *roofs*," Oliver said, scowling. "And Jackson needs to keep his nose out of our business."

The inn was *fine*. Sure, the roof leaked. The doors sometimes wobbled on their hinges. The pipes screeched when you turned on the hot faucet. But you put up with certain things in an old place like this, as Oliver kept insisting to the rest of his family, who were currently being useless in the guest common room while Oliver did paperwork.

Leo pushed himself up with a sigh, padding over to the front desk. Every step made his light-up sneakers glow even brighter.

He cocked his head, listening to the sounds of the party. Leo was full wolf, his hearing just as keen as Oliver's.

Oliver focused. He could hear every irritating noise through the twisting hallways: loud music, an aunt's grating giggles. Somebody roared in laughter, someone else roared with the distinct tones of an orc. And underneath it all were Grandmother's low tones, too muffled to make out. He wouldn't be able to hear them at all if she weren't his family. Werewolf senses got even keener when it came to pack.

Leo rested his chin on the counter. "Are you coming to the party, Uncle Ollie?"

"No," Oliver snapped. "I'm working."

Leo pouted. "Dad says you're only pretending to work so you don't have to talk to people."

"Well, your dad's a dick," Oliver said and winced. "Don't tell him I swore in front of you. He's still pissed about the A-hole thing."

"Asshole," Leo corrected proudly.

Oliver shushed him. His little brother Ben had gotten annoyingly uptight about swear words since Leo came along. Actually, he'd gotten so responsible that everybody started joking that maybe he could be alpha one day. When it first came up, Oliver had laughed along with the rest of his family. Oliver's place as the next alpha was inevitable. Grandmother was solid in her decision, and so was Oliver.

Then the fire happened, and the pack moved to Claw Haven. A proud new start, they claimed. For Oliver, it had been a guilty slink with his tail between his legs, sitting on a secret he could never tell the family. He started snapping at people, going off alone instead of airing out his problems to a trusted ear. His pack thought it was the guilt of an up-and-coming leader not being able to protect his family from a crazy hunter who'd tried to burn them in their beds. No one knew the real reason it shook Oliver so deeply. And if Oliver had anything to say about it, they'd never find out.

Ben came barreling into the lobby, his wife, Sabine, under his bulky arm.

"Wondering where you two got to," Ben said, leaning on the counter next to his son. "What's the holdup?"

Leo pointed at the roof. "Roof's gonna cave in!"

"It's not caving in," Oliver protested as they all looked up at it.

Outside, the wind howled. Oliver winced. The storm was picking up, cold air leaking through the thin insulation.

Sabine squinted, blond hair falling over her scarred eye. "I don't know about caving in, but that's definitely going to drip. Do you want to get the buckets, honey?"

"Okay," said Leo, rushing off. He was still excited about the inn, always asking what he could do to help. Oliver almost felt bad turning him down all the time.

Sabine pushed her hair out of her face. She'd never been embarrassed by the scar over her left eye, even when it was bright red and healing in the days after Ben found her in the woods mauled by a bear.

A scar means I survived, she'd told Oliver once. *Why would I want to hide that?*

Ben reached over the counter, tweaking an invoice Oliver was stacking. "Put down the work for five seconds, man. Come and have fun with us. Remember fun?"

"No," Oliver said sarcastically.

Ben snorted, stroking a line down Sabine's shoulder absently. Once upon a time, they used to throw parties, huge and lavish. Everyone would be invited. Ben and Oliver would shout and dance and run through the woods until their legs hurt. They'd even gotten matching tattoos on their elbows: *party animals*, with a howling wolf curling on top of the words.

Now here they were. Oliver was doing work so he wouldn't

have to go to a party, and Ben was ditching early to hang out with his wife and kid. How times changed.

"It's a great time up there," Ben tried. "The townsfolk are super friendly. I think you'd like them—don't roll your eyes, jackass; you *would* like them if you just talked to them."

"I've talked to them," Oliver said, shuffling his invoices again so he'd have to rearrange them in a second. "They won't stop talking to me. Every time I dare leave the inn, everyone's going *Hi, Oliver! How's it going, Oliver? Try my chocolates, Oliver; they're wolf-safe!*"

"Wow," Sabine said flatly. "What a bunch of jerks."

"I hate it when people give me free chocolate I can actually eat," Ben agreed.

"It's condescending," Oliver argued. "She keeps *asking*, like one day I'm going to change my mind about her stupid little chocolates—"

A throat cleared. Oliver looked up just in time to see Jackson Jay, dragonborn and roof guy extraordinaire, come around the corner. He looked awkward, scratching his scales in the way he did when he wanted to get out of a conversation. Which, in Oliver's opinion, wasn't often enough.

Then a woman followed after him, and Oliver understood why he looked awkward. Beth Haberdash was the hedgehog woman who owned the chocolate store on Main Street. She would be sweet if she wasn't so annoying. Always bumbling and stammering and getting all apologetic about selling her own chocolates, like she wasn't the one who opened the damn shop. And she kept getting things stuck on the spikes protruding from her back.

Oliver grimaced. This was what he got for not paying attention to his surroundings. He tried to be better nowadays, always on alert. But holy shit, always being on alert was *exhausting*.

"Hiya," said Jackson. "Just about to head out. Wanted to say goodbye to all the hosts first."

"Bye," Oliver said loudly.

Ben gave him an exasperated look, then turned to Jackson. "Thanks for coming, Jackson. Good to finally get everyone around for a housewarming party."

A particularly loud howl of wind made them all look around nervously.

Jackson pointed at the roof. "I'm telling you, one day soon that roof's gonna—"

"The roof's not going to cave in," Oliver said.

Jackson shrugged. "If you say so. If it does, I'll come help fix it."

"It won't happen," Oliver said icily. "I fixed it myself. It's a solid roof."

Another gust of wind rocked the inn. A breeze blew through, making Beth and Jackson shiver.

Ben gave him another pointed look. Oliver shuffled his invoices around, pretending to look busy. He didn't even know what he was stacking. He'd have to sort them out for real later. They looked important.

Sabine smiled over at Beth. "Are those the chocolates we were talking about?"

"What?" Beth shrank against the drafty wall, her back spikes poking into the wallpaper. There was a ripping noise, and Beth jumped forward, gasping. "Oh god, sorry."

"No harm done," Sabine said, holding her hand out for the bag of chocolates.

Ben turned to Oliver. "We're going to give them out to guests. You know, leave one on their pillow."

"Right," Oliver said. "For all the many, many guests who come through this...*charming* little town."

Ben gave him an irritating grin. The same grin he gave Oliver every time Oliver complained about their alpha dragging them to backwater Alaska to set up an inn in one of the only monster-centric towns on the West Coast. Oliver had half a mind to shut it down as soon as Grandmother transferred her role as alpha to him, which should be happening any day now. They wouldn't move out of town, of course—they were safe here. Oliver could put up with the annoying locals if his pack was protected. But they were losing money faster than they were earning it. Claw Haven was a safe place for quiet monsters, not a tourist trap. That was why they'd moved here. What was the point of having an inn in a town nobody passed through?

Oliver waited for Beth and Jackson to shuffle out into the cold. Then he turned to Ben and hissed, "Why are we even doing this? We opened *months* ago. This is stupid."

"Because Grandmother thought it was time," Ben said, fixing Oliver with a pointed look.

They were supposed to have the party when they opened. But Oliver kept putting it off, saying they weren't ready, there were still things around the inn that needed to be fixed.

Grandmother had seen right through him, obviously, but she'd let him have his way for a few months before finally putting her foot down.

We're an inn, she'd reminded him when she sent him to drop off invitations. *Our doors are supposed to be open.*

Not to the people who live *here*, Oliver had argued. The townsfolk of Claw Haven already had homes to go to. They were meant to take in tourists—if this town ever brought any in. As if Oliver would actually *want* any. Strangers were dangerous. Every one of their rare guests made Oliver's hackles go up. He had to stop himself from growling at the last one: a smarmy human businessman who was in town for his daughter's wedding and smoked in the lobby despite their very clear *No Smoking* sign. It had taken Oliver ages to get the ash out of the carpet.

Sabine made an impressed sound, digging in the bag of chocolates. "These are so good, Ollie. You have to try one."

"Give him the wolf one," Ben suggested.

Another drop fell from the roof.

Oliver groaned. "Where the hell is your kid with the bucket? We have an inn to fix, we don't need parties. Or chocolate."

"For someone who hates the inn so much, you sure talk about it a lot," Ben said. He scratched the counter, his nails too sharp. Not claws yet but getting there. Their wolf qualities slipped out if they got too emotional.

"You know, everyone put in a lot of work setting up this party. You're being a real—"

Leo burst into the lobby, carting a rusty old bucket, his light-up sneakers flashing.

"—A-hole," Ben finished hastily.

"Asshole," Leo said triumphantly, throwing the bucket down under the leaking ceiling, where the drips were turning into a steady stream thanks to the wet, heavy snowfall Oliver hated so much.

"Leo," said Ben and Sabine, whirling to scold him in unison.

Leo shrugged, sitting down on the floor next to the bucket. "What? *You* all say it."

A low, familiar voice made them turn around. "It's an adult word, Leo. You can use it when you're older."

Grandmother stepped into the lobby, her shawl wrapped tightly around her sturdy frame. She was wearing a sweater underneath it. She'd been covered up all winter. Oliver hadn't seen any of her various tattoos in months except for the ones on her hands: the spindly ends of branches starting at her knuckles and creeping under her sleeves. Werewolves ran hotter than most, and although the heating in Musgrove Inn was spotty in the lobby, it didn't warrant two thick layers.

"You look cold," Oliver said, finally putting the invoices to the side. "Do you need another shawl?"

Her thin lips curled up. "I'm fine. Pup, go get another bucket. This is a heavy-duty leak."

Leo ran off down the hall, almost tripping in his eagerness.

Oliver inclined his head respectfully at Grandmother as she

walked up to the front desk. "I'll work on the ceiling after the snow stops. I just need to—"

"Hire a professional?" Grandmother said wryly. She held up an arm to let Sabine step under it and give her neck a casual nuzzle.

Oliver cleared his throat. "I'm not having a stranger walk all over our roof."

Grandmother traded a look with Sabine, then with Ben.

"What?" Oliver snapped. "Sure, he's a monster. That doesn't mean he's *safe*. He's not pack!"

"Bro," Ben said. "You're acting like some territorial alpha who snarls at anyone who walks too close. Jackson's cool."

Oliver bared his sharpening teeth, feeling his eyes flash burning gold.

Ben blinked, startled. Before he could react, Grandmother touched his shoulder. "Why don't you go check on your boy? See how he's doing with that bucket."

Guilt curled in Oliver's gut as he watched his brother and sister-in-law walk down the hall after Leo. Grandmother had been the Musgrove alpha since before he was born. Standing up for the pack. Stopping conflicts before they started. How an alpha *should* be. Not growing fangs just because your brother was being annoying.

Oliver swallowed, teeth going blunt. "How's the party?"

"It's lovely," Grandmother said. She didn't touch his arm like she would have done a year ago. Out of everyone, she was the best about his new aversion to touch.

"Great. That's great." Oliver cleared his throat. "Are, uh... Are we, uh... I thought we were going to talk about the alpha ceremony tonight."

Grandmother appraised him silently. That pause was all it took.

Oliver gritted his teeth, still thankfully blunt. "You want to wait another year."

"I don't think you're ready," Grandmother said quietly.

"I'm working my *ass* off," he hissed. "And you're not getting any younger! What if your heart gets bad again?"

The exchange wasn't half as heated as the one he'd just had with his brother. But it was still ruder than he'd ever dared speak to Grandmother before they'd moved here, and shame flooded him reflexively.

Over in the corner, the stream of water dripped even heavier into the bucket.

Grandmother's hand twitched against her shawl. Like she'd started to reach out, then thought better of it. She curled it into her shawl instead, over the scar she'd come home from the hospital with five years ago.

"The surgery put a stop to that," she told him. "I'm fine."

"You're tired," he said flatly.

She gave him a stern look. "I...*might* be tired. But I'm still the alpha, and my heart's not giving out on me yet. I let you take care of the inn, but *I'm* the one in charge. I could go right over your head and ask Jackson to fix the room myself. But I trust you to do the right thing eventually."

"I do the right thing," Oliver muttered.

She looked at him with such understanding that Oliver wanted to hide from it. She'd raised him and Ben since their parents died when Oliver was eight. The rest of the pack had helped out—as good packs always did—but she was the one they'd lived with. The one who got them up in the mornings and was there to kiss them good-night.

"You don't trust people," Grandmother said sadly. "A true leader knows when to ask for help. You can't close yourself off just because one stranger tried to hurt us."

The guilt surged back, stronger than ever.

"You should go to the party," Grandmother continued. "Everyone's having fun. They're good people."

With that, she walked off down the hall toward the party.

Oliver took several deep breaths, the way she'd taught him so long ago, and focused his hearing on the party. Thumping music. Endless chatter. Another peal of shrill laughter from one of his aunts, high and irritating even through the multiple walls separating them.

Oliver took another deep breath. It didn't calm him down. Nothing calmed him down nowadays—not his pack, not working on the stupid inn, not running. He hadn't been able to shift since the fire, so he didn't even have *that*. He'd always judged the poor bastards who couldn't shift, wondering what you'd have to do to make your own wolf turn its back on you—and now he was one of them. Shifting would fix him, he was sure of it: not just fangs and claws that came out when he was annoyed, but a *full* wolf, running with his pack through the woods, being one with the forest and his family. He missed it like a phantom limb.

The water was reaching the top of the bucket. Oliver thought about doing something about it.

Instead, he turned and charged into the back rooms. Screw housewarmings, screw this inn, screw his family. A year ago, he would've been the *perfect* alpha. Now he was...what? Broken? Ruined? He couldn't even *shift*. What kind of adult wolf couldn't even shift?

He bared his teeth as he ransacked the back room, searching for the bottle he'd glimpsed when he was sorting things earlier today. It must've been misplaced party supplies, maybe an offering from the townsfolk. The bottle looked old—no label, maybe homemade—and it definitely wasn't supposed to be in the back room with all the inn's paperwork.

Oliver pulled the cork out. It smelled familiar. The bottle *looked* familiar, now that he had a proper look: slim and blue with a curled handle. It also stunk strongly of spirits. He'd been hoping for wine, something to ease him gently into drunkenness. But what the hell, he could cannonball into it instead. Better than going to the party and having to make small talk.

He tipped the bottle back and chugged. The glass caught the fluorescent light. For a moment, the liquid almost looked like moonlight.

Chapter Three

It was a pretty ugly sign. The font was too small, the edges gilded with cheap golden plastic. They didn't even have a logo. Not that it mattered now, since it was broken in half and rapidly getting covered in snow.

Luna shivered, looking up at Musgrove Inn. It was, as the reviewer had claimed, rough around the edges. The roof was crooked, the porch needed repainting and it had a general air of disuse.

She stumbled through the snow, clutching her suitcase and cursing herself for wearing such thin clothing. Her skirt was already getting soaked, snow leaking into her boots every time she stepped in a fresh bank. Her jacket was cute, but not nearly warm enough for a snowstorm.

She struggled up the ramp and burst into an empty lobby.

"Hello," she called, tugging her useless jacket tighter around her wet clothes. "Anybody here?"

No response. Luna dragged her damp suitcase toward the front desk, eyeing a pair of buckets that were catching a steady stream of drips from the ceiling. One of them was overflowing.

"Not a great start," she muttered as she stepped around the

puddle. "Helloooo? Very cold, wet and adorable woman here… I would love a hot towel!"

Nothing. Luna leaned over the desk and rang the service bell. Then she rang it again. Then a few more times just for good measure. She did *not* want to go back out in that snow. Also, she had to tell the manager she'd broken their ugly sign.

She was about to start yelling again when a man stumbled out of the back room.

Whoa, Luna thought. She'd been expecting a minotaur or some sort of bird dude. As far as she could tell, this guy glaring at her was…just a guy. A grumpy, stupidly gorgeous guy with a too-tight shirt who was glaring at her like she'd kicked his puppy. Maybe he was a vampire. Or a shifter. Shifters looked human, right? Luna knew a couple of cat people in high school. They'd looked normal, except that one time they got into a massive fight in the cafeteria and started growing whiskers and clawing each other. At least they hadn't shifted fully—Luna had never seen a monster shift all the way. Some people said it was horrifying. Others said it was beautiful.

"Hi," Luna started, trying to stop her teeth from chattering. "Do you have a room available?"

The guy stared at her. He still seemed annoyed, but mostly he looked confused. Luna realized with a start that he was holding a big fancy bottle and swaying slightly.

Luna let out an incredulous giggle. "Um, is there a party? I'd love to join, but I'm kind of freezing my butt off, so… Can I have a room?" She looked pointedly back at the overflowing buckets. "And can I expect my room to be as well-maintained as the lobby?"

The guy's eyes flashed gold. He bared his teeth, and Luna gasped as she saw a hint of fangs.

"You're a werewolf!"

"We all are," Hot Jackass said. He straightened, broad shoulders getting even wider. "Is that a problem?"

"No," Luna said. She lifted her chin, trying to remember her Power Pose training. "Wait, the whole *town* are werewolves?"

"What?" Hot Jackass scowled. "No. Just us. Figured Claw Haven needed some wolves."

"I hope they're just as friendly."

Luna gave him her cutest smile, curling a strand of hair around her finger as she tried to imagine this guy as a full wolf. In her mind, he kept those grumpy eyebrows.

"So…cards on the table," Luna said. "I crashed into your sign."

Hot Jackass blinked. He had very long eyelashes.

"What?"

"The sign outside the parking lot," Luna explained, wringing out her wet blond hair. She'd only been in the snow thirty seconds and it had already drenched her. "I crashed my car into it. I can pay for it—"

But Hot Jackass was already groaning, kneading his forehead with his hands. Big hands, Luna noticed with annoyance. Long fingers, big veiny hands connecting to toned arms—

"Tonight is the *worst*," Hot Jackass complained.

"I *said* I'll pay for it," Luna snapped, irritation cutting through the Cute Girl persona that got her backstage passes and free drinks and that one guy to watch her car for five hours even though he wasn't the valet. "Calm down! *God*. Also, do you have a phone? Mine's not getting any bars in this crappy— sorry—I mean *quaint* little town."

"Sure," Hot Jackass said, taking another swig of mysterious spirits. "Want anything else? A foot massage? My kidney?"

Luna let out another laugh. Who did this guy think he *was*?

"Look, asshole," she started. "I just got into a car crash; I'm wet, I'm freezing, *and* I just said I'd pay for your stupid sign, which doesn't even have a logo. News flash: Signs are supposed to be *eye-catching*."

Hot Jackass stiffened, looking behind her.

Luna turned.

A tall elderly woman wearing an envious number of layers smiled at her. Tattoos peeked out from her thick sleeves, winding down to meet her knuckles. She had this incredible air of calm about her, like she'd already been through everything and would gracefully offer you the solution to all your problems if you only asked.

"I'll show you to your room," the woman said. "Follow me."

She started down one of the hallways.

"Oh," Luna said. "Yay! Thank you!"

She grabbed her suitcase and stumbled after the mysterious woman, dripping on the carpet.

"I'm so sorry about your sign," she continued. "Seriously, I have five hundred in cash on me right now, you can have it—"

"You can worry about everything else later," the woman said, looking back toward the front desk. "Oliver, could you fetch another bucket for the leak?"

Luna expected Hot Jackass—*Oliver*—to sneer at her. Maybe roll his eyes. Something to match the overall vibe he'd demonstrated so far.

But he straightened up, placing the mystery booze on the desk. "Of course, Grandmother."

"Grandmother," Luna repeated as the woman led her down a beige hallway. "So, this is a family business? That's cute. I'm in one of those myself; you've probably heard of it—"

Her soaked boot caught on an uneven rug. She fell forward with a yelp only for the woman to grab her and haul her up effortlessly.

Luna blinked. Right. Werewolves. Super strong with killer reflexes. Luna tried to imagine this woman in her wolf form and came up with an elegant, lithe creature who moved every paw with purpose and grace.

"Thanks," Luna said, picking her suitcase back up. She shook her wet hair out of her face, trying to stop shivering long enough to give a good first impression. "I'm Luna. Luna Stack."

The woman gave her a curt nod. "Good to meet you, Luna. You may call me Grandmother. Everybody does."

She pulled open the door across from them. "I'll put you here. This hallway is for guests, and down that way are the family rooms."

Luna stepped into the room. It was…small. Plain. More peeling wallpaper. One twin bed, a bedside table and not much else. At least it had an en suite bathroom, though what she could glimpse from here looked equally unimpressive.

"Go get changed, warm up," Grandmother Musgrove continued. "Then, if you'd like, you can come and join the housewarming party. It's around the corner. Follow the noise."

Luna sniffed. The room stunk like mothballs. If she could smell it, how could the wolves stand it?

"Thanks," Luna said. "I'll see if I feel like it."

Grandmother Musgrove nodded. Before she could turn around, Luna gasped.

"Oh! Do you guys do massages here? *Not* feet—like, back stuff. Or a seaweed wrap? I'm pretty tense after this whole… *ordeal*."

Grandmother Musgrove's calm smile didn't change, but Luna felt like she was missing something important.

"Not tonight, obviously," Luna continued with a shivery laugh. "It's so late! But maybe tomorrow?"

Grandmother Musgrove looked her up and down. "I'll see what I can do."

"Thank you!" Luna smoothed down her ruined hair, smiling hard as she waved the woman goodbye. Destroying her inn's sign and getting into a fight with her asshole family member might not have been the *best* first impression, but Luna was sure she could salvage this. She was a Stack, after all.

★ ★ ★

The shower was awful. Weak water pressure that took forever to get past lukewarm. Then again, even lukewarm was a godsend after being out in the snow.

Luna stayed in the shower until the water finally got hot enough to scald her, then climbed out into the thankfully warm bathroom.

Which, of course, was when Luna realized the extent of her clothing troubles. Her suitcase was drenched from dragging it along the snow, and now half of her clothes were wet. She pulled on her warmest clothes: a gauzy long-sleeved shirt and the only full pair of pants she'd bothered taking because she'd packed for the *Bahamas*, goddamnit, not this Alaskan hellscape.

She was still too cold when she finished getting dressed. Lucky for her, there was a complementary robe in the built-in wardrobe. It was scratchy and a gross shade of off-white, but it would work until Luna put her clothes through a dryer. They had a dryer here, right? They had to. They didn't have a *hair*-dryer, even when Luna turned the place upside down looking for one, but they had to have a clothes dryer. That was just *basic*. Probably. Luna had never actually stayed at an inn before, and so far, it was starkly different than the hotels she was used to.

She called Hector on the landline, glaring at her out-of-service cell phone as she dialed.

"All coverage, my ass," she muttered as it rang.

And rang, and rang.

Luna groaned. "Come on, babe, I know you don't like picking up for unknown numbers, but your fiancée's call *did* just cut out in the middle of nowhere—"

Click. "Hello, this is Hector."

"Hector," Luna said. "Oh, thank god. I'm on a landline."

"Nostalgic," said Hector.

Luna paused. There was a lot of chatter on his end of the line, and a voice that sounded a lot like a flight announcement.

"Are you—are you at the *airport*?"

"I said I'd meet you in the Bahamas," Hector replied. "Did you find a motel, or are you being eaten by monsters?"

"Nobody's eating me," Luna said. She rubbed her robed arms, grimacing at the itchy material. She should be pulling up to the airport right now, getting ready for glittering beaches and warm air. Not this itchy, freezing crap.

"I found an inn," she said. "When I crashed into the sign right outside the parking lot. The front desk guy was such an asshole, but I met the owner, and I don't think they'll sue. I might have to smooth things over a little more, though, so I'm going to go rub elbows at some party they're throwing."

"Rough night," Hector said distractedly. "But no monsters?"

"No, there are monsters." Luna looked up as if expecting to find Grandmother Musgrove hiding behind a curtain. "Most of the townsfolk are monsters, apparently. This inn is owned by werewolves."

"Oooh. Watch out, they might go full wolf on you."

"Don't be mean," Luna chided, trying to pace and getting caught out by the landline wire. "They haven't even gone *half* wolf on me. Okay, the front desk guy was growly, but he didn't pull out any claws! And the owner seemed really nice! They're family-owned, just like us."

"Uh-huh," Hector said, letting her know he wasn't actually listening. "But the snow will clear up by tomorrow? They'll show you how to put chains on your tires, and I'll see you in the Bahamas?"

Luna rolled her eyes. "A little bit of sympathy, Hec! I crashed my car! I'm stranded in a leaky inn in the middle of nowhere, and all my clothes are ruined thanks to the snow!"

"Poor baby," Hector crooned immediately, and she could hear the smirk in his voice. "You want me to call your dad and get him to reschedule the flight?"

"No. Easier if I pay for it. I don't know when I'll actually get to the airport." Luna stifled a yawn. All this stress was exhausting. She'd make a quick appearance at the party, be her usual fun-loving self until she made sure the Musgroves loved her—most of them, anyway—then collapse into bed. Hopefully, they had electric blankets.

"Okay," he said, unaffected once more. She'd always liked that about him: Everything slid off Hector, no matter the issue. He was always there with an easy grin and a joke. It was what made them such a perfect match.

"Have a good night," he said. "Don't get—"

"I won't get eaten," Luna said. "*God*. Have a good flight, you warm bastard. Love you."

"Love you," he echoed like an afterthought.

The lobby was empty once again. The ceiling leaked a steady stream into a new bucket, the wood creaking. Faint music drifted in from the hallway.

Luna shivered, dragging her itchy robe closer around her. She was wearing socks, but she wished they provided complementary slippers along with this robe. And a hairdryer. Her hair was a limp, frigid press against her cheeks.

She was about to follow the music down the hall when a flash of blue caught her eye. She looked over and saw the mystery booze Oliver had been drinking perched at the edge of the front desk.

Luna paused. The bottle was pretty, all slim and curvy in ways that didn't match this shabby little inn. This was a bottle that belonged at a cool loft party. Or, Luna considered as she picked it up by its strange warped handle, a Halloween party. It wouldn't look out of place in some fairy ritual.

"Or werewolf ritual," Luna mumbled and snorted.

It didn't have a label, but that guy had been drinking it. It had to be safe. And if it had wolfsbane in it, Luna would just get drunk *a lot* faster.

She lifted the bottle.

The roof creaked again. This time, it was so loud it overtook the howl of snow outside.

Luna paused, the bottle resting against her lips.

After one more creak, the wood fell silent.

Luna shrugged and tipped the bottle back, liquid running into her mouth. It tasted…strange. Bitter with a fruity aftertaste. But the strangest part was that it was *warm*. Nothing in this room was warm. Maybe it was from the guy holding it, body heat leaching from his hand and through the glass, transferring into the liquid sliding down her throat.

Luna pulled back, smacking her lips.

"Huh," she said.

Then the ceiling fell in.

One second everything was normal, just a steady stream of water falling into the bucket. Then there was a horrible crack that made Luna jump, wood and metal collapsing into the carpet to reveal a hole in the roof.

Luna shrieked. Snow swirled in through the hole, cold wind whipping her robe. It wasn't *storming* anymore, but it was still snowing hard, and Luna immediately broke into goose bumps.

People came tearing around the corner. A vampire arrived first, his fanged mouth falling open in shock. Then an orc holding a beer bottle, with what looked like engine oil stains on his tight Henley shirt.

"Oh, shit," said the orc. He turned back toward the hallway, calling down, "Everybody owes Jackson ten bucks! The roof caved in!"

"The roof did *not*—" came that infuriating voice. Then it stopped, Hot Jackass coming to a standstill in the lobby as he stared up at the gaping hole in the ceiling.

Grandmother Musgrove arrived beside him, strands of hair falling out of her neat bun.

"What happened?" she asked. Her eyes widened on Luna. "Oh. *Oh*."

An older werewolf stumbled to a stop behind them, panting. He was wizened and hairy, a burn scar blotching his chin and neck. His gaze fell not on the hole, but on Luna, an ugly scowl creasing his face.

More monsters poured into the lobby. Minotaurs with party hats between their horns, dragons in scuffed overalls. Chimeras, gargoyles, orcs, vampires, a mermaid in a wheelchair.

Luna barely looked at them. She was too busy staring back at the ever-growing pack of werewolves, all of whom were staring right at her. The scarred old man was still scowling; several kids were frowning at their parents in confusion.

Oliver kneaded his forehead. Luna could hear his teeth grinding even over the wind and music, which nobody had turned off. The macarena drifted down the hallway, heading to a crescendo.

"What *happened*?" Oliver snapped.

Grandmother Musgrove cocked her head. She wasn't staring at Luna, she realized. She was staring at the bottle in her hand, her expression opening in puzzled wonder.

"The roof caved in," Grandmother Musgrove announced, turning to look at him. "Also, it seems you're married. Congratulations."

Chapter Four

Oliver waited for the punchline.

Grandmother Musgrove wasn't a very jokey woman, but she had her moments. This was, admittedly, a pretty weird moment to pick. But Oliver couldn't think of any other explanation for why she'd tell him he was *married* to the rude, spoiled stranger with giant bush baby eyes who'd crashed a car into his sign and called him an asshole within thirty seconds of meeting him.

The woman shivered pathetically, snow spiraling through the hole in the roof and landing in her damp hair. Even disheveled, she carried an air of entitlement and wealth. Her voice dripped with money, and her teeth were the kind of straight that only came from luxury dentists. Even the way she stood—anxious but still haughty like she expected to get out of this situation scot-free—screamed that she'd never had anything truly bad happen to her in her whole life. Nothing money couldn't get her out of.

Next to him, Ben gasped.

"Oh," Ben said. "*Ohhhhh.*"

"What?" Oliver snapped.

Ben pointed. The woman was holding the bottle he'd been

drinking from earlier. He must've left it there after he'd grudgingly decided to join the party long enough to shut his family up.

More gasps went up behind him. Oliver turned to find both his aunts clinging to each other with excitement and shock. Uncle Roy scratched the childhood burn scar on his neck and glared at the woman like he wanted to rip her pretty little throat out right there in the lobby. Even Sabine had her hands over her mouth. The only ones who looked as confused as Oliver were the kids pulling on their parents' sleeves for answers. Even a few nonwolves were getting it. The mermaid in the wheelchair had her hands over her mouth just like Sabine, eyes shining like she was watching the climax of a reality TV show.

"What?" Oliver asked again, turning to Grandmother. "What are you talking about?"

"You must be more drunk than I thought," Grandmother said. "Look closer."

She pointed at the bottle.

"Um," said the woman, still shivering like a leaf. "I assumed it was for the party... I can put it back—"

"Too late," Uncle Roy spat. "The damage is done."

A horrible realization rushed over Oliver fast, cutting through the drunkenness. He *did* recognize that bottle. That was the bottle that had been present in every Musgrove bonding ceremony since before Oliver was born, with the two betrothed sharing the sacred spirits made by Musgrove elders and left to age until the next ceremony. He'd never seen it when it wasn't draped in flowers and drizzled with oils somewhere in the woods, the bonded pair tipping the bottle into each spouse's mouth.

"But—" Oliver said. "But it was in the back room. With our filing cabinet and a bunch of crap we never use but don't want to throw out. Why was it in there?"

"A lot of things got misplaced during the move," Grandmother pointed out.

Oliver shook his head numbly. He couldn't have drunk that without knowing. It was sacred to their pack. He couldn't just uncork it and start chugging.

Next to him, Ben stifled a hysterical giggle. "Dude, that's—that's the *bond nectar*. How do you accidentally drink the *bond nectar*?"

Oliver ran his tongue around his mouth. Traces of the liquid were still there under the beer he'd thrown back at the party while waiting to leave.

"Uhhh," the woman said, clutching the bottle like it wasn't hugely important to the pack she was now in. "I'm sorry, can someone explain what's going on so I can curl up with an electric blanket and get this night over with? You guys do electric blankets, right?"

Another gust of wind came through the giant hole in the roof, sending a new wave of snow around the room. The woman—Oliver's *wife*, even though he didn't even know her *name*—jumped like she'd been stung, rubbing her arms through her robe.

The tiniest shiver ran through Grandmother, who turned toward the people behind them with a smile.

"I think the night has burned itself out," she announced. "Everybody might want to head home."

"Don't have to tell me twice," muttered Nick Wicker, an annoying orc who worked for the local mechanic and had only showed up for the free beer. "Come on, Jasper."

"Right behind you," said Jasper, a vampire who, if possible, was even more annoying than Nick. They both shot Oliver curious looks as they passed, and didn't look half as chastened as they should have when Oliver glowered at them. Claw Haven folk never did—the whole damn town felt entitled to everyone's private business.

Grandmother's hand hovered over Oliver's elbow as everyone filed out. "Come on."

"This is ridiculous," Oliver protested. He gestured up at the snow drifting down into the lobby, which was mercifully slowing down. "I—I need to put up a tarp. I need—"

"We can do that later," Grandmother said before walking over to the shivering woman.

Oliver gritted his teeth and followed. There was a strange warmth in his chest that burned hotter the closer he got to her, which was worrying.

"Luna," said Grandmother as she arrived in front of the woman. "Why don't you follow us someplace warmer? You look frozen."

Luna. Oliver had to bite his cheek to stop himself from groaning. Of course, she had a stupid moon name.

His brother was not as graceful. He snorted aloud as he followed the group down the hall toward their living quarters.

"Shut *up*," Oliver told him.

"Didn't say a word," Ben said, not bothering to wipe that stupid smug smile off his face.

Grandmother took Luna into Sabine and Ben's bedroom to pick out some warmer clothes. As they waited, Uncle Roy paced the Musgrove common room with his fangs bared.

"It's a trick," he snarled as he paced. "Somebody sent her to infiltrate the pack. Some illegal hunting clan back in Arizona—"

"Nobody's *hunting* us, Roy," Aunt Althea said, slurring from her attempts to fix her gold tooth. "And there *aren't* any hunters in Arizona anymore."

"That's what they *say*," Uncle Roy muttered.

"Roy," Aunt Althea said. "You're scaring the kids."

Uncle Roy snarled, only softening when he looked over at the kids—six-year-old Leo wrestling with his nine-year-old cousin, Darren. Next to them, sixteen-year-old Vida, Darren's sister, took her ever-present bulky headphones off to glare at Aunt Althea.

"Not a kid, *Mom*," she said. She shot Oliver an amused look as she slid her headphones back on. "Congrats on the wife, Uncle Ollie."

Oliver glared at her, then turned to the rest of the room. "It doesn't matter anyway. Grandmother will get this sorted. It's not—it *can't* be a real bond."

And yet there was that warmth in his chest, getting colder and colder. The cold hurt. He wanted to be warm again, to be *close* to her. It scared him. He didn't even *know* her, but some stupid ritual had decided that his body wanted to be next to hers, always. More than *next* to her. It wanted—

He thumped his chest, trying to make it stop aching. "Okay. Roof. We'll put up a tarp and wait for the snow to stop. We might have to replace the carpet in the lobby if the water stain gets too bad."

"You *really* should call Jackson," said Aunt Barney, who was sitting on the couch and braiding Aunt Althea's hair while the other woman continued to fix her gold tooth.

"He can consult," Oliver said. "But I don't want him working on the inn."

Aunt Althea and Aunt Barney traded knowing looks.

"Bad as Uncle Roy," Aunt Barney muttered, combing a gentle hand through her sister's thick, dark hair.

Oliver bit back the knee-jerk asshole response. Sure, he hadn't welcomed the annoyingly friendly townsfolk with open arms. But he wasn't as bad as Uncle Roy, who roamed the halls at night "in case of danger," scaring the hell out of the few guests who had stayed here since they opened.

He turned to Uncle Roy, who was still growling under his breath. "It's probably just some dumb mistake, Uncle Roy."

Uncle Roy gave him a betrayed look. "Here I thought you

were finally seeing sense this past year. Nothing good came out of that fire except you finally wising up."

Oliver fought back a shudder. "So what, Uncle Roy? She found a way to put the bottle in the office without us smelling her? Then she mind-controlled me to drink it? To leave it out in the open?"

Uncle Roy opened his mouth to go on another one of his rants.

Oliver cut him off. "Whatever this is, Grandmother will fix it, and then we'll never have to see that woman again."

"I like her," said Darren, letting Leo pin him to the carpet. "She's pretty."

"She's *rude*," Oliver barked.

Ben snorted again. "And I bet you did *nothing* to set that off."

Oliver scowled at him. Everyone was having too much fun with this situation except for him and Uncle Roy, who he did *not* want to be lumped in with. Uncle Roy had been scarred by wannabe hunters as a child and had grown up with a chip on his shoulder—not just for humans but for anyone who wasn't pack. Everybody had hoped he'd drop this attitude after he'd shocked the family by becoming involved with a human—even going as far as to *marry* her—and for a few years, it had seemed like he was softening. Then she'd left, and he'd gone right back to being suspicious of everyone outside the pack. Until last year, Oliver thought he was being dramatic. Then the fire happened, and Oliver found himself suspicious of anyone who tried to insert themselves into their lives. Which in this town was pretty much everyone.

Before Oliver could tell his brother exactly where to stick it, the hallway door opened. His heart skipped a beat, and he frowned. He didn't think he was *that* stressed.

"—hair looks fine," Sabine was saying as she came in with Grandmother. "What do you think, Ollie? How does her hair look?"

Luna strode in. She was wearing one of Sabine's sleep shirts and a baggy pair of sweatpants. She should've looked like a slob. Infuriatingly, she looked like a model showing off the latest in nightwear chic. Her hair had been freshly blow-dried, fuzzing up around her ears. She kept petting it like she wanted it to lie down, but it sprung back up every time. It looked so soft. Everything in Oliver wanted to touch it.

Luna raised her elegant eyebrows expectantly. "Well?"

"It's fine," Oliver managed, choking the urge down. *It's just the bond*, he reminded himself as his fingers itched. *It's not real*.

Luna gave him an exasperated look. "Okay, seriously. Thanks for the clothes and everything, but what is going on? I drink some weird liquor and suddenly I'm werewolf married? I'm not going to grow a tail, right?"

"You have to get the bite to become a werewolf," Sabine said. "Humans bond with werewolves all the time. You can take the bite if you want to—"

"Which she *doesn't*," Oliver said, alarmed. He glared at Sabine, incredulous. Was she honestly suggesting they turn some stranger?

"But it's not necessary," Sabine continued. She turned to Ben, who had slipped an arm over her shoulder. "I was already turned when we bonded. But even if I wasn't, I would've chosen it anyway. It's really up to you."

"Oookay," Luna said. "Well, we can go ahead and cross *that* option out. Speaking of crossing things out, I haven't signed anything. Is this legally binding?"

"It is," Grandmother Musgrove said. "Your souls are linked until you remove the bond."

"Our *souls*," Luna said with a breathy laugh. "Sure."

Oliver's stomach turned. He didn't like it any more than she did, but this was serious stuff. It shouldn't be laughed at.

"But is it *legally* binding?" she asked, nose wrinkling. "Like, do I have to get it removed? I'm getting married in two months."

"You'll be on the wolf marriage registry," Sabine said apologetically. "It just shows up. Sorry."

"We'll get it removed," Oliver said. He turned to Grandmother. "We can do the unbinding ritual soon, right? We have an elder, we have the ingredients—"

"Not the *Hyacinth confractus*," Ben piped up from where he'd taken his place next to Sabine, nuzzling gently into her shoulder. He only looked up from Sabine when he noticed everyone had fallen silent. "What? Grandmother asked me to check our supplies before we moved out here. I checked. We're out of confractus."

Aunt Barney paused in braiding her sister's hair. "That's the divorce flower, right? I can never remember the proper names."

"We can get some divorce flowers," Oliver said, desperately trying to remember his childhood wolf lessons. "We can order it in, right?"

"Nationwide shortage," Ben said. "That's why we haven't gotten any more. We're on a waitlist."

Oliver groaned. "It grows in Alaska, right? On mountains? I can go searching tomorrow!"

"You will go searching once the snow thaws," Grandmother corrected. "Unless you want to climb a mountain in the snow and start digging."

Oliver thought about it.

Grandmother reached up like she was about to grasp his jaw, half fondness, half frustration. Then she stopped.

"Oliver, honestly. You can last a few weeks until the snow thaws. It's basically spring already." With that, she inserted herself on the couch next to Aunt Althea and Aunt Barney, shaking her hair out of its bun and presenting it for braiding.

"Right," Luna said slowly. "And we'll just…keep this quiet until then."

"*Gladly*," Oliver said sourly.

Luna picked at her sleep shirt. She looked bewildered by the amount of physical affection happening between the pack: both aunts turning to braid Grandmother Musgrove's long gray hair; Darren and Leo wrestling right up against Vida's leg while she tried to kick them away from her; Sabine and Ben nuzzling each other. The only ones not touching anyone were Uncle Roy and Oliver, and *goddamn* if Oliver didn't hate that. Once he would've been braiding Grandmother's hair with his aunts or wrestling on the ground with the kids. Now he was standing off to the side, arms crossed, face stuck in a scowl he couldn't seem to wipe off.

Luna sucked in a breath, giving the room a brisk grin. "Okay! So, this was super lovely, even with all the roofs caving in and the cold and the yelling and the accidental werewolf marriage. It was nice to meet you all."

Aunt Althea made a noise of protest as Luna started slinking toward the door. "We've barely met you! Come, sit. Have some cocoa. Can we get some cocoa in here?"

"I'll go," Ben said, untangling himself from Sabine.

Luna watched him leave, looking somehow even more uncomfortable than when she was watching everyone touch each other.

"I'm *really* tired," she said, patting her frizzy hair down.

"But you're part of the pack! Until the snow thaws, anyway." Aunt Althea patted the scant space left on the couch. "Who are you? What do you do?"

"Um…" Luna looked out at the sea of expectant faces. Her gaze lingered on Oliver, but only for a moment. Just long enough for the warmth in Oliver's chest to burn hotter. Then she looked away, and he went cold.

Luna bent into a curtsy. Oliver couldn't tell if it was ironic or not.

"I'm Luna Stack. I'm a Gemini, and I like noodles and *warm* weather. My family runs Stack Appliances."

Sabine gasped. "Oh, you guys make such cool stuff! That

vampire family over the way has a Stack hot tub, it's fantastic. They make those fancy armchairs I showed you, remember, Aunt Barney?"

Aunt Barney asked, "Do we get a friends-and-family discount?"

Luna laughed awkwardly. "Um…"

"No discounts," Oliver said. "She's not pack. She's a mistake."

He hadn't meant to say it so sternly. The room fell silent anyway.

"Wow," Luna said flatly. "What a way to treat your new wife."

He stared at her.

Luna giggled. "I'm joking! Obviously. I would never marry you, even if I didn't already have a fiancé."

Then she beamed. Oliver could feel the sacred liquor at the back of his throat, sweet and scalding. Did she feel him? She wasn't a wolf, but she'd still feel it. A little piece of him. A shard. A sharp little prick irritating her insides.

"Thanks again for the clothes," Luna said into the silence. "So cute and cozy."

She did a little shimmy, exposing a flash of her long, flat stomach. Something deep and primal stirred in Oliver's stomach. Oliver told it to shut the fuck up and tore his gaze away from the pale skin as it vanished under her sleep shirt.

"I'm going to bed," Luna continued. "Toodles."

Ben came back into the room, brows raising when he took in the strained silence. Luna grabbed the mug off him as she passed, flicking everyone a tiny finger wave as she escaped into the hall.

"So," Ben said, flexing his newly empty hands. "Ollie married a woman who says *toodles*. Unironically."

"It was ironic," Oliver protested. "It *has* to be ironic."

"Maybe it started ironic, and it became sincere," Sabine suggested, ducking back under her husband's arm.

"Yeah, she seems *really* sincere." Oliver pinched the bridge of his nose.

"Oliver," Grandmother Musgrove said, soft but stern as her hair was braided by four hands at once. "That's your wife."

Anger sparked through Oliver in a wave.

"That's not my wife!" he exploded. "That's a spoiled LA heiress who's never had to work a day in her life. I know everybody finds it so *funny*, but I don't. Alright? I'm bound to some stranger. This isn't *funny* to me."

"Hear, hear," said Uncle Roy quietly, the first words he'd spoken since Luna came back in the room. "The further away she stays, the better."

Hear, hear, Oliver thought. But before he could say anything, the warmth in his chest went so intensely cold that it made him grunt.

"As far away as she *can* stay, anyway," Uncle Roy continued with a frown. "Is it hitting already? She's only down in the guest hall."

"I know," Oliver gritted out. He rubbed his chest. The ice in his rib cage was throbbing now, radiating out to the rest of his body. The tips of his fingers ached from the cold.

"Maybe she's exploring the house," Uncle Roy said, eyes going steely. "Looking for our weaknesses."

Grandmother Musgrove cocked her head, listening. "She's in her room. Mumbling something about the quality of our sheets."

Oliver kept rubbing his chest. Why did he already know she was in her room? It made sense, but it was more than that. It was a knowing, deep in his heart. The bond was reporting back to him, letting him know where his bondmate was. *God*, that was going to be annoying. He'd be trying to focus on paperwork, and the bond would be blaring like the world's most annoying Google pin, alerting him to where his other half was. Even though he *hadn't asked*.

Ben winced in sympathy. "That's strong, dude. I had to be on the other side of the house before it started hurting."

"Great," Oliver muttered.

Ben laid a big hand on his shoulder. "It's strongest when the bond is new. It'll get easier with time."

"It'd better," Oliver said. He rubbed his chest harder, hoping it would soothe the numbing cold. It didn't. Nothing would—except getting close to the last person in this inn he wanted to get close to.

Chapter Five

There was a chocolate wolf on the pillow the next morning. It would've been sweet, Luna considered as she waited for Hector to pick up, if it didn't mean that someone had snuck into her room while she was sleeping.

The landline clicked. "Stranded fiancée?"

Luna laughed, twirling the cord of her bathrobe. "Are you just answering every unknown number like that?"

"Every landline number with an Alaskan area code," Hector said. "How was the night? No nibbles?"

"No one ate me," Luna replied, turning the wolf chocolate over in her hands. She popped it into her mouth and chewed. "Oh *wow*, that's delicious."

"Hmm?"

"Nothing." Luna swallowed, already missing the bitter taste. She didn't usually like dark chocolate, but this was delightful. "Do you remember that time you invested in those terrible cheese graters—"

"There's still a market for graters that scream when you grate things, babe."

"My point is," Luna said, licking chocolate off her teeth. "I didn't laugh at you *that* hard. Because I love you."

"Alright," Hector said. There was the sound of a glass clinking on his end of the line, and Luna groaned as she imagined him sitting on some beach in the Bahamas. "What did you do?"

"*I* didn't do anything." Luna bit her thumbnail, wincing when it pulled a strip of pink manicure off. "But say I stumbled into a totally unwanted, unconsummated marriage with a werewolf who hates me almost as much as I hate him. Would you be mad?"

There was a long silence. Then Hector snorted.

"I said not to laugh," Luna whined. "This isn't funny!"

"Clancy will find it hilarious," Hector said. "And your dad's going to laugh and then tell you to sue the hell out of them."

"I'm not going to *sue* them," Luna argued, fitting her feet into the snow boots Sabine had given her last night. "They're nice. *Weirdly* nice, actually. Not the guy I'm stuck with, but everyone else. Also, are wolves super affectionate with each other? Because I spent ten minutes around them, and they are *constantly* touching. I thought that was just when they were in full wolf form?"

"Nope, even when they're in human form," Hector said confidently. "Wait, back up. What the hell happened at that party?"

"I didn't even make it to the party. The roof caved in."

"What?"

Luna sighed and explained the rest of her night. The mystery booze, the snow, the roof. Her scowling, closed-off husband, who seemed just as enthused about the situation as she was. His sweet family, who had treated her alarmingly nicely, even if the uncle was super goddamn creepy.

"And they dragged my car out of the snow and fitted the wheels with chains, and I think they want to take me to buy warmer clothes," she finished. "And they keep joking that I'm family! At least until the snow thaws and they can go up the mountain to get the weird divorce flower."

Hector started giggling.

"Shut up," Luna told him. "I'm *suffering!*"

She rubbed her chest. Sabine had mentioned that when they were in her bedroom gathering clothes. *You'll be able to feel him*, she'd said. *It won't be as powerful since you're not a wolf. But you'll be able to feel him a little. Right there in your chest.*

And there it was. It had been warm when they'd been in the same room. Now it was cold, a small sliver of it right in the center of her chest. Trying to make her go toward him. He wasn't far. Still on the property. Wait, why did she *know* that?

"So," Hector said when his laughter trailed off. "When you say *unconsummated*—"

A knock on the door drowned the rest of his words out.

"I have to go," Luna blurted. "Love you. Hope the mai tais are tolerable!"

She threw the landline back into its cradle, relieved by the distraction. Any other time, she would've welcomed Hector's teasing, but for some reason, she didn't want to hear him make fun of her for this. It felt weird. Like she was doing something wrong. Which she hadn't, obviously. She'd never even touched the guy, let alone slept with him. And still, she had this strange guilty feeling as she flung the door open.

Sabine waved a thick jacket at her. "Hey! Just wanted to drop this off."

"Thanks," Luna said, pulling on the jacket. It was *heavy*, perfect for the Alaskan weather she hadn't packed for. "Oh my god, this is amazing! Thank you."

"No problem." Sabine brushed her hair out of her eyes, and Luna made sure not to stare at the deep scar that rode over her left eye. She pulled it off, at least. Luna had been taught young that if you were confident, you could pull almost everything off. Sabine wore quiet confidence in spades.

"Was that your fiancé I heard?" Sabine asked. "He sounds cute. What's he like?"

"He's great," Luna said. "His family makes kitchen appliances."

Sabine waited. "But what's he like?"

Luna tried to remember what his most recent magazine interview had said about him. She didn't often have to tell people what Hector was like; they already knew who he was.

"He's cute and funny," Luna said. "And so, *so* fun. That's why we're perfect together. He found out that his fiancée got accidentally werewolf hitched, and he laughed his butt off."

"Wow. Sounds like a laid-back guy."

"He is. He'll be on a deck chair in the Bahamas right now, soaking up the sun. Or moon. I don't remember what time it is over there."

She headed into the hall. Sabine fell into step beside her easily.

"I can take you into town after I drop Leo off at school," Sabine offered. "Or an aunt can take you. They have knitting club with the minotaurs later."

"I was actually looking forward to some me time," Luna said, trying to wince as cutely as possible as they headed through the lobby. "Thank you, guys, *so* much for snow-proofing the car. And lugging it out of the ditch. I'll throw in a tip when I pay for the sign!"

"Thanks," Sabine said slowly. "Are you sure? Californians don't have the best luck on Claw Haven roads in the winter."

"I'm sure," Luna said as she opened the front door, shivering at the slap of cold air. At least it wasn't snowing anymore.

"Wow, that's icy. This jacket's a lifesaver. Well, bye!" She closed the door in Sabine's hesitant face. She didn't even make it down the snowy ramp before a familiar voice stopped her.

"—can tell me how to do it," Oliver said from above her. "But *I'm* gonna be the one doing it. Alright?"

Luna strode out into the driveway and craned her head.

Oliver stood on the snowy roof, looking far too assured for

someone standing on a holey roof in the snow. In *ripped jeans*, no less. Luna eyed his toned, hairy thighs through the gaps in the denim. She wanted to squeeze them. She was pretty sure most of that want was her own. The bond in her chest pulsed with heat, melting the ice that had been building up while she'd been apart from him.

"'Course," said a voice to Luna's left. She looked over to see a dragon standing in the driveway, smoke drifting up from his scaly nostrils.

She was almost tempted to take a picture—she had never seen a dragon so close before. They were the most common kind of monsters: the kind that stayed in the same form their whole lives. There was no getting rid of his tail, or his snout, or those strong wings tucked tight against his back.

"Just want to save you trouble down the line," the dragon continued, thumbing his belt. "Not worth fixing anything properly until the snow melts. Too damn slippery up there."

"Werewolves heal fast, Jackson," Oliver reminded him, frowning at the tarp he was nailing down over the hole.

The dragon's wings twitched like he was expecting to have to use them soon.

"I know. Still doesn't mean you should give yourself a broken leg when you go tumbling off—" He noticed Luna and stopped. "Well, hey, stranger. You must be the wife. I'm Jackson. Heard you're stuck here until the snow thaws. Luckily, you got here just before spring. How're you doing?"

He stuck out a hand. Luna shook it, surprised at how smooth the underside of the dragon's palm was. No scales, just supple, leathery skin.

"I'll be better once I'm someplace where they don't know how to put snow chains on car tires," Luna told him, trying not to glance back at Oliver's toned thighs. "I'm an LA girl at heart."

Jackson laughed. "Well, let us know if we can make your

stay more enjoyable. The Musgroves are a good bunch, but they don't know all the spots us locals know."

Luna's eyes lit up. If she was stuck here until the snow thawed, she'd need to kill time until then. "That would be amazing! Do you guys have a spa around here? The inn doesn't do massages."

"No spa," Jackson said after a moment. "We have restaurants, cafés, a bakery, a flower shop. Movie theater. Bookstore. We got a lot of beautiful spots if you're willing to walk. Mountains—great for hiking once the snow clears. The ocean's right over there... I guess that's too cold for humans right now."

Luna kept her smile intact. Hopefully, this guy was just bad at pitching. There had to be *something* worthwhile to do around here.

"Everything except the freezing ocean sounds *great*," she chirped. Then, because she was still shivering despite her thick coat and her skin could really use some soothing, she added, "So, like...not even a mud pool? Somewhere that does body wraps? Facial treatments?"

"We have a skincare store," Jackson replied.

Luna clenched her teeth. "Alright! Well, thank you so much. I'll keep that in mind. So nice to meet you, Jackson!"

"Nice to meet you, Luna," he replied. He tipped his head up toward the roof again. "Oliver, sure you don't want to escort this young lady into town? You did say you were going in for supplies."

"I'm sure," came the immediate reply.

Luna made sure Jackson couldn't see her as she rolled her eyes. She strode toward the parking lot, ignoring the warmth in her chest. It ebbed with every step, replaced by a numb cold that the car heater did nothing to help.

Luna shivered as she walked down the sidewalk with her shopping bags. She was bundled up, but the cold in her chest had spread to her fingertips. She hoped Oliver was having fun in his stupid ripped jeans. Why wasn't *he* affected by the weird cold that kicked in whenever they were apart?

She pulled her jacket tighter, focusing on the town around her. It was a lot cuter when she wasn't battling through a snowstorm. Someone had already plowed the main roads, so Luna had been able to cruise slowly down the street without worrying about skidding. The middle of town was small enough that she could park in one spot and walk around, getting everything she needed without tiring herself out. It was nice. She loved LA, but it was annoying having to get into a car every time she wanted to go somewhere. If the weather was better, she could've walked into town from the inn. Admired the mountains on one side of town, the ocean glittering on the other. Sure, there wasn't a lot to do here, but it was pretty damn beautiful.

Luna paused in the middle of the sidewalk. Shopping bags dangled from her arms as she wrestled her phone out, snapping a picture of the snowy scenery. She still didn't have much data on her phone, but her laptop worked fine if she sat on the side of the room closest to the inn's router. She could post the photo to her Instagram later.

She turned back and instantly bumped into a huge orc carrying an armful of flour.

"Crap," Luna said, barely managing not to spill her bags of clothes all over the cold bricks. "Sorry!"

She shrank back from the orc with a wince. He was *huge*, all bulging muscles and oil stains on the tight shirt he had on under his winter coat. Then he opened his mouth, and his flustered tone made it clear she had nothing to stress about.

"Shit, that's on me," the orc said distractedly, steadying her with the hand that wasn't locked around his giant flour bag. "Are you good?" He shuffled the bag around, then paused. "Oh shit! You're that human from the Musgrove Inn."

Luna recognized him, now that she looked closer—he'd had

engine oil smudged on his shirt back at the inn, too. He'd been the second one to come in and gape at the hole in the roof.

"Everyone's talking about you," the orc continued.

Luna sighed. "Everyone?"

"Well, not *everyone*. Just the bored ones. So yeah, actually. Everyone." The orc gave her a rakish grin. "Not a lot to do in Claw Haven but shoot the shit. I'm Nick, by the way. Nick Wicker."

"Luna Stack," Luna said. She held out a cautious hand for a handshake and then paused to look at the flour bag in his arms. "Are you baking something?"

"What?" Nick looked at the flour he was carrying and balked, letting out a strange laugh. "Me? No. I can't bake for shit! This is just…for lifting weights. Bye."

He ignored her outstretched hand and bustled off, clutching the flour bag to his chest like he was trying to hide it.

Luna had to stop herself from staring after him—first because that was a weird reaction to have about a bag of flour, but mostly because there were so many monsters out for a morning walk: people covered in wings or feathers or scales, nodding at each other or stopping in the middle of the street to chat. If you stopped in the middle of a bustling LA street, you'd get yelled at.

She readjusted the bags on her arms. She had everything she'd come into town for, plus a few extras. Time to get out of the cold. Hopefully, the ache in her chest would die down when she was under the same roof as that jerk.

She turned back toward her rental car and paused. There was a chocolate shop across the street. *Prickles*, the sign declared. A chocolate cartoon hedgehog curled up next to the word, smiling out at the street.

Luna headed into the shop. A bell rang over the door, and Luna felt a strange thrill. *I'm in a little chocolate store in a little town that has a little bell over the door. This is the most whimsical thing that's ever happened to me.*

Maybe, she considered, there *was* something to do in Claw Haven. But only if you were a tourist. She would never want to *live* here.

The store smelled like sea salt and dark cocoa. Luna took a hearty sniff as the hedgehog woman behind the counter whirled around, her spikes skimming the scratched-up chalkboard behind her. Luna couldn't help but feel sorry for the woman—werewolves could present as human. But monsters like this woman, or the dragon back on the inn roof, couldn't hide even if they wanted to. It would make dealing with prejudiced jerks much harder.

At least this monster looked cute, with her twitching muzzle and her big black eyes, even if the spikes bursting out of her back looked annoying, her apron clipped around them.

"Oops," said the hedgehog woman, eyes wide. "Hi! Hello! Can I get you anything? We have samples."

"Don't mind if I do," Luna said happily. She stepped toward the bowl that the woman was holding out and paused. She recognized those little wolves. "Oh, hey! These are yours? I had one this morning, and they were delish."

"Oh," the hedgehog woman said, flushing all down her muzzle. "Thank you so much! They're a new recipe."

Luna popped a chocolate wolf into her mouth and gestured around the empty store. "New business?"

The woman toyed nervously with her apron. "We're still getting the word out."

"Yeah? Newsletters, ads, sponsorships…?" Luna watched as the woman's eyes got wider and wider.

"Um," the woman said. "Kind of just…posters. We're not a very touristy town."

Luna frowned. "You could be. You guys have mountains *and* seaside *and* forest. And that whole monster wonderland going on, for people who are into that kind of thing. You could do a lot with it."

The woman nodded. Luna got the feeling she would've nodded at anything Luna said. She seemed the type.

"I'm Luna," Luna said.

"Beth." The woman's tiny hedgehog hands twisted tighter in her apron. "I'm sorry, but are you the human staying at Musgrove Inn? Everybody's talking about it."

"Great," Luna muttered and pulled up a sunny smile. "That's me!"

"Oh." Beth's shoulders hunched. "Where's Oliver? Is he not with you?"

Luna laughed. Beth must not have the whole story if she thought Luna's accidental husband would want to tag along into town with her.

"No, he's back at the inn. Hopefully not falling off the roof."

"Oh," Beth said again. Her brow furrowed. "I hope he's alright. I had werewolf friends who got bonded in college, and they couldn't be on the other side of the house before the pain set in."

Luna waited for that baffling sentence to make sense. When seconds passed with nothing becoming clear, she asked, "Excuse me? Pain?"

"It's a side effect of the new bond," Beth explained hesitantly, as if afraid she was being tested. "Did—did he not tell you that?"

Luna thought back to Oliver up on that roof, hammering down a tarp and not looking at her once. Of the cold in her chest, spreading to her fingers and making it hard to hold her bags. Of Sabine saying, *It won't be as powerful since you're not a wolf.*

"No," she said icily. "He didn't."

Chapter Six

One annoying thing about having a close family, Oliver mused as he dragged the broken sign into the lobby, was that they kept *bothering* you. Ben had asked how he was feeling five times in the last half an hour, and if he did it again, Oliver was going to wolf out and jump on him. Never mind that he hadn't been able to properly wolf out in a year. He'd do it out of sheer brotherly rage. Anything to distract him from the overwhelming ache pulsing through his body, the cold so intense it went all the way back around to burning hot. It made it hard to focus on the broken sign he was holding.

Ben took a deep breath behind him.

Don't, Oliver thought as he sat on the carpet, bending over the sign. His hand shook around the superglue tube as ice throbbed through his body.

"Are you *sure* you're okay?" Ben asked.

Oliver growled up at him. "I'm fine."

Ben eyed him dubiously. Oliver straightened, trying to look normal. In control. Not stress-sweating at *all*, and definitely not shaking. The pain was like an icy fist around his heart, squeezing hard. He wanted to crawl into a corner and shiver until it stopped. But he had shit to do, and he wasn't going to let an unwanted bondmate's distance stop him.

"Kinda risky," Ben said, toeing the lobby carpet where the sign now lay. "Having her so far away."

"She's not *far away*," Oliver protested, easing the broken sides of the sign back together. "I can sense her. She's coming back from town."

Sweat dripped down his forehead. He wiped it away with his forearm and grunted as a fresh wave of cold agony rushed through him.

"Still," Ben said. "You could've gone with her."

Oliver gritted his teeth. "I refuse to let—"

Another wave of pain washed over him. Oliver bent over with the force of it, a gasp ripping out of his throat. The superglue dropped onto the newly repaired sign, tumbling down the wood onto the carpet.

Ben rushed forward. "Ollie?"

Oliver shook his head. It was starting to ebb, just as fast as it had come on. In seconds, the pain turned from agony all over his body to a hard throb localized in his chest.

"She's close," Oliver said. He could already imagine that shiny rental car turning into the parking lot, sliding even *with* the chains on her tires. *I like* warm *weather*, she'd snarked at them last night. That spoiled valley girl would *not* be good at driving in the snow.

"Good," Ben said. "Means you can stop walking around looking constipated."

Oliver picked the glue back up. "I don't look—"

The front doors slammed open. Luna charged through, her arms ladened with bags that she immediately dropped to the floor. Her gaze was fixed on Oliver, so bright and fiery that his relief at not being in pain anymore was completely overshadowed by a spark of lust. He wanted those blazing eyes on him, her face lit up in ecstasy…

Shut up, he told the bond in his chest. Those images had been mostly its fault. He'd been attracted to her before she drank the bond nectar, but that had been a low, simmering thing. Not this white-hot lust that made it impossible to focus on anything else. He shoved it down, trying to focus on how much she pissed him off.

"Luna," Ben said. "Hey. How was your—"

Luna cut him off, glaring at Oliver. "You don't want to be around me *so* much that you'll be in pain for it? You don't even *know* me!"

It was easier to concentrate on his annoyance after that. Oliver laughed, climbing to his feet. "*Exactly!* I don't know you, Valley Girl! Why should I follow a stranger into town because she didn't think to pack anything warm when she was driving around *Alaska* in the winter?"

"I was heading straight from my hotel to the airport," Luna yelled. "It's not my fault there are all these windy roads and snowstorms in the way!"

Ben took a cautious step toward the hallway. "I'm gonna…"

Oliver ignored him, stalking forward. The cold in his chest eased with every step, which only pissed him off more. He'd been so *cold*. He wanted to run up to her and fold her into his arms, feel the warmth spread through his whole body.

"You're so *annoying*," he growled, fighting the urge off. "Who drinks random liquor off a front desk?"

She gaped at him. "Well, who drinks at *work*?"

"I live here! It's my house!"

"It's not your house. It's next to your house!"

"It was after hours," he argued. "And don't tell me you care about drinking at work. If you've ever worked a day in your life, I bet you're knocking off at 2:00 p.m. with cocktails!"

She glared at him with an outrage only accessible to people who had just been accused of something that was entirely true.

The lobby wasn't soundproofed like their bedrooms were.

Oliver was fully aware that any wolf who wanted to listen could do it from any corner of the inn, especially with how loud they were yelling. But it was hard to care as he stared down at her, heart pounding in his chest.

She was panting. Her cheeks were flushed from the cold, and she smelled *delectable*. She smelled like *his*. Oliver wanted to throttle his past self for drinking out of some random bottle out of the back room and then leaving it on the counter for unsuspecting rich girls to find.

She looked behind him and squawked. "Oh my god. You're *infuriating*."

"*I'm* infuriating?"

"Yes," she snapped, storming behind him to where the sign was lying on the ground, the superglue sitting sadly next to it. "I said I'd pay for that sign! Don't try to glue it back together, are you crazy? It's a terrible sign! It has *no* flair. You'd be better off painting a rock! At least a rock has texture. This has *nothing* to draw the eye!"

Oliver couldn't think of anything to say to that except, "Oh, go straighten your hair."

She gasped at him. Then she patted down her fluffy hair, like *that* was her biggest priority in this shitshow of a day.

"*You* go straighten your hair," she yelled. "And give me this stupid sign!"

She bent down toward the sign he'd just painstakingly stuck together.

Oliver ran up, trying to grab it off her. "That's my property!"

"I *said* I'd pay for it!"

The sign snapped in half. Luna stumbled back holding one half, Oliver with the other.

He stared down at his broken half, rage simmering into an inferno, so hot it drowned out the part of him that wanted to pin her to the nearest wall and ravish her.

"It was *fixed*," he snarled. He could feel his teeth sharpen, helpless to stop it. The small part of him that wasn't consumed with rage worried that he'd scare her—all wolves were taught at a young age to keep their fangs away from humans. He waited for Luna to gasp, to shrink away with her hand over her lip-glossy mouth. Or to lean into her party girl persona, the one she'd been flinging around yesterday evening, all laid-back and cute and *stupid*.

But Luna did something shocking.

She snarled *back* at him. Bared all her blunt teeth and her five-foot fury, throwing her half of the sign to the ground.

"No, it *wasn't*," she yelled. "That sign sucked! Just like these drafty walls and the complete lack of art on this shitty wallpaper and your zero hairdryers and your hole in the roof *sucks*! Do you *want* your inn to suck? Is this on *purpose*, so you'll go out of business and not have to run an inn anymore?"

"Maybe! I wanted to own an inn when I was a dumbass kid, not *now*. I only agreed because everyone outvoted me! You think I want to be stuck with all these ridiculous chores and ungrateful guests? You think I want all these strangers in my business all the time, telling me what I should be doing, how I should protect my pack?"

He rubbed his chest. The ice was gone, but at what cost? The agony was worth being away from this woman.

"Screw this." He threw his half of the sign down and marched toward the front doors.

Luna lingered behind him, clutching the broken wood to her chest. "Where are you going?"

"To get the divorce flower," he barked, not looking back. "I'm not staying tied to you for one more day."

"It's still snowy," Luna protested. "And you can't get too far away!"

Oliver threw the front door open and turned, shooting her a hard smile. "How about we try?"

Then he slammed the door in her outraged face and took

off running, ignoring the warmth that turned to ice before he even got down the driveway.

He picked up speed as he cleared the parking lot. His wolf form would get him there faster, but he was still speedy even if he was stuck on two legs. He ran on the side of the road, where they had already cleared the snow, not bothering to look at the passersby trying to make eye contact as he sprinted past.

Why couldn't everyone just leave him *alone*?

The ice in his chest grew spikes, sending blistering tendrils out through the rest of his body. His feet ached as they struck the wet pavement. His hands shook at his sides. He was starting to sweat in ways that had nothing to do with how fast he was running. His shirt stuck to his back, tiny gasps of pain falling out of him as he got closer and closer to the mountains.

Asphalt gave way to a thick layer of snow. His steps became harder, and somehow it wasn't the snow holding him back— this felt like his very bones were protesting the distance between him and the spoiled woman back at the inn who had tied them together.

The mountain loomed in front of him. A few more minutes of running and he'd be at the base, ready to climb.

His vision tunneled. He stumbled, knees hitting the snow. He knelt there for a moment, spots dancing in the corners of his vision.

"Come on," he panted, his lips numb. "Come on. Gotta be strong. Gonna—gonna be an alpha."

He *was*. This past year was just a hiccup. He'd known he was going to be the next alpha since he was a teenager. That wouldn't change just because Oliver was playing it safe.

He tried to stand. His knees collapsed under him, then his arms. He fell to his stomach and stared up at the mountain, dazed, head lolling. It was still too far away. Even if he made it, it was covered in snow. He wouldn't be able to find the flower like this.

Ben is never going to let me live this down, he thought.

Something surprising sprung up amongst the pain: worry. Not his own. The bond was making her stupid emotions leak into his.

Oliver pulled up his walls. Her worry faded, and he felt himself smile.

Then everything went dark.

Chapter Seven

Guys had run out on Luna before.

She was a *lot*. In the best ways, obviously. The fun, entertaining ways. Even so, some guys couldn't handle it. There had been her high school boyfriend, who hadn't liked that she danced on tables at parties. Then her college boyfriend, who had gotten mad at her for *accidentally* throwing out his granddad's ashes so she could have a free vase for the beautiful bouquet she bought herself as a half-birthday present.

But she'd never made a guy chase guaranteed agony just so he wouldn't have to be in the same room as her. She couldn't help but feel a little bad as Ben came striding into the living quarters with Oliver hanging over his shoulder, still unconscious.

"Sooo," Luna said as she stared at Oliver's limp form. "When you say 'in pain'…"

"It's a very vulnerable time," Grandmother Musgrove said.

She stood back to let Ben get past her. Luna was relieved it was just Grandmother Musgrove here, no weird uncles or prying aunts or boisterous kids. She was a little sad Sabine wasn't around. She'd joked with Luna last night while they were getting clothes from her room. Luna could use some jokes right now to offset the annoying and baseless guilt. It wasn't her fault, *obviously*. But she couldn't help but feel a little bad as she watched Oliver's limp body bounce against Ben as he carried him to their quarters.

"Pain is only the most immediate symptom," Grandmother Musgrove continued. "If he stayed away, he would get sick. Perhaps die."

Luna stared at her. "Oh my god, *seriously*?"

"In rare cases."

She started down the hall. Luna trailed after her, wincing when Ben banged Oliver's head on a door frame.

"You can stay with us free of charge," Grandmother Musgrove announced, adjusting her thick sleeves against her tattooed wrists. "I'm sorry this happened now and not a year ago. He was different before. Sweeter. More open. Less prone to snapping at things that didn't require teeth. You would have liked him."

"Before," Luna repeated. "Why, what happened a year ago?"

Grandmother Musgrove stopped, staring down the hall at the closed door that Ben had carried Oliver through.

"You should go to see him," she said. "The closer you are, the less he hurts."

Luna squirmed. The door to her room lay behind Grandmother Musgrove, empty and tempting.

"I totally will," she said. "After I call Hector."

She rushed into her room, closing the door behind her. The ice in her chest was small, almost unnoticeable. Oliver would be fine until she got back. She could still sense him through the bond, dead to the world in the Musgrove's common room.

She twisted the phone cord around her finger as it rang. *The closer you are, the less he hurts.* Grandmother Musgrove made her sound like morphine. A soothing balm. A warm shower for a shivering traveler. She'd never been that for somebody before. It felt like a lot of responsibility.

She wasn't a *balm* to Hector, she was…fun to have around. Arm candy. Something adorable and pampered and delightful, like a purebred puppy who very rarely peed on the carpet. Hector never wanted anything else, and neither did she.

"Stranded fiancée," came Hector's greeting down the crackling line. "How goes the snow? Melted yet?"

Luna glanced out at the thick snow outside the window. It wasn't actively snowing, but the sky was looking worryingly overcast.

"Not yet," she said. "Hey, did you know about the werewolf bond…proximity thing? Like, it hurts them if their… ugh. Bondmate, spouse, whatever. It hurts them if they get too far away."

"Shit, seriously? I thought that was just Hollywood." There was a slurping noise, and Luna sighed.

"Are you drinking on the beach right now?"

"Toes in the sand, baby."

Luna groaned, flopping back against her cold bed.

Hector laughed. "What happened? Did you go for a walk, and he freaked out?"

"We, uh…" Luna coughed. "He flipped out at me over nothing and stormed off. Then his brother had to go after him and carry him back because he, um, passed out."

Hector whistled. "He passed out? That's intense. So, what, you gotta hug him once a day, or he gets sick? That's what happened in the movie I saw. What's he like, anyway? Your new husband."

"Ha, ha," Luna said loudly. "We're not *married*-married, just wolf married. They do separate marriages for the human paperwork; we haven't signed *anything*. And he's a jackass. He's rude and he argues about *nothing*, and he's so stubborn about the stupidest shit."

"Uh-huh."

More slurping. Luna sighed, eyes dropping closed as she

imagined a golden beach, her toes wriggling through gloriously warm sand.

"Is he hot?"

Luna's eyes flew open. "What? He's—he's fine."

"Oookay." Hector paused. "Not used to you playing things *down*."

"Well, what am I supposed to say? *Yes, beloved fiancé, the guy I'm magically bonded to is smoking hot.* He's still a jackass! I mean, apparently, he's going through a lot right now, but who isn't, right?"

There was a long silence. Luna toyed with the scratchy sheets, looking longingly over at the bags of clothes she had yet to unpack. Her hair straightener was still in its box, waiting.

"And you two have to be close, or it hurts him," Hector said. "And it's *bond magic*."

"Ye-e-es," Luna said. She squinted up at the ceiling, which was the same hideous color as the walls. They badly needed to hire an interior designer.

"You know our rules," Hector said. "As long as you don't fall in love with him, it's fine by me."

"I'm not going to *sleep* with him," Luna said. She rolled over on her bed, ignoring the excited little flutter in her stomach. A hundred images rushed into her mind—Oliver's strong legs, his broad shoulders, his dark stubble. The biteable line of his chin and the constant strain of his pecs through his too-tight shirts.

Hector had proposed an open relationship six months into their dating after Luna had mentioned liking a waiter's hairstyle. *I'm not a jealous guy*, Hector said when Luna had gaped at him. *If it's just sex, I don't care. If you start to fall for him, that's another issue.*

She'd asked if he wanted to sleep with other girls. He'd shrugged, saying he did but wouldn't if she didn't want him to.

Luna had thought about it and realized she didn't mind if Hector slept with other girls, as long as he let her know and it didn't turn into anything deeper. It had surprised her. She'd always privately assumed she would be possessive about this kind of thing, the same way she didn't let her brother play with any of her toys growing up.

I have your heart, Hector told her when they talked about it later. *That's what matters.*

It was the sweetest thing he'd ever said to her. Luna still thought about it whenever she got cold feet about the wedding. Not that she did often. They were a good match. It was just daunting to consider being with one guy forever. She'd feel that way about any guy, she was sure.

"Sure," Hector said, in that exact tone he'd used when she said she wasn't going to sleep with that waiter with the good hairstyle. She had, but mostly so she could joke about it with Hector afterward. The waiter had been pretty disappointing in bed.

"So," Hector continued. "When you said you weren't going to get eaten in Claw Haven…"

Luna laughed louder than she had since arriving in this freezing, admittedly picturesque little town as she imagined Oliver's head between her legs. Those dark eyes on hers as he licked at her, stubble rasping against her thighs.

"And I stand by that," she said, still giggling to distract herself from the heat pooling at her core. "I'm going to go."

"Tell him hi from me," Hector said, amused.

Luna was still giggling about the phone call as she headed into the Musgrove living quarters. They had *fun* together, she and Hector. They so rarely fought because they never bothered dwelling on things that would lead to a fight. Life with Hector was one long holiday. And when she married him, that would be the rest of her life: fun and jokes and mai tais on the beach, never lingering on the serious stuff. What kind of guy told his fiancée to go sleep with the hot werewolf she was accidentally bonded to? Hector, that was who.

Not that she was going to. Probably. Maybe. *Definitely* not if he still hated her.

She raised a hand to knock on the door to the Musgrove common room.

It flew open. Ben stood behind it, already waving.

Right, Luna thought, dropping her hand. *Werewolf hearing*.

"Great, you're here," Ben said, leading her over to the couch where he'd dropped Oliver face down. "I've never actually been around a case this bad before; everyone usually sticks close to each other after their bonding. You know?"

Before she could decide if his tone was accusatory or not, he held out a paper bag.

Luna took it and looked inside. A cluster of chocolate wolves sat at the bottom.

"Give him a few, get his blood sugar up. I'll be in the laundry room doing lazy boy's chores." Ben gave Oliver an exaggerated look like they were both in on the joke. "Yell if you need us. This room isn't soundproofed."

"Got it," Luna said. Then she frowned. "Wait, are the *other* rooms soundproofed?"

Ben laughed, heading for the door. "At *our* end of the inn? Are you kidding me? We got it put in with the insulation. I don't know how any wolf survives without it. We'd have to live in different houses otherwise, and who wants that?"

He ducked into the hallway, closing the door behind him.

Luna stared down at the unconscious werewolf lying face down on the couch. It was too small for him, and his wet sneakers dangled off the edge. He'd never looked less menacing. And she realized, as she sat gingerly on the couch arm next to his head, he'd never looked more at peace. Other than a wrinkle in his brow, his face was lax.

The closer you are, the less he hurts.

Luna paused. Then she reached out and cautiously touched his hair.

The wrinkle in his brow smoothed.

Whoa, Luna thought as the warmth in her chest expanded. *It's actually working.*

She stroked his hair away from his forehead.

His eyes snapped open.

"Oh my god!" Luna snatched her hand back, the paper bag rustling in her lap.

Oliver's head twisted, and he stared up at Luna groggily. He wore a look of deep relief, but there was confusion behind it. Like his body was telling him something and his brain was taking a second to wake up.

"You're safe," Luna said hastily. "You're on your couch. Ben carried you back."

He squinted up at her. Then his expression lapsed into exhaustion, and he slumped back down on the couch.

"Oh my god, you're *such* a drama queen." Luna took a chocolate wolf out of the bag and tossed it at him. "Eat this."

The chocolate bounced off his cheek. He picked it up, glaring incredulously. She waited for him to scoff, but he just heaved himself up and stared at the chocolate, so tiny in his large hand. Then he ate it in one bite.

"Surprised you're not allergic," Luna tried.

"'S wolf-safe," he said, still chewing.

A strand of dark hair fell over his forehead. Luna's fingers twitched, itching to push it back like she'd done before. The warmth in her chest was tugging in little lurches. It wanted her to touch him even more than she did. It was strange, being able to sense something else's wants on top of your own. The less she focused on it, the less she could tell them apart.

"Sooo," Luna said. She shifted down so she was sitting on the actual couch, not just the arm. Leaving a sensible distance between them, of course. "Nobody told me about the proximity thing. Any other *bond* crap I need to know about? I thought it just meant I was on a magical wolf registry and would have a little Tinkerbell warmth in my chest."

Oliver sighed. "It varies from couple to couple. Some people can feel each other's emotions. Some of them read each other's minds—"

"Read each other's *minds*?" Luna laughed shrilly. "You are not getting into *my* mind, wolf boy."

"Back at you," Oliver snarled. He had a very expressive face. Like someone had designed it purely to reach optimum scowl.

She threw the bag of chocolate into his lap. "Okay, rude. I'm not *disgusting*, you know. I'm fun, I'm hot. I'm a *riot* at parties. One time, I was auctioned off at a charity dinner, and a woman paid twenty-five thousand dollars just to have lunch with me. And that was just *lunch*. Do you know what people would pay to be *married* to me?"

He gave her an unreadable look, like he wanted to say something but he had too many ideas to settle on one.

"I don't," he started. His hands flexed around the paper bag. "I don't *know* you."

"Yeah, I don't know *you*. That doesn't mean we have to scream at each other about it."

"*And* you have a fiancé," he continued like she hadn't spoken. "*And* I don't want to bow to the whims of bond magic just because it wants us to…"

He trailed off, rubbing his chest. He looked exhausted. Maybe he *hadn't* wanted her before the bond, Luna realized with a sinking stomach. Maybe her attraction to him had been one-sided. She'd met a few guys who were immune to her charms. Most of them were gay, but there had to be some straight ones out there who weren't into her brand of cool, fun and hot. Maybe he could only get off with tall, dark-haired women. Maybe he was only into MILFs. You never knew.

"Okay," she said, squeaky. She cleared her throat, flashing

him a winning smile. "What do you want? Not the magic. You."

She meant it as a getting-to-know-you question. Then he turned to face her, eyes dark and half-lidded. Any notion that he wasn't attracted to her before the bond was wiped from Luna in an instant.

Luna's mouth went dry. Her smile faded, forgotten, as the warmth in her chest started to pulse. Neither of them spoke.

Then Oliver looked away, and the moment was broken.

"I want my pack to be safe and cared for," Oliver said. "I want… I want to fix the roof in the damn lobby."

"You said you wanted an inn when you were younger," Luna said. "What, does the reality not live up to your expectations?"

He gave her a sideways look.

Luna rolled her eyes. "I'm sorry, is *that* too personal? Excuse me for trying to be polite for five seconds."

His mouth flickered. He scratched it, but Luna glimpsed the curious smile he was hiding behind his hand. Even if it was gone when he dropped his hand back into the bag of chocolates.

"I didn't think about all the upkeep when I was younger," he said, popping another chocolate into his mouth. "I just… I don't know. Liked the idea of offering a safe harbor."

Luna couldn't help it: She cooed, bright and teasing.

"Shut up," Oliver said with the automatic reflexes of someone who had grown up in a big family.

"What? That's sweet. That's the first time you haven't been a complete asshole around me. A girl could get used to this."

She rocked sideways and bumped their elbows together. They both went stiff, Luna's arm blooming with delighted warmth. She looked over to see the muscles in his arm working where she'd touched him.

She leaned back. "Sorry. Or…not sorry?"

"I don't want to drag you into this," he admitted. "You did get yourself into this mess—"

"Okay, if we're going to blame somebody, let's blame the guy who started drinking mystery booze at work—"

"But you didn't actually ask to be stuck here," he said over her. "Especially not with some…asshole who passes out if you get too far away. My point is I won't interfere. You're already with someone, no matter what our magic says."

She risked another look over and found him staring determinedly at the wall, jaw flexing. She wondered what the bond was doing inside him. Was it pulsing like hers? The others said it was more intense for him since he was a wolf. Maybe it was churning. Burning. Calling out. She could still sense a faint yank inside her own chest, drawing her toward him.

She watched him, considering. She was stuck at an inn until the snow melted. This was basically a holiday. Her last holiday before she got married. Hector had already given her his blessing, and if it was for the guy's *health*…

"About that," Luna began. "Hector actually said he was fine with it."

Oliver stopped, his hand still in the chocolate bag. "Fine with what?"

Luna hesitated. Then she put a hand on his denim-clad leg. Her hand tingled, unable to stop herself from squeezing the firm muscle there.

A groan cut off in his throat. He blinked hard, collecting himself. "Seriously? He's *fine* with his fiancée sleeping with another man right before their wedding?"

"We have an arrangement."

Oliver shook his head. His leg shifted under her touch, but Luna could feel the heat in her chest getting warmer. Shifting. Curling outward, wanting closer.

"I can't imagine being fine with giving what's mine to someone else," he said.

Luna snorted. "Okay, *some* people aren't territorial, wolf boy."

"It's not a wolf thing," he argued. He made a face. "It *really* isn't. I know way too much about my cousins' love lives. Some of them have multiple bondmates." He sighed. "Let's not get into it. My point is we're not all territorial like that."

She dropped her voice a few octaves, letting it go soft and sultry. "Just a you thing, then."

He didn't say anything, looking down at her palm on his thigh.

She squeezed it again, enjoying how his muscles jumped underneath her hand. It had been a long time since a guy had made her feel this delicious anticipation. Some of it was even from her, she was pretty sure. At least half of that want was bona fide Luna Stack—no bond required.

"You're not disgusting either," she told him. She shuffled closer until their legs were touching. "Actually, I thought you were kind of hot when I met you. Before I knew you were drunk and super rude."

"I was having a bad night," he said. His gaze dropped to her mouth. His pupils were huge, almost drowning out the dark brown surrounding them.

Luna grinned. "And it only got worse." She reached up, tweaking that piece of hair she'd stroked off his forehead earlier. "We could make the best of a bad situation. What do you say?"

He blinked. He still looked disbelieving, but it was rapidly being taken over by a haze that Luna knew all too well. She could feel it, too, making the world narrow down to the two of them on the couch, their legs touching.

She leaned in.

"Wait," he said.

Her heart fell, the golden warmth behind it coiling in protest.

"Not here," he continued, standing up. "No soundproofing."

Chapter Eight

Oliver dragged her into his bedroom and immediately stumbled over a sneaker.

Luna giggled, looking around his room. "Wow! Messy."

"Yeah, yeah." Oliver kicked the sneaker under his bed, which was…also less tidy than he'd like it. "Sorry, I don't have a maid."

"I don't have a maid," Luna groaned. "She's a cleaner, and she only comes once a week."

"Jesus Christ, stop *talking*. We were finally getting along." Oliver grabbed under her thighs, hoisting her up.

Luna yelped. It quickly turned into a gasp, dimple denting her stupidly adorable cheek as she grinned down at him. *Probably never had someone pick her up before*, Oliver thought as he held her. He'd had girlfriends who wanted him to use his superstrength to their advantage. Oliver eyed the wall behind her. Later, he decided. Right now, he wanted her splayed out on his messy sheets.

Luna let out another shocked laugh as he dropped her onto the mattress.

"Rude," she said, brushing hair out of her eyes. "You treat all your girls this way?"

"Only the ones who really, really annoy me," Oliver said.

The bond pulsed in his chest as he crawled on top of her. He wondered if she felt it as strongly as he did. She couldn't, being a human and all, but it was tempting to imagine that the bond was lighting her up just like it was doing to him. Tugging at him to get closer. To get *more*.

Luna's mouth was still curved in that flirty smile. For a second, Oliver thought he saw an edge of uncertainty, but then she blinked and it was all hunger again.

She dragged him down into a kiss. The bond in Oliver's chest pulsed so hot he gasped, jerking back.

Luna stared up at him, pupils huge. Her cheeks were bright red. She was already panting.

"Oh," she said. "Oh, *wow*."

She dragged him back down. Oliver didn't pull back this time, even as the bond lit a wildfire inside him. Surging, throbbing, wanting him to get closer. He felt drunk with it. He hadn't felt like this with anyone, not even with—

He didn't dare finish the thought. He focused on Luna underneath him, every touch making warmth spiral over his skin.

Luna grunted against his mouth. "Mm. Clothes."

"Yeah," he agreed, fingers already working at the hem of her shirt. She was still wearing Sabine's sleep shirt, which was weird. He quickly forgot about the weirdness as he stripped it off, smoothing his hands down all the exposed skin.

Luna moaned, head tipping back. "Oh my god. They should *sell* this shit. This feels…"

She yanked at his shirt, and he pulled it off in one swift motion. Then he was on her again, kissing her mouth, her cheek, her neck. Everything felt so *good*. The simplest touch turned him molten.

Then all of a sudden, Luna laughed, tugging at his arm.

"What?" Oliver pulled back to see what she was pointing at. "Oh, come on."

Luna giggled, teasing a finger over his one and only tattoo: *party animals*, with a howling wolf curled on top.

"It's *so* stupid," Luna crowed. "Were you a frat boy?"

"No. Shut up." Oliver leaned down again, the bond spasming in delight as he pressed an open-mouth kiss to her shoulder. She let out a small moan, but it was quickly overrun by another laugh.

He made an annoyed noise into her collarbone. "It's not that funny!"

"No, it's just…" Luna cackled. "Hector joked about how I was gonna get eaten in a monster town."

He looked at her blankly.

"You know," Luna said. Her tongue flicked out. "*Eaten.*"

I should not find that charming, Oliver thought as he watched her tongue waggle. And yet his traitorous mouth twitched.

"Do me a favor," he said flatly. "Don't talk about your fiancé during this."

Luna's laugh turned into a yelp as he slid off the bed, pulling her with him by her knees. He nuzzled her bare stomach, tugging her sweatpants down.

"This is gonna be weird," Luna said as he slid her underwear off. "Right? With the bond? I can feel it. It's like…spreading? Can you feel that?"

He nodded. The warmth in his chest spread with every second he was touching her. His skin buzzed with it. It wasn't *making* him want, it was just…adding fire to the flames. Looking at the soft pink of her cunt would've made his cock jerk any day, not just because they were tied together. He took a moment to admire her: the neat landing strip, the nub of her clit already hard and peeking out at the top of her folds.

He gave her thigh one last kiss and then buried his face between her legs.

Luna moaned, breathy and surprised.

"Fucking *tingles*," she marveled. She ground her hips against his mouth, another moan stuttering out of her.

She was so *wet*. He was already slick from his nose to his chin. He stiffened his tongue, fucking it into her, and felt her get even wetter. He gathered the wetness on a finger and lifted it to her clit, working tight circles around the nub.

"Oh my god," Luna panted. Her hands tightened in his hair, hips working faster. "Oh my god, oh my *god*."

She reached up, tugging her breasts out of her bra cups to twist her nipples. A strange sensation rocked through Oliver. For a second, it felt like *he* was the one lying on the bed, twisting his nipples and getting eaten out. He froze in shock, groaning at the twin sensations.

"Oh, wooooow," Luna said, voice high. "That was—okay. *Wow*. Why'd you stop?"

She twisted her nipples again. Oliver felt the faintest twinge in his own chest, shuddering at the pleasure that followed. The bond sang through them, linking them up to the same buzzing wavelength.

"This is so *weird*," Oliver said.

Luna grinned smugly. "I'm not complaining!"

She nudged him with her heel. He huffed, leaning back in.

The sensations came faster now. Mostly his own—the delight of burying his face in her pussy, his cock pulsing in his jeans, her nails scratching his scalp. But some of it was hers. He could feel the orgasm building up in her core, the bond pulsing hotter with every passing second.

"I'm gonna—" Luna gasped.

He could feel it, the almost unbearable pleasure. The incredulity that she was even telling him since the bond made sure he already knew. And then, finally, the peak.

It took everything in Oliver to keep working her clit and fucking her with his tongue. Her orgasm was sparking at the edges of his mind, so close to setting all of him ablaze.

Luna relaxed against the bed, still moaning. Oliver had to look down to check he hadn't come in his jeans like a teenager. There had been moments when Luna had blurred into him so intensely that he wasn't sure who the pleasure belonged to.

"They *really* should bottle that." Luna let out a hysterical giggle and pulled on his shoulders. "Get up here. I'm not done with you yet."

Oliver felt a growl rumble up his throat. He stumbled up, crawling over her. He kissed her stomach, sucked her nipple, sank his blunt teeth into her shoulder.

Luna yelped, delighted. "Should I be worried about waking up tomorrow covered in fur?"

"I'll never break the skin," he assured her. "It gets drilled into us in every sex ed class."

"Ooooh, tell me more about werewolf sex ed," Luna said, leaning up to take her bra off properly. "What, do you howl when you come?"

He didn't answer. He was too busy yanking his jeans off and throwing them much harder than he meant to. Oliver winced as they smacked into the wall, his belt denting the wallpaper.

"Wait," Luna said. "*Do* you?"

"It was—" Oliver paused, unable to stop a groan as he freed his throbbing erection from his boxers. "It was a onetime thing."

He bent down to kiss her. She stopped him, a hand on her chest.

He pulled back, about to ask what was wrong. Two things made him pause: One, the hungry look on her face as she stared at his cock. And two, the pulse of borrowed lust that raced through the bond.

Luna looked up at him, eyes all pupil. "Fuck me."

The bond *yanked*. Oliver followed it gladly, devouring her mouth with a frantic passion. Her hands knotted in his hair, her naked body so soft and hot against him that it almost hurt to pull away long enough to grab a condom from the bedside table.

Luna marveled at his chest hair as he shuffled through the infuriating drawer.

"You're so hairy."

"Genetics," he said distractedly. He made a noise of triumph as his hand closed around a familiar foil packet. He gripped the edge—

—then proceeded to tear the whole thing in half. She was kissing his chest, each touch of her lips a spark threatening to consume him. He cursed, grabbing another condom. That one tore, too, and Luna's devastating lips curved up around his nipple.

"Having fun?"

"So much," Oliver said, annoyed. "Just…"

He trailed off as she took the next condom from him and opened it easily, sliding it onto him with a practiced air that would've looked unaffected if he couldn't feel her need through the bond, impatient and eager. She wanted this as much as he did. She was just better at acting like she didn't care.

"Ah-ah," she said as he started climbing on top of her. She patted his hairy flank. "Doggy-style. To suit the occasion."

He rolled his eyes as blatantly as he could, letting her up. "How many more dog jokes are you going to throw at me?"

"I'm surprised I held out this long," Luna said, rolling onto her hands and knees. She tilted her ass into the air, wiggling tantalizingly. "Now be a good boy and fuck me."

Oliver hoped she didn't feel the excitement that raced through him as she said that. Judging by the smug grin she flashed at him, she absolutely did.

He knelt behind her, rubbing her hips. Part of him wished she'd let him fuck her face-to-face. He wanted to touch every part of her that he could reach, wanted to watch her face crease and her neck strain. Wanted her to clutch at him, her haughty composure in ribbons as he fucked her. But she was still wiggling her ass, and he was only human.

Well. Sort of.

A gasp spilled out of her as he dragged his cockhead against her swollen pussy folds.

"Shit," she hissed. "Oliver. Get in me. Come on, you want it just as bad, I can feel it. I can *feel*—"

She broke off on a groan as Oliver pressed inside. He echoed it, the bond thrumming between them. He could feel her tight walls around him, but he could also feel how it felt. Getting fucked.

"So *weird*," Luna whispered gleefully. "Ohhhh man. I feel *awesome*."

"Yeah," Oliver said nonsensically and pulled her further onto his cock.

Luna jolted. Her spine arched, teeth flashing up at him. "Give me all of it."

Something snapped inside of him. He pulled her up, locking an arm around her torso to hold her up. He plastered his chest against her back, hips jackrabbiting into her. He usually took it slower than this, but he could feel her emotions through the bond: shock, joy, hunger so deep it made him bare his teeth.

"Oh, fuck," she gasped. "Oh shit, *Oliver*—"

He growled, crushing her closer. He shoved his nose in her hair, breathing in salt, roses, the shitty soap they stocked in the guest bathrooms. His first time with someone wasn't usually like this. Before, he'd always been quiet, cautious, searching. Stopping to try out different positions and angles, seeing what made them moan. There was no stopping this. The bond was too powerful. Oliver could do nothing against it but hold her and fuck her and groan like an animal, arms clamped around her torso. And all the while, Luna's pleasure flowed through him: her utter joy at being fucked, her dazed excitement at feeling what it was like for him. An echo chamber of ecstasy, dragging them higher and higher.

Oliver came first, holding her close as he pumped into her and stilled, shaking. The bond echoed his orgasm between them. He was fucking her, and he was being fucked. He was Oliver and he was also Luna, and when their visions tunneled, they fell down the chasm together, entwined so close they couldn't tell each other apart.

Oliver woke up an indeterminate amount of time later, still inside of her.

"*Whassapaning*," he mumbled against her shoulder.

"*Mrgh*," Luna replied, muffled against the pillow. She was underneath him, her back pressed into his front. "*Gedoff.*"

He lifted himself on wobbly elbows. He felt strange. The bond was still there, a warm glow in his chest. But it was tamer now—sated—no emotions leaking through. His cock was soft inside of Luna, except there was a strange throb at the base. It felt tight. Swollen. Almost like…

He froze. It couldn't be.

"Um," Luna said. She squirmed, and the movement made his mostly soft cock twitch inside of her. "What's happening? Are you hard again?"

"No," Oliver said, hushed. "It's…a side effect."

Luna frowned. "Of the bond?"

"I guess." Oliver waited, hoping against hope that it would go back down.

Luna squirmed again.

Oliver winced. "Just a second! It'll go away."

"Seriously," Luna said, still moving against the mattress. "It feels like… I don't know what it feels like. Did you get *bigger*?"

"I didn't mean to," Oliver managed.

Luna tried to push herself up, gasping in pain when the

giant bulb at the base of his cock stayed inside her. She fell back against the bed. "Oliver! What is *with* your dick?"

"It's a knot," he said miserably. "It's…locking us together. For, you know."

Luna froze. "That condom will hold, right?"

"It's reinforced," he said. "Built for any sized knot."

"Thank god for werewolf-reinforced condoms," Luna muttered. "Remind me what this is again? They didn't mention monsters in my sex ed class."

"You *know*," Oliver said desperately.

"I know it's for breeding," Luna replied with a wince. "But, like…how long will it be like this?"

"I don't know," Oliver admitted.

"You don't know?"

"It varies," Oliver said, trying to remember the most mortifying of his wolf lessons. "Maybe ten minutes?"

He dropped his head onto the pillow above her, mortified. He was *knotting* her. What kind of stupid werewolf biology was at work inside him? Did it sense a bond and think *alright, time to go*? Knotting was supposed to be something impossibly intimate. Some werewolves *never* knotted. And here he was, knotting a woman he'd literally run away from an hour ago. It didn't matter how gorgeous she was, or how her dimple made him want to pin her to the wall and scent her until she was covered in him. He didn't *know* her. She shouldn't be stuck under him, unable to move while they waited for his knot to go down.

"Fuck," he spat, cheeks burning. "I'm sorry. This has never happened before. It's not supposed to happen like this."

Luna chuckled. "Bet you say that to all the girls you knot."

"There are no other girls! This isn't—" He shuddered as his knot throbbed deep inside of her. "*Shit*."

Luna twisted toward him. He avoided her gaze, but they were stuck so close together. It was impossible not to see her small smile.

"Oliver," she said. "It's *fine*. Stop freaking out."

"I'm not freaking out," he snapped. He clenched his jaw. "Does it hurt?"

"No." Luna swiveled her hips experimentally.

He gasped, another wave of unbearable pleasure rolling through him. "Stop *moving*."

Luna stilled. But not for long.

Oliver frowned as she pushed at him. "What?"

"Roll over."

Oliver glared at her.

"Not a dog joke this time," Luna said. She kicked his leg. "Seriously, do it."

Oliver turned onto his back as carefully as he could. Luna followed clumsily, still locked onto him. She straddled him, hips working gently back and forth. The long line of her back was mesmerizing.

Oliver groaned, grabbing her thighs from behind. "What are you doing?"

"What does it look like?" She turned to shoot him a wink, leaning down to scratch her manicured nails through his leg hair. "I mean, since you're already stuck in there."

She rolled her hips harder.

Oliver made a noise like he'd been sucker-punched. His cock twitched again, growing ever-so-slightly thicker.

Luna grinned. "Sensitive?"

He nodded wildly. The bond made Luna's emotions bleed through once more: bone-deep satisfaction, hunger, and an odd tenderness about seeing Oliver so vulnerable.

Then Luna rolled her hips again, and the tenderness was swallowed up by renewed hunger as Oliver groaned.

"Good," Luna said sweetly. "Me too. Now be a good boy and hold still while I get myself off."

Chapter Nine

Luna dragged her finger in a lazy circle through Oliver's chest hair, humming contentedly. She was sore and satisfied and warmer than she had been in days. They'd had sex twice more after the knot finally went down—until she'd lost count of how many times she'd come, and the bedframe was scored with scratches from Oliver digging his claws in.

She looked up to watch Oliver's sleeping face. There were no tired bags under his eyes, no wrinkle in his brow. His face was smooth, utterly relaxed. Luna bet the guy hadn't been this relaxed since the mysterious incident last year that had made them all move here. It made her oddly happy. The guy was so pent-up, and he deserved some stress relief. Especially if it came in the form of making Luna incoherent with pleasure.

Oliver let out a sleepy grunt. "Quit it. Tickles."

Luna circled her finger around his nipple.

Oliver squirmed, cracking one eye open to glare half-heartedly at her.

Luna grinned. "Sorry. Got bored."

"Y'r like a golden retriever," he muttered. His head tilted sideways, lips brushing her forehead. He was half in a dream. Luna could almost feel the edges of it in her mind. Hazy and dark, lit up by flickers of flame. A woman with dark hair and a bright smile—

"Don't," Oliver snapped.

Luna startled. She'd gone deeper than she'd meant to.

"Sorry," she said as Oliver struggled underneath her. "I didn't mean to. The bond—"

He sat up, shoulders tight. There was nothing half-hearted about his glare this time.

"Don't," he said, softer. "If the bond lets us in too deep, we block it. Got it? Some things are private."

"Totally," Luna agreed. She dragged a hand through her messy hair, shaken. Who *was* that? Whoever it was, they had triggered horrible feelings. Maybe he'd left a bad relationship back in Arizona.

She could still feel his emotions, barely-there echoes of guilt and anger. She shoved up a mental block until they faded into nothing. No more Oliver leaking through the bond.

A heavy knock made them both jerk.

Oliver frowned. "Is it dinner already?"

Luna checked the clock on the bedside table. "Yeah. Wow. Guess we tired each other out."

Oliver made a sleepy noise of agreement and sat up. He rubbed his eyes, only dropping his hand to give her a sideways look. "When you say you're telling your fiancé about this… He doesn't get *details*, right?"

Luna laughed, shooting up to dig her chin into his shoulder. "Why, are you into that?"

"*No*," he said flatly.

Right, Luna thought. *Possessive*. Even if he only had her until the snow thawed.

The knock came again, loud and insistent. Luna wondered why they were knocking so loud, then remembered the soundproofing.

Oliver gave her arm another unhappy look and climbed out of bed to search for his pants.

"We eat dinners together," he said as he pulled his boxers on. "You don't have to come."

Luna leaned on the bedframe, admiring the pronounced curve of his ass as it vanished under his boxers. "Am I invited?"

Oliver made a face like she was, and he was exasperated about it.

"Then I'll come," Luna said.

It didn't occur to her to be nervous until she was heading down the hallway with him. What was she doing? She'd spent the day in his room. Even if they didn't know, they could *smell* him on her, right? They knew she had a fiancé. What was she supposed to do, blurt out their arrangement right there at the dinner table?

It didn't help that Oliver looked just as nervous as her, his shoulders getting higher and higher with each step.

"You don't have to," Oliver said as they reached the common room door. "My family can be…a lot."

Before Luna could remind him that she was *fully* aware, the door swung open.

Vida stopped, her headphones clamped securely over both ears. She turned back toward the bustling common room and yelled, "Never mind! They're here!"

"You don't need to yell," Oliver reminded her.

She gave him a droll look only achievable by disdainful teenagers.

"Whatever," she said and paused. She gave a small, almost subtle sniff. Then she looked at Luna with such a smug, knowing look that Luna's heart sank.

She *definitely* smelled it.

"Whatever," Vida said again, ducking her head to hide a shy grin. Then she fled back to the crowded table.

Everyone had already taken their seats: The kids clumping together, with Vida joining an argument involving Leo, who tried to slide his broccoli onto a complaining Darren's plate. The aunts were next to them, deep in conversation. Then Ben and Sabine, with Ben plucking an eyelash off Sabine's scarred cheek. Uncle Roy had pulled his chair away, surveying the scene with a scowl. One hand kept drifting up to his chin, scratching his burn mark. It looked old—much older than Sabine's slashing scar. Like he'd gotten it when he was very young.

Grandmother Musgrove sat at the head, cutting her steak into tiny squares. She looked up, waving a graceful hand at the two empty chairs beside her.

"Come and sit."

Luna followed Oliver to their seats, wishing she'd put on deodorant. It might not have covered up the Oliver stink that everyone was obviously smelling, but it may have helped with some of the nervous sweat she could feel as she sat down. She and Oliver were seated next to each other, tucked in so tight that their legs and elbows brushed.

"Sorry," Oliver said, pulling his leg and elbow in so he wasn't touching her. Pretty rich for a guy who had been inside her *multiple* times today. He looked out at the table, which was heavy with food. "You could've come to get me. I would've helped."

"We decided to let you have the night off," Ben said, flicking his wife's eyelash off his finger. He looked considerably less smug than Vida, who kept sneaking glances at Luna and stifling a giggle.

"You seemed busy," Sabine added. She was smiling, but she looked confused.

Everyone was smiling, Luna noticed. Smiling and looking at each other, all conspiratorial and smug. Even Leo and Darren had picked up on something, sniffing the air once they noticed all the adults acting weird. Darren let out an amused snort, averting his eyes. Leo just kept sniffing, cocking his head at Luna in bafflement.

Grandmother Musgrove asked, "How was your first proper day in Claw Haven, Luna?"

"Great," Luna said, as bright as she could muster. "Oh, that reminds me! My fiancé wants to thank you guys for being so nice. I've been telling him everything that's been going on, and he's super happy with it. *Super* happy."

Ben's eyebrows hit his forehead. "Huh. To each their own, I—"

He cut off with a grunt like someone had kicked him under the table. Luna couldn't tell if it had been Sabine or Oliver, the former looking at him far too innocently and the latter glowering at him almost as hard as Uncle Roy was glowering at Luna.

Luna flashed Uncle Roy her prettiest smile. His eyes narrowed, and he dug one sharp thumbnail into the old burn mark on his chin.

Yikes. Luna looked down at her plate instead. Medium-rare steak, a salad that was mostly lettuce, a bread bun and a dollop of buttery mashed potato. A little boring, but Luna was starving, and she doubted there were many Uber Eats options in a town this small.

She picked up her fork.

Grandmother Musgrove cleared her throat.

Luna looked up. Everybody was holding hands, even glaring Uncle Roy. Grandmother Musgrove held out a hand on one side of her. Oliver sat stiffly on the other side, hands on his lap.

"She doesn't have to," Oliver said.

Luna rolled her eyes and grabbed his hand. She wasn't a grace kind of girl, but when in Rome.

Grandmother Musgrove nodded at Leo. "When you're ready."

Leo sucked in a big breath. "Thank you, everybody, who made our food tonight. It isn't chicken like I wanted, but I guess

I'm grateful anyway. Thanks, everyone." Then he blinked, looking over at Oliver. "Wait, you weren't here. Thanks, everybody but Oliver. And hello to our temporary pack member, Luna. You're very pretty and sophisticated."

Luna giggled. "Wow. Thank you. You're pretty too. I love your truck shirt—so chic."

"Thanks!" Leo beamed at her, then looked across the table toward his parents. "Can we eat now?"

"Yes," said Sabine, hiding a smile. "We can eat now."

Everyone at the table lapsed back into chatter. Luna ate her boring food and tried to remember the last time she'd had a homemade family dinner. She didn't think she ever had. The Stacks were a takeout family who ate in their separate rooms. They went out to restaurants sometimes, but only for birthdays and the occasional business milestone celebration. Hector once mentioned that it was strange that such a fun-loving family didn't bother getting together much. Luna didn't think so. They all had their own parties to attend.

Oliver rarely spoke. His family tried to drag him into conversations. Leo asked about a movie they watched last week, and Ben goaded him about some embarrassing moment from high school involving a wardrobe malfunction during a football game. But each time one of his family members spoke to him, he'd give them a one-word answer and shut it down. He kept tensing up whenever Luna reached for her water glass or leaned over to grab more salad. It was a strange tenseness. Like his body wanted him to relax but his mind wanted the opposite. Like he still thought she was a threat.

What would have happened if she'd been bound to him last year, when he wasn't so closed off?

It was probably good he wasn't more open, she considered as she ate her terrible salad. If he actually let her in, she might feel something more than physical. Something that had nothing to do with the bond tying them together. Then she'd *really* be screwed.

"So, Luna," Sabine said, cutting through a steak that was noticeably less cooked than Luna's. All the others were, now that she looked closely. "What do you do?"

Luna tried to remember her official role at her dad's company.

"A little bit of this, a little bit of that," she said with a smirk. Then, because she would be out of here soon and was still riding the high from earlier, "And I do a little marketing."

"That sounds fun," Sabine said, with the polite eagerness of someone who had no idea what that entailed. "What's that like?"

"*So* fun," Luna gushed. "Don't tell anybody, but I was the one who designed that little logo on our most recent rebranding. Logos are *very* important."

She looked over at Oliver, who was watching her with a dry expression that meant he remembered her sign outburst in the lobby.

"I'll bet," he said.

Darren picked a piece of meat out from between his buck teeth and asked, "Uncle Ollie, can we still go to the movies this weekend?"

"Uncle *Ollie*," Luna whispered, delighted.

He gave her another exasperated look.

"Sure," Oliver said. Then he paused, fork scraping to a stop against his plate. "Uh, Luna will have to come."

"Duh," Darren said, like he was offended Oliver thought he had to be reminded. "*I* pay attention in wolf lessons."

"The bottle wasn't supposed to be in the back office," Oliver argued. "And I've never seen it when it wasn't covered in flowers! It looked different!"

Darren rolled his eyes. "Ooookay, Uncle Ollie."

"*I* would never accidentally drink the bond nectar," Vida

muttered beside him. She still had her headphones on, though she'd relegated them to her neck at her mother's request.

Luna looked over at Grandmother Musgrove. "Wolf lessons?"

She nodded. "Every second Saturday from the ages of five to thirteen, we get the children together and tell them of our history—Musgrove, of course, but also wolf. Family stories, rituals. What they should expect as they grow."

"Aw! That's sweet." Luna beamed around the table. "You guys are *so* nice. I always heard werewolves were all, like, *rowr!* with each other."

The table fell silent.

"Not, like…" Luna giggled nervously, making a clawing motion with her manicured hand. "Not, like, *bad*. Just…*rowr!* You know?"

"We can be," Uncle Roy said gruffly.

"Oh, don't be like that, Roy." Aunt Barney took a napkin out of one of her million pockets and dabbed at her mouth. "Some of us are, dear. Just like any family."

"What is yours like?" Aunt Althea asked, gold fang flashing as she spoke. She tucked her hand into a fake claw. "Are they *rowr*?"

"We're rowr-dy," Luna said. It got her a decent laugh. "Yeah, we have tons of fun. We don't do family dinners, though. This is so cute!" She gave them another smile, extra-bright to make up for the awkwardness. One lesson she learned young: If you acted cute enough, people let you get away with anything.

She snuck a glance at Oliver. He was chewing slowly, ignoring Ben, who was trying to make pointed eye contact with him from across the table.

Sabine asked, "Are you close?"

"I mean… We work together, technically." Luna poked at a stray piece of tomato, wondering why she felt so exposed. She talked about her family all the time at charity events. It was what everyone knew her for. *Luna Stack, daughter of Henry*

Stack. Then they'd ask how he was, and she'd say he was great, even if they hadn't talked in months. Which happened often enough. Not on purpose, obviously. They were just busy with their own awesome lives.

"Everyone has their own things going on," Luna continued. She busied herself with sliding more salad onto her fork, feeling weirdly exposed. The Musgroves lived together and plaited each other's hair, and they went to the movies and ate dinner together every night. Luna couldn't be bothered driving forty minutes to her parents' place. Last year, she'd been in the neighborhood for a bachelorette party and dropped in to say hi. Their first questions when they saw her in the foyer were *What are you doing here? Did something happen?*

She watched Darren poke his big sister with a fork. Vida poked him back, scowling. It made Luna miss her own little brother, which was weird. She didn't usually miss her brother. She didn't miss her family, period—until she started watching the way the Musgroves fit together.

Aunt Barney and Althea whispered together, their voices getting louder and louder until Althea said: "Yes, you do! It's that little blue logo we see sometimes at the hardware store. Cute little logo, I always said. Most logos are dull as dishwater; yours actually has some pizzaz."

Luna gave her the biggest smile she could manage. Nobody else knew she had designed that logo. Her dad had laughed in her face when she admitted she wanted to work in graphic design and marketing.

Don't worry your pretty little head about it, he'd told her. He wouldn't be happy if he found out she was "meddling," as he called it whenever she tried to have a say in the company he'd built.

"Totally," Luna said. "Um, thank…thank you."

Leo spoke up. "Hey Grandma, is Uncle Ollie gonna be alpha this year?"

The table went silent again. Oliver's grip went white around his fork, then forcibly relaxed. He didn't look up at Grandmother Musgrove, who gave Leo a warm smile.

"Maybe next year," she said.

"But you said that *last* year," Leo pointed out. He gave Darren a knowing look, who frowned back at him like he was annoyed at Leo for saying it.

Sabine cleared her throat. "I like your hair, Aunt Althea. New beads?"

Aunt Althea gasped, holding up the beads she'd woven into her hair.

Luna stared at Oliver. He was nodding blankly, barely pretending to be interested as the others admired Aunt Althea's hair. Luna always assumed somebody had to die to replace an alpha. Was it just like handing over a job? Had he been on track to be alpha, then something happened to make Grandmother change her mind? Everybody had gone silent, so what was the story there?

Darren shoved the last piece of broccoli on his plate and stood.

"Chocolate time," he announced, heading over to a drawer and emerging with the paper bag that Luna had been holding only a few hours ago.

"That's for guests, honey," Aunt Althea reminded him.

Darren pouted. "But Uncle Ollie ate them!"

"We can buy more tomorrow," Grandmother Musgrove said. "It would be nice to support local."

Darren ran around the table, distributing wolf chocolates.

"Oh, I love these," Luna gushed as Darren handed her one. "Beth gave me another sample when I was in town before. She's adorable, and her chocolates are *delish*."

"She's a wonderful chocolatier," Grandmother Musgrove agreed. "It's a shame she might not be able to keep that store open."

"What?" Luna asked. "Why?"

"Not enough tourists," Ben explained.

Oliver shifted in his seat, careful not to let his elbow skim Luna's. Luna thought back to what he'd yelled at her about wanting the inn to close, then what he'd said later on the couch. Safe harbor.

"This place should be crawling with tourists," Luna said. "You guys have mountains; you have forests, and a *beautiful* ocean view. Throw in the monster schtick, and you have a hook!"

"*Claw Haven*," the kids chorused. Even Vida, though her tone was heavy with sarcasm. "*For the monster who wants some peace and quiet!*"

Luna clapped. "Exactly! You can totally capitalize on that."

Luna rolled the chocolate in her hands, feeling the wolf's rounded muzzle. An idea was brewing; she could feel the images coming together the way they always did before she reached for her secret sketchbook.

"About your new sign," Luna said. "I could design it. Free of charge."

Another series of looks got traded around the table.

Luna tucked her hair behind her ears self-consciously. "It's no big deal. You *are* letting me stay here for free."

"Because I pass out if you leave," Oliver said.

She cocked her head at him. "Is that a 'no'?"

Grandmother Musgrove spoke up. "That would be lovely, Luna. I look forward to seeing it. Thank you."

"You're welcome!" Luna popped the chocolate wolf into her mouth and beamed.

Fondness pulsed through her, fast and reluctant. It took Luna a second to realize it wasn't her own. She looked over at Oliver, surprised.

He wasn't looking at her. All his limbs were pulled in tight so he wouldn't touch her, eyes on his plate. For a second, Luna thought she might have imagined it. Then his mouth twitched, and she caught the faintest echo of fondness once more.

She averted her eyes. She'd promised she wouldn't pry. She didn't want him messing around in her head as much as he didn't want her in his. She chewed her chocolate, and the next time she caught the echo of an emotion—annoyance at Uncle Roy's opinion on the movie they watched last night—Luna blocked it out.

Chapter Ten

Oliver stood in front of Luna's door the next morning, hands flexing at his sides.

Just knock, he told himself. *Why the hell are you nervous? The worst that can happen is she says no and you have to reschedule. Get over it.*

He startled as the door at the end of the hall opened, Ben strolling out of the hallway with his car keys in his hand and his work apron tossed over his shoulder, yawning widely.

Oliver tried to look like he was examining Luna's doorframe for paint chips.

No dice. Ben ran up to the guest hallway, yanking his work apron off his shoulder and smacking Oliver in the stomach.

"Jesus, dude, just *knock*."

"Shut up," Oliver hissed.

"*You* shut up."

Then they were wrestling. Oliver had been surprised to learn that most human siblings grew out of play-fighting when they were adults. His grandparents had wrestled with their siblings until they died of old age.

At least they were keeping it quiet, Oliver considered as he shoved his little brother into a headlock. They were being mature about it.

Ben twisted out of the headlock and straightened. "Just talk to your wife, man. You got through the whole dinner without yelling at each other, that's progress. Not to mention that you two were fucking like rabbits—"

Oliver swiped at him.

Ben leaped out of the way easily. He was always the agile one, speed to Oliver's strength.

"Go to work, jackass," Oliver whispered. "And she's not my wife!"

Ben skipped the rest of the way to the lobby, like an asshole.

"You need to start running again," he yell-whispered from the lobby. "You're insufferable when you don't go for your runs. Like a golden retriever."

Oliver gestured helplessly at Luna's door.

"Bring her along," Ben continued to yell-whisper and skipped out of the lobby.

Oliver stood silently in the hall, listening. Luna's room wasn't soundproofed, and there were no signs that she'd heard. Just the same scribbling noises that had been happening since he arrived in front of her door. The occasional swear and the sound of ripping paper.

Oliver gritted his teeth and knocked.

Another swear, then, "Uhhh, come in!"

Oliver opened the door.

Luna threw a notebook under the pillow and stood, hair bouncing. She'd straightened it, and she was wearing her style of clothes again, all stylish and sleek. But this time it was a pencil skirt and a flowy blouse, like she was going for businesswoman instead of summer fun. She'd gone around every single clothes shop in town while Oliver shook in freezing agony back at the inn.

Oliver asked, "What's that?"

"What's what?" Luna twirled a strand of hair around her finger. She did that a lot, Oliver noticed—tried to be cute to distract whoever she was talking to. It would have worked if Oliver wasn't so stubborn.

He pointed at the edge poking out from under the pillow. "It looked like a notebook."

"Oh, *that*." Luna waved at it dismissively, shoving the notebook fully out of sight. "It's...my ideas notebook. For marketing stuff."

"Top secret?"

Luna laughed, short and sharp. "You could say that. It doesn't matter anyway—not like I'm going to use any of it."

She tugged on her hair, her shiny lips pressing into a thin white line. She was nervous, he realized. He almost wanted to tease her for it. But she looked so uncharacteristically shy, and he didn't want to piss her off before asking the next question.

"I was heading into town," he said. "Do you want to come?"

She squinted at him. "I feel like the actual question is *Can you come with me into town so I don't pass out on the side of the road?*"

He waited. "And?"

"I'm thinking."

He sighed. Of course, she wouldn't make this easy.

Luna hummed. Stroked her chin. Hummed some more.

"I do actually have things to do," Oliver started.

She spoke over him. "What do I get out of it?"

Then she stood there, twirling her damn hair. Oliver wished he didn't find it so hot. Since when was he into spoiled-rich-girl chic, which clung to her even when she was wearing Sabine's sleep clothes?

"I'm still pretty disappointed you guys don't do massages," she continued. "I was just about to leave a Yelp review."

"Fine," he said. "I'll give you a damn massage. Can we go now?"

She blinked, hand pausing in her hair. She'd been expecting

him to turn her down, he realized. But before he could take it back, her pouty mouth curved into a surprised smile.

"I look forward to it," she said, bending to grab her handbag from beside her bed. "You have taken a course, right?"

"I have a certificate."

"What, really?"

"No," he said flatly. "Let's go."

After an argument over how long it would take to put on makeup that led to Luna muttering under her breath as she applied foundation in the car and *another* argument over how spindly Luna's arms were, Luna got to push the cart around the hardware store. Oliver didn't even know how that last one had turned into a fight. He *didn't* care who pushed the cart. But suddenly, he was yell-whispering outside of the hardware store.

Luna was such a sore winner about it, too. Humming all happily, pretending not to strain under the weight with each addition to the cart.

"Are you going to get Jackson to help?" she asked, doing a terrible job of looking unaffected as she pushed the heavy cart down the aisle. "*He* seemed to know what he was doing."

Oliver thought hard about wrestling the damn cart off her.

"He's already told me what to do," he said. "I can handle it myself."

"Right, sure. Totally get a novice to do it when there's a professional right there," Luna said. Then she frowned. "Wait. I thought you couldn't work on it until the snow thaws?"

"I can't work on it until it's stopped snowing," Oliver corrected her, scanning the aisle for the type of nails that Jackson told him about. "Just need to get the snow out of the way."

"Still sounds slippery."

Oliver squinted at the rows and rows of nails. Why were there so many? How many different types of nails could people possibly need?

A-ha. He grabbed a packet of the correct nails and started, "I heal—"

"Fast. No, I remember." Luna grimaced as she pulled the cart over, then pretended she hadn't when she noticed Oliver looking. She even draped herself appealingly against the cart, resting her chin in her hand like she wasn't panting at all.

"If you get hurt…" she said. "Do I feel it? Because I think I felt a lil' something when you passed out."

Oliver's fingers twitched around the packet of nails. His family was going to shove that in his face for the rest of his life. Then he processed the last part of that sentence.

"You what? What did it feel like?"

Luna shrugged. She scratched the corner of her mouth, which was sticky with gloss yet again. He wished it didn't look so appealing.

"It didn't feel like *passing out*," Luna said. "I just…knew that something happened. Is it more intense for you since you're a wolf?"

Yes, he thought. He hadn't been so lost to the whims of his wolf since he was a teenager. He was attuned to her scent, keeping an ear out for where she was in the inn and having to stop himself from burying his nose in her neck when she passed. And that wasn't even counting the bond, which dialed everything up to eleven. He could sense where she was and feel her emotions if he focused, and sometimes even when he didn't. There had been so many moments during sex where they'd leaked through, her passion blurring into his so easily that he hadn't been able to tell the difference.

"Not if I don't focus on it," he said, dropping the packet of nails into the cart. Then, when she raised her brows expectantly, he added, "Like I said, it depends on the bond. Ben and Sabine know what each other is feeling and where the other is most of the time. Grandmother and Grandfather could read each other's minds without even trying. Uncle Roy and his wife, too. They had to block it out. Even when they severed the bond, they could still hear echoes for years."

"He was *married*?" Luna laughed, then covered it up badly with a cough. "What was she like? Long-suffering?"

He bit his cheek to stop his smile. "Georgia was sweet. Funny. Didn't put up with his crap."

"Wolf?"

"Human," he corrected. "It didn't end well. He still won't tell us why, but we're betting it was his own damn fault."

"Shocker," Luna muttered. She was so busy watching Oliver that she didn't notice the orc she was about to run into, and Oliver had to grab the front of the cart and yank it to a stop.

"What are— Oh!" Luna's irritation slid quickly into awkwardness. "Hi! Oh my god, sorry!"

"Don't worry about it," said Nick Wicker with a dismissive wave. He had engine oil on his shirt yet again, and Oliver wondered if this guy ever washed his clothes.

Nick winked at Oliver. "Ollie! How's life with the new wife?"

"Not my wife," Oliver said hastily. "Bye, Nick." He tried to push the cart away. But Luna was already talking.

"We didn't even know each other's names when we got 'bonded,'" Luna said. "I have a fiancé, so…"

"Ooookay," Nick said with a nervous laugh. He was still smiling, but all of a sudden he looked like he regretted bringing it up. "That's…modern."

"My fiancé knows everything that's happening," Luna continued, eyes and smile far too wide. "He's *very* happy."

Nick's brows hit his hairline. "Wow! Okay! That's great for you guys."

Luna nodded. "And how's the weight lifting going?"

Nick's grin twisted in confusion. "Uhhh. It's fine?"

"Are the flour bags working?"

Whatever the hell that meant, it wiped the smile off Nick's face.

"I gotta go," Nick blurted, and headed into the next aisle so fast his cart wheels screeched.

Luna caught Oliver looking and started, "When I ran into him the other day—"

"I do not give one single fang about Nick Wicker," Oliver assured her, pushing the cart back into a straight line. "Why do you have to say it like that? *He's very happy?*"

"I don't want everyone thinking I'm a cheater!"

"Well, you're making it sound like your fiancé has a *thing* for you sleeping with werewolves," Oliver hissed, hoping that anyone with hearing as good as his was busy chatting with someone or sifting through some loud wind chimes.

Luna groaned, shoving the cart forward. "Fine! I'll say it differently next time! There's going to be a next time, right? Everybody here is so nosy."

"Right?" Oliver said, his annoyance with Luna overpowered by the annoyance from all his months in town. "What happened to everyone minding their own business? I feel like every time I turn a corner, somebody is asking me how I'm doing."

Luna nodded vigorously, forcing the heavy cart around the corner. "If you all just ignored each other like *normal* people— Oh!"

She cut off with a yelp as a familiar hedgehog woman appeared in front of them. Oliver grabbed the cart just before it could slam into her.

"Oh, gosh." Beth curled into herself, her spikes puffing out like a puffer fish's.

Luna let out a noise so high-pitched that Oliver winced. "Beeeeth! Hiiii! We were just going to drop by your cute little shop to buy your adorable chocolates!"

"I'm not there," Beth said, uncurling. "I— Obviously,

because I'm here. My employee works there a couple of days a week."

Luna leaned over the cart and tweaked one of Beth's shoulder prickles. "*Love* that for you. Have you ever thought about getting on socials? Doing some promo?"

Oliver shot her a look. Luna ignored him, twirling a strand of hair around her finger in a way that was definitely meant to annoy him. Here she was, getting annoyed at people for getting in her business, and now she was butting into Beth's.

"Um," Beth said. "I—I don't know. I feel a little weird about shoving it in people's faces."

"Gotta let people know it exists," Luna argued. "Look, I took a photo of one of your wolf chocolates yesterday. Isn't it cute?"

She got out her phone. Oliver leaned over and saw a picture of Luna posing with the wolf chocolate, winking at the camera.

"I also took a photo of your store," Luna continued. "Look, I'll post about you on Insta. *Just bought the cutest monster-themed chocolates from the most adorable store in Alaska...* Copy-paste your deets... Do you do online orders?"

Beth brightened. "Yes! We ship anywhere in the USA and Canada."

"Perfect," Luna sing-songed. "And...posted."

The loading sign stayed on the screen.

"When my data allows it," Luna continued, teeth gritted. She shot another smile at Beth. "Anyway, it was so great to see you! Bye-bye!"

Oliver waited until Beth walked off, almost colliding with a *50% OFF* sign on the way because she refused to stop waving until Luna did.

Luna looked back at her phone with a triumphant noise. "Posted! Finally. This place needs a better connection. The mountains aren't *surrounding* you, so what gives?"

Oliver used the distraction to take the cart off her, pushing it easily the rest of the way around the corner.

She caught up with him fast, her irritated glare sliding off when she noticed how he was looking at her. "What?"

"Why'd you do that?"

She looked down at her phone, where the notifications were already pouring in. How many followers did this woman have, anyway?

"I'm bored?" She shrugged. "There isn't a lot to do in this town. Excuse me for finding a pet project, *Ollie*."

He squirmed at the nickname, twisting the cart handle. Nobody called him that outside of his family. People tried, but he always politely rebuffed them. At least, he did up until a year ago. These days, he usually just glared.

"What, they didn't give you anything to do while you're stuck here?"

"I don't actually—" She stopped, biting her lip. She twisted to look around the empty aisle. "I just consult. For the marketing team. And that's only because I gave them all fruit baskets and got them tickets to baseball games so they'd give me a chance. If my dad knew how often they emailed me to fix a problem…"

He frowned as he pulled the cart to a stop in front of several stacks of wooden slats. "He doesn't want them to?"

She laughed again, running a hand through her hair. She looked genuinely nervous—no distraction-through-cuteness this time.

"He wants me to stay out of the way. He thinks the only thing I'm good for is posing for pamphlet photos." She held up her manicured hands. "These lil' paws aren't made for work, you know? They're made for leisure. And I'm *very* good at it."

She said it with a grin. But there was a bitterness underneath, like she wasn't fully on board with her cruisy lifestyle.

He sounds like an asshole. Oliver bit his tongue, reaching up to grab a wooden plank from behind her head. He'd assumed she wouldn't know what work was if it ran up and bit her.

However, she'd actually gone behind her dad's back to find work—admittedly, at his own company, but still.

"Weird," Oliver said instead. "I guessed he was smart. Since he runs a company and all."

She blinked. For a second, he thought he'd overstepped—just because she was ragging on her dad didn't mean he got to. But then she grinned at him, nothing coy about it.

"Are you being nice to me?"

"No," he replied, heaving the plank into the cart. "I'm insulting your dad. Problem?"

She shook her head. Her stare was so hypnotic that Oliver found it difficult to tear his gaze away and reach up for the planks again. The bond fluttered in his chest, growing hot tendrils.

He pulled another plank out, distracted. He didn't notice the other wooden planks sliding forward until it was too late.

"Shit," he barked. There were too many to catch at once. He grabbed Luna, bending over her just in time. The planks slammed into his back, making him wince. *That* was going to bruise. For about ten minutes, but still.

Luna yelped, jumping closer as they rolled off him and onto the floor.

"Oh my god," she yelled.

"It's fine," he said, strained. He pulled back. "You alright?"

She nodded. "Are *you* alright?"

"Sure." He grimaced, rolling his shoulders. "Takes more than that to hurt me."

A minotaur stomped into the end of the aisle, dressed in a staff uniform.

"I got it," Oliver called. "Don't worry about it."

He looked down. Luna was clinging to his shirt. She looked down as if she hadn't noticed. Her arms dropped back to her sides, and she took a large step back.

"Very, uh..." She coughed. "Very alpha of you. Why doesn't

your grandmother want you to be alpha, anyway? That seemed like a whole…thing. You were *going* to be alpha, right?"

"I still am," Oliver said shortly.

Luna gave him a dubious look. "Sooo…what happened?"

Oliver clenched his jaw. He might like her a little better this morning, but he wasn't about to spill his guts about the fire. Some things were private.

He bent down and scooped the wooden planks into his arms, tiptoeing to slide them back into place above their heads. "*A good alpha relies on others,*" he recited flatly. "*A good alpha isn't an island. A good alpha lets everyone stick their nose into his business.*"

"Well," she said. "You're…very protective. So that's one alpha thing to cross off the checklist."

He looked down to see if she was making fun of him. But there was no trace of irony in her face, just an uncharacteristic shyness.

The warmth in his chest rolled, trying to expand into his rib cage. He squashed it back into place. The snow was thawing. She'd be out of his life soon enough.

Chapter Eleven

Luna stumbled to a stop, panting.

"I'm going to die," she moaned.

For a moment there was no reply except a chilling wind. Then Oliver came plodding back, looking just as annoyed as the last time he had to come back for her.

"You're not dying," he said flatly. "You're just a human trying to keep up with a werewolf."

Luna thought about berating him. She gave herself a few extra wheezes before straightening up, rolling her eyes when she noticed how irritatingly hot he looked. A fine sheen of sweat made his too-tight shirt stick to his skin, accentuating his muscles and coarse hair. The bond pulsed inside her, almost indistinguishable from her own lust, both wanting Luna to walk up and grope his pecs right there in the middle of the forest.

She wisely held herself back. She wasn't an animal. More importantly, she wasn't about to give him the satisfaction. She would have every chance later when they slept together, which was quickly turning into a daily occurrence in the week since she had arrived.

"You said you could run," Oliver continued.

"I *can* run. On a *treadmill*. Not at werewolf speeds up a *cliff*!"

Luna gestured wildly at the steep forest incline she had been struggling up. "Can't you just run a *little* slower? You're lucky I even agreed to go for a run with you. I *should* be driving next to you at snail speeds."

"I'm not running on a sidewalk," Oliver argued, repeating an argument they'd already had twice the day before. "I go for runs to get away from it all, not to wave at nosy townsfolk. And you *know* they'll wave."

Luna sighed. Every time she went into town, which wasn't often, there were more and more monsters waving at her. It *was* annoying. But Luna couldn't help but be a little charmed. She'd never lived in a place where grocers asked how your family was doing. Or in Luna's case, Oliver's family. It seemed like everyone in town knew about their situation now and had readily accepted that Luna was stuck with the Musgroves until the snow thawed.

"Still," Luna said, adjusting her admittedly cute sports shirt, which she had found at a boutique in town. "You should be more grateful. I didn't have to do this."

"You did if you didn't want me to go stir-crazy," Oliver said. "If you think I'm an asshole now, I'm even worse when I don't get to work out."

Luna gasped, the noise made less effective when she immediately wheezed, "You mean this is the *cure* to your assholery? Oh my god, if you'd told me that I would have started running that first night!"

It was a low blow. But Luna couldn't help it. They'd been bitching at each other all day, and it wasn't like they could properly get away. Every time they tried, Oliver turned up with his tail between his legs, looking just as reluctant as she did. But agonizing pain was a great motivator.

Oliver's jaw twitched. Luna waited for him to bark at her, or even just take off again, making her trudge after him up the steep incline.

"Come on," he said instead. "We're almost around the cliff. Then it's an easy loop back down to the inn. They'll be waiting on us."

He ran off, jogging slower than before.

"Waiting," Luna repeated, her whole body groaning in protest as she started lagging after him. "What for?"

"We're having a family outing," Oliver said in a flat tone that implied he wanted it just as much as she did.

Luna groaned. "Can't we just stay home? We could say I'm tired! We won't even have to lie!"

Oliver said nothing. Luna watched the muscles in his back flex with each step he took, and admitted to herself that he had slowed his pace for her.

"No," Oliver said finally. "I haven't come along on a family outing for a while. I owe it to them."

Luna mustered up enough oxygen for a groan. But even as she trudged up the forest cliff after him, she couldn't help thinking how sweet it was. Who the hell went on "family outings"? Not *her* family, for sure.

"What are we doing?" Luna panted.

"Don't know," Oliver said. "But it's Claw Haven, so our options are limited."

Luna huffed a breathless laugh. She opened her mouth to deliver what was surely a witty addition about the lack of entertainment in this tiny town, only for her foot to catch on a rock and skid.

Luna yelped. She threw her hands out, her mind whirling as she prepared to hit the rocky forest floor—

—only to find herself wrapped in Oliver's sweaty arms, staring into his intense eyes.

"Careful," he barked.

Luna said nothing, her chest heaving. He'd been a few steps ahead. Werewolf reflexes were good, but not *that* good.

Unless you're linked, she reminded herself. He probably felt her fall, his own stomach dropping along with hers.

Oliver pulled her up. His blazing touch lingered on her arms, and the bond rejoiced. Luna's head swam with the urge to lean up and kiss him. And not for the first time, she wasn't sure if the urge was hers or the bond's.

Oliver cleared his throat, stepping back. It felt like plunging into an ice bath, the cold air making her shiver again.

"Let's head back down," he said. "We've kept them waiting long enough."

Sweethelm Books was cute enough, Luna considered as she pretended to be interested in a shelf of history books—especially if the bookstore cat Leo kept talking about, Mosey, showed up. That cat sounded *adorable*.

"Are you a very bookish family?" Luna asked as the younger kids chased each other around the comics section and Vida ignored them both and read a young adult book on a nearby couch.

"Not much," Oliver admitted. "But it's somewhere to be. Even if we have to put up with Chester being a dick."

"Chester?" Luna asked, craning her head to watch the kids tussle far too close to a display of comic books.

"The owner," Oliver said. "He's a dragon. And a dick."

Grandmother Musgrove tutted, making Luna jump. She hadn't even known she was behind them—she'd thought Grandmother Musgrove was over in the self-help section with the aunts and Uncle Roy, reading out the titles they thought were the stupidest. Or looking at travel books with Ben and Sabine, who had apparently traveled a lot before they had a kid.

"Chester is not a dick," Grandmother Musgrove said with dignity, pulling her shawl tight despite the warm air coming from the vents in the bookshop. "He's a sweet man with a gruff disposition. Like another man I know."

Oliver did a very good job of ignoring them both. He nodded over at the kids, who were now clambering over Vida while she crouched protectively over her book, still determinedly reading.

"I'm going to go rescue Vida," he announced.

He stalked off toward that corner of the bookstore. Luna watched him go, the bond stretching forlornly between them.

He's just going to the other side of the store, she told it. *Calm down*.

But the bond continued to turn in fretful circles inside her chest, trying to make her walk over and join him. For some reason, it only got worse when the younger kids started climbing on Oliver instead. Oliver stood there with a long-suffering expression, but it quickly turned to a reluctant smile as they worked farther up his legs and hung off his waist. To everyone's surprise, even Vida joined in, and he lifted her off her feet as she clung to his arm. The kids all shrieked with laughter, and Luna's breath caught in her throat as Oliver grinned reluctantly.

A sweet man with a gruff disposition. Catching her when she fell, being a climbing gym for his nephews. Making his family dinner every night he wasn't with her. What else was Oliver hiding under all that annoyed glaring?

"Luna," Grandmother Musgrove said. "Is the bond acting up? You look flushed."

Luna forced whatever was happening to her face to cut it out and gave Grandmother Musgrove a sunny smile.

"It's just warm in here," she said, fanning her cheeks. She looked around desperately for a distraction and found one in a human woman about her age standing on a stepladder and shelving books in the fiction section.

"Oh good," she said. "I had a question. Excuse me, ma'am!"

Luna jogged over, her mind reeling, trying to think of any possible question she could have for a bookshop employee. She couldn't even remember the last time she was *in* a bookshop. If she wanted a book, she had it shipped to her doorstep.

The human woman looked down from the stepladder. "Yes? How can I help?"

Luna paused. The woman was wearing a shockingly stylish vintage skirt, plus a purple hair ribbon that made her look like she'd stepped out of a Librarian Chic Pinterest board. It had been so long since Luna had seen someone whose fashion style she envied, it took her a second to remember her fake question.

"If I see something I like," Luna started, "but I don't decide I want it until I leave town, could I buy it online and get it shipped to me? I'm going away soon."

"Oh," the woman said, climbing off the stepladder. "We don't do that. Sorry."

Luna paused. She *didn't* want anything, but the idea that she couldn't order something online shook her.

"You don't have an online store?" Luna asked, aghast.

"The owner is old-school," the woman explained.

"What about your customer base outside of Claw Haven?"

"We don't have that," said the woman with a perfect customer-service smile. "Can I help you find something?"

Before Luna could decide whether she wanted to slink back to the others or inform this woman of all the business she was missing out on, Leo streaked past them and started scaling the bookshelves.

"Hey," Oliver barked. "Leo! Get off of there!"

Leo twisted to blow a raspberry at him, already as high as Luna's head. But his grip got muddled as he reached for the next shelf, and the woman let out a yelp as the kid's hand sank into her hair instead.

"Whoa," Luna cried, grabbing Leo as he started to panic and yank this poor woman's neat bun undone. "Everything's peachy! Can you give me your hand, bud?"

Leo stilled. Luna worked his hand free and set him on the ground.

"Okay," Luna said, trying to figure out what to say next.

What would she want to be told if she had done that as a kid? "Uhhh. Did you hurt your hand?"

Leo giggled at the absurdity of her question. "No!"

"No," Luna agreed, and turned to the bookstore employee. "Did you hurt your hair?"

"No," the woman said sunnily, untying her purple ribbon from its ruined knot.

"Then no harm done," Luna said, tapping Leo's shoulders. "Off you go. No more climbing!"

Leo raced back toward Oliver. Luna looked up to find him watching her with a strangely soft expression, and the bond flared in her chest. Then Darren tackled him from behind, and Oliver's expression turned exasperated again as he whirled to drag Darren off.

An old, croaky voice echoed from the back room of the bookstore: "Are you in one piece, Vi?"

"I'm fine, Chester," the bookstore employee, who must be Vi, called back. She fiddled with her purple ribbon, her customer-service smile slipping as the silky material escaped her fingers. "Damn."

"I got it," Luna offered. She stepped behind Vi, and only after she felt her stiffen did she realize that she was majorly invading this woman's space. But Luna already had the ribbon, undoing the tangles that Leo had accidentally created and redoing a proper knot around Vi's dark hair.

"There," she said. "Now you're perfect again. Vi, was it? I'm Luna."

She held out a hand, wondering why she had even done that. It wasn't in her nature to get in other people's business like that. If someone needed help, she let them figure it out for themselves. But it had seemed so natural. She was there, wasn't she? So she might as well.

If Vi was still weirded out by the invasion of personal space, she hid it quickly.

"Nice to meet you," Vi said, the picture of politeness with not much behind it. Then her expression faltered and she reached up to touch her newly done ponytail. "And thank you."

"No problem!" Luna beamed, oddly proud of her little act of helping. She waved over at the kids, who were back to clambering over Oliver. "Little rascals. They're usually super sweet."

"They are," Vi said, her practiced smile turning warm. "They come in a lot. They don't buy many books, but it's good to see them anyway. They make me glad I'm—"

She faltered, blinking hard. Her smile went back to its perfunctory self. "Anyway. Can I help you with anything else?"

Luna nudged her, her curiosity piqued. "Glad you what? Come on, you're the first Claw Haven local who hasn't started getting super personal within thirty seconds of meeting me! Except that orc with the flour, I guess. No idea what's up with him."

"Orc with the—?" Vi shook her head, stepping back. For a moment Luna thought she was going to make a quick exit. Then she hesitated, looking back at the Musgroves peppered around the store.

"I'm just glad I moved here for my sister," Vi said finally. "She's going through a hard time and it's good to be here for her. That's all I was going to say."

"Oh," Luna said, touched. "That's...that's so nice."

Vi patted her hair into place self-consciously. "And how have you been? You're the woman who's been staying with the Musgroves, I assume."

"That's me!" Luna posed, only feeling a little like an idiot as she did it. Especially after Vi had gotten sincere with her like that. "It's been...uh..."

She had been about to give her usual schtick about how she was making the best of it. That the family were so nice it made up for the grump she was chained to until the snow thawed. But looking around the bookstore, she suddenly felt oddly vulnerable.

"Weird," she confessed. "Like, this is a *family outing*. Who *does* that? They already spend all their time together at home! It's—it's *ridiculous*."

She stammered to a stop as a familiar arm bumped up against hers, the bond squalling inside of her as she looked up to see Oliver raising his dark brows at her.

"What did I miss?" he asked, so casual it threw her. This was a totally different man than the one she'd been stuck with: a softer, more giving version that only seemed to come out when he was with his family and ignoring Luna's existence. But he wasn't ignoring her now. Having some of that softness aimed her way made Luna tongue-tied.

"I was just saying how ridiculous you guys were," Luna said, trying desperately to make it clear she wasn't insulting him this time. "You know. All your super-cute family outings and dinners and board game nights, as if you don't already spend all your time together."

To her surprise, Oliver didn't even roll his eyes. He just cocked his head, like she had a point.

"It *is* pretty ridiculous," Oliver said after a moment. "But wolves will be wolves, I guess. Are you ready to go? Leo's going to throw a tantrum if he doesn't get dinosaur nuggets soon."

"Oh, that child and his dinosaur nuggets!" Luna giggled, still stupidly flustered for reasons she couldn't fully understand. She waved at Vi. "Good to meet you, Vi. Stay chic."

Vi made a face like she had never been called *chic* before. But like everything else, she hid it quickly under a mask of professionalism.

"I will," she said. "You, too."

Luna struck another pose. Usually it made her feel cute and silly. This time it made her feel like she was an actor who didn't know her lines. Luna always knew what to say—until Claw Haven. Until the Musgroves. Until Oliver, who took her off guard with everything he said—even the nice things. *Especially* the nice things.

★ ★ ★

She couldn't help staring at him as they climbed into his car. Oliver glanced over at her. "What?"

"Nothing," Luna said. "I've just never seen you so relaxed."

"I'm not relaxed," Oliver said instantly. "Would *you* be relaxed around that?"

He pointed at the van in front of them, which the rest of the Musgroves were piling into. Uncle Roy was scowling at a self-help book the aunts had got him, seemingly as a joke. The younger kids were still trying to chase each other, only stopping when Ben grabbed them and hoisted them into the back seat. Sabine was helping Grandmother Musgrove into the front while Vida ignored everyone and bobbed her head to music trickling out of her giant headphones.

"No," Luna admitted. "But wolves will be wolves. Right? With your cozy little packs. All protective and whatever."

Oliver said nothing. His hands tightened on the steering wheel, his gaze fixed on his family with an intensity that made Luna think she'd said the wrong thing.

She leaned forward to meet his eyes. "Was that speciesist or something? You *are* cozy. Insufferably so, some might say."

The insult jolted Oliver back from whatever he had been spiraling into. "What? Right, no, sure. Put your seat belt on."

And *there* was the Oliver she was used to.

"I was getting to it," Luna complained. She clicked the seat belt into place, watching the Musgrove van pull into the icy street. She waited for Oliver's car to follow them. Nothing happened.

"Are we waiting for a reason?" Luna asked.

Once again, Oliver said nothing. Luna looked over to see him twist the keys in the lock. Then he did it again. And again.

"Shit." Oliver sighed, wrenching the keys out. "I think we're going to miss Leo's dino nuggets."

Chapter Twelve

"I can text the Musgrove group chat," Luna said from the passenger seat. "They can swing back around, it'll take five minutes."

"In five minutes I'll have this fixed," Oliver called from under the car hood. He stared at the engine, trying to remember what Grandmother had taught him when this happened last time. But *last* time it had been an issue with the battery, which looked fine to him. So did everything else. The car wasn't even giving him any warning lights; it just wouldn't start.

He heard the passenger door open and close. The bond twisted joyously inside him as Luna came to lean against the car, her arms crossed and her expression unimpressed. He wished he didn't find her glaring at him so attractive. It made him want to pull her in and kiss her right here in the cold street. But he held himself back. There would be plenty of time for that later. Luna had been coming to his room after dinner all week, then badgering him until he gave in and pulled her inside.

He told himself he was annoyed by it. But he couldn't ignore how much he wanted her in his bed, bond or no bond. Even if he would rather run away from her and pass out again than tell her that.

"I don't know," Luna said, considering. "Your eyebrows say otherwise."

Oliver scowled at her. "My eyebrows?"

"Those aren't the eyebrows of a confident wolf," Luna said flatly. "Those are the eyebrows of someone who's going to keep us here in the freezing cold for *ages* because he's too proud to call his family for help. And after I just had that whole speech about you guys being so close and cozy!"

"I'll fix it," Oliver said. He turned back to the useless engine, ignoring the bitterness that rose up in him when Luna spoke about their family like that. They *had been* close and cozy, once. And the rest of them still were. But Oliver was on the outside now. He couldn't trust himself to be close with them after what he'd almost allowed to happen back in Arizona.

Heavy footsteps approached from behind. A familiar voice called, "You guys having trouble?"

Oliver sighed and turned. Nick Wicker, orc mechanic and free drinks opportunist, was waving a wrench at them from the sidewalk.

"I can push it to the shop," he said, gesturing down the road to the mechanic shop where he worked. "Or I can have a look at it here."

"We're fine," Oliver said.

Luna smacked him in the chest. "Ignore him! We would *love* your help. Thanks so much, Nick!"

Nick looked at her, surprised. Oliver got the feeling that tourists didn't usually bother remembering his name. Then Nick broke out in a toothy smile, the one that Oliver tried to find annoying but kept finding endearing instead. It was just so damn *goofy*.

"It's no problem," Nick said as he swaggered up to the popped hood. "You're actually doing me a favor. It's boring as hell back there. I was just telling my boss how close I was to coming out here and sabotaging a car just to have something to do."

Oliver and Luna traded a look as he bent down over the engine.

"Which you didn't," Oliver said warily. "Right?"

Nick jerked up so fast he smacked his head on the hood. "Ow! Shit. Ha-ha, no sabotaging here! That maybe wasn't the best thing to say when your car just broke down. So tell me what happened!"

"Nothing. It just won't start."

Nick hummed, his eyes surprisingly keen as they roved over the engine. "Give me a minute to go through all the usual—"

Then he broke off, his head almost slamming into the hood again.

"Vi! Hey!"

Oliver turned. A short human with a purple ribbon in her hair and the most precise smile he'd ever seen was approaching them, beaming.

"Hello," said Vi from the bookstore they had just walked out of, not looking at Nick. "My boss sent me out to see if there was anything I could do to help."

"We're fine," Oliver said again.

Luna rubbed her arms with a too-loud laugh. "A blanket would be great! Something nonscratchy, if you have it."

"You don't need a blanket," Oliver told her.

Luna rolled her eyes. "There's *snow*!"

"It's mostly melted," Oliver insisted, glancing at the remnants of slush on the sidewalk.

Luna huffed. "We can't all have werewolf body heat, okay?"

Before Oliver could talk himself out of it, he wrapped an arm around her and pulled her close. Werewolves ran hot—Oliver couldn't count how many times he'd helped a human like this. Mostly in high school, waiting on the field for a winter game to start.

Luna's breath hitched. Oliver wondered if her bond was reacting like his, rioting in his chest like Fourth of July fireworks.

He had to stop himself from squeezing her tight. Instead he rubbed her arms, keeping it quick and effective.

"Better?" he asked.

Luna nodded. For a moment she looked dazed. Then she shot him a grin. "My very own personal wolf heater. They should hire you by the hour."

"It was nice to see you, Violet," Nick hollered.

Oliver looked over to the bookstore door, where Vi was going back inside. Everyone had paused to look at Nick, who was waving at Vi with a desperation that made Oliver wince.

"You too," Vi said after a moment, her smile straining. Then she ducked back into the store.

Luna gave Oliver another pointed look, her mouth curling in delight. Oliver narrowed his eyes at her. He was *not* going to get involved in some weird orc's crush just because Luna was bored.

"So," Luna started. "Nick! Tell me about yourself. Do you have any lucky girl—?"

Nick made a triumphant noise under the car hood. "A-ha! I see the bastard. Wait here, I'll go grab the replacement part."

Oliver frowned. "Do you need me to push it to the shop?"

"Nope," Nick called, already jogging down the street. "I got it! It'll take two minutes!"

Luna sighed as he ran toward the shop. "Damn. Finally something interesting was happening in this town."

She shivered, burrowing deeper into his arms. Oliver always forgot how sensitive humans were to the cold. He held her tighter, and the bond in him spasmed in joy. It wanted him to turn her around and pull her close. Wanted him to nuzzle her shiny hair. It was getting harder to tell which was the bond and which was just him liking her hair, which was concerning.

Another set of footsteps approached them from a different direction. Oliver looked over to see Emma Curt, grouchy owner of the Grotto Café across the road, sporting a new pixie cut and glaring at them with two cups of coffee in her hands.

"Heard there was a breakdown," Emma said stiffly. "Hope you like black coffee. If you don't, hold it anyway. It's warm."

"Oh," Luna said. "Um, thank you?"

"Don't thank me," Emma said. "Come buy a coffee later. From *us*, not from those other cafés down the street."

"You got it," Luna said.

Emma handed the coffee over.

"It's not actually *that* cold," she told Luna. "You know it's basically spring, right?"

With that, she walked off.

"And yet there's still snow," Luna called after her.

"Barely," Emma yelled back.

Luna glanced over at the mountains hopefully.

"Don't get your hopes up," Oliver told her, glaring up at the snow-covered mountaintops in the distance. "If we tried to get the flower now we'd be swimming through snow."

"Aw," Luna said, faux-sweetly. "Keep that up and I'll think you want to keep me here."

"Don't count on it," Oliver said flatly.

Luna watched Emma vanish into her café and then twisted in Oliver's arms to give him a look. "You really can't do anything in this town without everyone getting in your business."

"Says the woman who was trying to pry into Nick Wicker's failure of a love life," Oliver replied.

"He seems sweet," Luna defended. "Weird, but sweet. He was so squirrely about that flour last week. Who gets sketchy about *flour*?"

"Don't know, don't care," said Oliver, who was determinedly disinterested in the personal lives of the townsfolk, no matter how much they tried to involve him.

Sweethelm Books' door swung open again. Vi marched out

carrying a knitted blanket festooned with tiny white cats with leathery wings.

"Oh my god," Luna cried. "That's *adorable*! Is this that bookshop cat the others were telling me about?"

"That's Mosey," Vi agreed.

"It's so cute," Luna gasped. "Thank you!"

She grabbed the blanket, wrapping it around herself and burrowing back into Oliver's arms.

"I could just let you go now," Oliver threatened.

"Shush, werewolf heater," she replied.

It shouldn't have been cute. Oliver had to bite his cheek to stop a smile anyway.

"It's nice of Nick to help us out like this," Luna said to Vi. "Don't you think?"

Vi paused just long enough to confirm what Oliver had suspected: She hated the guy's guts.

"Sure," she said politely. "He's coming back?"

As if on cue, Nick came running into view, a car part Oliver didn't recognize clutched in his big green hand.

"I got it," Nick said with a level of enthusiasm usually reserved for golden retrievers. He came to a stop in front of the open hood, staring not at the car, but at Vi. There might as well have been stars sparkling in his eyes, and for a moment Oliver actually felt bad for the guy. He'd always assumed Nick was an empty-headed grunt who only cared for free beer and his noisy motorcycle. But the look on Nick's face was so open and vulnerable that Oliver didn't want to see it get stomped on.

Then Nick cleared his throat, and the look vanished under a smug grin. "Still with the hair ribbon, huh?"

Oliver frowned. Was he trying to insult her? It sure *sounded* like an insult. But that didn't make sense with everything else he had just seen.

Vi's smile tightened. She looked back at Luna. "I have to head back in. Let me know if there's anything else I can do."

"Later," Nick called after her, his hand clutched in his oily shirt, right over his heart. He watched her vanish back into the bookstore, and Oliver had to avert his eyes so he didn't cringe with secondhand embarrassment.

Nick hadn't been trying to insult her. He was just *that* bad at flirting. At least Luna seemed delighted, her hand over her mouth like she was watching a play.

Nick stared at the closed door for several seconds, rubbing his shirt anxiously. Then he whirled around to face them, giving them a toothy grin that didn't reach his eyes.

"Back to work," he said, and bent over the hood.

"How much will we owe you?" Oliver asked.

Nick made a dismissive noise, waving a giant green hand at them. "Ah, forget about it. Barely a five-minute job."

"Are you sure?" Oliver asked. He wanted to give the guy *something* after that pathetic display. He'd almost give the guy a hug, if he was the kind of person who hugged non–family members.

"At this point, I'm close to paying you for giving me something to do," Nick replied. "Only so many times I can dust the toolboxes, y'know?"

Oliver nodded and let the guy get on with his work. Luna tugged on his shirt, and Oliver looked at her, puzzled, as she grinned up at him.

Leave him alone, Oliver mouthed.

Luna stuck her tongue out at him, of all things.

But before Luna could grill him properly, Nick snapped something into place and straightened, narrowly avoiding hitting his head on the hood this time.

"Done," he announced. He slammed the hood shut. "Well, would you look at the time! I need to get back. Lots of work to do."

"You just said you were so bored you were thinking of sabotaging a car," Luna called after him.

But it was too late. Nick was already jogging across the road toward the mechanic garage. Oliver could see two orcs poking their heads out to watch, bemused, as Nick ran toward them like he was fleeing from something. Which, Oliver guessed, he was.

Luna rested her cheek on Oliver's chest. "Aw. Just when it was getting interesting."

"That wasn't interesting," Oliver replied. "That was *sad*. Get in the car."

Luna pouted. She unwound the blanket from her shoulders and headed to Sweethelm Books, leaving it in a bundle on a shelf just inside the door. Then she ran back and climbed into the passenger's seat, rubbing her arms.

Oliver twisted the keys in the ignition. They both let out a sigh of relief when the car rumbled to life.

"We don't *actually* think Nick sabotaged the car," Luna asked. "Right?"

"I doubt it," Oliver said. "But I don't know the guy that well. Even less than I thought, apparently."

Luna hummed, turning the heater on full blast and sitting back in her seat. She looked so happy Oliver wanted to kiss her about it. He pushed the urge down and focused on putting the car into gear.

"Okay," Luna said. "*Maybe* small towns are good sometimes."

Oliver scoffed, pulling into the street. "You just want to know people's business. You sound like a local."

"So? It's *fun*." Luna grinned, and something flared in his chest that had nothing to do with the bond. "And... I don't know."

She went uncharacteristically quiet. Oliver looked over to see her picking at her pristine nails, also so out of character that he frowned.

"What?"

"Nothing," Luna said. "Just...you know. Family bookshop trips where everybody knows who you are. It's cute."

"We had that in Arizona," he reminded her as they coasted down the Main Road. "No small towns needed."

Luna said nothing. Oliver itched to look over at her again, but he kept his eyes on the road.

"You're different around them," said Luna in a rush.

"Different?"

"Yeah," Luna said, her voice oddly soft. "You're sweet."

The bond spasmed behind Oliver's rib cage. He had to clench the steering wheel so he didn't do something stupid, like reach over and pull her into a kiss while he was driving.

"Don't get used to it," he managed.

Luna giggled. Oliver tried to be annoyed. It didn't work.

"No, I see you now," Luna said. "You're…how did your grandmother put it? A sweetheart with a gruff exterior. Next you'll be bringing me my handbag and massaging my feet!"

"Don't count on it," Oliver said.

Luna made a considering noise. She leaned over, resting her chin on his shoulder and ignoring his warning glare.

"I don't know," she said. "You *did* promise me a massage."

Chapter Thirteen

Luna hummed in blissful satisfaction. She was topless and lying on top of her bed, Oliver kneeling over her with his slippery hands kneading gently at her back.

"You're better at this than I thought," she said, twisting lazily to look at him. "What'd you do, watch a YouTube tutorial?"

Oliver ignored her, his hands sliding oil over her shoulders and pressing to loosen the knot of muscle there. He'd already worked on her legs, which were still stiff from the morning runs he'd been dragging her on. They'd had a brief setback the other day when Luna had sat down and refused to move, and Oliver could only go so far without stumbling in pain. He'd only lasted a few moments before grudgingly stalking back.

Luna let out another happy hum. "Whatever, it feels good. Does it feel good for you?"

She gave him a sly look. Oliver had been sporting an impressive erection since the first few minutes of the massage. He'd been gentlemanly about it, hovering over her so it didn't press into her ass. Even without the physical evidence of his arousal, the bond inside Luna was thrilled to have him so close. They had slept together last night, but the bond was already urging her to get close again. Even now, with his hands smoothing up and down her bare back, it wanted him closer. He had to be feeling the same thing.

"'S fine," Oliver said. He shifted above her, still not allowing himself to grind down against her towel-covered ass.

Luna rolled her eyes. She was about to ask him to take the towel off her when her phone vibrated next to her head.

Luna grabbed it, grinning as she saw the text from Beth. It was another message thanking her for posting about her chocolate store. She'd sold out on the very first day. In the weeks since then she'd been playing catchup, queuing orders and buying more packaging so she could ship across the country.

"*A-ha*," she said, holding her phone up to show Oliver. "What'd I tell you?"

Oliver glanced down at the text. "I'm still surprised that your followers care so much about monster chocolate. Most of your photos are about iced coffee and your new clothes."

"Coffee and chocolate go great together," Luna said distractedly, typing out a string of kiss emojis to Beth. Then she paused. "You looked at my socials?"

"No," Oliver said immediately.

Luna giggled at his harshness. Like he'd rather get his fingernails pulled out than admit he looked at his temporary wife's social media.

She put her phone down. "We need to go to the store tomorrow. I'm doing a consult for Beth. I think I can talk her into doing some cute lil' coasters and mugs. And I'm in talks with a few other brands for some promo swaps."

"Can she afford all that?"

"I'm doing it for free," Luna admitted. Then, when Oliver's hands stilled on her back, she added, "I'm *bored*, Oliver! There are only so many times I can go to the movies with you and Leo. Or go shopping in town. Or get dragged on runs. Or play Connect Four with Sabine. Everyone's busy with their own lives, and I'm *stuck* here while you do laundry."

"You could help with the laundry," Oliver suggested dryly, his hands resuming their firm, gentle press.

Luna laughed again. "I was thinking of something actually *fun*."

She turned over. The sheet fell, exposing her breasts.

Oliver had the gall to look away. Just for a moment, his mouth tugging down into a frown as he examined the headboard. It didn't have the gusto of his usual frowns. Like he was putting it on for his own benefit. Then he looked back at her, gaze drifting down to her exposed breasts, and the frown went slack. His eyes flashed with hunger, something she'd seen several times in the weeks since she arrived at Claw Haven. She'd reach up to adjust her necklace, and that hunger would flicker over his face as his gaze dropped to her collarbone. Then it would be gone, the conversation continuing like nothing had happened. Like he was still trying to shove against that bond pulling them together, even though they'd already given in to it most nights she'd been stuck here.

"What?" she said as he tried to scowl. "You saw that weather report this morning. The snow will thaw soon. We should make the most of the time we have left."

He didn't move. *Maybe he just enjoys torturing himself*, Luna considered as she toyed with the sheet pooling around her bare stomach. He seemed the type.

Luna's phone rang. She sighed.

"Hold that thought," she said, gesturing at his erection. "Hello, this is Luna!"

A crisp, chipper voice came down the staticky line. "Hi, Luna. I'm Vi Harper. I work at Sweethelm Books, we met the other day."

"Right," Luna said, snapping her fingers. "You gave me that adorable cat blanket! I remember."

"Right," Vi said. "Beth said you helped her out with some marketing issues she'd been having."

"Well, I love those adorable little chocolates," Luna said. "I'm actually crazy busy right now, so you might have to talk fast."

Oliver folded his arms over his chest. Luna winked at him.

"Of course," Vi chirped. "I won't take up too much of your time. I just wanted to call and ask if you know much about setting up an online store, like you mentioned. I'd do it myself, but it's not my area of expertise, and I've been—"

She paused, her polite tone faltering. She cleared her throat.

"Too busy to learn," she continued.

Luna nodded. "With your sister."

"Right," said Vi, sounding oddly flustered, like she regretted telling a stranger that news in the first place. Unlike the rest of Claw Haven, Vi didn't seem like the type of person who told strangers about her personal life.

Vi continued, "My boss—"

Another voice cut in on her end of the line, old and croaky. "Is that that rich lady who bagged the grumpy werewolf? Tell her we're fine! People need to get off their butts and come into bookstores, that's the problem!"

Luna snorted. Oliver's hands paused on her back, proving that he was listening in to her phone calls like he always said he wasn't. Luna turned to give him a smug look, which he resolutely ignored.

"Thank you, Chester," Vi said. Then, into the phone, "Sorry about that. We've been running into a lot of problems. I've been doing what I can, but it's not exactly my wheelhouse."

Chester's voice echoed over the line again. "Every step needs you to do a hundred things first! I have a life, you know! I don't know how to validate a domain! I don't even know what a domain *is*! And the website helpers are no real help. It's like they're speaking gibberish—"

"We were wondering if you'd be available to help," Vi said over him. "An online store is a good idea."

Luna sighed, twirling her hair around one finger. She'd only let the phone call go on this long because she was entertained by the old guy's ranting. And because—if she was honest with herself—she did kind of want to help. Maybe if she knew more about setting up an online store, she would have thought about it. But that wasn't her area, and she wasn't particularly interested in learning.

"Vi," she started. "Unfortunately, I don't work with website design or any of that. But I'm sure you can find someone else."

Vi paused. For a second, Luna thought she might get more of that strain that she'd gotten a glimpse of when Vi mentioned she was too "busy" to learn. But when Vi spoke, her voice was as crisp as ever.

"Of course. Thanks for your time."

"Byeeee." Luna hung up, throwing the phone back down on the bed and lying down next to it. "Now. Where were we?"

Oliver didn't move. He didn't even look down at her breasts, still prominently displayed above the sheet. "Who was that?"

"Vi. You know, the human from Sweethelm Books. The one Nick has a huge crush on." Luna reached up with her bare foot, skimming his hip. "Do you think I should set those two up together? I think they could be *tres* cute."

"Please don't." Oliver stepped aside. "What did she want?"

"I don't know," she said, chasing his hip with her foot until she could hook her toe into his belt strap. "Boring stuff."

"Boring stuff?"

"Website stuff. Online store crap. It can get stupidly complicated. I let everyone else deal with it for me. Good luck if she's going to do that herself; she did *not* sound like she was having a good time—hey!" She pouted as he unhooked her toe from his belt loop and pushed her foot away.

"I thought you wanted something to do," Oliver said.

"I do," Luna replied. "But I'm not *that* bored."

She sat up, reaching for his shirt.

He stepped out of the way a second time. "So, someone gave

you something to do, and you're going to go back to painting your nails, looking at spas you're going to book when you get home, and complaining about how bored you are?"

Luna beamed. "Yes!"

Oliver gave her a flat look. He tried to dodge a third time, but Luna grabbed his shirt and held him fast, leaning in to skim his cheek with her nose.

"Since when," she asked, tongue darting out to lick his stubble, "do you want to help these people?"

"I don't," Oliver said hastily.

She smirked against his cheek. He would have, once. Maybe last year, before he got surly and closed off. Even now, he would help Vi if he genuinely gave a shit about her. She'd seen everything he did for his family—cleaning, cooking, driving the kids around, helping with homework, endlessly fixing up the inn.

"Then it sounds like you should stop arguing," Luna said, kneeling up so the rest of the towel pooled around her knees. "And get on me."

A low growl rumbled in his throat.

Luna grinned. She tugged the back of his neck, and he followed her down onto the bed.

That phone call was still in her head as she watched Sabine make lunch later that day. The frustration in Chester's croaky voice, the strain behind Vi's polite tone when Luna told her she couldn't help. She *probably* could. She didn't know how to set all of that up, but she could find out. A few YouTube tutorials and a call to her secret marketing team and she'd have it sorted. And Vi seemed sweet when she let her guard down. Luna was shocked to realize she truly did want to help her.

"You look serious," Sabine commented from the counter where she was chopping carrots. "Never seen you look so serious before!"

"I'm serious," Luna replied.

Over on the common room couch, Uncle Roy snorted. He'd been glaring daggers at her since she dared step into the room. He did it less when Grandmother Musgrove was around, but she was taking a nap right now, which meant he could glare to his wrinkled heart's content.

Luna sidled up to Sabine. "Can I help with anything?"

"Don't," Uncle Roy called. "Sabine, I'm *telling* you."

"He thinks you're going to put lethal amounts of wolfsbane in it," Sabine told her dryly, dumping a handful of carrot slices into the pot boiling on the stove. "Come over here, squeeze some lemons. We're making lemonade later."

"Don't," Uncle Roy snarled.

Sabine turned and growled at him, teeth sharpening. Luna wondered how her slashing scars only made her look more beautiful when Uncle Roy's burn scars made him look so vicious.

"She's *fine*, Roy," Sabine said, teeth still sharp. "If she tries to drop anything in the soup, I'll slap it right out of her hand."

Uncle Roy bared his teeth and lurched off the couch. He stalked into the hallway, slamming the door behind him.

"That's him taken care of," Sabine said, teeth back to normal. She motioned toward the lemons next to her on the counter. "Go on."

Luna started chopping the lemons and pressing them into the squeezer, relieved that she knew how to do this, at least. She'd squeezed lemons for cocktails before. If Sabine made her help with anything more advanced, *then* she'd be in trouble.

"What's his deal?" Luna asked as she squeezed another lemon half into the bowl Sabine had set out. "I thought he was just like that with me, but we went grocery shopping yesterday, and he snarled at a mom for letting her kid walk too close! The poor kid behind the counter asked how his day was, and I thought he was going to take him out."

Sabine groaned, emptying another handful of carrots into

the pot on the stove. "Ignore him. He's even more suspicious of outsiders than ever. Especially after last year."

Luna latched onto the opening eagerly. She'd been meaning to bring it up during one of their Connect Four games, but there was always a kid or an aunt or an Oliver around making it difficult.

"What happened last year?"

Sabine's knife paused on the next carrot. "Did Oliver tell you why we moved?"

"Yeah, he's a real open book," Luna deadpanned. "Can't stop him talking about personal stuff."

Sabine laughed. It died fast. She wiped the carrot slices off her knife and turned to face her. "Someone burned our house down."

Luna's smile dropped off her face. "Oh my god. Like, on purpose?"

"Very much so." Sabine headed back to the stove, stirring the pot as she continued, "It was a totally normal night. Dinner, movie, bed. Then around midnight, Oliver wakes us up, yelling at us to get out. The flames had blocked off the halls, so we had to climb out the windows."

"Oh my god," Luna said, heart racing. She hadn't even considered something like that. "That's awful. I'm so sorry. Was it a hunter? Those people are crazy. Isn't it illegal here?"

"Very illegal," Sabine agreed. "She turned off the alarms. If Oliver hadn't gotten up in the middle of the night for water and noticed the smoke…things could've gone a lot worse." Sabine scratched her scar, the skin pulling tight as she gave Luna a strained smile. "We lost almost everything. I think it dragged Uncle Roy back to his childhood. Hunters tried to burn him. That's why he has that scar. We heal a lot slower with fire. It's a hunter's go-to for wolves."

Sabine gave the pot one last stir and went back to the cutting board, wiping it down with a washcloth.

"Lemons are looking good," she said. "I'll get the sugar."

Luna startled. She'd completely forgotten about the lemons. She placed the next half in the squeezer, mind racing. The woman Oliver had been dreaming about, the one with dark hair and a bright smile, who had triggered all those terrible emotions...was that her?

"I didn't know things like that happened anymore," she admitted. "Did they catch her?"

"She's in jail," Sabine confirmed. "Life sentence."

Luna sagged in relief. "Good."

"I'm just glad we found out about Claw Haven," Sabine said, bending down to slot the cutting board under the sink. "The mayor's family were old friends with Grandmother. Once he heard about our situation, he reached out. It wasn't our only option, but Grandmother liked the idea of a fresh start in a town that celebrates monsters instead of just tolerating them. The town's built for us, you know? Big doorways, ramps for mer in wheelchairs, horn polish at every corner store. And everyone's been so welcoming. You don't have to worry about getting side-eyed when you're shopping or having a parent pull their kid away from you on the bus. And the townspeople have helped, even with Oliver turning down any of the big things. Beth's chocolates, Jackson consulting for free. Claw Haven knows how hard it can be to get started."

Sabine dropped a massive bag of sugar onto the counter. "Alright! Let's get this party rocking."

Luna kept squeezing lemons, nodding along to Sabine's instructions and watching her pour sugar into a saucepan. But Sabine's words kept rolling over in her head: *Everybody's been so welcoming. Claw Haven knows how hard it can be to get started.*

She found Oliver fixing a bedframe in room 8. His nose wrinkled as she walked in. "Why do you stink of lemon?"

Luna wiped her hands on her jeans. Obviously, she hadn't

scrubbed as hard as she'd thought. She'd been distracted, eager to get out of the kitchen and find him.

"Can you take me into town after you're done? I want to talk to that bookstore lady."

Oliver looked up from the wooden slat he'd been sliding into place. "Why?"

Luna rolled her eyes. "I want to look into her online store stuff, okay? It's not a big deal."

She leaned on the doorway, all casual. If this was anyone else, they would've bought it. But Oliver just stared at her with an unreadable expression.

"Thought you weren't that bored," he said.

"Maybe I am," Luna replied. "It's *really* boring here."

She examined her nails. He was still watching her with an intensity that made her nervous. Like he could see right through her. For a moment, she panicked that he'd call her out on it. She almost wanted him to. For him to drag it out of her: *Fine, I wanted to help. Are you happy?*

She felt a strange rush of disappointment when he turned back to the bedframe, fixing the slat into place.

"Give me five minutes," he said.

Chapter Fourteen

The bond rejoiced the second Luna walked into the room.
Cut it out, Oliver told it sternly.

The bond pulsed once, as if in rebellion. Oliver crossed his arms tight over his warm chest, sitting back against the couch. He already had the full moon jitters to deal with tonight. He didn't need more bond bullshit.

"Let's get this over with," he said.

Luna gave him a judgy look. As did everyone else in the room, because Luna had insisted that this should be a family event. *It's Musgrove Inn*, she'd pointed out when she floated the idea last night. *Not Oliver Inn. Everybody should see what's going into it.*

And everyone had agreed and filed into the common room like they didn't have better things to do tonight. Like everyone wasn't twitchy and fidgeting with the full moon, ready to wolf out and roam the forest.

"Take all the time you want," Grandmother said, pulling her long sleeves over her hands. "We have a busy night ahead, is all."

Luna brightened. "Of course!"

She struck a pose next to the whiteboard she'd dragged Oliver into town to get two days ago. It had a towel draped over it, thick and fluffy since Luna had talked them into buying better ones for the guests.

"In one word," she started. "How would you describe Musgrove Inn?"

"Drafty," Ben called.

Oliver glared at him. Ben beamed, slinging an arm around his wife's shoulders and knocking Oliver in the head in the process.

"Cool," Darren tried, his homework abandoned in his lap. He was tearing tiny strips off the edges of the paper, restless and ready for the night.

"Boring," Vida said from where she was sitting on the floor, headphones angled so she could listen with one ear. She'd had her music on full blast all day. Oliver had caught her headbanging in the lobby earlier.

Luna clapped. "Great ideas. I was thinking something more like…"

She turned and whipped the towel off the whiteboard. It had multiple lists scrawled down it. Two words sat at the top of the board: *COZY MONSTERS*.

"*Cozy*," Leo yelled. He ran and leaped up across both his parents' laps, burrowing his face into his dad's stomach.

Ben grunted, patting his back. "Okay, bud, save it for later."

Leo growled, digging his nose in harder. Fur sprouted over his arms.

"*Save it*," Ben reminded him. He nodded pointedly at Luna. "Go on, Luna."

Luna blinked. Then she pulled up another shining smile, stupidly charming for someone who looked like she'd fit in on a TV game show, holding a suitcase full of money.

"So," she said. "I looked at your online presence, and I think we need to work on your branding. What you have so far is fine, but it needs a little *sparkle*. Something to tie it all together, let people know what they should expect in a few short words."

Uncle Roy raised a grudging hand.

Luna blinked again, her smile going slack with shock. "Roy! Do you have an idea?"

Uncle Roy pointed at the whiteboard. "Where's the logo? You said you'd give us a logo."

"I'm still working on it!" Luna preened, ruffling her sleek blond hair. "I'm still deciding what's going to work best for your branding. Which, I think we can all agree, should be centered around this."

She tapped the whiteboard.

"Now, we can work on what's inside the inn later. Obviously, we need to up the cozy factor and get more cute. Armchairs instead of those things you have out in the guest common room. Maybe some adorable little monster-themed cushions and knick-knacks around people's rooms. But anyway, let's focus on everything *outside* the inn. You have a beautiful mountain view! The ocean's a ten-minute drive away! *And* you have that gorgeous forest at your doorstep! You have a bakery where dragons bake the bread, you have a minotaur with a flower shop and you have Beth's sweet little monster chocolates. There's so much to explore."

Sabine spoke up, ruffling her son's furry arms. "You should present this to the town, Luna."

Luna paused. "Excuse me?"

"We've all heard you talking about how the town could... how did you put it? Rebrand," Sabine continued. "We have a town meeting coming up. You could do a presentation. If Sweethelm Books and Prickles are interested, I bet others would be, too."

"And you should talk to the mayor," said Aunt Barney, undoing her sister's braid. "Christopher will talk to anyone who wants to uplift the town. He's the one who organized that beautiful mural you were taking photos of, Luna."

Aunt Althea frowned. "Christopher's on his honeymoon, remember? Won't be back for a while."

"Oh. Right."

"I'll make a note of it," Luna said. She turned back to the board. "Anyway! When your guests are done seeing all the wonders of Claw Haven—"

"Which you will only make more wonderful," Aunt Althea said. She twisted to look at Aunt Barney. "When was that town meeting again?"

"In two days," Aunt Barney said. "Luna, you could make something like this for the town in two days, right?"

Luna hesitated. "Um. I...guess?"

"She doesn't have to do anything," Oliver said, glaring at his nosy family. "Luna, don't listen to them. You don't have to do any town meetings if you don't want to."

"Right," Luna said. But her eyes were tracking in that way they did when she was planning something. Then she blinked, her smile coming up again. "Anyway! Once everyone is done seeing Claw Haven, they can come back to Musgrove Inn and get cozy by the fire!"

"The fireplace is walled up," Oliver said flatly.

Luna pointed at one of the bullet points on her list. *FIX FIRE*.

"I like that idea," Aunt Althea said, gold tooth glinting. "We could bake potatoes."

"Hear, hear," Ben said quietly.

Leo dug his nose into Sabine's arm, letting out another low growl. She stroked his hair absentmindedly, watching Luna with a smile so fond it made Oliver's stomach twist. They shouldn't treat her like this. Like she was part of the pack. The snow would melt any day now, they'd go up the mountain and get the divorce flower and this whole mess would be over. Oliver would be free of this warmth tying knots in his chest and making him ache with cold whenever he dared stray too far, and

Luna would go back to her comfortable life as an heiress to an appliance company. They'd never have to see each other again. Which was a good thing, no matter what that traitorous bond in his chest said about it. She had a fiancé. She had a *life*. She didn't belong here in this tiny town in the middle of nowhere.

It took Ben nudging him for Oliver to realize that everybody was looking at him. Waiting. All of them fidgeting, restless, ready to shed their skin and become one with the night.

Everyone except him.

Oliver cleared his throat. "You're still doing all of this for free, right? We're not going to find a giant consulting bill when you leave?"

"Depends how nice you are," Luna said. Then she folded. "No bill. I promised."

"Plus, you're bored," Oliver said.

"Plus, I'm bored," she chirped, smile still fixed in place. That damn dimple appeared next to it. Oliver's heart thudded hard in his chest, hot and powerful.

Around him, his family squirmed. The moon was bright and gleaming, with no clouds to hide behind. They didn't have long.

Oliver's fingers dug into his thighs, forcing his nails to stay blunt.

"Okay," he started. "That's—"

"That's enough for now," Grandmother Musgrove said over him, standing gracefully. "Thank you for this, Luna. We can't wait to see the rest of what you have planned."

"At the town meeting," Aunt Barney added.

"Oh!" Luna twisted her smooth hands together. "I was kind of hoping to explain the socials tonight. And some tweaks you might want to add to your website. I have a *lot* of ideas on how to improve your interior design. No offense to whoever set this up, but if you're maximizing coziness, you're gonna want—"

She fell silent as Grandmother Musgrove rested a hand on her shoulder. Oliver could see the moment she clocked it: The old woman's teeth were a little too sharp, her eyes brighter than usual.

"Another night," Grandmother Musgrove said. "Or, if you wish, at the town meeting. I think you have a lot to offer, Luna."

Luna flushed. "Oh! Um, thank you."

Grandmother Musgrove turned toward the rest of the room, the air crackling with excitement. "Shall we?"

Leo let out a small howl and bolted for the door. Darren followed, the two of them colliding in a wrestling match, fur sprouting over their skin as they tumbled into the hallway.

"Wait until you're outside, please," Sabine called, nosing at her husband's chin.

Aunt Althea and Aunt Barney followed them out, giggling like schoolgirls. Even Uncle Roy cracked a smile as he left, tugging Vida's headphones off her head and dodging the bite she aimed at him.

Grandmother Musgrove was the last to leave. Her gaze lingered on Luna for a moment before she turned to Oliver, who sat stiff and unmoving on the couch.

"You'll be alright?" she asked softly.

"Always," he replied.

Her mouth quirked. She gave them both a considering look. Then she headed into the hallway, closing the door behind her.

"Wow," Luna said. "Here I thought you guys were exaggerating when you said the full moon got you riled up."

"Nope," Oliver said flatly.

Luna looked toward the closed door. "Aren't you going with them?"

Oliver swallowed. The wolf inside him prowled the edges of his skin, the moon pulling it toward the surface. But whenever he reached for it, his wolf retreated.

"No," he gritted.

He gave it another second, waiting to hear his family spill

out the front door, their joy a knife in his stupid, bitter heart. Then he ripped the door open, storming down the hall toward his room.

Luna called out for him.

He kept walking.

Oliver shut himself in his room and hoped.

Hoped she would come.

Hoped she wouldn't.

Both of these hopes warred in his chest, equally violent. He'd spent every full moon since the fire alone in his room. It wasn't like he hadn't tried. Those first few months he'd run with them in his human form, but it wasn't the same. Not with the wolf prowling inside of him, wanting out but not trusting him enough to hand the reins over. He couldn't take another night of his family trying to include him in their puppy piles and running insultingly slowly so he could chase them. He didn't need their pity.

Luna knocked on the door. The bond writhed hopefully behind his rib cage.

Oliver smacked his chest, annoyed. "What?"

Luna flung open the door and waltzed in, perching next to him on the bed so closely that Oliver jerked away on instinct.

"I saw a full wolf heading toward the lobby," she said. "I know it's natural, but is that safe? All of them wolfed out, running around? It's probably fine, I just heard—"

"The wolf can be hard to control if you're not used to it. Or if you're emotional. That's why we run in packs; there's someone there to keep you in order if you lose it."

"Fab," Luna said distractedly, tracing patterns in the carpet with her shoe as she pretended not to watch him.

Oliver gritted his teeth, waiting for the inevitable.

Luna hesitated. "Sooo…you don't shift?"

"I *can't*," Oliver huffed bitterly. "Not anymore."

"Oh," Luna said quietly. "That's… Oh."

Oliver ignored her. He couldn't hear the howling from his soundproofed room, but he could imagine it: racing through the trees, the kids tripping over their own paws. Even Vida let go of that aloof teenager crap on full moons, tongue lolling out of her mouth as she chased her brother and cousin around. Sabine and Ben would be nuzzling each other, Uncle Roy lingering around the edges of the pack until someone goaded him into chasing them, usually one of the aunts. And Grandmother would plod proudly behind them, keeping watch. Making sure the play didn't get too rough, with no trees or skin broken tonight. They'd end the night exhausted and happy, filled with gratitude that they'd been born into a family that got to have this.

And Oliver would be here, cold and alone. He *was* happy for them, really. But he couldn't help the bitterness that welled up in him every full moon as he watched them bound outside on four paws. It was so much *simpler* being a wolf. He missed it with every part of himself.

Luna sniffed, breaking him out of his thought spiral. "When I was fourteen, my family went to Monaco, and I had to stay home with a broken leg."

Oliver stared at her. He couldn't tell if she was joking. Then, finally, her mouth twitched.

"I'm just saying," she continued. "I *totally* understand."

"Poor little rich girl," he deadpanned. "Having to stay home from a family holiday. What, no maid to bring you caviar on a silver platter?"

"We did have a maid. But I dismissed her. *I* wanted to sulk in solitude." Luna bit her lip. At first, he thought she was going to proposition him like she often did when they were alone. But her expression didn't fit. She looked…strangely vulnerable. Her chin lifted defiantly, the same way it had when she asked him to bring her into town to talk to Vi. Like she was waiting for him to make fun of her.

"You should quit pulling away so much. You're making them sad. And you're making *you* sad. You should let yourself have something nice for once. Even if you don't—" She stopped, lips pressed tight together.

He stared at her. *Even if you don't think you deserve it.* He was terrified that was what she was about to say. He didn't want her to see him. He didn't want her to see the guilt curdling inside him. Did she *know* the truth about the fire? They'd agreed not to go too deep. He rarely got her thoughts, just glimpses of sensation when they were having sex. The occasional slip when they were sitting too close during dinner. Images of her family, tinged with a strange sadness as she watched the Musgroves immerse themselves so deeply in each other's lives. He tried to block it out as best he could, just like they promised. But some things leaked through.

Luna laughed, high and self-conscious. "Whoa! Where did that come from? I've been watching way too many Lifetime movies with you guys."

She paused, biting her lip. "They weren't serious about the town meeting thing, right? That was just…being polite."

Oliver snorted. "Do you think Grandmother would 'just be polite'? When she says something, she means it. But don't do it just because you feel pressured."

"I never have," Luna said absentmindedly. She ran a hand through her hair, her gaze distant. She was considering it, Oliver realized. She didn't look too happy about it, which confused him. Why would she do it if she didn't want to?

Her mind brushed against his inside the bond. Oliver shied away, as usual. She stayed out of his mind, he stayed out of hers.

"You don't have to," Oliver repeated. "We don't even go to the town meetings most of the time. Just ignore it."

"Right," said Luna. But she still looked troubled. Then she

shook her head and slung a leg over him, settling into his lap. "Anyway! Since we have this side of the inn all to ourselves…"

Her nose brushed his. The bond sparked eagerly in his chest, his hands coming up to squeeze her thighs automatically. There was an emotion in her face he didn't quite recognize, but then she kissed him, and everything melted away except for her soft skin, her clever hands and her glinting eyes.

Something was trying to leak through the bond. Oliver didn't let it in. By the time sensations started to spill through over into him, Luna had locked whatever it was away, and the only glimpses he got of her mind were pure pleasure.

Chapter Fifteen

Luna stared into the crowd, a sinking feeling in her stomach. It wasn't even a big crowd. Despite word going around that all business owners in Claw Haven should attend, only about forty of the fifty or so chairs were occupied. And the first row was entirely Musgroves, who looked far too eager to watch Luna make a fool of herself.

Oliver kept frowning at her. He could sense her anxiety— he would probably sense it even without their bond, with how obvious Luna was about it. She kept wringing her hands and staring at the presentation she had covered up on the small stage like it would emerge from the sheet and bite her.

It wasn't a great presentation. She'd only had a few days to put it together, after all. But the Musgroves seemed so eager, and she *did* have a lot of ideas about how to make the town shine. The more she thought about it, the more excited she was.

And nervous.

She gnawed on her lip as townsfolk took their seats. There was Beth Haberdash, of course, waving eagerly when Luna looked her way. She had agreed to help Beth with her presentation, along with Vi Harper, who was sitting in the second row next to a grumpy old dragon who must be Chester, the owner of Sweethelm Books, who looked just like Luna had imagined when she spoke to him on the phone these past few days. Then Emma Curt, standoffish owner of the Grotto Café on Main Street, pulling at her pixie cut. And several orcs in stained overalls, including Nick. He looked deeply uncomfortable except for when one of his coworkers was talking to him—then he would break out in a toothy smile that would vanish as soon as he thought no one was looking at him.

Luna checked her phone and blew out a shaky breath. Two minutes until presentation time. Were they going to boo her off the stage? Or worse, *laugh* at her? Luna would take contempt over ridicule any day.

Oliver got out of his chair and climbed up on the tiny stage.

"Hey," he said, voice lowered. "You alright?"

"Sorry," Luna said with a nervous laugh. She suddenly wished she had worn more deodorant. She was sweating despite her deceptively thin jacket. Maybe the weather *was* getting warmer like the townsfolk kept insisting. Or maybe Luna was just panicking.

"You must be feeling all my—my *blaaaaah* through the bond," Luna continued, waving her hands to signify the *blaaaaah*.

"Some of it," Oliver said, crossing his arms so distractingly that Luna's stress temporarily faded to make way for burning lust. Then Oliver kept speaking, and the stress came rushing back.

"Since when do you worry about this kind of stuff?" Oliver asked. "You love talking to people."

"Not like this," Luna said in a high voice that bypassed chipper and went all the way to demented. She turned toward her covered presentation, hugging her arms. "I've never done a project this big! Hell, I've never *proposed* a project this big! What if they think it's stupid?"

"It's not stupid," Oliver replied. He took her shoulders, and the bond whirled inside Luna's chest. "Hey. You're great at this. Everyone will see that. And if they don't, then who cares? You're not getting paid anyway."

Luna giggled faintly. "True. I guess it is just…a side project. While I'm stuck here."

"Exactly," Oliver said. "Low stakes."

"Low stakes," Luna whispered. "Right."

It was probably the nicest Oliver had been to her since she got stuck in Claw Haven. For some reason it made Luna want to blush like a schoolgirl.

"Thanks," she said awkwardly. "For not making fun of me."

Oliver frowned. "I'm saving that for later."

Heath, a dragon who owned the bakery Scales N' Scones and made being grumpy seem a shared dragon trait, piped up from the middle row. "Is the meeting starting yet? It's 6:01."

"You'll do great," Oliver said.

He dropped Luna's arms. The anxiety came rushing back, and Luna had to clench her teeth to force her usual smile.

Low stakes, she reminded herself. But it didn't feel low stakes. Especially not with Oliver's warm touch fading and his entire family watching. She was stupidly fond of this little werewolf family. She didn't want them to crash and burn.

She whirled on the crowd, arms spread. "Hello! My name is Luna Stack. I'm here today to present you with an incredible opportunity."

Oliver motioned at her subtly. *Tone it down.*

But it was too late: Heath the bakery dragon spoke up again, smoke drifting out of his unimpressed snout.

"Why?" he asked flatly. "What do you get out of it?"

Luna kept her smile in place as she stepped back toward her covered presentation. "I'm glad you asked! As many of you already know, I didn't plan to spend my winter in Claw Haven. But due to a mishap with some bonding nectar, I'm stuck here until the snow thaws. Isn't that right, accidental husband?"

"You got it, accidental wife," Oliver said immediately.

Luna giggled, unable to stop herself. She looked over at the rest of the Musgroves, who were all watching with varying degrees of encouragement. Except for Uncle Roy, who was glaring around the town hall like he expected someone to pull a wolfsbane crossbow.

"And since I'm in the marketing business," Luna continued, "I started to see an opportunity in Claw Haven. My first client was Beth Haberdash. Beth?"

Beth stood, shrinking against her spikes as she waved at the crowd.

"Beth's sales have increased by *five hundred percent* since I helped spruce up her online store and expand her mailing list and socials," Luna started.

An interested mutter went around the crowd. They didn't look very surprised—Luna guessed most of them had already heard about Beth's sudden success.

"And just last week," Luna continued, "I helped Sweethelm Books set up an online store so they can ship books all over the world. Vi?"

Vi Harper stood, straightening her purple hair ribbon. "It's still in its fledgling stages. But we've had a lot of interest. And most of that is because of how much Luna has helped us get the word out. She has some really useful contacts."

Another interested murmur. Luna preened, even more of her confidence returning as people took an obvious interest.

"So what I'm proposing," she said, "is that we take this rebranding to the whole town."

A huge, timid hand raised. Joshua Haberdash, minotaur owner of the local flower store, brushed fur out of his eyes and asked, "Excuse me. But what is 'rebranding'?"

"It's changing a brand," said Emma Curt, frowning at a too-long strand in her pixie cut. "You redo it. Like how every James Bond is different. It's a new representation of your store."

Luna pointed at Emma triumphantly. "Exactly! My idea is

to turn the whole town into this cohesive brand. All the stores will have some version of it."

"What's the brand?" came a voice from the back row.

Luna craned her head to see Sam, a twentysomething guy who worked at the local tattoo salon, Inky Talons. At first Luna had thought *he* was a human, only for Aunt Barney to tell her that Sam was an incubus. Apparently he was very squirrely about it and Luna shouldn't bring it up.

"Great question, Sam," Luna called back.

She held her breath and turned toward her hidden presentation. She whipped the sheet off, and it fell to the tiny stage to reveal a propped-up board.

"*Claw Haven*," Luna read out. "*For the monster who wants some peace and quiet.*"

"We already have that," called Chester, his tail swishing around his chair legs. "It's on the sign when you come in."

"Exactly," Luna said. "And what kind of place does this slogan make you think of?"

There was a moment of silence where everybody thought about it. In the front row, Leo squirmed until he couldn't take it anymore and sat up in Ben's lap.

"Cozy!" he yelled. "Cozy monsters!"

"Thank you, Leo!" Luna cried, turning over the board to reveal the second side. She was suddenly relieved she had done a practice round with the Musgroves before presenting in front of a bunch of strangers.

"Claw Haven has this amazing untapped potential," Luna started. "First of all, it's *beautiful*. Mountains and forests and ocean, all at your doorstep! But most importantly, it has *you* guys. A close-knit, cozy monster community full of people who care about each other and want to offer their hospitality. Everything's already here, you just need to turn it up a notch. Like... Heath! You could add little cartoon dragons on your bakery aprons!"

Heath Astarot's scaly brow furrowed. "It's not that kind of bakery. We take ourselves seriously."

"You can do cartoon dragons and still take yourself seriously," Luna argued, too on a roll to get set back.

"I think it would be cute," Beth Haberdash whispered.

Luna turned to her. "Thank you, Beth! And for anyone who goes cozy, you could even use your interlinking brands to lift each other up! Sweethelm Books now sells Beth's chocolates at the counter. You could have Joshua's flowers next to the cash register! You could have posters about the Sweethelm Books book club! Emma, you could rename your café to something like the Cozy Grotto. *Grotto* is already so cozy, it's halfway there!"

Emma grunted, eyeing the presentation skeptically. "So what, we make ourselves all cutesy and people will just magically come here?"

"No," Luna said. "That's part two of my marketing plan. In very simple terms, step one is organizing everything—products, websites, logos—but the next step and arguably the most important one is getting the word out there. How many of your businesses have social media accounts?"

A few hands went up. Luna pointed at secret-incubus-Sam. "Sam! How are Inky Talons' socials doing?"

"We have an Insta account that last posted six months ago," said Sam awkwardly.

"We can up that frequency," Luna said. "Especially if you do flashes! That's the word, right? Flashes? Anyway, flashes! Of cozy monster tattoos that people can come and get in this amazing cozy monster town! We could open Claw Haven up to the world. I've been here for a while now, and I *know* people would come."

Uncle Roy's growly voice echoed through the hall. "But we don't *want* outsiders to come. That's the whole point of Claw Haven."

The town hall went quiet. Several people exchanged tense looks. Uncle Roy sat back and glowered at Luna, his gaze just as distrustful as that first day. Even if nowadays it seemed he had to work at it.

"Claw Haven is 'cozy' because it's a safe place for monsters," Uncle Roy continued. "We protect each other. We take care of our own."

"I know," Luna said. "And that's what makes this such a great, supportive community."

"But we would like *some* more tourists," muttered Emma Curt.

"Even if they are rude bastards," added Heath Astarot.

"Hear, hear," said Chester. "I despise tourists. But without them, my bookstore would be kaput. And this…ugh. This online store *has* opened up a lot of business opportunities. If people want to buy from us, who am I to deny them?"

"I don't have a problem with more tourists," said Joshua Haberdash quietly, pushing the fur out of his eyes yet again. "Actually, I'd love some more tourists. We can have the most interesting chats."

Uncle Roy twisted to glare at them. "Your funeral."

The murmuring started up again. Luna stepped forward, surprised when the noise immediately died down and all eyes turned to her.

Oliver gave her a small thumbs-up. Luna felt something push at the bond and realized that he was trying to send her something. It felt a lot like pride.

Luna suppressed a flood of butterflies and went back to her presentation, pulling down the board to reveal a second one hiding underneath it.

A gasp traveled through the town hall. It was a picture of Main Street. But Luna had scribbled in some important additions: adding *Cozy* in front of *Grotto Café*, adding signs telling people about attractions, old and not-yet-invented, signs displaying what adorable things were waiting for them inside. Scales N' Scones had a sleeping dragon painted on the shop window. Sweethelm Books had a painting of Mosey, the majestic bookstore cat that had been prowling elsewhere every time Luna visited. Prickles had a chocolate-tasting station, and there was a tour guide dragon flying overhead with a minotaur strapped to its belly, pointing out the sights. The street was a winter wonderland of light and color, and Luna's heart swelled as the crowd broke into excited whispers.

"You really have something in Claw Haven," Luna said. "It took me a while, but I see it now. Claw Haven is…"

Luna suddenly forgot every adjective she had written down on her notes app. She paused, baring her teeth as she tried to remember. The Musgroves laughed from the front row, and Luna realized that she had picked up one of their wolfy habits. She hid her teeth with a self-conscious laugh, but not before she spotted Oliver. He was chewing on his cheek, but not enough to hide his amusement.

Luna broke out into a smile. Not the flashy one she usually walked around with. But something small and private that she almost felt embarrassed to show the crowd.

"Claw Haven is *comforting*," she continued. "It's quiet, it's friendly, it's this perfect little escape. People need that. They *always* need that. And if we show them what Claw Haven can be—what Claw Haven *is*—I think people would really love it. Monster and human."

Sabine whooped. After a small nudge, Ben whooped with her. Then the whole Musgrove family broke into whoops, excluding Uncle Roy, who glared at the floor, and Oliver, who watched Luna with a look of such pride she felt it more than the loudest whoop.

Nobody had been proud of her before. It was overwhelming.

When the whoops finally died down, Emma raised her hand.

"So," she said. "What is it you do? Like, you're a...marketing guru?"

"Basically," Luna said. "I'm a marketing consultant slash graphic designer. And if we run into something I don't know how to do, I can point you to somebody who can."

Secret-incubus-Sam stuck up his tattooed hand next. "How much are you charging?"

"Oh, while I'm stuck here? It's free."

The hall exploded into questions, hands flying up. Luna giggled, giddy with relief. She took a moment to look at Oliver, who was watching her with those dark, steady eyes. Then she turned to the crowd and started pointing for people to speak.

Chapter Sixteen

Oliver stared at his family, unimpressed.

"You don't have to hide right *now*," he pointed out. "It's the common room. We can hear her coming."

Everyone shushed him. Leo, Darren and even Vida were crouched under the table. Ben and Sabine were hiding behind the kitchen counter. The aunts were standing against the wall where the door would open to cover them. Even Grandmother was joining in, peeking out from behind the curtain with the cake.

Oliver sighed. "You all look like idiots. You know that?"

Luna's light footsteps sounded down the hall. Oliver tried to bolt underneath the crowded table, only for the kids to shove him away.

"Get your own hiding place," Darren hissed.

"You're a bad nephew," Oliver told him. He looked around the room, cursing himself for leaving it too late. Then he ducked behind the curtain next to Grandmother.

"It's the best spot," she whispered.

"Not obvious at all," replied Oliver, whose feet were sticking out from the bulging curtain.

Sabine shushed them. Everybody fell silent, and Oliver

wondered if they'd made a huge mistake. Luna had been busy all week helping Claw Haven to "rebrand." He'd been dragged along to so many meetings he couldn't count them all. He now knew how to set up a mailing list, what the best newsletter hosting sites were according to five different categories, and how to properly wrap a book for inter-country transportation. All against his will.

But it was nothing compared to everything Luna had to deal with. She might be so tired she wouldn't even want a surprise party.

The door opened. Oliver braced himself.

"Hellooo," Luna called. "Um. Guys? I got a text—"

Her words broke off in a shocked shriek as everybody leaped out from their hiding spaces. Except for Oliver and Grandmother, who stepped out at a normal pace—Grandmother because she had the cake, Oliver because he wasn't about to jump out looking like an idiot.

"Surprise!" everyone yelled, some more enthusiastically than others.

Luna fell against the door, her hands clasped dramatically to her chest.

"Oh my god! What's happening? Oooh, is it someone's birthday?"

She gasped, her eyes lighting up on the cake. It was a cartoon wolf curled up on the plate, his iced muzzle lying on his admittedly adorable marshmallow paws.

"It's for you," Grandmother Musgrove admitted. "Heath wanted to thank you for all his success this month. We thought we'd make an occasion out of it, to celebrate everything you're doing for the town."

She set the cake down on the table, which was laden with everything Luna had taken a second helping of during dinners: gleaming green beans and herby roast. There was also strawberries and cream, since she had brought it up more than once in that first week when she was longing openly for room service.

Luna's mouth dropped open. She stared at the table of food, then at everybody standing around giggling.

"*Heath* did this?" Luna asked, pointing dubiously at the adorable dragon cake. "Scales N' Scones Heath who gives you eye contact like whoever looks away first loses?"

"Ah," Ben said. "He's a sweet guy under all that."

"Right," Luna said faintly. "Gruff disposition. Lot of those in Claw Haven."

Oliver shifted self-consciously. But Luna wasn't looking at him—instead her gaze traveled around the room expectantly.

"Where's Uncle Roy?"

"He had something on," Grandmother Musgrove said.

"He didn't want to come," Oliver said over her.

Luna sniggered. Oliver ignored his grandmother's wary look and walked over to Luna, the bond in his chest shoving for him to close the distance properly.

Sure, he felt annoyingly fond of her tonight. But that didn't mean he was about to get too close, no matter what the bond wanted. He had to draw the line somewhere.

"Well, he missed out," Luna said. She touched the table, which had been draped with a plastic tablecloth left over from one of the kid's birthday parties. Oliver waited for her to make a smart comment, but Luna just stood there, touching the tablecloth with a strange look on her face.

Oliver probed the bond. She wasn't disappointed. She was… *touched*. Touched and trying very hard to hide it.

She cleared her throat, pulling up a hasty smile as she turned back to them. "Aw, you guys! You didn't have to do all this. I haven't even done much yet."

"Nonsense," said Grandmother. "Joshua said those bouquets you posted after visiting his flower store have been flying off the shelves."

"Same as Heath's sleeping-dragon croissants," Ben added. "I saw him *smile* yesterday when he was making them. It was weird. And I think he's coming around to your logo idea."

"Chester said books have been going like hotcakes since you set up their online store," Sabine said. "Especially after you helped them with those pesky packaging issues!"

"And newsletter trouble," Oliver finished. He'd listened to Luna rant about admin issues for too long not to bring it up.

"All in a day's work." Luna struck a goofy pose, color high on her cheeks. "And now I know how to send a paperback from Alaska to New Jersey with minimal bending! Never expected to learn *that* when I got stuck here. Ahem."

She was downplaying it. Oliver had been following her around town while she set everything up with various store owners, and he'd seen how hard she worked. She got results. Oliver kept expecting her to brag, and sometimes she did. But most of the time, she was shockingly bashful about her work, like she was waiting for someone to tell her she wasn't very good.

"We hope this is alright," Grandmother continued, waving at the little table of food. "We'd like to do a town-wide celebration one day—"

Luna laughed, loud and nervous. "Aw, come on. Who needs the town when I have you guys? You guys are…"

She trailed off. The bond spasmed between them, and Oliver had to dig his nails into his palms so he didn't reach out and comfort her.

"This is so nice," Luna said quietly. "Nobody's ever—I mean, I've had parties. Tons of parties! You know me, I'm a party gal! But never for something I did. Something I'm, like, actually proud of."

She blinked hard, a wobbly smile spreading over her face. "I really do think Claw Haven is great! I think—I think you guys are great."

She sniffed. The common room fell silent, and Oliver couldn't help himself. He reached over and touched Luna, rubbing her shoulder. The bond flooded him with warmth, and he could feel Luna's gratefulness even before she laid her hand over his.

"Thanks," she said softly. Then she looked back at the others. "Thanks to *all* of you. I couldn't have been trapped in a better town. I'm almost sorry I have to leave soon!"

It was like a bucket of water over Oliver's good mood. He could feel his family's eyes on him, and he resolutely ignored it. He refused to accept their pity. Especially when he knew all along this was coming.

Luna was always going to leave. Why did this reminder feel like an icepick in his heart?

"Group hug," Leo yelled.

Before Oliver could warn him off it, he was throwing himself forward and wrapping his arms around Luna's legs. Darren followed suit, much more bashful, and soon everyone was clamoring in and enveloping Luna in a tight group hug.

Oliver rested his chin on her head. He was in the middle of the huddle, trying to fight down his instinct to shove his way out. For some reason, having Luna close made the intimacy easier. The bond thrummed between them, and for a ridiculous moment Oliver thought their hearts were beating in time. Then the hug ended, and Luna pulled away with eyes she would always deny were wet, and the feeling faded.

Oliver was on his second slice of dragon cake when Luna sidled up behind him.

"So this is why you were asking me how much icing sugar I liked in my whipped cream," she murmured.

Oliver forced back his dark mood. He wasn't about to ruin the night just because she'd reminded him she was leaving.

"And you never even suspected," Oliver replied with forced levity.

"Well, no. You asked it so mockingly," Luna said, and offered him her finger. There was a dollop of whipped cream on the end of it, the sweet smell wafting tantalizingly as she waved it in front of his mouth.

Oliver glanced over at his family. None of them were looking at him. And hell, this would *definitely* cheer him up.

He leaned in and sucked it off her finger, watching Luna's eyes darken.

Luna lowered her voice. "Want to get out of here and *celebrate* me some more?"

Part of Oliver wanted to say no. To put some sensible distance between them. Make her inevitable departure easier. But it wasn't closeness she was offering—it was pleasure. Oliver could bury himself in that and ignore the stupid, stubborn disappointment that she wouldn't be around much longer.

"Race you," Oliver replied quietly.

Darren piped up from the couch with a giant grin. "Eeeeew! Uncle Ollie!"

"Shut up," Oliver told him. "We're going to go play cards."

"In his soundproofed bedroom," Ben added.

Oliver shot him a side-eye and followed Luna out of the common room. They were in the hall before he noticed he had a hand on the small of her back. He dropped it, even though he would be touching a hell of a lot more in a minute. He couldn't get too used to these casual little touches, not with the snow thawing more every day. Every time he glanced out the window, that snow was thinner.

It wouldn't be long now.

The bond roared between them as Luna rode him, her head thrown back.

Oliver ran his hands over her breasts. His claws pricked into her flushed skin, their sharpness echoing back to him through the bond. He squeezed, and they moaned in unison.

It should have been rushed. It had started out rushed, every night ending with a race to the finish line. But somewhere along the line it became slower. Almost sweet, if they were the kind of people who could be sweet together.

"Oh shit," Luna whispered, grinding her hips against him. "Are you close? I can feel it."

She meant the bond. He could feel her getting close too, their orgasms always chasing each other through their connection. But she also meant his knot, which was barely starting to swell at his base. She had gotten better at being able to feel the barely-there swell of it just before he came.

"That's it," Luna said as she bounced on him. "Come in me. Make me feel it."

Oliver groaned and came. Luna trembled on top of him, her thighs clenching as the orgasm echoed through the bond, showing him exactly how it felt to get filled up with his own knot. The sensation of filling and being filled raced between them like a spark racing around a circuit. Oliver dragged her down, burying his face in her neck and trying to keep the feeling.

Then it ended. As always.

Luna settled down against him, humming contentedly. Basking in the bond, Oliver knew. The bond was always happiest like this, the two of them bare and pressed together as deep as they could be. Oliver couldn't even bring himself to be annoyed by it anymore. For the first time in a long time, he simply let himself be happy.

Then Luna spoke up and ruined it.

"You know, you're totally screwing me over with this whole 'bonded sex' thing. You're telling me I never get echoing orgasms after we get that divorce flower?"

"Guess so," Oliver said. He shifted against the bed, Luna moving with him as his knot pulled at her stretched hole. It never got any less intimate, and thanks to what Luna had said, it felt just as scary and overwhelming as the first time.

He would never have this again, after her. This strange melding of their minds and bodies, echoing each other's feelings back at each other. He would never trust anyone enough to bond with them. Unless someone tricked him into a bond a second time, Luna was it for him. And she was never truly his in the first place.

"Whoa," Luna said, lifting her chin off his chest. "What's that about? You got all…"

She scrunched up her face.

"I'm fine," he said. "Quit poking at the bond."

"I'm not poking," Luna insisted. "Your grumpiness is flooding into me. Stop harshing my vibe."

"I would never," Oliver said bitterly.

He twisted as far away from her as he could, which mostly meant he looked away from her. His gaze caught on the view outside the window: the mountains in the distance, only a hint of snow on their very tips now.

Luna touched his cheek, turning him back.

"Seriously," she said. "What's wrong? I thought… I thought tonight was great."

The shyness in her voice made him pause. He stroked her cheek, something he could only get away with when they were locked together like this. The moment stretched, Luna's eyes getting big and vulnerable.

She was so beautiful. Oliver hated it.

"Luna," he said.

Luna blinked, closer to him than any other person would ever get. "Yes?"

Oliver hesitated. Then he finally said it, the thing they had both been waiting for for a long time.

"I think it's time."

Chapter Seventeen

The Musgroves gathered on the porch to wave them off the next morning.

"We don't want some big send-off," Oliver said as they headed for the car. "You can go back to bed."

"We're already up," said Darren grumpily, leaning against Vida so hard that whenever she tried to move he almost fell over.

Luna couldn't help but look back as she got into the car. *Her* family would never have bothered to get up this early to see her off before a trip, no matter how important.

"Safe travels," Grandmother Musgrove called as Oliver pulled out of the inn parking lot with their hiking gear in the back seat.

Luna waved until they were out of sight. Then she turned to Oliver, her toes flexed in her fashionable but practical hiking boots. "You know, you'll probably have to carry me if this hike takes more than three hours."

"What, *you*?" He snorted. "I suspected as much, princess. Those boots are worn in, right?"

Luna flexed her toes harder. They weren't, but she was wearing double socks like Sabine had advised her the other day. That made her safe from blisters, right? She suddenly wished she'd gone on all those hiking trips her LA friends had invited her on. The longest hike she'd done was two hours, and she'd spent the last forty minutes whining for Hector to carry her.

Ten minutes later, they pulled into the parking lot at the base of the mountain. Luna stared up at it as Oliver checked their supplies in the giant backpack he'd insisted on taking with them. The mountain was shockingly beautiful, even if it was going to be hell on Luna's poor feet.

She snapped a photo on her phone.

"For the website," she explained when Oliver glanced over. "Gotta have good pictures of all the attractions."

Oliver went back to zipping up the backpack. "Right. Because you're going to revamp us whether we want you to or not."

"You'll thank me one day," she said cheerily. "Unless you still want your family business to go down in flames."

His head snapped up. It took Luna a second to realize why the phrasing might've freaked him out.

"I mean," she said hastily, trying not to imagine the inn burning thanks to some crazy woman with a prejudice against werewolves. "Wouldn't want all that laundry and roof-fixing to go to waste, right?"

She headed toward the start of the mountain path, which was helpfully marked with a sign. After a second, he followed, and Luna felt the bond hum in satisfaction.

"There's still a little bit of snow up there," she pointed out. "We're sure it won't start snowing again before we get down?"

"If the weather forecast has anything to say about it, no," he said.

"And you're sure you can guide us up there okay?"

Oliver rolled his eyes. "It's hardly guiding. The path is straightforward, and there are flowers all over once you get high enough." He hitched the backpack further up his shoulders. "Come on. If we're lucky, we can make it back by dinner."

He set off up the trail. Luna sighed and followed, feet already sweating in her double socks and boots.

Three and a half hours later, Luna had seen several disgusting bugs and zero flowers.

"Just keep an eye out for a white flower with a red center," Oliver said for the dozenth time, looking like he was considering tossing her off the mountain. Luna almost wished he would. Her feet *hurt*, she was sweaty and gross, and her nose was freezing. The bond helped a little, warming her up from the inside out whenever she got close enough. But it wasn't a match for the chilly air surrounding them.

"I didn't even ask for this," she complained as she trudged after him. "Why am *I* the one going up the stupid mountain for the stupid breakup flower?"

"Because *I'm* going," he reminded her. "Which means you have to come too, or I would've passed out before I even got to the parking lot. Hurry up."

"*You* hurry up," she muttered. She clutched her jacket closer to her chest since he had no room in his backpack and had refused to carry it for her. When she'd asked what the hell was even *in* that giant backpack he was lugging around for a one-day hike, he'd given her a look like she was the biggest idiot in the world and started listing off first aid equipment, blankets, a flare and nonperishable foods.

Luna came to a stop, wheezing. "Okay! I'm done! We *need* to rest."

"*You* need to rest," he corrected, hopping easily up a rocky bit of path. "The faster we get this over with, the faster we can break this bond and go back to our lives. Come on."

Luna frowned, oddly stung. Oliver had been...*different* today. As in, he had been more like his old self.

It didn't make sense. He *was* fond of her; Luna was almost sure of it. So why was he acting like she was a thorn in his side again? Was he trying to make her inevitable departure easier on himself by reverting into the asshole who had scowled at her that first night at the inn?

If so, that was stupid. Luna was *always* going to leave. Why couldn't they make nice until then? They'd been doing so much better lately. Until Oliver woke up this morning and decided to be a jackass again.

Well, Luna thought. *If he's going to be immature about this, so am I.*

With that, she flopped down on the ground.

Oliver paused. Luna wondered if he'd stopped because he heard her sit down or because the bond had started to stretch, urging him to go back. Luna could feel it in her chest, warm tendrils reaching out toward him.

"Flowers all over the mountain," Luna said. "Really?"

"Once you get high enough," Oliver answered. He turned and sighed when he saw her sitting in the dirt. "Can you just get over yourself for five seconds? Your feet hurt, boo-hoo. When this is over and you go back to your life, your feet will never hurt again. You could *pay* someone to carry you up a hill."

Luna thought back to Hector, who hadn't carried her the rest of the way no matter how hard she'd begged. He'd tried joking his way out of it, but the more she'd begged, the quieter he'd gotten. Finally, he'd turned around and said, *Babe, you're not making this very fun right now.*

It had made Luna go quiet for a full five minutes. They were, admittedly, the *fun* couple. It was what drew them to each other. It wasn't just her; if Hector ever got too serious, which didn't happen often, Luna would tell him to go back to normal. *Being serious is for boring people*, he liked to say.

But this was *Oliver*. Their tentative truce was almost over. Luna had yelled in his face so many times, what was one more?

"I will get a *train* of people to carry me," she hissed, surging to her sore feet. "I can't *wait* to get back to normal! Being bonded to you has been the worst month of my life."

Oliver's jaw twitched. For a moment, she thought she might have hurt his feelings.

Then he snarled. "Here I thought you were enjoying yourself. Worming your way into my family, remaking the inn in your own image—"

"Excuse *you*, I'm making it better!"

"Nobody *asked* you," Oliver argued. "Just pay for a new sign and leave!"

"I would love to," Luna yelled. "Unfortunately, *someone* decided to drink the bond nectar and—"

She stopped. There, on a cliff face over a steep drop, was a small flower poking out of the rocks. A cluster of white with a red center.

Luna cried out triumphantly. "Divorce flower! *Yes!*"

Oliver whipped around to look. His scowl melted into shock when he saw Luna was not in fact joking. Then it set into steely determination.

"Whoa," Luna said as he stalked toward the cliff edge. "Um… Bit of a drop."

"It's fine," he replied. He didn't even look down at the steep drop between them and the cliff face. A log protruded over the gap, thick and rotting.

Luna winced as Oliver stepped onto the log, testing its give. "Are you seriously going to walk out on that?"

"No," Oliver said. "Of course not."

He got down on the ground and started to shimmy across the log.

"Oh," Luna said. "Much better."

She padded cautiously over to the edge of the cliff. Oliver was halfway across the log, clinging like a spider monkey. The drop loomed below, maybe ten feet of empty space before it came to an abrupt stop at the patch of path where they had briefly stopped to have an impassioned argument about the dubious usefulness of double-socking.

"Are you sure this is the best way to get it?" Luna asked as Oliver climbed across the log.

Oliver shushed her. "I almost have it."

He stretched out, straining toward the flower. His fingers skimmed the white petals.

Luna grimaced. "I don't know. That log looks a little—"

A sharp crack rang out as the log snapped in two. Oliver scrambled back, but it was too late. The log fell, taking Oliver with it.

Luna shrieked. She rushed to the edge of the cliff. The bond inside her chest spasmed with pain as she peered over.

Oliver lay on the path below them, the log splintered around him. He was groaning, clutching his ankle.

"Oh my god," Luna yelled. "Are you okay?"

"I'm great," Oliver croaked, face twisted in agony.

Another pulse of pain rushed through the bond. Something was very wrong.

It took her several minutes to rush back down the path. Her cell phone signal never went higher than one bar, flickering in and out of service and not sending a single one of her emergency texts.

When she finally reached the spot where Oliver had fallen, she found him sitting up against a tree clutching his phone morosely. The backpack was resting beside him.

She dropped to her knees next to him. "Are you okay? Did I go too far?"

"Nope," he said through gritted teeth, arms curled protectively around his legs. "Are you getting any signal?"

She shook her head, looking him over. She couldn't see any broken bones.

"Where are you hurt? I felt something when you hit the ground."

"Wolves heal fast," Oliver said.

Another jolt of pain through the bond. Luna thought about jabbing him in random places until he howled. Then she remembered they were stuck on a mountain together and decided against it.

"Show me," she demanded.

Oliver sighed. Then he lifted his arms to reveal his ankle, which was swollen to the size of a grapefruit.

Luna shrieked again.

"Calm down," he told her. "Last time I broke an ankle, I could walk on it after a day."

"A *day*?" Luna laughed, incredulous. "You said we'd be back before dinner!"

Oliver tipped his head back against the tree, wincing when it jostled his leg. "We have supplies."

Luna wanted to whine like a little kid. She maturely held back.

"Oliver," she said, only the faintest whine leaking into her voice. "I *really* don't want to sleep out here."

"There's a cave down that way." Oliver pointed down the path. Luna vaguely remembered him pointing it out and saying that Vida veered off the path to smoke in it during her first and only hike last year.

Luna snorted in disbelief. "You want *me* to stay in a *cave*?"

She gestured at herself: peppy ponytail, stylish jeans, cute yet durable boots that were *killing* her.

"We have blankets," he reminded her. "And I'm a furnace, remember? I can spare some body heat."

Luna scoffed. "You just want to cuddle."

It was something Oliver would have laughed at a few days ago. Now he only glared, his jaw tightening.

"Your family will send someone to find us," she tried weakly.

"My family knows I pack like this." He slapped the backpack sitting beside him. "And it's not long until dark. If they *do* send somebody up before I can make it back on foot, they'll be able to smell us from the path."

Luna glared at him.

Oliver sighed. Suddenly, he looked exhausted, all the fight going out of him.

"You can keep walking if you want. Another hour, maybe two, and you'll find a flower somewhere less dangerous. Then you can come back for me. But I'll still need somewhere to stay tonight. And unless you've seen a hotel behind a tree somewhere…"

He trailed off, staring up at her expectantly. He expected her to leave him, she realized. Leave him injured and helpless in the middle of some hiking track for a few hours while her distance put him in even more pain than he already was.

"It would hurt," she said. "A few hours of me walking away, you'd pass out again."

"And I'd be fine once you got back," he argued. "This trip can't be for nothing."

She went cold, imagining it: walking back and finding him limp and unconscious, his ankle still swollen. Alone, just like he insisted he wanted.

"I can't get Spotify up here," she said.

He frowned. "What?"

"I'm not going on a hike, *alone*, with no music to keep me company," she said, grabbing the backpack and hauling it on. "We can get the flower once you're healed. Come on."

She held out a hand.

He stared at it. "There is no way you can lift me."

"Then help me out!" She slapped his shoulder.

He huffed a pained laugh. Then he reached back, pushing himself up on the tree behind him. At Luna's urging, he slung a toned arm around her shoulders. Luna ignored the bond singing in satisfaction inside her chest and took a step.

He stepped with her, face tight with pain.

"You have to lean on me," she told him.

He rolled his eyes and muttered something about flattening her. But he leaned harder, Luna grunting under his weight as they shuffled forward another step.

"There," she said, panting. "Better."

It took forty minutes of slow, painstaking shuffling to reach the cave. It was further off the path than Luna had expected—she couldn't even see the path from its entrance—but Oliver assured her that his family would be able to smell them easily if they walked up the path.

He unzipped the backpack, ready to lay out the blankets before Luna swatted him aside and took the blankets out of his hands.

"Let the girl with two functioning legs do it," she said, standing up and snapping the blankets out, letting them drift onto the thankfully dry ground.

Oliver shuffled onto them. He reached for the backpack again, this time pulling out a bag of snacks.

"Lot of time to kill waiting for that to go down," Luna said, nodding at his swollen ankle. "And I can't answer all the work emails that are *definitely* piling up. I have this pottery company in London that seems eager for a newsletter swap. I think they'd be good for... Anyway. Want to play I Spy? I spy something...green."

"Tree," Oliver said, not looking up.

Luna gasped. "Oh my gosh, you *did* it."

Oliver handed her a juice box and several strips of jerky.

Luna blinked at them, weirdly charmed. "Thanks."

"Thanks for the blankets," he replied, leaning up against the cave wall. He bit into his own strip of jerky, chewing loudly.

"Well, thanks to me for bringing them. Thanks for taking two seconds to lay them out."

Luna rolled her eyes. She bit into her jerky, picturing him here with his family. Dealing out juice boxes, orange slices, jerky, trail mix, and everything else she'd glimpsed in that snack bag he was pushing back into the backpack for later. Showing them how to identify bugs, which he'd started talking to Luna about before she threatened to push him off the mountain. Maybe teaching them how to light a fire. He took care of his pack. She had to give him that. He was gruff and growly, and he didn't let anyone in, even the people he was closest to. But he took care of them.

Luna sipped her juice box, trying to quell the fluttering in her stomach. It had nothing to do with the bond—she just couldn't remember the last person who'd made her feel cared for.

"So," she said, settling against the cave wall beside him, their elbows touching. "About that whole…not shifting thing. Is it because of what that woman tried to do?"

He stiffened. "Who told you that?"

"Sabine," she admitted, putting every inch of casualness she could into the word. Everything was easier to talk about if it wasn't important. "It's not a big *deal*. I mean, obviously, it's a big deal someone tried to kill your family, and now you can't shift. But like, it's not a big deal if you tell me about it."

She took another bite of jerky, chewing through the tough texture.

"What am I gonna do about it, right? So, if you want to tell me…"

"Nothing to tell." He shoved the rest of his food into his jeans pocket, scowling. He looked shaken.

Luna bit her pinkie nail. It was bright blue, thanks to Darren's efforts several nights ago. The polish was patchy, but she hadn't redone it yet. She kind of liked looking down and remembering his gap-toothed grin as she let him slide the brush over her nails.

It was going to be a long day. Luna thought about giving up, starting another game of I Spy, or better yet, seeing if they could get physical without jostling his broken ankle. But something about Oliver made her want to continue. She could *see* this great guy under all his gruff and bluster. She wanted to coax him out. If he snapped at her, who cared? She'd be out of his life soon.

"Okay," she said. "But it wasn't your fault. You're acting like you did something. You didn't do anything, that crazy lady did."

He looked over at her. "Where did this come from?"

"I just…" Luna paused, trying to remember how Grandmother Musgrove had phrased it during one of their breakfast talks a few days ago while Grandmother sliced a tinned peach into pieces. "I want you to get out of your own way."

"What's that supposed to mean?"

She groaned. "I mean you have these moments where you're this cool guy who loves his family and can actually make jokes! Then you smother it in your stupid grumpy shit. You don't need to blame yourself for something that wasn't your fault. Let yourself be happy. It's easy! I'm happy all the time."

She finished with a dazzling grin, propping up her chin with her hands and fluttering her eyelashes.

He barked a laugh. His eyes were still guarded, but some of the tension leaked out of his shoulders.

"You are *not*," he said.

She stabbed a finger at him. "You've only seen me outside my normal life. I'm *so* happy when I'm not here."

He snorted. It was less dismissive than she'd expected. If it was anyone else, she might call it fond.

"You like Claw Haven," he said, tugging at the frayed cuff

of his battered shorts. "You've spent the last few weeks singing its praises to anyone who will listen."

Luna scoffed weakly. "That's just…marketing. I love its market potential."

It sounded hollow, even to her. She hadn't lied when she'd gotten up on that stage during the town meeting and insisted that Claw Haven was special. She didn't like it only because it could make a pretty penny for tourists, but because she liked *being* here. The beautiful scenery, the quaint streets, the eccentric townsfolk who wouldn't keep their noses out of your business: Minotaurs in the grocery aisles, dragons baking bread, succubi flicking through greeting cards. Merpeople pushing themselves around in wheelchairs and fairies flitting around crosswalks. Vampires in coffee shops and adorable hedgehog women running chocolate stores.

And, of course, the Musgroves. She still couldn't believe they threw her that little party last night. And she *really* couldn't believe she had almost cried over it.

"Maybe I do like it," she admitted with a sigh. "Okay? It's sweet. And the people here are sweet. It's, like…a novelty. Fun for a holiday away."

"But not to live in," Oliver said.

"Right." She looked over to find him closer than before. He still had that fond look on his face. Like he could see straight through her lies and into the truth: Claw Haven seemed like a nice place to live. Just not for someone like her. She saw how everybody looked at her—they thought she was adorable, sure. But she also saw how baffled they were by her big-city demeanor: her accent and her clothes and all her comments about room service and spas. As nice as the townsfolk were, she wouldn't be surprised if they made fun of her behind her back. She had made fun of them behind their backs—why wouldn't they do the same?

She didn't belong in Claw Haven. No matter how much

she was starting to like the idea. Luna shivered. The bond tugged inside her chest, wanting her to lean in and be filled with warmth. Luna was finding it hard to figure out where it ended and she began.

His fond look collapsed into a frown. "Are you cold? We can get some of the blankets."

He reached down to tug at the blankets under them.

Luna put a hand over his. "It's fine. It's just the, um…" She dragged up a flimsy smile, trying to make herself sound just as peppy as before. "I know a way to keep warm," she said, sliding a finger under his shorts. "I'll have to ride you, though. Keep that ankle out of the action."

He made a low rumble in his chest. He started to lean in, but Luna caught his chin.

"Do you have condoms?"

He scoffed. "Of course I have condoms."

The incredulousness in his voice made her pull back even farther. "You brought condoms on our day hike?"

"Always be prepared," he said, eyes dark and full of intent. He caught her around the waist and pulled until she was straddling him.

Luna's breath hitched in her chest. She forced the strange vulnerability away and grinned down at him. "How's that ankle?"

"Fine," he said, only a little strained. He'd obviously jostled it while he was hauling her over him. He slid a hand up her shirt, then paused. "Are you sure you won't be too cold?"

She shot him a wry look and yanked her shirt over her head, gratified when his eyes went half-lidded. She pressed her chest against his. His skin was hot, but the bond was hotter, lighting her up inside.

She ran her hands through his hair, reveling in the heat. "What were you saying about keeping me warm?"

Chapter Eighteen

The next morning rolled around surprisingly fast and, thankfully, snow-free.

Oliver told himself he wasn't disappointed. *Luna* certainly wasn't, whooping in celebration as she clipped her bra back on.

"If the forecast was wrong," Luna said, yanking on her jeans and scanning the cave for her missing shirt, "I'd still drag you up to root around in the snow. I did *not* spend a night in a *cave* to come home empty-handed."

"I don't know," Oliver said. "You seemed like you had an alright time."

"Yeah, back at you," Luna snickered. She scanned the cave one more time and sighed. "Have you seen my shirt?"

Oliver shook his head. He hadn't looked, but he wanted to see Luna like this while he still could. Until she started shivering, anyway.

Still shirtless, Luna bent down to scrape her notebook off the ground. She'd been drawing in it when he woke up, hands flying to cover the page when she noticed him looking.

He pointed at it as she tucked the notebook into her back pocket. "You can at least let me see the Musgrove logo. You'll have to let me see it eventually."

"They're just—"

"Concepts. I know." He held back a smile, remembering how she'd flung herself over the notebook, shrieking loud enough for him to come all the way awake.

"I won't make fun of you," he said. "If that's what you're worried about."

Luna scoffed like that was the most ridiculous thing she'd ever heard. Like she didn't get all weird and self-conscious anytime someone brought up her work.

"I won't," he said.

Luna paused. Her eyes narrowed. For a moment, Oliver thought he would get an eye roll and a dismissal; maybe she'd pretend to knock his ankle as she stepped over him. Instead, she reached into her back pocket and took out the notebook, flinging it at him.

It bounced off his chest. Oliver caught it, surprised.

"Wait," Luna said, dropping to her knees beside him as he flipped through the pages. "Some of them are bad. Give it back and I'll—"

"These look fine," Oliver said, holding the book out of reach. Some were more fleshed out than others. A dozen little versions of *MUSGROVE INN*, another dozen doodles of wolves below it.

He held the notebook out and tapped the page. "I like this one."

Luna grabbed it off him and paused. "This?"

He nodded. Luna looked quizzically at the paper. It was one of the more detailed logos: a fully-shifted wolf sitting in a cozy armchair with a fire roaring behind him. A mug sat in his hand, steaming contentedly.

Luna hummed. She took out a pencil from her back pocket and drew two thick eyebrows on the wolf.

"There," she said, satisfied. "*Now* it's you."

He pointed at the mug. "It's not my mug."

Luna laughed. "Right! That stupid party-hat mug you insist

you hate until someone else tries to use it." She scribbled a tiny party hat onto the mug and leaned back. "Now it's *really* you."

She giggled. The bond in Oliver's chest throbbed, making his arms twitch. He wanted to reach out and touch all that bare skin still on display.

As if on cue, Luna shivered.

Oliver laid a hand on her lower back. The bond in his chest kicked up, humming happily.

"Ah," Luna sighed. "Thank you, werewolf heater."

She tipped her head back, basking in it. Then she frowned, twisting to look at him, still lying naked in the blankets. "Is your ankle still hurting? You said it was okay to walk on!"

"It is," he reassured her. He rotated his ankle obligingly. It ached in protest, but it was a dull ache. No agony like yesterday.

She waited. "Well, what's the holdup? You're just lying there."

He *had* just been lying there, he realized. It hadn't even occurred to him to move. He'd been having fun watching her get dressed and cheer about the lack of snow. He wanted to watch her while he still could.

The faster they got the flower, the faster they could get back to their lives. But for some reason, he was liking the idea less and less. He was still eager to get the bond removed and stop being magically pulled toward a woman he didn't even know last month. But he didn't want Luna to walk out of his life. She was…good to have around. Even if she annoyed the hell out of him. Sometimes *because* she annoyed the hell out of him. She pushed him in ways he needed to be pushed. And she fit in great with the family, even if she was trying to drag them all into creating a tourist trap.

She was *fun*. And there were times when she was *more* than fun. When she finally dropped that spoiled, airy personality and let something real seep through.

Luna raised her eyebrows expectantly. She smelled like old

sweat and bug cream, and Oliver wanted to lick her until she smelled like him.

Not that it mattered. She had a life to get back to, and he couldn't lie here forever.

"Nothing," Oliver said finally. "I'm getting up."

Luna blinked. For a second, he thought he caught disappointment flashing over her face. Then it was gone, and Luna let out a triumphant cry, pointing at a far corner of the cave.

"My shirt!"

Hiking went a lot faster when you didn't have a broken foot.

Oliver expected they'd keep walking to find a higher point where flowers were more common and easier to get. But Luna stopped at the edge of the cliff, staring at the flower growing across the gap.

"Hear me out," she said as Oliver headed back to her. "You put me on your shoulders and I, like, *lean*."

He made a face.

"Come on!" She pouted, holding up her boots. "I don't want to walk another two hours up, and then, what—five hours down? I want to get this over with already! Put me on your shoulders and don't drop me. What is your superstrength even *for* if not to lift hot women?"

Oliver thought about bringing up that time he'd fucked her up against a wall. Then he knelt expectantly.

"Fine," he said. "Hop on."

For a second, there was nothing. He heard her breath hitch.

He started to look up, but she was already behind him, hooking a leg over one of his shoulders. Then the other.

He stood slowly. Luna let out a tiny trill, arms out.

"Tense your core," he reminded her.

"No shit," she told him. She giggled. "I think this can actually work. Let's do this!"

He stepped up to the edge of the cliff and bent over, keeping an eye on her as she stretched into the empty space he'd fallen into. He eyed the steep drop. He'd gotten off lucky with just a broken ankle. What would happen to *her* if she fell?

His hands tightened on her legs. They'd never find out.

"Little more," she said, strained. "Little…bit…*yes!*"

He looked up to find her wagging a flower in his face. Before yesterday, he'd only seen them in wedding photos and the occasional sketch in Grandmother's dusty old books: a cluster of white petals with a blood-red center.

He walked them away from the edge and dropped to his knees. She climbed off him and jumped triumphantly.

"We did it! Divorce flower, you're beautiful!" She smacked a kiss to its many petals, shaking it in victory.

"Careful," he reminded her.

"Oh. Right." She stilled, holding the flower out expectantly.

He took it. For a moment, he felt a strange swooping sensation, like all his younger years were tunneling into this one: He hadn't expected to hold one of these for a long time. *Maybe* on his wedding day. More likely when he was an elder and it was his responsibility to make the sacred nectar for his pack. Grandmother Musgrove was still yet to teach him.

Then the feeling was gone. He tucked the flower carefully into the side pocket of his backpack, next to the water bottle.

"Mission accomplished," Luna said. She looked oddly flustered, a blush breaking out over her tanned face. "So…homeward bound?"

"Homeward bound," he agreed.

He waited for her to start down the path. But she just stood there, staring at him. If she were anyone else, he would say she looked shy.

"Unless you want to stay here and let my family send a search party," he continued.

"What? Right!" She let out a high-pitched laugh and started down the path. He followed, trying not to notice how heavily she smelled of him. If he focused on it, he'd want to obey the bond swirling in his chest and move closer, tuck her against him as they walked. This wasn't the time. From here, they would only get further away from each other.

Luna made it a heroic forty-five minutes before she declared that her feet were too sore and they had to stop.

"Not all of us have werewolf endurance," she complained as she sat down on a hefty rock, squeezing her feet through her boots. She looked up at him hopefully. "Snack break?"

He told himself he wasn't charmed by her big eyes and sighed, pulling his backpack off. They had enough trail mix to last them several more days, but they were down to their last strip of jerky. More fool him for eating so much of it last night.

He snapped the strip in half and handed the bigger half over.

"Thanks," she said distractedly. She placed it on her knee, carefully shimmying out of her boots.

"What are you doing?"

"Nothing. Snack break." She pulled off her socks next, grimacing at the stale sock smell. Then she started massaging her feet, fingers moving with the clumsiness of someone who had never given a foot massage before.

Oliver swallowed his half of the jerky and sighed audibly.

Luna frowned up at him. "What? Sorry for not having super-speedy regenerating foot muscles."

Oliver climbed down on his knees silently, taking her foot out of her grip.

Luna resisted, grimacing. "Ew, quit it! My feet are gross!"

"I licked your sweaty neck an hour ago," he reminded her. "Get over yourself."

Luna grumbled but stopped trying to pull her foot away. After a moment, she even relaxed into him, letting out a breath of relief as he dug his thumbs into the tender muscles, careful of the blister forming near her big toe.

"You should offer this at the inn," she said. She picked up the jerky strip off her knee and paused. "Wait, was that all the jerky you're eating?"

He nodded at the half strip in her hand. "That's the last of it. I have trail mix if I get hungry."

"Trail mix doesn't hit the spot like jerky," Luna said with the confidence of someone who had been forced to sit through too many of Uncle Roy's speeches about the importance of werewolves eating protein.

She nudged the jerky into Oliver's cheek. "Here you go. Come on."

"I'm fine," he insisted, still working his thumbs against the ball of her foot. "Wasn't the jerky the only thing you didn't complain about last night? You even said the oranges were 'chalky.'"

"They *were* chalky," Luna said. She nudged the jerky more insistently into his cheek. "Open up."

"We're almost home," he pointed out.

She just kept nudging the jerky harder into his cheek. It did smell good. And he *was* hungry. He turned his head, and Luna whooped as he let her slot it into his mouth.

"Good boy," she praised, ruffling his hair.

He rolled his eyes, pretending like the praise didn't do anything to him. The bond in his chest rejoiced, throwing sparks. But there was also a heat in his stomach that kicked in whenever anyone told him he'd done a good job.

Luna went suspiciously silent. He took her other foot, still chewing. When she still didn't say anything, sarcastic or otherwise, he looked up.

She had her chin in her hands, looking down at him with a pleased little smile.

He swallowed his jerky, fighting back self-consciousness. "What?"

She shook her head. "Nothing. I just think you're going to make a really good alpha."

He ducked his head. If he kept looking at her, he might do something stupid, like blush.

"I bet you say that to every werewolf who massages your feet," he said.

She kicked him gently. "Seriously. You're good at taking care of people."

"When I get out of my own way," he prompted.

She beamed at him. "Exactly!"

He slid her socks back on, rolling his eyes again at the face she made at putting on dirty socks. Then he pulled her boots on for her, even doing up the laces.

"A *very* good boy," she cooed.

"Shut up," he told her, cheeks burning. "I just want this over with. I saw how long it took you to do these up before." He finished the second boot and stood. "Ready?"

She straightened, easing her weight from one foot to the other. She was smiling, but he could see the wince. She was spoiled, sure. But it *did* hurt.

He sighed. "Alright."

He slung the backpack around to his chest.

"What are you doing?" Luna asked. "What's—"

Her question cut off with a yelp as he hoisted her onto his back. Her flailing arms locked around his neck, legs coming up to circle his waist.

"Oh!" she said. "This is—this is *happening*. Okay."

"You *could* say thanks. You whined about this for an hour yesterday."

"Yeah, well, I didn't think you'd actually…" She trailed off in a mumble. "How's your ankle? Is this too much weight?"

"It's like lifting a bag of chocolates," he assured her.

She made a strange noise behind him. Half laugh, half stammer, hands squeezing together over his heart.

Chapter Nineteen

Luna was still clinging to his back when they made the last turn that would lead them into the parking lot. She could even see the car through the trees.

Oliver stopped. Luna assumed this was her sign to get off, even if he hadn't let go of her yet.

"Thank god," she sighed, climbing off him and stretching mightily. "I was cramping from holding my legs like that for so long."

She mostly said it to make him roll his eyes. But he didn't even look at her. His head was cocked, his nose flaring.

Luna shivered, rubbing her arms against the chill. "What?"

He shook his head and set off down the path. Luna jogged behind him, eyeing his ankle warily. He'd been limping for the last hour, denying it every time she brought it up. She'd been tempted to start kicking his leg just to prove herself right, but they'd already been stranded here for one night. If she got them stuck out here for another, he'd harp on about it until she was waving Claw Haven goodbye in the rearview mirror of her rental car.

She turned the corner into the parking lot and came to a skidding halt.

There was another car sitting opposite theirs. Sabine and Ben stood next to it with one back door open. Ben carried a light backpack while Sabine munched on a peach.

"Oh," Ben said. "Hey. There goes that plan."

He tossed the backpack into the back seat and slammed the door shut.

"Told you," he said to Sabine.

She shrugged, biting another hunk off the peach. "Good morning! How was your night?"

"Fine," said Luna and Oliver in unison.

Sabine and Ben traded a knowing look. Luna grimaced, trying to imagine how she smelled to these wolves after a night of sex and hours of being plastered against Oliver's back.

Ben asked, "Did you get the flower?"

Oliver rummaged in the side pocket of his backpack, resurfacing with a squished but still perfectly intact flower.

Ben grinned. "Sorry to see you go, Luna. But it looks like you'll be unbonded to this lug by dinner."

"Promises, promises," Luna said dryly. She rubbed her arms harder, goose bumps standing up on her skin. It had been warm when she'd clung to Oliver's back. It was so much colder without him. It had been freezing last night, but she'd barely felt it. Oliver hadn't let her go that whole night. She'd fallen asleep to him absentmindedly nuzzling her neck, the way he'd seen Ben and Sabine do to each other.

Oliver frowned. "She can really make the spirit so fast?"

"That's what she said before we left." Ben opened the passenger seat door, ready to climb back in. "Said she needs a few hours and some privacy. And the ritual tools, obviously. Otherwise, yeah. Unbonded by dinner."

A knot tightened in Luna's chest. She couldn't tell if it was the bond rebelling or just her own body. She *would* be relieved to get back to her life. But she'd be lying if she said she wouldn't miss Claw Haven and everything that came with it.

She looked over at Oliver, pulling up a smile. She was about to say it had been arguably nice knowing him, but a wet spot on his cheek made her stop. Was he *crying*?

Oliver frowned, looking up. Another wet spot landed on his forehead.

It was snowing, Luna realized. She held out a hand. A snowflake landed on her palm and melted down her wrist.

Sabine hummed, a snowflake hitting her face and running down the thick scar over her eye. "It's earlier than the forecast said."

"It doesn't matter now," Oliver replied, shielding the flower from the snow. "We have what we came for."

Ben whistled. "Hell yeah. That's enough for a generation of divorces. Let's go!"

Luna followed Oliver to the car. He handed her the flower, and Luna laid it carefully on her lap.

"A generation of divorces," she said as they drove toward the inn. "This little thing?"

She poked its tiny white petals.

"Quit picking at it," he said, eyes still on the road. He flicked on the windshield wipers, snow smearing over the glass. "That's what Grandmother says. A small pack only needs one flower to last a lifetime."

Luna rubbed her cold arms, staring down at the flower in her lap. Tried to picture Uncle Roy's wife, who called maybe twice a year. She couldn't imagine walking out on this family. Being a part of it—*really* being a part of it, not her accidental visit—and then leaving. If she was married to Uncle Roy, sure. But if she had someone else…

"What?"

Luna startled. They were stopped at a red light, Oliver watching her as snowflakes fell around the car.

"Nothing," she said hastily. She touched the flower again,

more gently than she'd ever touched anything. "It's beautiful. For something so sad."

He didn't reply. She looked over at him, expecting him to be watching the flower. But he was still staring at her, his expression unreadable.

Luna swallowed. "The light's green."

"Huh? Oh." Oliver stepped on the accelerator. The car lurched forward. Luna fell back against her seat with a shiver, thinking of Oliver's molten arms around her all night, keeping her warm.

Hector answered on the eighth ring. "Stranded fiancée? Did it work?"

"Minor setback," she told him, drumming her chipped blue nails on the handset. There was no way she was coming back from that ordeal with perfectly polished nails. "So, we're only getting back now—"

"What? Did you stay overnight on the mountain? I thought you said there wasn't a hotel up there."

"It wasn't a big deal," she said quickly. "Anyway, we're back! Yay! His grandmother is getting the breakup ritual ready now. I'll be yours again in no time. *Only* yours, I mean. Obviously, I was still yours through all this."

She let out a nervous titter. It wasn't like she thought Hector would get mad—he *never* got mad unless he could make it *fun*. But she still felt weirdly guilty. Like he should get mad at her. Even though he'd given his blessing a hundred times to sleep around before the wedding. Something about sleeping in Oliver's arms, his hands soothing the sore muscles in her feet, felt more illicit than the sex. Like she was betraying Hector somehow.

"So," she said before he could say anything in response. "How was *your* week?"

He made a noncommittal noise. "Well, I'm running out of things to do at this resort."

"Maybe work? Which is what they brought you there to do?" For some reason, it was harder than usual to keep her voice playful. Her default voice for most things was fun. Why was this suddenly difficult?

"Ha, ha. Anyway, I booked a helicopter ride. Got some beautiful photos of the islands."

Glass clinked on his end of the line. Luna thought of suntans and mai tais. They didn't fill her with longing like they did weeks ago. Instead, they made her think of Grandmother Musgrove's hot chocolate, full of spices and a crumbled-up Flake bar.

"Anyhoo," he continued. "How was *your* week?"

"Great," she said automatically, toying with the comforter tucked around her. "I think this town has something, Hec. Like, it's got the It factor. Claw Haven: for the monster who needs some peace and quiet, sure, but also the perfect escape for the busy traveler! The monsters only make it more cozy. Like when you put foil behind a jewel to make it shine better. Have you ever seen a minotaur in a winter scarf? It's *adorable*."

"It sounds adorable," he said distractedly.

"And it'll be even more adorable when they start implementing my marketing strategies," she continued. "I've been doing some consulting on the side—don't tell Dad."

"Wait," he said. "For the inn? I thought you were just replacing their sign."

"I am!" Luna replied. "But you know how small towns are. You're out and about, you get to talking, someone asks for advice, and suddenly everybody wants a piece of you. I'm a *very* hot commodity here."

"Do I know how small towns are?" Hector repeated, incredulous. "Do *you* know how small towns are? You've been there a month!"

"It's been a *very* full month," she said defensively. She reached down and pulled her duvet tight around her, determinedly not imagining a certain pair of arms around her instead. In another month, this would all be a distant memory. She'd be back to her old life, in her old house, with her brand-new husband. Back to charity galas and parties and to secretly emailing the marketing team and falling into whatever fun Hector had planned every weekend. A nonstop party. That was how Hector had proposed: *Let's keep this party going*, he'd said with a grin and a giant, glittering diamond ring that was currently sitting at the bottom of Luna's handbag. For safekeeping, of course.

"Whatever," he said dismissively. "Do they tip well? They'd better. The way you made it sound, that inn is another bad year away from going under. Not even *mentioning* Claw Haven."

Luna bit her lip. She hadn't told him she was doing all that marketing work for free. "You know how I said I was bored?"

He was silent. Then he let out a laugh so loud Luna had to hold the phone away from her ear.

"You're doing it for nothing? Oh, *Lu*."

"Don't *Lu* me," she said. "I'm *so* bored, Hector! By this point, I would've paid *them* to give me the reins. There's nothing to do here when you're chained to a werewolf who passes out if you want to go on a walk without him!"

"I mean," he said. "Not *nothing*."

"Hush," she told him, neck prickling with heat where Oliver had kissed her this morning.

He snickered. "How is that going, by the way? Should I be worried?"

"No," she said, too fast.

There was a pause.

"Uh," Hector said. He laughed, uncharacteristic nerves trickling into his tone. "Ooookay."

She grimaced, burying her face in the duvet. Could she *sound* any more suspicious?

"It just feels weird," she said. "Like, our arrangement was

only ever meant for onetime flings. Right? If you hit it off with someone at a party, or—or you wanted to hook up with a waiter in a hotel room. One night only. This is…"

Hector's voice went soft in a way she rarely heard it. The last time was after his aunt had a stroke and he was talking to her on the phone, trying to decipher her words as she slurred with the one working half of her mouth.

"Lu," he said. "Are you falling for your accidental husband?"

Luna scoffed as loud as she possibly could.

"For *Oliver*? God, no. He's still that same rude jackass who snarled at me that first night. He's good in bed, but that's pretty much all he's good for. You don't have anything to worry about."

"Okay," he said, relieved. Glass clinked again, and Luna imagined ice against his sun-warmed mouth. "That would've been depressing. Everybody already has their flights booked for our wedding, babe."

Luna almost said something about how everyone would make the trip anyway. If a destination wedding got canceled and the flights were still booked, their guests would turn it into an impromptu holiday. At least, that was what Luna and Hector did when their college friends broke up the day before their destination wedding in Hawaii. Luna and Hector had spent two days sprawled out on a beach drinking rum out of coconuts.

I'm kind of glad they broke up, Luna had told him as she rested shirtless on a beach chair. *This is way nicer than that awful vegan spread they told us about. Seriously, who has zoodles at a wedding?*

Carbs or bust, Hector had agreed.

Then they'd toasted to it with the twelve-hundred-dollar bottle of champagne they had been planning to give to the not-so-happy couple.

There was a knock on the door.

Luna jumped up. "That might be them now! That was fast. Love you, bye!"

"Have a good divorce!"

Luna hung up and raced for the door. She flung it open to reveal Oliver, even more steely-faced than usual. He wouldn't look at her.

Her heart dropped into her stomach. Had he heard her trashing him on the phone?

"You look stormy," she said, her smile strained. "What happened? Did you lose the flower?"

His jaw clenched. He finally met her gaze, eyes flat and guarded.

"Come with me."

Chapter Twenty

He didn't bother slowing as he strode down the hall.

"Wow, okay, we're in a *hurry* then," Luna said, jogging to catch up. "What happened?"

"Don't know," he replied, not looking at her. "Grandmother said to meet her in the common room. She said it's about the flower."

"What, is it defective? Did we grab the wrong one?"

He ignored her. If he looked at her right now, she might be able to see the idiotic hurt on his face. Or worse, feel it through the bond.

He should've known better, he berated himself as they headed for the common room. This was why he didn't trust strangers. You never knew what they were thinking. He'd been stupid enough to believe they were letting their guard down around each other, that they knew each other, that they might even *care* about each other. And all along, Luna thought he was that same rude jackass who yelled at a woman for trying to find a place to stay during a snowstorm.

"Um," Luna called behind him, still jogging. "Hello? Am I going to be able to make my wedding next month or not?"

"You'll make it," he snapped.

His claws popped out. He forced them back into his nail beds, gritting his teeth. Was she lying to him when she said she thought he'd be a good alpha? Was there *anything* true about her, or was she really only helping Musgrove Inn because she was bored?

He stalked into the common room. It was empty apart from Grandmother Musgrove, who was standing in the middle of the room with her shawl pulled tight around her despite wolves' hot blood and the heater on full blast.

"Hello," she said as Luna ran in behind Oliver. "The door, if you wouldn't mind."

Luna closed it. Oliver could feel her questioning gaze on his face. He didn't look at her.

Grandmother cleared her throat. She stroked a hand down her shawl, a thick multicolored garment that had been around since before Oliver was born. It was one of the only things they'd managed to salvage from the fire back at their old home. Grandmother had dug it out of the rubble, covered in ash but otherwise unscathed.

"The flower was unfortunately destroyed," she started. "During the preparation process. I'm so sorry your hike was a waste. Next time will surely be a success."

Oliver waited. He couldn't have heard that right.

"Wait," Luna said. "The *whole* flower got destroyed? I thought you only needed a bit of it!"

"We do," Grandmother replied. "There is a part of the preparation process where the petals must be burned at the edges. I thought I would save some time and do every petal at once. But I slipped, and the flower was destroyed. I'm so sorry. My hands aren't what they used to be."

She squeezed her shawl, her bony fingers locking around the old wool.

"It is getting warmer now. With any luck the snow should

thaw a few days after it settles. I'll send Ben up next time. You shouldn't have to go twice."

"Tell him to go up further than us," Luna said. "Get a bunch. A *bouquet* of divorce flowers."

"I will." She came forward and laid a hand on Luna's arm, apologetic. "The snow *will* thaw soon," she said again. "It's spring, after all."

She leaned in, pressing a kiss to Luna's forehead. Then she leaned up and did the same to Oliver, hand brushing his hair before she trailed out of the room, still clinging to her shawl.

Oliver watched the door close behind her. Something was itching at the back of his head. He couldn't figure out what it was.

"I guess you should call your fiancé back," he told Luna.

He risked a glance at her to find her watching the door as well, her eyes narrowed.

"What?" he asked.

She shook her head. Started for the door. He followed, trying to identify that strange itch at the back of his head.

"That was weird," she said finally as they walked down the hall. "Like, *she* was weird. Right?"

"What do you mean?" Oliver asked.

Luna gave him an expectant look. Before Oliver could ask again, realization jolted through him in a sickening wave: It was suspicion. *That* was the itch. His and Luna's, tangling together through the bond.

"She's not a liar," Oliver said. "If she says she slipped—"

"*I've* never seen her hands shake," Luna insisted, folding her arms over the baggy shirt she'd changed into after the hike. "Have you?"

He paused. She was slower these days, but he'd never seen her hands shake either.

"It wouldn't have gone up in flames all at once," Luna continued. "There would be *some* petals left. Enough for us."

"She wouldn't—" Oliver cut off, wetting his lips. "Why would she lie? Your wedding is coming up."

"I don't know," Luna said slowly. She toyed with a strand of blond hair. "Maybe she wants to keep me around. Free marketing."

She flashed him an impish smile. There was an edge to it he didn't recognize, but Oliver was too awash in a realization he didn't want to dwell on.

"You think she's *making* you stay? She wouldn't."

Luna hummed consideringly. She came to a stop in front of Grandmother Musgrove's door, the farthest door on their side of the inn. Just like back home. The home that had been in the Musgrove pack for six generations, the home that was nothing but ash because Oliver was a gullible idiot.

"We don't go into her room," Oliver said. "That's her private space. It would be disrespectful."

Luna made a face. "You know what else is disrespectful? Trapping an innocent woman with your grandson."

She reached for the doorknob.

Oliver pushed her aside, grabbing it himself. If there was going to be someone invading his grandmother's privacy, it would be better if it was family. Real family, not whatever Luna was.

"If it will make you be quiet," he said.

Then he opened the door.

For a second, he wasn't sure what he was seeing. Then he heard Luna make a sound, not quite a gasp and not quite a squeak. She was shocked. Even though she'd said it—she'd *said* it—she didn't truly expect it.

Grandmother stood beside her desk, frozen. Her hands cupped a golden bowl, a fire burning down inside it. They had come in just in time to watch the last of the white petals shrivel to ash.

Oliver wanted to yell. What came out was a hoarse and horrified whisper. "Grandmother. What are you *doing*?"

Grandmother winced. She stood in front of the desk as if that would cover up her crime. As if that would hide the smoke still drifting up behind her.

"I can explain," she started.

Luna laughed. "You can *explain*? He broke his *foot* getting that thing! Do you know how hard it is carrying a limping werewolf down a hiking track?"

"You did *not* carry me," Oliver said weakly.

"Whatever." Luna shoved her blond hair back, letting out a noise not unlike a tea kettle whistling. "I can't— I don't— What the *hell*? You're so nice! I *trusted* you! Were you the one who put the bond nectar in the office in the first place?"

"That was an accident," Grandmother said hastily. "Your entire bond was an accident. But I believe it's a happy one. If you just had more time—"

"What?" Luna blurted. "I'd throw over my fiancé, my whole *life*, to come and stay here with *Furrier by the Dozen*? With *him*? That's—that's ridiculous!"

She even laughed, the noise strange and shrill.

Oliver felt it like a knife. The shock was gone. In its place was anger, deep and raging. She'd seen him unconscious after he ran away toward the mountains. She'd seen how he struggled with the bond, with *Luna*, and she wanted to lock him in for *more* of it?

"You chained me to a stranger," he hissed.

Grandmother sighed, resigned. "You chained *yourself* to a stranger. I only wanted—"

"She could be anyone," Oliver said, the panic growing in his chest. A dozen images blurred through his head: Standing at Luna's door listening to her laugh and say he was only good for sex. Luna looking down at him while he rubbed her feet, telling him he'd make a good alpha. Luna grinning gleefully as she showed him how many chocolate orders Beth got after her latest round of social media posts. Luna near tears after they threw her an impromptu party celebrating her successes. Luna shivering and dripping and scowling at him at the front desk, a rich, spoiled socialite about to launch into a life of nonstop fun and zero responsibility.

"She could be anyone," Oliver raged. "She's been living here *with* us! She could have done *anything* to us!"

"Um," Luna said uncertainly. "What? I know I'm a bit of a culture shock, but I'm not *that* bad."

She laughed again. Softer than last time. It still sounded strange, the bond pushing at Oliver to feel her roiling emotions.

He locked them out savagely. He didn't need a bond to know what she was feeling. She'd been clear on the phone call, let alone here in the hall.

"Luna is good for you," Grandmother pleaded.

He bared his teeth at her for the first time since he was a child. His voice was rising, and he could hear others padding down the hall to see what the fuss was about, Ben muttering something to Sabine about pressure cookers.

"You don't know that," he yelled. "She just showed up out of nowhere! We don't *know* her. She's not *safe*."

"Not everybody wants to hurt us, Ollie. That woman was a fluke. And she's in prison now; she can't hurt us. I don't understand why it got this big of a reaction from you. You didn't even *know* her."

Grandmother reached to touch his cheek.

He jerked back. It surged out of him like an explosion: "*I gave her the key!*"

The hall went silent.

Oliver's ears rang. He stared at the carpet, vision swimming. He didn't look up. He didn't dare.

"I did know her," he heard himself saying, the words finally tumbling out. A torrent after a year of keeping them at bay.

"Alexis didn't break in; I gave her a key. She never came over, but I thought—I thought it was romantic. She said she would wear it as a necklace. *Key to your heart*, she said."

A hand touched his chin. He flinched.

Grandmother tilted his head back up. Her gaze wasn't horrified like he'd thought it would be. It was warm and unbearably tender.

"Why didn't you tell us?"

He laughed bitterly. "She said her family wouldn't approve. Better to keep it under wraps from everyone."

"But—" Grandmother wavered. "*After—*"

"How could I? I endangered the pack. I'm next in line to be alpha, and I almost got us all—" He stopped, the word choking off in his throat. He could hear Ben saying something, but it was lost in the blood rushing in his ears. He turned, storming back down the hall. Past his aunts wringing their hands and Sabine and Ben with their arms around each other, past Uncle Roy looking shellshocked.

"Oliver," Luna called.

The bond inside his chest spasmed. Wanting him to go back. He kept walking.

Chapter Twenty-One

If Luna was the type of person who enjoyed ASMR, she might've found the current atmosphere soothing. A snowstorm was raging outside, and she could hear the soft sounds of people chewing Prickles chocolate as everybody stared silently at the lobby carpet.

But she wasn't, and if somebody didn't speak in the next ten seconds, she was going to flip her shit.

"So," Luna said around the chocolate minotaur she was chewing. "I told my fiancé it would take a few more days. Do we think that's realistic?"

The snowstorm howled outside. The roof vibrated, and everybody stopped chewing to stare up at the repaired patch of wood.

The howl died down. The wood stopped shaking.

"Maybe another week," Ben said.

"It *is* quite late in the year for snow," Sabine added. She held out a hand for more chocolate. Ben tipped another minotaur into it.

"How did Hector take it?" Sabine asked, covering her mouth while she chewed.

Luna shrugged. "It's Hector. He can take *everything* in stride."

She laughed, trying to make it sound like she was her usual carefree self. It sounded just as hollow as all those laughs she had flung out during their confrontation with Grandmother Musgrove. She had gone right back to the woman she was before Claw Haven. She hadn't realized how…*callous* that woman was until now.

Ben nosed at Sabine's jaw. "If this happened before *our* wedding, I'd be camped out in your room with you. Not on some beach—"

Sabine nudged him, giving him a severe look that made Luna think they'd talked about this before.

"I mean, that's cool," Ben said hurriedly. He turned to shoot Luna a wide grin. "We love a guy who rolls with the punches. Sounds like a cool, cool dude."

Grandmother Musgrove sighed. She was leaning against the front desk, gripping her shawl so tight her fingers were white with pressure.

"I think it's been long enough," she announced. "One of us should go talk to him."

Luna looked over at Ben. Everybody else looked at her.

Luna laughed. "Me? Not, I don't know, his *brother*? No, send one of the kids! He can't yell at Leo! Not without feeling bad about it later."

"I'm adorable," Leo agreed, stuffing another chocolate minotaur into his mouth.

"I'll go talk to him," Uncle Roy offered. He shot Luna a dirty look. He'd been shocked by the revelation in the hall, but there was something triumphant in his twisted expression. Like all his suspicions had finally been validated in the worst way.

"I think it's best if he talks to someone who wasn't directly involved in…" Grandmother Musgrove trailed off.

"Why?" Uncle Roy glared at her. "He doesn't trust her. And he shouldn't! She's not pack."

"She sure as shit *smells* like pack," Ben muttered.

Uncle Roy sneered. "That *bond* is about as real as Althea's gold tooth. It never should've happened, and you had no right to stretch it out."

"I thought it would be good for him," Grandmother said quietly. She rubbed her forehead, leaning back against the front desk once more. She looked exhausted.

Ben frowned. "Grandmother? Can I get you something?"

"No. I'm fine." She gave him a faint smile, then turned back to Luna. "You don't have to. You'd be fully justified to not do anything I ask for the rest of your time here."

Part of Luna wanted to agree. Wanted to stamp her foot and leave a bad review on Yelp. But it was a very small part. Everything else in her felt nothing but sympathy for this woman who had to watch her grandson close in on himself and not know why. Of course she wanted to see him open up again. Even if she had to use a blonde heiress who was getting married to another man.

Luna swallowed the fresh sting of betrayal and smiled back at her.

"I can go," she said. "Just...don't be surprised if he throws me out."

Ben snorted. "You can hold your own. If he yells—"

"Yell back. I know. I'm good at that." Luna shot them all another smile, this one more strained. Then she turned and headed down the hall, only pausing to grab another two chocolates from Ben's paper bag.

Luna knocked on the door.

No response.

"Typical," she sighed. She knew he couldn't hear her through the soundproofed door, but she was nervous. She wasn't the girl you sent to talk about something serious. She was the girl you sent when you needed to liven up a party. What was she even *doing* here?

She knocked again. Nothing.

Luna sighed. Then she started drumming the beat to Shakira's "She Wolf," which she had spent a good thirty minutes singing on the hike this morning, only stopping after the fifth time he threatened to drop her.

The door flew open. Oliver stood behind it, teeth bared in a snarl.

Luna held up the chocolates. "Last chance. They're going fast."

Oliver's face twisted. He started to close the door.

Luna threw herself in the way. "Come on! I promise not to talk about anything you don't want to. I just got sent down to make sure you're not eating the curtains."

"The curtains are fine," he said dully. "Get out."

"I still need to check." She batted her eyes at him. She even propped herself provocatively against the door, which would be more effective if he wasn't still half-heartedly trying to close it.

For a moment, she thought he would tell her to get out again. Then he sighed, the pressure of the door easing.

"I'm fine," he said. "You can tell them I—"

Luna swanned in and plopped herself on the bed, dropping the chocolates on the bed beside her.

"So," she said briskly. "How about that snow?"

He stared down at her. He still looked raw, like he had out in the hallway. Luna had never carried a secret that huge for that long. *That kind of secret would eat my soul*, she thought. She didn't know how he had coped.

"Luna," he said flatly. "Could you just...*not* do this?"

"Do what?" She struck her cutest pose, the one that made Hector smirk and forgo whatever they were disagreeing on to kiss her. But like all her other cuteness attacks, it didn't work on Oliver. Even with the bond burning inside him, tempting him closer, he stayed away.

"I heard what you said on the phone," he said. "Alright? You don't have to pretend that you care."

Luna's smile froze. Shit. She knew he'd heard through her stupid, non-soundproof room.

"You heard what I said to my *fiancé*? About the guy I'm *sleeping* with?" She tossed her hair dismissively, letting it fall over her face in that hot and appealing way she'd practiced in the mirror. "He's not a jealous guy, but come on. Guy's gonna feel a *little* insecure if he hears we're actually getting along."

His hands twitched at his side. There were little spots of red in his palm from where his claws had dug in. Luna had seen them pop out while he was yelling in the hall. The skin would be healed by now, she reassured herself before she could do something dumb, like reach for them.

She laughed awkwardly. "It hasn't been *that* bad, right? Being stuck together?"

He just stood there, staring down at her. His shoulders were hunched.

Luna tried to think of a joke. Something sweet or ironic to get that guarded look off his face. But the longer the silence stretched, the emptier her mind got.

She sighed, picking up one of the chocolates she'd dropped on the bed next to her.

"Look," she said. "I know I'm not...the person to talk to about heavy stuff. I'm Party Spice, you know? But I'm here. If you do want to talk."

She rolled the chocolate between her fingers, pressing a nail in between the minotaur's tiny horns.

The bed dipped beside her. Oliver had picked up the other chocolate and was sitting down, almost close enough for their legs to touch.

"You're not *that* fun," he assured her. He slid the chocolate into his mouth.

Luna said, "Okay, again, you've only ever seen me in a *very* different context to my usual—"

"I don't want to talk about it," he said over her. He bent over, elbows pressing heavily against his knees. "I can't believe I— God. I can't believe I *told* them."

Luna hummed. "Probably good you did. It was obviously weighing on you."

"What, almost getting my entire family killed? Yeah, Luna, it was *weighing* on me." He rubbed his forehead in a move that reminded her so much of his grandmother she had to smother a smile.

Luna had to stop herself from reaching out to touch his arm. "How did you two meet?"

Oliver glared at her like she had just insulted him. Then he sighed. "We ran into each other when I was out for a run. We just…hit it off. At least, that's what I thought. Later she told me she orchestrated the whole thing. Researched what kind of girl I liked. Exes, that sort of thing. Then she wormed her way into my life. She'd tried to do it before, but that guy figured her out. He was smarter than me, I guess."

"That's not fair," Luna said gently.

"I don't care if it's *fair*," Oliver snarled. "I almost got my family killed! If I'd just asked more questions, if I'd done a background check, if I hadn't given her the fucking key—"

He stopped, gritting his teeth.

"I don't want to talk about it," he continued. "I just… I want— Wait. What the hell were you saying about Party Spice?"

"Like the Spice Girls," she explained.

His brown eyes narrowed. "There *is* no Party Spice. There's Sporty Spice, Scary Spice, Baby Spice— Wait, no, I take it back!"

But it was too late. Luna was laughing, head thrown back with the force of it.

"You know their naaaaames," she crowed.

He scowled. "Everybody knows their names."

"No, they don't!" Luna giggled. "This is great! Did you have a favorite?"

"Shut up and eat your chocolate," he said. But the haunted look had drained out of his face. Some of the tension had left his shoulders.

She nudged him. "See? *This* is what I'm good at. Livening up a party."

He snorted. It was a weak shadow of his usual impassioned snorts, but she'd take it.

"You can't be all fun all the time," he pointed out.

"Well, *you* can't be grumpy all the time." She popped her chocolate into her mouth, sighing happily as it melted over her tongue. "Everything's *fine*, Oliver. Your family's fine. That awful woman is in jail. The inn will get a lot better once you fix it up. Once you start implementing my genius ideas, money will be rolling in by the barrel. So, something terrible *almost* happened. So what? You're okay. Your family's okay. Everything's good."

Oliver was silent. Luna looked over to find him watching her, exhaustion shot through with something she couldn't quite identify.

She smiled reflexively. "What?"

He shook his head. He reached up to touch her cheek, and Luna's heart stuttered in her chest in a way that had nothing to do with the bond unfurling inside it, eager as always for his touch.

"Chocolate," he explained. He drew his thumb back, sucking the spot of chocolate he'd lifted off Luna's cheek.

Luna nodded, dazed. She couldn't stop looking at his thumb, still shiny with spit. She wanted to put it in her own mouth. Wanted him to touch her again, smear that shiny thumb all down her collarbone. He was still watching her, and something strange washed over her.

Relief, she realized. Luna was relieved she was still here. That she wasn't in her rental car right now, finally on her way to the airport.

Still…there was something strange about the relief. Like it wasn't fully hers.

Oliver dropped his gaze. Then he looked at the door and groaned. "They're all waiting for me, aren't they?"

"*Oh*, yeah," Luna said. She let out a nervous laugh and stood. "Come on. Nobody's mad, I promise."

"They should be," he muttered.

She held out a hand.

Oliver glared at it. But it was a tired glare, one born out of habit rather than actual annoyance.

She wiggled her fingers.

He sighed loudly. Then he took her hand, letting her pull him to his feet.

The kids were clustered on the ground, with Darren picking at Leo's light-up sneakers as Leo and Vida commenced a thumb-war, quickly stopped by the aunts just as Luna and Oliver entered the lobby. Grandmother Musgrove was off in the corner with Uncle Roy, their hushed conversation dying as both of them looked up. Sabine turned toward them, in the middle of crumpling up the empty Prickles bag. There was no one beside her. Where had Ben gone?

The roof creaked. It was a statement of how anxious Oliver must've been that he barely even glanced at it, his hands fisted at his sides.

Luna looked down. No claws out, no blood in his palms. Then she looked back up at the pack. They all looked encouraging. Except for Uncle Roy, who was still glaring at Luna, and Grandmother Musgrove, who was watching Oliver with a sorrowful expression.

For a moment, the only sound was the wind howling outside.

"We don't have to make a big deal about—" Oliver stopped, turning to watch Ben push past him with his arms full of towels. "Where are you going?"

"Delivering more towels to room 12," Ben replied. "The new fluffy ones. Luna was right, the guests love 'em."

Luna swallowed her nerves and posed, sending him a wink.

Ben winked back. He was terrible at it, but that didn't stop him from doing it to Sabine at least once a day.

"Somebody's gotta take care of the guests," Ben continued. "Since we actually have guests now. That woman who heard about us from Luna's Instagram story is staying for another three days."

He swayed sideways and headbutted Oliver fondly in the shoulder, reminding Luna oddly of a cat. "If you're planning on some grand apology, forget about it. You got conned by a crazy lady. We have a new home now. No score to settle, brother."

Then he headed off, arms so full of towels he had to shove them down with his chin to see where he was going.

"He's right," Sabine said, stepping aside to let Ben down the guest hall. "You don't need to apologize."

Oliver growled. "Just let me say it!"

"You said it after the house burned down," Darren said, going back to toying with Leo's light-up sneakers.

"Over and over and over," Leo added, kicking gently at Darren's fingers. "It was so *annoying*."

"Yeah, well…" Oliver's jaw tightened. "You all kept saying it wasn't my fault. You didn't know."

"It *wasn't* your fault," Sabine told him. "It was Alexis. Like Ben said, you got conned. No one got hurt—"

"But you could've! I put the pack in danger just because I was stupid enough—"

Grandmother Musgrove spoke up. "To fall in love? To trust someone?"

The lobby fell silent once more as she walked up to him,

laying a hesitant hand on his arm. He stiffened underneath it, but he didn't pull away. Not this time.

"Those were brave things to do, Oliver," Grandmother Musgrove said softly. "Just…the next girl you fall for, get us to vet her first."

No one looked at Luna, but it was a very pointed avoidance. Luna even caught Vida ducking her head to hide a very un-Vida-like smile.

Luna felt her cheeks heat. She glanced at Oliver to find him already looking at her. She wanted to make some joke—*Do I have chocolate on my face again?*—but her throat was suddenly tight. She couldn't speak if she wanted to.

The roof creaked louder. Luna frowned. Was that uneven plank of wood from Oliver's patch job moving, or was that just her?

Ben emerged from the guest hallway. "The guy in room 3 spilled his drink. We still keep the carpet cleaner in the top closet, right? Or did Ollie have another fight with Sabine about where to keep cleaning stuff?"

"It wasn't a fight," Sabine argued.

"Um," Luna said as the uneven patch of roof bulged. "Guys?"

Ben slid an arm around Sabine's waist, smacking a kiss on her forehead. "So, I'm going up the mountain next time the snow thaws, huh? I'll repack that backpack."

Oliver sighed. "Sometimes I really hate—"

"*Guys*," Luna yelled.

The roof cracked open. Snow piled into the lobby, right on top of the carpet Oliver had cleaned a month before.

"Snow," Oliver finished flatly.

Chapter Twenty-Two

Oliver bumped into three birdhouses on the way to Jackson's front porch.

"They're *everywhere*," he hissed when Luna turned around to glare at him. "Not everybody is as small as you!"

He expected her to preen. Maybe strike a pose like she was so fond of doing, as if waiting for someone to take her picture. Instead, she just looked at him, gaze lingering on his broad shoulders.

"No, they are not," she said impishly and turned to knock on Jackson's front door.

Oliver tucked his elbows in and shimmied past another cluster of birdhouses. There were several dozen of them littering the yard, each of them hanging from a display with a dewy price tag attached, the plastic misty from last night's snow. It only came up to Oliver's ankles, which told him a lot about what he considered *normal*. Once upon a time, snow up to his ankles would've been a surprise.

He made it to the front porch, shaking snow off his boots, just in time for the door to creak open.

"Oh," said Jackson, already wearing overalls despite the early hour. His wings twitched where they were folded behind his back, a claw coming up to scratch self-consciously at his scaly snout. "Hello."

"Hi!" Luna fluffed her blond hair, which she'd insisted was ruined by the hood she'd been wearing in the car on the way over. The drive hadn't been long enough for the heater to warm up properly.

"Sorry to interrupt your Saturday morning," she continued. "Beth gave us your address. I hope that's okay. Oliver has something to say to you!"

She turned to him, smiling widely. She had been annoyed by the roof caving in again, like everybody else. But she'd been delighted to prove herself right in saying that he should've let a professional handle it, even if she tamed her reaction down yesterday. *Since you were having an emotional time and all*, she'd said on the way over.

Jackson looked at him, waiting. He looked expectant, and Oliver sighed as he realized they all knew what was coming.

"The roof caved in again," he admitted. "We put up a tarp, but it's about to give out."

"Oh, wow," said Jackson mildly. "The roof caved in? During the storm? Wow. Who could've seen that coming?"

"Truly nobody," Luna said brightly.

Oliver squeezed the bridge of his nose. At least Jackson was doing his best to hide it. Luna was bouncing smugly in her boots.

"Look, you don't have to rub my nose in it," Oliver said. "Just...tell me how much it'll cost to get you to fix it."

Jackson's eyebrows rose up his scaly forehead. "Fix it? Not just consult?"

Oliver waited, hoping he would keep going and he wouldn't have to humble himself further. But the silence stretched. Luna dug an elbow into his side.

Oliver glared at her megawatt smile. It dimmed slightly, like she was reminding herself that he had gone through something very emotional yesterday. Oliver told himself he wasn't touched and turned back to Jackson.

"Seems like a waste of time for me to fix it again if it'll just collapse during the next storm," he admitted.

Luna's smile turned into something even smaller. Almost proud. Oliver couldn't look at it for long before he had to turn away.

Jackson fiddled with the straps of his overalls. "Sounds about right. I can come now if you want. I just need to grab some supplies first."

"That would be *great*," Luna chirped. Then she winced, nodding for Oliver to take over.

"That would be great," Oliver repeated at a normal level of peppiness for this time in the morning. "Are you sure? The snow's stopped, so the tarp will hold if you have other things to do this morning."

But Jackson was already shaking his head. "Can't have guests walk in and have that hole in the roof be the first thing they see. Heard you're getting more lately."

"We are," Luna said triumphantly. "I mean, *they* are. I'm just the marketing girlie."

Oliver stared at her. "You pick *now* to be humble?"

Luna shot him a coquettish look over her shoulder. It faltered after only a few seconds. That had been happening a lot. She'd start with something irritated or coy or flirty and then it would turn into something small and tentative. In those moments, Party Girl Ready for a Camera was gone, and Luna stood in her place.

Jackson cleared his throat. Oliver tore his gaze away from Luna to see the dragonborn watching him with a knowing smile.

"Uh," Oliver said. He straightened his coat. "So, we'll see you soon?"

"Soon enough," Jackson replied. "You kids go on now."

Oliver bumped into another three birdhouses on the way out. Luna laughed, but they were short, snippy laughs, like her mind was elsewhere.

Breakfast was in full swing back at the inn, and the pack gathered in the common room around the table.

Oliver sat down in his usual seat, looking at the empty chair where Grandmother always sat.

"Where's Grandmother?"

"She's not feeling well," Leo told him with the snide tone of a child who wasn't sure the adults had told him the complete truth.

Oliver frowned at Ben, who shrugged.

"'S what she said," he told Oliver, digging into his cereal. Bran and banana because he was "taking care of his health now," and pancakes on the side because "pancakes don't cancel out the healthy shit, dumbass."

Luna leaned over. "Why do you look constipated? People get colds, Oliver."

"Not werewolves," he replied. "If she's sick—"

He stopped himself as every adult at the table glared at him. He'd been about to explain Grandmother's heart condition, which had required an operation five years ago.

"Which she isn't," Oliver said hastily, but the damage was done.

Leo slammed his spoon down. "This is stupid! I'm not a baby; you can *tell* me if she's dying."

"Leo," Sabine and Ben snapped as one.

"She's just tired," Uncle Roy said from over by the coffee machine. "Hey. Don't listen to anybody who says she's sick. Alright? Grandmother's tough as fangs. That includes her heart."

Leo went back to his colorful cereal, grumbling under his breath. Vida and Darren traded worried looks across the table, pausing over their toast.

Oliver wiped the anxiety off his face. "Hey, never mind that. People get tired all the time. Like Uncle Roy said, she's tough as fangs. Eat your breakfast."

The other kids went back to their food, still trading silent looks. Beside him, Luna was picking at her toast and trying not to look concerned. She was doing a very bad job of it, tearing absentmindedly at her crust and staring at the table with a thousand-yard stare. Even without reaching through the bond, he could see her running through a mental catalog of every health issue she might've overlooked since she arrived, while Oliver was doing the exact same thing.

Oliver nudged her leg under the table.

Luna looked up, startled. Her toast was in shreds on her plate, picked apart by her nervous fingers.

He shook his head. *It's fine*, he mouthed.

She smiled back at him. It was the kind of smile that wanted to be comforted but couldn't quite get there. It did make her start eating her toast, so he was counting it as a win.

Oliver fought the urge to push through the bond to see what she was feeling. They'd *agreed*. He wasn't about to ignore that just because he wanted to know how to make her feel better.

Ben cleared his throat. "So did you have to grovel?"

Oliver blinked. "What?"

"With Jackson," Ben explained, scraping up the last spoonful of cereal and pulling his pancake plate closer. "Did he make you grovel?"

"You know Jackson," Oliver said dryly. "He's a petty dragon."

Ben stabbed his fork toward Luna. "I hope you took photos."

"So many," Luna said. She kicked Oliver in the ankle.

Oliver looked over, expecting to be let in on their continued joke about Jackson. But Luna was making pointed eye contact with something across the room, mouth pulled awkwardly tight.

Oliver turned. Uncle Roy was staring daggers at him from the coffee machine. As soon as he met Oliver's eyes, he jerked his head toward the hallway door. Then he strode toward it, obviously expecting Oliver to follow.

"Good luck," Luna mumbled into her toast.

Oliver didn't bother reminding her that everybody in this room could hear that. He got up, swiping a piece of toast from his plate. He was even more worried now, but he was also starving.

Oliver managed to stuff the entire piece of toast into his mouth before they made it to the lobby, eyeing the crumbs falling to the carpet with the weariness of a man who would be vacuuming later. He needed to hire some cleaners. Maybe he would do that when the idea of letting someone else into the inner workings of the inn stopped making him want to tear his hair out. He'd asked Jackson to work on the roof, which was a good first step.

"Hey," Oliver said as soon as they got out of earshot. "What's up with Grandmother, really? Is she alright?"

Uncle Roy waved a dismissive hand. "She's fine. Look, we didn't get to talk last night. You're not getting stupid over this human, right?"

"What?"

Uncle Roy gritted his teeth. "I just— Everybody wants you to *open up*. Because they're stupid. You *did* open up. Opened up the door to that woman who tried to burn us in our beds."

Oliver went cold. He'd thought this was behind them. There had been a moment last night after he'd pinned the tarp back in place, when he'd come back inside to everybody drinking hot chocolate. They'd gathered around him, rubbing their faces against his cheek like he was a little kid, under the guise of warming him up. But he knew it for what it was: telling him there was no harm done. That all was forgiven. Even Luna had joined in, giggling about his stubble. Uncle Roy had stood off in the corner, and Oliver hadn't thought anything of it. It was hard to get Uncle Roy to join in on anything, especially physical affection. Oliver had caught him glaring at Luna, but as soon as he noticed, Uncle Roy would go back to sipping his hot chocolate.

"Luna isn't dangerous," Oliver tried. "She's a spoiled priss, but she won't hurt us."

It went against every scared instinct he'd built up in the last year. But as soon as he said it, those instincts that had fueled him to yell at his grandmother yesterday shrank back. It was easier to see his beliefs, his *real* beliefs, behind the fear. Luna wouldn't hurt the pack. Not if she could help it.

Uncle Roy growled, the noise rumbling low in his throat. "Look. Say she *isn't* dangerous. She still isn't one of us. Don't let them convince you she is. Don't let *her*."

"I'm not," Oliver said, ignoring the bond writhing sadly in his chest. "She isn't."

"She's a tourist at best," Uncle Roy continued over him. "She'll probably put this inn on her portfolio to convince her daddy to let her do some actual work for once. That stunt our alpha pulled yesterday? That was the stupidest shit I've ever seen."

"*Hey*," Oliver snapped, hackles going up.

Uncle Roy held up his gnarled hands. "I didn't call *her* stupid. I said she *did* something stupid. Why drag this out? That woman is *leaving*, and we will be here long after she does. *We! Pack!*" He thumped Oliver's chest hard, the way he used to do before football games in high school. "The only good thing that came out of that fire is it finally got someone else in this family to agree with me. Do not let outsiders in! You're going to be alpha one day. Are you putting the pack first?"

Oliver fought back another wave of defensiveness. *Good alphas hear their packmates out.* But they'd all learned to tune out some of Uncle Roy's more colorful opinions, even if Oliver had listened more closely in the past year.

"I always put the pack first," he argued. "But Luna—she's good for the inn. She was talking about doing some official partnerships with some stores around town."

"You hate this town! You said the townsfolk were annoying busybodies!"

"They are," Oliver said. "But I think they genuinely want to help! Jackson dropped everything to come and spend his weekend fixing up our roof. He texted me on the way over to say he's only going to charge me half of his usual rates."

Uncle Roy let out another growl and started pacing. "Do you *hear* yourself? You're getting soft again."

"It's what our alpha wants," Oliver reminded him.

"Our alpha is *wrong*!" Uncle Roy came to a sudden stop. He squeezed his eyes shut with a shudder. Before Oliver could tell him how far out of line he was, Uncle Roy looked back up with a snarl. "She's shoving that woman at you, shoving that fake bond at you. It makes you feel like you need that woman. You don't!"

"*You* bonded with a human," Oliver reminded him. "*You* brought a 'stranger' into the pack, you giant hypocrite!"

"I never should've," Uncle Roy roared. "That bitch tricked me. Georgia never loved me, she just wanted me to make her a werewolf and knew I'd never do it without bonding with her first."

Oliver stopped. He had never heard anything about that. He'd assumed Uncle Roy's ex-wife had left because of his constant grumpiness. And his trust issues. And his inability to open up.

"What the hell are you talking about?" Oliver demanded.

Uncle Roy grinded his teeth. "I... Never mind. Don't repeat that."

He turned away. Oliver caught his arm, dragging him back.

"Whoa, hey," Oliver said. "What do you mean? Georgia never wanted to be a werewolf. She liked being human."

"She wanted a pack," Uncle Roy muttered. "Didn't care whose it was. Would've married *you* if I didn't fall for her fool tricks. So be lucky it was me she suckered into that bond."

Oliver stared at him. It couldn't be true. Could it? Even if it wasn't true, one thing was certain: Uncle Roy sure as hell believed it.

"Georgia made me swear not to tell you," Uncle Roy said in a rush. "Said she didn't want to 'taint your memories' of her. Know where she is now? Huh? She's in New York with whatever dumbass pack took her in and turned her like she wanted! Could've been anybody. *Anybody.* Never gave a shit about me. You can't trust humans, Oliver. Even if they're not gonna hunt you, they'll still screw you over."

Oliver shook his head, reeling. All of Uncle Roy's bitterness was starting to make sense: He had finally opened his heart only for his wife to prove he'd been right all along: trusting someone only got you hurt.

It sounded appallingly familiar. Oliver watched his uncle's face twist, a sickening realization growing inside him.

"I never should've agreed to that bond," Uncle Roy spat. "It's poison. Worming its way into your bones, making you think you have something with a—a *stranger!*"

Oliver couldn't tell if he was talking about Luna or Georgia. That realization from before was expanding, cold and queasy, until it finally revealed itself in full:

This snarling, bitter old man in front of him…was *him*. This was what he would turn into if he kept heading down this path.

Oliver held back a shudder as he imagined it: not becoming alpha, everybody rolling their eyes behind his back when he spoke. Zoning out when he went on yet another angry rant. He thought he was being smart when he'd closed himself off after the fire. Now he had a horrified suspicion he had doomed himself.

But it wasn't too late. Right? Luna had proved that. Even

if she walked out of his life today, there was his old self left in him. He just had to hold on to it. A growl ripped out of Oliver's throat, loud enough to make Uncle Roy twitch.

"It didn't make me think shit," he snarled. "It made me want to be close to her, sure. But it didn't make me *like* her. She did that all on her own. I know it won't last, alright? I'm not an idiot. I just think—"

He stopped, the words sticking in his throat.

Uncle Roy stared at Oliver, his eyes wet and wounded. He really *had* been excited to have someone in the family who agreed with him, even if he was more enthusiastic about it than Oliver was comfortable with. He'd tried to bring it up with Oliver, only for Oliver to make the first excuse he could think of and leave him to his ranting. But he couldn't leave this. Not without sticking up for Luna. Not without sticking up for himself. He wasn't going to turn into a resentful old man who didn't let anyone in just in case they betrayed him. He was better than that.

He had to be. Even if he never saw Luna again.

Oliver swallowed thickly. "Maybe she's good for us, Uncle Roy. Maybe we're good for her. Is that so bad?"

Uncle Roy sucked in a wet gasp. The burn mark on his cheek was white and faded with age. And yet, standing there under the harsh lobby lights, it had never looked brighter.

The lobby door creaked open.

Oliver turned to watch Jackson step in. He stopped as he took in the two men, who were standing as tight as clenched fists.

"Ah," Jackson said. "Is this a bad time?"

"No," Uncle Roy snarled. "Come right in. Have your run of the place, why don't you?"

"Uncle Roy," Oliver said. "That's *enough*."

Uncle Roy snarled at him, teeth sharpening into fangs. For a second, Oliver's hackles went up, and he thought he might have to genuinely fight his uncle right here in the lobby.

Then Uncle Roy's face fell. He stared over Oliver's shoulder with such slack shock that Oliver whirled immediately.

Grandmother stood in the hall, swaying on the spot. She had three shawls wrapped tightly around her body. Her only exposed skin was her face, which was slick with sweat. She looked dazed.

Oliver rushed forward, taking her gently by the arms. "Grandmother! What's wrong? Does something hurt?"

It took her a moment to focus on him. It filled him with fear to see those eyes, usually so keen, clouded over.

Her lips came unstuck with a wet noise.

"I think…" she began weakly.

Then she collapsed into his arms.

Chapter Twenty-Three

Luna was pretty sure they were over the limit for visitors.

She leaned over to Sabine, who had graciously given Luna one of the few seats available in the tiny hospital room. "Should I…go?"

Sabine looked down at her, surprised. "What? Why?"

Luna gestured helplessly at the room. Only she and Darren were sitting on chairs. Everybody else was standing around Grandmother Musgrove's bed. Or in Leo's case, sprawled over her legs. Grandmother Musgrove was pretending her foot was a snake under the sheets, and Leo giggled as he pounced on it over and over.

"It just seems kind of crowded. I feel like I'm intruding," Luna whispered. In a room full of humans, that would've been private. But she was in a room full of werewolves, so everyone immediately chimed in with a chorus of denials from around Grandmother Musgrove's bed.

Uncle Roy glared at her silently. He was leaning against the wall, one eye on the door.

"Anyway, the furthest you can go is the parking lot," Ben added once the denials died down. "If you're lucky. How far did you get last time you tried?"

Luna looked over at Oliver questioningly. The last time they'd tested it, they'd stopped when Oliver started stumbling from pain. She'd wanted to stop before that, but he had been stubborn.

"She could get past the parking lot," Oliver said thoughtfully. "I think she could make it halfway home before I passed out."

Luna laughed. Mostly to get the weird icky feeling in her stomach to go away. It had formed as soon as Uncle Roy rushed in announcing that they needed to go to the hospital right *now* and had remained as they drove with an unconscious Grandmother Musgrove in the back seat and Oliver white-knuckling the steering wheel so hard it almost cracked.

Uncle Roy spoke up. "Someone's coming."

Everybody looked to the door just in time for a nurse to come in. It was the same nurse as last time, a middle-aged succubus with a tail so alarmingly tall it towered over her stout head. Luna had to squint at her name tag again to remember her name: Maeve.

"Hullo, Musgroves and co.," Maeve said in a dubiously Irish accent. "I'm just gonna do a wee checkup. Your doctor will be in shortly."

Uncle Roy snorted derisively. "Has he treated a lot of werewolves?"

Maeve shot him a bright smile as she moved around the bed to check the machines hooked up to Grandmother Musgrove. "Dr. Gert actually ran a clinic for monster youths back in San Fran. You're in good hands."

"Oh," said Uncle Roy, some of the aggression dropping out of his tight shoulders. "Uh, alright."

An orc walked in wearing an impeccably fitted white coat, her hair tied in an elegant knot between her horns. She saluted them all with her clipboard. "Hi, everyone. I'm Dr. Gert. Mrs. Musgrove, how are you feeling?"

Grandmother Musgrove folded her hands neatly in her blanket-clad lap. "That depends on what you tell me next."

Dr. Gert laughed. "Well, you don't need surgery at this stage, but I'm afraid we are going to keep you for a few days. Just to check your heart is still doing okay after that scare back there. How does that sound?"

"Sounds like I ought to get comfortable."

Leo immediately scrambled up the bed and started patting her pillows. Luna couldn't hold back a grin.

"Looks like you have help with that," Dr. Gert said. "Well, I'll let you get back to it. Let me know if you have any questions."

She headed into the hall, Maeve the nurse on her heels.

Grandmother Musgrove lay back against the pillow Leo had fluffed up or otherwise punched into submission. "*Some* of you have to go home."

Another chorus of denials rose. Even Uncle Roy joined in on this one, though he limited his to muttering.

"Luna was right about one thing," Grandmother Musgrove said over them. She twisted to look at Luna, giving her a warm smile. "We *are* a little crowded."

Luna smiled back. She didn't quite forgive her for burning the flower, but it was hard to be mad at a sweet old woman lying in a hospital bed. Once Luna got past the shock of it all, it was kind of touching. She couldn't imagine *her* family trapping her with someone on the off chance that they forced her to improve as a person.

Grandmother looked over at Oliver next. He frowned before she could even say anything.

"Go home," she said before he could protest. "Jackson can show you a thing or two about roof repair. But don't touch anything unless he tells you to."

Oliver took a deep breath, obviously about to argue.

She gave him a hard look.

The breath left Oliver in a rush. "I'll come back tonight."

He hesitated. Then he bent down and pressed their foreheads together, rubbing his skin against hers.

She held the back of his head. "Looks like you might have to be alpha sooner than we thought."

"You're gonna be alpha until I go gray," he replied softly.

Luna averted her eyes. They were burning, she realized with no shortage of embarrassment. She sniffed hard. Before Claw Haven, she couldn't remember the last time she'd cried in front of anything except a movie screen.

Oliver straightened, looking expectantly at Luna.

"Coming," she squeaked. Then she winced, hoping she didn't just give away how close she was to bursting into tears in the hospital room full of someone else's family. She rushed out the door, only pausing to squeeze Grandmother Musgrove's foot through the sheets like Leo had been doing earlier.

Luna spent the ride home staring out the window at the thin layer of snow, thinking about the Musgroves showing her how they put snow chains on her rental car's tires. Everybody had come out to watch Ben demonstrate, Oliver glowering at his side and not saying anything. Vida had pretended not to care, but Luna saw her taking notes on her phone. Darren had goaded Leo into a snowball fight with the aunts. Uncle Roy kept trying to interject with lessons on engine maintenance, which Sabine shut down with a glance at Luna that implied she knew just how much Luna knew about cars: a big fat zero. Grandmother Musgrove had stood at Luna's side, rarely talking, so wrapped in shawls it looked difficult to move.

At the time, Luna was bemused and cold, and she was eager to get back inside and call her cell phone provider to see if she could talk them into being less shitty. She had barely paid attention to the lesson, still convinced she'd never need those skills and would be on a sunny beach within a week. She'd been wondering what these people could want from her. Now she knew they'd just wanted to show her how to put snow chains on her damn tires so she wouldn't crash into somebody else's sign the next time she drove in the snow.

"You're quiet," Oliver said.

It took Luna a second to process what he'd said. Her head was still back in that parking lot, watching the kids pummel each other with snowballs.

"I thought you'd be grateful," she replied.

"Oh, I am," he assured her. "Just worried we're having another medical event. You couldn't deal with five minutes of silence on the hike."

She rolled her eyes. "Okay, just because I'm not singing the Spice Girls…"

Oliver's stomach growled loud enough to make her jump.

"Oh my *god*," she said. She let out a surprised laugh that quickly turned into a gasp. "You didn't have breakfast! I *told* you to eat something before we went to Jackson's!"

"I had toast," he said quickly.

His stomach rumbled again.

"Shut up," he told it, scowling.

Luna grinned. The anxiety from the hospital trip was finally leaving her. She didn't know when Oliver's scowl had become comforting instead of rage-inducing, but she was relieved. It made her feel like things were going to be okay. Oliver had been so pale in the hospital, so still and blank-faced as he paced at a speed that had Ben joking about him wearing a tread in the linoleum. She'd take scowling Oliver over blank Oliver any day.

Jackson was on the roof. He'd offered to come with them to the hospital, but when that got denied, he said he'd get to work.

"Hi," Luna called up to him. "Oliver's going to come up there later; he has to have a snack first."

Oliver's face twisted as she pulled him into the lobby. "I have to have a snack first? What am I, in grade school?"

Luna ignored him, dragging him down the Musgrove's hallway and into their kitchen.

"Shut up and eat something," she said. "What do you want? We got Pop-Tarts, we have…" She poked at the solidified eggs on the kitchen table, which hadn't been cleared in the rush of getting Grandmother Musgrove to the hospital. "Cold eggs. Cold toast. Oooh, we have cheese. Do you want a grilled cheese? That's *so* comforting."

"I'm fine," he replied. He reached into a box of bran cereal and popped a piece into his mouth.

They both grimaced. It sounded like he was chewing rocks.

"Cut that out," she told him as he reached in for another handful of dry cereal. "Let's make you an actual meal."

She yanked open the fridge and yelled in triumph to see multiple types of cheese. "Aw, you guys took my cheese advice! You won't regret it. A fridge isn't complete without soft cheese, hard cheese, feta cheese, and weird blue cheese that only tastes nice if you pair it with something."

"Luna," Oliver said. "What are you doing?"

Luna's grin dimmed. She ducked out from behind the fridge door. "I'm admiring your cheese collection. It's finally adequate."

"Darren wouldn't shut up about it after your fancy cheese rant when we had nachos," Oliver said. He walked over and closed the fridge, leaning against it. "I can make myself something. Don't worry about it."

Luna kept her smile in place; however, she couldn't help but let steel leak into her voice as she said, "Your Grandmother is in hospital. You broke your ankle—"

"My ankle is fine!"

"—and you told your family something that's obviously been

crushing you for a full year," she finished, voice rising. "So shut up and let me make you a grilled fucking cheese!"

Oliver blinked.

Luna slapped a hand over her eyes. "Wait, shit, I take that back. I was meant to be making this nice for you, not yelling at you. Go sit down so I can stop yelling at you."

Oliver snickered.

Luna dropped her hand to find him laughing, head tipped back against the fridge.

"You're exhausting," he told her. "I can't believe everybody back home thinks you're just a party girl."

Luna frowned, stung. "I'm not usually like this! I'm *breezy*. I'm *cool*. I'm…"

She floundered, fully prepared to start in on what she was like back home: poised and giggly, all fun all the time. The girl you called if you wanted a baby shower to be a hit without those creepy diaper games. People *loved* her back home. She was constantly invited to dinner parties, movie openings and birthdays. Rooms erupted into cheers when she walked in. She wasn't the person you went to if someone needed a first aid kit or a shoulder to cry on, but goddamnit, she was *fun*. She was so annoyed that Oliver made her *not* fun. Made her into the kind of person who yelled and gave away her last piece of jerky and knew how to put snow chains on her tires.

Oliver cut her off before she could say any of it, those dark eyes so soft on hers. "You could be."

Luna groaned. "Loud and aggressive and angry?"

He cocked his head, considering. "I just don't think you're really…fun party girl all the time. Nobody is."

Luna's heart thudded in her chest. The bond was trilling, as it always did when Oliver was close. But her heartbeat was stronger, overpowering the vibrations thrumming down her ribs.

She pulled up another hasty smile. "Wanna bet?"

Then she turned toward the cupboards to hide the blush growing on her cheeks.

"Sit," she told him, pulling open the cupboard doors and making a show of peering through the canned goods.

A chair scraped out behind her. "If you're taking requests, I'd… I'd love some cheesy broccoli soup."

His voice was so tentative that Luna couldn't help but look back. Oliver was sitting in his chair from this morning, toying with a shredded piece of crust from Luna's plate.

"My parents used to make it with us before the car crash," he explained. "It's one of the last memories I have of them. Cheesy broccoli soup is a Musgrove family staple."

Luna tilted her head, considering. She'd had cheese in soup before and hadn't been a fan. But if this was the Musgrove version of a comforting grilled cheese, then so be it.

"I can swing that," she said, taking out her phone. "What do I google? Do you have a favorite recipe?"

"I do," he said, standing up. "I can tell you while we make it. Come on," he added when she glared at him to get back in the chair. "I'll feel better if I can do something with my hands."

Luna looked down at his thick fingers. For a second, she thought about taking one into her mouth, telling him she had a better idea of what he could do with his hands.

Then his stomach rumbled again, and all thoughts of his big fingers were put aside.

"Fine," she said. "What do we do first?"

He opened the fridge and handed her broccoli and a potato.

"Start with these," he said.

Five minutes later, they had onions browning on the stove. Oliver's doing, of course. Luna was still busy with the broccoli and potatoes. Oliver had had to teach her how to sharpen a knife after he noticed it was getting blunt. Then Luna got temporarily distracted by the eyes on the potatoes, which she'd never had to deal with before and spent an inordinate amount of time carving out.

She stood back, admiring her cutting board proudly. "Done!"

"Great," Oliver said, looking over her shoulder. "Now we can…"

He trailed off.

Luna looked back at him self-consciously. "What?"

"Nothing," he said.

Luna glared at him. "No, what? Those are perfectly chopped vegetables!"

"Uh-huh," he said. He scratched his mouth, not quite hiding how it twitched. "Luna. Have you ever chopped a vegetable in your life?"

"Yes," Luna snapped. She had chopped bell peppers and pickles for charcuterie boards. Cucumber for cucumber water. Fruit for late-night snacks. She was practically an *expert* in chopping.

"It's fine," he said, taking the chopping board. "Everything's getting blended anyway, so it won't matter that they're chunky."

"They're *fine*," Luna insisted. She moved past him to watch as he slid her vegetables into the pot and then covered them with hot water. It hissed as it hit the pot, and Luna winced. But apparently, that was what was supposed to happen because Oliver's face didn't change once as he placed the lid on top and turned the burner down.

They cleaned the table as they waited for the pot to finish boiling. Oliver ate a handful of grated cheese, a cold piece of toast, and a few more handfuls of dry cereal until Luna threatened to pelt him with a cold fried egg. He ate another handful of cereal, and Luna seriously considered doing it before remembering she'd only agreed to make soup to be *nice* to the guy, and throwing a cold egg at him might cancel that out.

Cleaning was boring. Cleaning had *always* been boring, which was why Luna got a cleaner to do it at home. But Luna couldn't help feeling a little satisfied when she stood back to see the table clean and shining, no crumbs or bits of egg left from their rushed exit. The pleasure of a job well done. Like posting a good story on Instagram and watching the likes roll in. Like Beth texting her that this week's sales were even better than the previous week's and it was all because of Luna. The most she did back home was secretly design a successful logo or throw a baller party. Cleaning a table and making soup was…small compared to that. But it felt good to think of the Musgroves coming back and finding a clean kitchen and their favorite comfort food waiting on the stove.

They added stock next. Then cream and cheddar. Then they blended it all with a stick blender that Luna did fine with until the very end when she pulled it out too soon, splattering half-blended broccoli chunks over the stovetop.

"It's soaking into my shirt," she complained as Oliver swabbed soup off the stove. She picked a chunk of wet potato off her wet shirt and flicked it into the sink. "Ugh."

"Don't waste it," he told her. He took a spoon and dipped it in the pot, bringing it up to his mouth for a taste.

Luna waited. "Good?"

He nodded, turning the spoon toward her.

Luna bent in. The soup was thick and a little saltier than she would've liked, but it was warm, cheesy and cozy.

"It's nice," she said quietly. It sounded too earnest, so she cleared her throat and grinned. "Just like home?"

"Just like home," he said quietly. His dark gaze dropped to her mouth.

Luna's breath hitched. She kept her smile up. "Do I have soup on me?"

He shook his head and leaned in, dragging his nose down her cheek.

She squirmed. "Cut that out. I smell like soup."

"No, you don't," he said quietly. His hands settled on her hips, pressing her into the counter.

She shivered, tipping her head back so he could nose at her neck. "No? What do I smell like?"

He paused. His mouth was over her pulse point, breath flooding over the fluttering skin.

"Mine," he murmured.

Then he dragged her in. The bond in Luna's chest bloomed as their mouths met, her fingers tangling in his hair. His big hands slid under her thighs, and Luna gasped as he heaved her up onto the counter.

"Aren't you—" She stopped, allowing him one more tantalizing kiss before pulling back. "Aren't you hungry?"

He nuzzled her neck. Luna shivered as he reached her ear, biting the lobe and tugging.

"Starving," he promised.

Chapter Twenty-Four

Luna was lost in the sensations: his big hands under her thighs, holding them open. Oliver's mouth slowly but surely devoured her own. His sweat-slick body was on top of her while his hips ground slowly against hers. His cock was soft, but his knot was still swollen, so he could only manage the smallest thrusts. Every time he went to pull out, his knot bulged tantalizingly against her opening. So big. *Too* big, stretching her to the point where she didn't know if she could bear it—and then he'd push back in.

Luna whined. Every once in a while, she caught a flash of Oliver through the bond: how good she felt against him, how her big wet eyes made him want to pin her down and fuck her until she wailed.

Luna squeezed around him hopefully. Oliver's thrusts stuttered, his knot pulsing inside of her. One word drifted through the bond, low and growling: *mine*.

Luna shivered. She sent a wordless agreement back through the bond.

Oliver's hips stilled. He pulled back, fixing those dark eyes on her. "You have to block it out. Don't go too deep, remember?"

"I'm blocking," Luna said. She squeezed her eyes shut,

focusing on closing herself off. It took more effort every time. But Oliver faded obediently from her mind, the warm glow of the bond replacing it.

"There we go," Luna said. She bumped their noses together, giving him a shaky smile. "Hey. It's not like I can see anything shocking, right? I already know all your dark secrets."

He frowned.

Luna bit his chin. "Hey, none of that. Tell me what I smell like."

His eyes went half-lidded. "Mine."

"Yeah," Luna said, squirming. She could feel his knot going down, his cock hardening up inside the condom. "That's right, big boy. All yours. Oh, *shit*!"

His knot popped out of her, then back in. She thrashed against the pillows. It was one of her favorite parts: the knot not completely gone but small enough to fuck her properly.

"Yours," Luna gasped, the noise verging on a sob. "Oh my god, Oliver—*fuck*—make me yours!"

Oliver growled into her neck, hips snapping harder. The knot popped in and out, cock finally hard enough to press that spot inside of her that made her cry out.

Luna clung to him, whimpering. It was getting harder to tell what was her and what was him, the bond twisting them together as their pleasure mounted. Luna was getting fucked, and then suddenly, she was doing the fucking; her knot was going down, and the bedframe creaked under her hand as she carved new splinters in it with her claws.

It was impossible to block each other fully when they were twisted together so closely. Luna let it wash over her, only distantly aware of tears spilling down her cheeks as he emptied himself inside of her for the second time. Oliver licked her cheeks clean, and Luna tasted salt.

She lay there, quaking, his cock softening once more inside of her. They were both putting their walls back up, but Luna still caught it before they slammed the door shut on their bond: longing. Oliver wanted to keep her. For one moment, lost in their combined pleasure, Oliver had wanted her to stay with him in Claw Haven.

Luna swallowed over her thick throat as he pulled out. People thought all sorts of things during sex. It didn't make it true once it was over. And if it *was* true, that was…not ideal. She wasn't staying. She *couldn't* stay. She had a fiancé waiting for her. She had a *life*, filled with maids and spas and places to buy coffee if you got a craving at 10:00 p.m.

Oliver touched her cheek, catching a stray tear. "You okay?"

"Yeah!" Luna pulled up a hasty smile, wiping her face. "That was intense."

He touched her cheek again, and for a moment, Luna thought she must've missed a tear. But his thumb stayed there, resting against the corner of her eye so tenderly that Luna almost welled up again. For a second, she let herself entertain the fantasy. Staying here in Claw Haven and having breakfast at a crowded table every morning. Nodding at everyone in the street and helping stores to set up marketing campaigns. Going to sleep every night wrapped in Oliver's arms, warm and safe and *seen*…

Oliver's stomach growled. The look on his face made Luna burst out laughing, only a little watery.

"Luckily, we have soup," she giggled. She pushed at his shoulder. "Come on, the microwave awaits."

They brought their warm bowls back to bed. Oliver scarfed it down and went back for seconds before Luna was even halfway through.

He was strange when he got back. Stiff and awkward, keeping a distance between them like he had in her first few weeks at the inn.

"Let's not do that again," he said finally.

Luna froze, spoon halfway to her mouth. "What? But we don't have the flower yet."

"No, not..." He gestured toward the tangled sheets they were sitting on, which would have to go in the wash for the third time this week. "The *mine* crap."

Luna snorted, her panic dying down. She wasn't ready for their last time yet.

"It's sex," she said. "Stuff you say during sex doesn't mean anything."

He shrugged, digging into his second bowl of soup. "Still. Feels weird."

Luna arched her brows at him. Then at the huge borrowed shirt she was wearing on her sweaty body, and then the claw marks in the bedframe.

He aimed an equally pointed look at her engagement ring.

"Oh, whatever." Luna twisted the ring around her finger, feeling it pinch. She had fished it out of the bottom of her bag earlier—it felt like the right thing to do, with what was waiting for her. "I *am* kind of yours. Until we get that flower, anyway."

He grunted into his soup. "I'm not counting my chimeras until the ritual's over and done with."

"True." Luna sighed. "It'll be weird not having that little squirmy warmth in my chest. I was getting used to it."

"Yeah, well." Oliver opened his mouth like he was going to say something else. Then he crammed another spoonful of soup into it.

Luna resisted the urge to push at the bond and see what he was holding back on. She stretched out, her toes skimming his leg. "Then again, it'll be good to get back to normal. No more being stuck together. No cold front when you dare go more than a dozen feet away. No more feeling you get annoyed when that dog food commercial comes on."

"A border collie would never abandon its owner for a treat," Oliver replied. "They're very loyal."

"I know," Luna said, her throat going thick again as she contemplated a future where she never talked to him again. She swallowed until it was gone, then repeated more softly than she ever meant to, "I know."

Chapter Twenty-Five

"I know this is a lot of work," Oliver said as Jackson flipped through the notebook. "I can pay you your usual rates."

Jackson shook his head. "Claw Haven discount, Oliver. Everybody needs help when they're settling in. I'm not hurting for money."

He flipped through the plans Oliver had given him—replacing the carpet, windows, wallpaper—coming to a stop on the insulation page. He tapped the bullet-point list Oliver had scribbled. "Look, foam's a lot faster to install. But you'll run into problems down the line. Better in the long run to fix insulation boards to the exterior walls and cover 'em with new sliding."

"You're the expert," Oliver said.

Jackson kept flipping. He landed on the fireplace page and chuckled, tapping the sketch. "*That* one might be difficult. I'm not a sculptor."

"We'd just need you to get the fire up and working again," Oliver said. "You don't have to do the, uh, flourishes."

The bond in his chest flared with warmth. Oliver turned to see Luna rounding the corner into the guest common room, lighting up when she saw who Oliver was talking to.

"Jackson!" she yelped. "Just the dragon I was hoping to see. Are you looking at the fireplace?"

"Sure am," Jackson replied. "This your work?"

He held out the notebook. The fireplace in the sketch had been decked out with fangs and bricks painted to look like dappled scales.

Luna grinned, swanning over to admire her sketch. "It is! I wanted to check in with you—dragon mouth fireplace, cute or offensive? Or just gaudy? I want to lean into the monster themes, but is it too much? What do you think?"

Jackson tucked his scaly hand into his overalls pocket, tail swishing behind him. "I'm not an interior designer, ma'am. But I think it looks neat. My granddad had one just like it."

Luna shot Oliver a smug look. Oliver shot her an eye roll back. He'd been teasing her when he suggested the dragon mouth fireplace might be offensive. Mostly.

"Well," Jackson said, loud enough to make Oliver realize they'd just been standing there making faces at each other. "I better go get those supplies ready. I'll come over in a couple of hours. We'll do insulation first, then windows. Start from the bottom, work our way out."

He handed Oliver the notebook back. "By the way, how's your grandmother doing?"

"Fine," Oliver said automatically. Then he remembered he was trying to give fewer one-word answers to the townsfolk when they asked this question since they just kept *asking* otherwise. "Her heart's on the mend. We're taking her in once a week for tests, but so far, everything's fine."

Fine was a white lie. Grandmother Musgrove was still tired all the time and had to sit down if she walked for more than ten minutes in one stretch, but she wasn't getting worse. Oliver was trying to be more open, sure. But that didn't mean he had to spill his family's health issues every time someone asked.

"Glad to hear it," Jackson said. "Well. See you in a few hours to start on those walls."

Oliver watched him leave. One thing he appreciated about Jackson, he wasn't the kind of guy who slapped him on the shoulder as a greeting or a goodbye. There were too many of those in town, and somehow *Oliver* was the asshole for making it known that he didn't want some stranger touching him.

Luna kept flipping through the notebook. It wasn't her special work notebook—she'd bought another one specifically for Musgrove Inn. She even decked it out with pink-and-white glitter that spelled out *MUSGROVE DREAM HOME*, which Oliver had to be told was a Barbie reference.

"A few hours is enough time to go into town," she said. "We can pick up some of those paintings I told you about, the ones reimagining famous paintings with monsters in them. We can put them in storage until after the walls are done. Oooh, Vi from the bookstore said they finally have those cute little wolfy bookmarks, and we can put those on the bedside tables."

She was bouncing with excitement, face flushed as she ran down her list to monster-fy the inn. Oliver watched her fondly, the bond whirring happily in his chest as she stood beside him. It still wanted him closer, but ignoring it was second nature by now. It was harder to ignore the desire behind it. Bond or no bond, Oliver itched to touch the small of her back or brush her honeyed hair out of her eyes. Small touches, nothing touches. The kind of touch her fiancé would give her when she returned to him after the snow thawed. The kind of touch he shouldn't let himself indulge.

"—and we need to stock up on seaweed; that last mer ate the last of it," she finished, eyes bright. She looked over at him and paused. "What's *that* face?"

Oliver desperately rearranged his face into something less incriminating. "What face?"

"The…" Luna frowned. For a moment, Oliver felt something

brush up against the bond. Before he could ask her what the hell she was doing, the touch was gone and Luna averted her gaze.

"Sorry," she said thinly. "My bad. Let's go!"

Luna kept up the chatter as they darted around the stores on Main Street, handing him bags to carry.

"Careful with the paintings," she reminded him as they ducked into Sweethelm Books. "And hold *that* bag perfectly straight, it might leak otherwise."

"I got it," Oliver assured her.

Luna did a distracted little shimmy. Oliver had to hide a smile. The shimmy was an unconscious tic that cropped up whenever she was stressed about veering too far away from Un-Fun Luna, a tactic to convince others, or maybe just herself, *we're all having a good time, right?*

"Busy," Oliver commented as he closed the door behind him. "Nice work."

"Aw, it wasn't all me." Luna grinned, cheeks flushing as she surveyed the crowded bookstore. Tourists were *everywhere*, cooing over fountain pens and debating whether they should get into poetry.

"It was mostly you," Oliver pointed out, holding his bags out of the way for yet another tourist to come through. A day tripper, Oliver assumed. If they weren't, then they were yet to book into the inn.

"I heard you on the phone last week talking her through putting the ad up," Oliver continued.

"Yeah, well." Luna's grin went uncharacteristically shy. She bit her lip, and Oliver felt it echo through the bond. His tongue darted out to swipe his own lip. Luna's gaze dropped down to it, and Oliver had a bizarre moment where he considered kissing her right there in the supplies aisle with his arms full of bags and everybody watching.

Then Luna cleared her throat, whirling to inspect the shelves.

"Wolf bookmarks," she murmured under her breath as she stalked the aisles. "Bookmarks, bookmarks, bookmarks…"

Vi Harper appeared behind Luna, smiling politely.

"Hi there," Vi said. "Are you two looking for bookmarks?"

Luna whirled. "Vi! Oh my god, hi!"

Vi's smile suddenly became more solid. "Luna! It's so good to see you in person again. I feel like I've sent you a hundred emails."

"Right?" Luna darted forward and tweaked Vi's hair ribbon. "Aw, it gets cuter every time I see it. Where's my favorite dragon?"

Vi pointed. "Chester's out back."

Oliver concentrated. Sure enough, he could hear the old dragon swearing under his breath in the back rooms about an "idiot customer who wanted the stupidest edition" of a book. Oliver didn't get out much, but it was hard not to know about Chester, the elderly dragon who ran the bookstore. Apparently, Ben had had the misfortune of mentioning he liked Lee Child books once, while handing Chester a croissant. Then he'd been treated to a ten-minute rant on the downfall of modern literature. Oliver was in no hurry to see that dragon again.

"You've done such a good job," Luna gushed to Vi. "Look at you, back in your natural busy habitat! How are you? How's your sister?"

Vi blinked. Her smile was still in place, but it was her pause that let Oliver know she likely didn't love talking about personal matters with people she'd only talked to over email. If he remembered Vi correctly, she had moved to town to look after her sister after her husband died unexpectedly. Oliver wouldn't want to talk about that either.

"Sorry," Luna said apologetically. "I've become that small-town person I keep making fun of. I can't help it; everybody knows each other's business!"

"I suppose I'm still getting used to it," Vi said graciously. "Gabby's fine. Thank you for asking."

She turned toward the back counter, slipping expertly between the crowd of customers. "I have your bookmarks behind the counter. We threw in those pens you liked."

Luna preened. "She threw in the pens I liked," she whispered to Oliver.

"I'm right here," Oliver pointed out, trying and failing to hide his smile. "And my hearing is better than yours."

Vi emerged from behind the counter holding a neatly folded paper bag. "And while you're here, we're having another problem with the shipping website. If you're not busy, could you come around next week and teach me how to fix it so that I know what to do when it comes up again?"

Luna paused. "Sure! If I'm here next week."

"Of course," Vi said apologetically. "I'm so sorry, I've been crazy busy lately. Right, the snow will have melted soon. You can go and get that flower any day now."

It took Oliver a second too long to realize he should be smiling. He pulled one up, hoping it looked real. Judging from the surprise that flickered through Vi's expression, it looked about as real as it felt.

"Great," Luna said, voice too high. "Well, thanks for the bookmarks, Violet! Do we owe you anything?"

Violet's smile twitched so hard Luna startled.

"Whoa," she said. "What did I say?"

"Nothing," Vi said hurriedly.

The old dragon's voice echoed from the back of the store: "She hates being called Violet! Only Vi!"

Oliver immediately thought back to Nick Wicker, desperately trying to gain Vi's approval by calling her Violet and being a smug jackass.

"Oh," Luna said. Her mouth curled, and Oliver knew she was thinking the same thing. "Sorry, Vi."

"It's fine," said Vi in a tone that implied she would have put up with the name no matter how much she despised it.

A throat cleared behind them.

Oliver turned, almost whacking a passing child with his numerous bags.

The chimera had glasses, a sweater vest and giant horns sticking out of his golden mane. His feathery wings were folded tightly behind him so that he didn't touch the bookshelves.

Vi nodded at him. "Mayor. Good to see you back from your honeymoon."

"Good to be back, Vi." Christopher gave her a prim nod, then turned to Luna. "Hello. I heard you wanted to speak with me."

Chapter Twenty-Six

"I'm so glad I ran into you," Luna gushed to the mayor over their table at the newly dubbed Cozy Grotto Café. "I thought I'd be long gone by the time you got back from your honeymoon. I was supposed to leave last week, but something went wrong with the breakup ritual—"

She paused to stare at the cup of hot chocolate the owner, Emma, had placed in front of her. There was a tiny chocolate dragon nestled next to the cup, slowly melting against the ceramic.

"Oh, yay!" She gave a delighted clap. "They're using Beth's chocolate! I told them to do that. Thanks, Emma!"

Emma glanced back at her, several plates stacked up her arms. She looked annoyed, as usual, but she also looked genuinely grateful as she nodded at Luna.

"Should've done it earlier," Emma called. "Been great for business—hey, watch where you're going!"

She glared at the bewildered minotaur who had almost walked into her, who noticed her angry expression and made an immediate beeline for the door. Emma Curt had that effect on people.

Luna gasped, pointing at the counter where they had rows

of pamphlets she had made. "And they put out pamphlets for the inn, too!"

She turned toward the window, waving until she caught Oliver's eye through the glass. He paused his phone conversation to look at her in exasperation. Luna pointed at the inn's pamphlet lined up on the café counter.

Oliver squinted. His mouth twitched, and he gave Luna a brief thumbs-up.

"I helped design it," Luna told Christopher, giving the pamphlet another proud look. "Yay!"

"Yay," Christopher agreed, his voice deep and pleasant and ever-so-slightly British. He sipped his hot chocolate, a drop clinging to the golden fur above his lip before he wiped it off with a napkin. "Yes, I heard about your situation. That must've been very inconvenient for you."

"It's not so bad," Luna allowed, taking a sip of steaming hot chocolate. "The Musgroves are great. Being bonded to a stranger right before my wedding is less great, but we've made it work."

Christopher nodded. His nostrils flared. His polite expression didn't change, but Luna knew he wasn't smelling the hot chocolate. He was smelling Oliver all over her.

Luna set her cup down with a broad smile. "My fiancé is very understanding."

"So I've heard," Christopher said neatly. "When is— Oop!" He pulled his wings in to allow Emma to get past him with another armful of plates. "Apologies, Emma." Turning his attention back to Luna, he asked, "When is the wedding?"

"A month," Luna replied. Then she stopped and counted. "Three weeks? Wow, it's really coming up. We're having a beach wedding."

"Balmy." He touched the wedding band around his furry finger, his smile going soft and private as he stared out the window. Luna didn't have to ask who he was thinking of—she'd seen Instagram photos of them together, gazing at each other like nothing else existed.

She touched her engagement ring self-consciously. Wearing it made her feel less like she was doing something wrong.

Christopher cleared his throat, blinking out of his haze. "I'm glad I ran into you too, Luna. Everyone has been getting in touch to tell me how you've been helping the town. Setting up websites, designing merchandise, getting them interviews, helping them grow mailing lists. I have to admit, I've been so focused on the residents of the town that I neglected the fact that we need people visiting to keep us afloat. Then I go away for a month and when I get back, the streets are busier than ever. Even this café! I've never seen the Grotto—sorry, the *Cozy* Grotto—so packed. You've done incredible work."

Luna beamed, playing at bashfulness. "Aw, you're sweet. I'm just getting the word out about what a cool little town this is. Claw Haven did the rest."

She plucked her melting chocolate off the plate and popped it into her mouth, chewing happily. It was nice to be praised for something that lasted for more than one night and didn't require cleanup in the morning. Not that Luna ever stuck around for the cleanup.

Christopher smiled at her again. He radiated kindness and calm that reminded Luna of Grandmother Musgrove, or maybe of a cartoon king from a movie she fell in love with as a child. Regal and simple, not afraid to get amongst the common folk. She understood why the town had picked him for mayor. She'd vote for him too.

"Luna," he said, leaning forward on his elbows. "I think we have an opportunity here. I was told that you first started reaching out to local businesses because you didn't have anything to do."

He waved a hand at the street outside, crowded with tourists. "If *this* is what you do when you're bored, I'd love to see what you can do when you're invested."

Luna's grip tightened around her cup. She *was* invested, she wanted to argue. She was maybe *too* invested in this charming little town with terrible cell reception that was covered in snow for half the year. She was even invested in the people who lived in Claw Haven—all these too-friendly busybody monsters who'd gone looking for a refuge and ended up here.

She pulled her focus back to Christopher, who obviously had an angle. "Am I hearing a proposition?"

"How would you feel about helping me organize a fair? A reintroduction to Claw Haven, let's say. Show off our new 'brand' you've helped us set up."

Luna blinked. It sounded like a lot of admin, but she'd already been learning so many new skills this month that didn't usually fall under her "secretly marketing" wheelhouse—setting up subscriber buttons, ordering bookmarks in bulk, organizing the ETA for clay shipments to arrive by plane instead of boat. She'd even learned a little bit of coding to help people set up their online stores.

"I'd love to," she said, mind already running through a dozen different poster and slogan ideas and brands that would be interested in sponsoring them. Then she looked out the window at the snow. Or more precisely, the lack of it. There was sludgy ice around the edges of the street, but that was it.

"I might have to coordinate a lot of it over email," she said. "Once the snow's thawed, I'm… I'm gone."

"Email sounds great. I look forward to working with you," Christopher replied with that easy, trusting smile. It wasn't difficult to smile back, even as anxiety strangely grew in her gut, appearing whenever she talked about leaving Claw Haven.

"Please tell me you're getting paid for this," Oliver said as they jogged through the forest several hours later. "It sounds like a hell of a lot of work."

"I'm getting paid," Luna panted. "He even paid me more

than I asked for! Said it was back pay for everything I've done so far. One of Claw Haven's suspiciously nice residents strikes again."

"He's the nicest guy I've ever met," Oliver said. "I hated him for months."

Luna laughed. Her elbows jostled his as they turned around the forest path. Each touch sent a small fissure of warmth up Luna's arm. How did werewolves cope with this in the summer? Arizonan summer, anyway. She doubted Alaskan summers got anywhere close to the heat they were both used to.

"Seriously," Oliver said. "I could not believe this guy was for real. He had to have something hidden up those tight sleeves. But nope, he's just this weirdly polite, devoted dude who loves his wife and wants this town to be okay."

They skirted around a tree and fell back into place next to each other. Luna was getting faster, to be sure. But Oliver was also better about slowing down these days.

"He looked eager," he added. "Never seen the guy look so excited about anything but his wife."

Luna preened. "He was very impressed with my work! He said even *he* didn't know this much about the local businesses. Said I was *very* skilled." As soon as she registered the pride, caution rushed in behind it. "I mean, a lot of it is just knowing people, you know? Emailing people that I talked to at parties two years ago and asking if they want to sponsor a skincare store. Did you know Arthur Pineclaw used to live in Claw Haven? Like, *the* Arthur Pineclaw. You know, the chimera from *Mane Suspect* and *Just Kitten Around*. His agent hasn't gotten back to me yet, but my fingers are crossed! Anyway, it's not me so much as it is talking to the right people."

Oliver huffed. "Why do you do that?"

"Do what?"

He shook his head, eyes on the trees ahead of them. "You're so cocky about everything. Then you bring up your work, and you start saying all these disclaimers. *It's not me, I didn't do anything.* Bullshit. You did everything! Half of these people didn't know what a mailing list was or how to design a Facebook ad before you came along."

Luna eyed her sneakers, cheeks burning. She was used to getting praise—everyone told her how gorgeous she was, how fun, how sophisticated—but she wasn't used to getting praise for *this*. Her family treated her degrees like something she'd done to feel smart. Whenever she tried to make a marketing suggestion, she got an eye roll and a quick subject change.

Their elbows brushed. Luna shivered as another burst of heat ran up her arm and into her heart.

Oliver sighed. "Don't tell anyone I said this. As much as this town pisses me off, you've started something here. I think your family are idiots for thinking you can't do this. You've done a lot of good in Claw Haven. It's really going to make a difference."

Luna looked over at him, shocked. He was still staring up at the trees ahead, which were thinning out as they got closer to the ocean. There was a muscle fluttering in his jaw like he was clenching it.

"You can speed up, you know," Luna said. "We can put some real space between us now. Last time you even went out of sight!"

"And you immediately got lost," he reminded her.

Luna's phone rang.

"Told you it was worth it to buy sports leggings with pockets," she told Oliver as she fished it out. "Hello?"

"Hey," said Ben. "Oliver with you?"

"Obviously."

"Great," Ben said. "Tell him I'm going up the mountain tomorrow. It's flower time."

Chapter Twenty-Seven

A distraction, Grandmother Musgrove called it. Something to take his mind off Ben and Sabine's trek into the mountains. Oliver had assumed she would show him a mysterious stain she'd discovered in one of the rooms or get him to fix the bell at the front desk. He didn't expect her to lead him into her room—his hand on her arm in case she fell again—to find her desk covered in the instruments he was never allowed to touch as a child: a slim blue bottle with a curled handle, a battered golden bowl, a small silver knife, pungent dry herbs tied in bundles. The smell reminded him of those nights when he'd climbed into her bed in the months after his parents died. Ben came too, and he'd fall asleep with his face buried in Grandmother's hair and Ben's foot sticking somewhere uncomfortable and the scent of those dried herbs hanging in the air. It smelled like safety. Like being stuck in his head, unable to climb out, only to have his grandmother reach a hand down and lift him free.

He touched the sleek blue bottle that had gotten him into this mess. "What's all this?"

She gave him a soft smile. "I think it's past time somebody in this family besides me learns how to break a bond."

Oliver swallowed past the sudden lump in his throat. They'd talked about doing this eventually, but she hadn't brought it up in the past year. Not since he'd pulled away and she'd started doubting his abilities to be alpha. He wanted to ask if this meant she'd changed her mind—if she believed in him again—but the words caught in his throat.

"Now," she said. "The first thing you'll want to do is pour the bond nectar into a glass. I'll show you how to make the nectar later, it's a much longer process."

She set a pristine glass on the desk and picked up the bottle, which still had the cork firmly in place.

He watched her mime pouring it. "Is the glass important?"

She stared down at it. "Well, otherwise you'd get it all over the desk."

"No, I mean..." He gestured down at the delicate glass, its gentle patterns vaguely familiar. "Would any glass work? Is it a special glass? If we lose that golden bowl, can I buy another one from Pottery Barn?"

She considered as she set the bottle back down. "You don't *have* to. If it's an emergency, you can use whatever receptacle you have lying around. Use a McDonald's cup if you have to. But Musgroves are proud to use the same items our ancestors have used for centuries."

"Of course," Oliver said hastily.

"I'll put you in touch with your cousins; they have more where these came from." She tapped the golden bowl, a sweet sound ringing through her room. "Now we take the flower and burn the edges."

She lit a match. Then she met his eyes, and he knew they were both thinking about the debacle that had gone down in the hallway a few days ago.

"You only need a few petals," she said, miming shaking her hand out into the golden bowl.

"A few," he prompted.

"Two," she said. "Well, *traditionally* two. Really, it's one for every person breaking the bond, so it depends on how many are in the bond. Then crush them in with the herbs."

She picked up the dried herbs and crumbled some into the golden bowl, mashing it around with her fingers.

"Then you empty it into the glass," she continued. "And you bleed into it."

He made a face. "*Bleed* into it?"

"Yes." She held out the small silver knife to him. "Traditionally, the un-bonding pair will do it. Symbolizing that they are severing from each other."

Oliver shifted uncomfortably. He took the knife, feeling the short, slim blade. This had to be the knife that had cut the bond between Uncle Roy and his wife. The knife that had cut the bonds between however many Musgroves throughout however many generations.

He'd always assumed he wouldn't bond with anyone. It was too intimate. He'd get married, of course. But not every married couple bonded. He'd always been worried that it would be too much, constantly being able to feel their presence or the lack of it. Feeling the echoes of their emotions, maybe even knowing what they were thinking if the bond lasted long enough and ran particularly deep. After he left Arizona, he'd doubted whether he'd even get married. If he'd ever trust anyone enough to date again. He never thought he'd stumble into a bond. Especially not with someone like Luna, whose world was so separate from his she might as well have been from another planet.

He rolled the knife in his hand, imagining pressing it into her thumb. She wouldn't heal fast like he would. She'd have to bandage it. He wondered if it would scar. The idea filled him with deep dread and equally deep want. He'd never let it happen; he'd cut her shallowly and briefly, barely enough for the drops of blood they needed. But he wanted something tangible for her to remember him by. He wanted her to lie in bed at night with her husband, rubbing her finger over the scar and remembering their time together. A stolen two months in a strange, snowy town where she'd once arranged a fair. Would she forget all about them when she left? Would she forget him?

"Oliver."

Grandmother's voice dragged him back. He placed the knife back on the desk, giving her a tight smile. "Is that it?"

She paused. Then she touched his arm, squeezing gently. She'd done it a million times before, yet Oliver still stiffened.

He wanted to be the guy who leaned into his family's touch gladly. He used to be, once. He wanted to be Oliver from a year ago, who hadn't betrayed them all by opening up to the wrong person and wasn't this broken husk of a wolf who couldn't even shift. Who felt like he didn't deserve his family's affection to the point where he got angry if they tried to give it to him.

He tried to make his arm relax. But it was too late, Grandmother's hand dropping back to her side.

"Yes," she said. "That's it. The bond will sever, and you'll be back to yourselves once more."

Back to ourselves, Oliver thought. He rubbed his chest. It was getting warmer. Luna must be closer than he'd thought.

Grandmother cleared her throat. "So, she's staying until the fair?"

"She's thinking about it," Oliver said, trying to yank back the respect and awe he'd felt at being shown the rituals of his family and banish all the stupid, useless regret that had risen when she gave him the knife. "It'd cut it pretty close, is the thing. The wedding is the day after."

She hummed. Her gaze was back on her desk again, looking over the bottle, the knife and the herbs crushed at the bottom of the golden bowl.

Oliver swallowed. "Grandmother. Showing me all of this. Does this mean you still—"

The warmth in his chest pulsed, and he cut off as the door swung open.

"Found you," Luna trilled, with a bright grin that said she'd been playing Hot and Cold with the bond to locate Oliver. "Do you know— Oh! You're doing secret ritual stuff!"

Her hands flew up to cover her eyes. Her nails were covered in bumpy silver nail polish. She'd let Darren or Leo at them again last night, one child on each hand as they watched *I Love Lucy* reruns in the common room.

"I can't see," she announced. "I'm blind."

"It's fine," Oliver said as Grandmother Musgrove draped a nearby dressing gown over the table. "What's up?"

Luna dropped her hands and broke into another bright grin. "Aunt Althea says you know where the drill is. The bookshop needs it for their fair stall!"

"We're loaning drills to Sweethelm Books now?"

Luna nodded. She clasped her hands under her chin, rocking side to side in a way that Oliver would deny was cute until the end of time.

He sighed. "It's in the basement. I'll show you."

"Oh, you can keep..." Luna waved a hand at the cloth-covered table. She looked anxious, and he didn't blame her. The last time she'd been in here, Grandmother was burning her only ticket out.

"We're finished for now," Grandmother said. "Give Chester and Vi my best."

She patted Oliver's back, light and fleeting.

Luna looked at Grandmother's hand. Then she looked at Oliver, eyes widening pointedly. The bond in his chest flared hopefully, a distant echo of what she was feeling as she watched them.

Oliver clenched his jaw. Then he turned, catching Grandmother's hand and squeezing—the first time he'd reached out to her in a year.

"Will do," he said, leaving before he could see her surprised expression turn soft with warmth.

★ ★ ★

Luna didn't stop grinning all the way down the hallway.

"Quit it," he told her.

She butted her head against his shoulder, wolf-style. "That was so *cute*! She got *so* happy, oh my god. You should hug your whole family tonight; I want to see their faces—especially Uncle Roy's."

"He'll think you talked me into it as a part of your secret plan to take down the family," he reminded her.

"Probably," she agreed, still bouncing along happily beside him. She even twirled.

He stood back so she didn't crash into him. "*You're* in a good mood. You know Ben and Sabine aren't back yet, right? They might've gotten kidnapped. Or fallen off a cliff. Don't count your un-bonding chickens before they hatch."

She shook her head. "I just got great news from a sponsor! They're giving me all the money I asked for, *and* they're promoting us all over Alaska! This fair is going to be amazing! Everyone's going to see how incredible Claw Haven is."

She twirled again. He didn't step away this time, letting her elbow graze his chest. It sent a spark of heat into his rib cage, and Oliver tried not to wonder how many more times he'd get to have this. He still wasn't used to the bond flourishing inside of him, sending out pulses of warmth whenever she got close. But it would be strange to never feel it again.

Luna yelped, foot skidding on the carpet. Her twirl turned into a fall, and Oliver reached out automatically to catch her. "Careful!"

She blinked up at him. She was pressed against his chest, her hands splayed on his stomach where they'd flown out to catch herself. In the last few weeks, she'd touched him more than anyone had in a full year.

Oliver stepped back, nodding at the door at the end of the guest hallway. "Uh…basement's down here."

"Right," Luna said. Her cheeks were flushed again. She'd been blushing more lately, which was odd. She'd touched his chest often enough. She'd touched his bare skin, touched it sweaty and heaving, touched him while he was inside her. There was no reason for her to stand there blushing after he did something so innocent as stopping her from stumbling.

"Don't fall," he called behind him as he headed down the basement stairs.

"Ha, ha," she said, following him down. She sounded distracted, but she was back to her usual peppy self when she continued, "You remember we don't all have night vision, right? It's dark down here."

"We don't have *night vision*," he said. "We just see—"

"Better, I know. Lights please!"

He flicked on the light switch.

Luna squinted in the dim light. "Not much better. Okay! Where's that drill?"

Oliver headed over to the workbench and pulled open a drawer.

Luna frowned around at the basement, which was mostly bare. "Looks a little empty."

Oliver looked up from the drawer, expecting Luna's face to light up with apologetic realization.

"Because your house burned down with all your stuff inside it!" She winced, giving him another stupidly cute smile. "Got it."

He waited for the anger to surge back. It was definitely there, the same way it always was whenever someone brought up the fire. But it was a distant simmer compared to the raging heat it used to be.

He snorted, grabbing the drill out of the drawer and handing it over. "Do you know when we can expect this back? I'm not borrowing Jackson's."

"A few days. Maybe. I don't know how long a stall takes to

put together, and I don't think Chester does either. He's a bookstore guy, not a building guy." She looked at him, expectant.

"No," he said automatically.

She leaned on his shoulder, batting her eyes.

He groaned loud enough that she giggled. "Jesus. Fine."

"Thank you!" She twirled again, and he eyed her warily as she came to a stop on the concrete. "I'm going to miss this place. It's so nice doing things for the community. If I want something at home, I just go and buy it!"

"Yeah," he said flatly. "That must suck."

"Ha." She shrugged, her smile dimming. "It's just nice, is all."

She bit her lip, tucking the drill under one arm. He thought about asking her if she'd ever held a drill in her life. Then he thought about Uncle Roy, never letting himself have an earnest moment. Luna was leaving soon. He could get over himself for a sentence or two.

Oliver sucked in a bracing breath. "Everybody's going to miss you."

She blinked. The disappointment drained from her face in an instant, replaced by a teasing grin. She set the drill on a desk next to her, sliding a finger over the metal tip. "Everyone?"

"Sure," he said, trying uselessly to stop his heart from speeding up as she walked closer. "Sabine finally had someone as competitive as her in board games. And Leo had someone who would let him paint their nails."

He told himself he wasn't disappointed. Just because he'd resolved to not end up like Uncle Roy didn't mean he had to walk around with his heart on his sleeve like an idiot.

"Right," Luna agreed. She came to a stop in front of him, their shoes touching. Even in the dim light, she was beautiful. Even bundled up on a hike or panting on a run. Even when she was yelling at him that first night, when she was nothing but a stranger he'd been chained to, he hadn't been able to tear his eyes away.

The bond fizzled in his chest. It was so close. It wanted closer. Oliver couldn't pry it apart from his own want, burning just as bright.

"Are..." He tore his gaze from her tempting mouth. "Are you staying for the fair?"

She blinked. Her pupils were huge.

"I need to ask Hector," she said. "He still thinks I'm leaving as soon as the bond is broken. So..."

He frowned, indignation sneaking through the lust. "What? Why haven't you told him about the fair?"

"Hmm?" Luna broke out into an aw-shucks smile, the fake one she used when she wanted to change the subject. "It's nothing. I just—"

"Did you not tell him it was important?" He scanned her face, trying to look under the cuteness crap. "Or did you tell him it was important, and he didn't believe you?"

"Um," Luna said quietly, voice climbing several pitches. "That's—that isn't—"

She shook her head, leaning up. She slid her hands up his shirt again.

"How about," she started, "we don't talk about my fiancé when we were obviously just about to— Whoa, hey, why are you so tense?"

He shook his head. Someone was coming toward the basement door. He didn't recognize the scent, but there was an uncanny feeling sinking into his bones as the footsteps approached.

"Seriously," Luna said. "Is someone holding the front desk at gunpoint, or are you just still weirded out every time I talk about—"

She cut off with a gasp as the door swung open.

"Hector!"

Chapter Twenty-Eight

Luna blinked hard.

Hector was still there. Cleft chin, tanned skin, and a heavy jacket, which she would bet he bought at the airport when he realized that his suit jacket wouldn't stand up to Alaska in the spring. He was grinning on the stairs, arms raised like he was waiting for Luna to run into them. They did that when they met at airports. They'd turned it into a game, with one of them yelling "You're finally home from war!" or "You cheating bastard!" or something equally silly before running into the other's arms. They'd devolve into a shouted reunion full of fictional garbage until they got the giggles. It was one of Luna's favorite things in the world. And yet she stayed rooted to the spot, staring like she'd never seen her fiancé before.

"Hector," she said faintly. "You're— Hi! You're here! Why are you here?"

Oliver cleared his throat. Luna realized too late that she still had her hands all over his muscled chest. She stumbled back, hoping she didn't look too guilty.

"You said it was happening today," Hector said. "For real this time. I wanted to surprise you."

"Oh," Luna said as he descended the steps and walked over, pressing a kiss to her red cheek. "That's—wow. So thoughtful."

Hector squeezed her shoulder. The silence stretched as Luna tried to think of something, *anything* to say.

Hector laughed. "Is this a bad time?"

"No," said Luna and Oliver in unison.

"Right," Hector said. He let out another laugh, raising a hand toward Oliver. "I'm hoping you're the husband."

"I'm not," Oliver said. "Not in any way that matters."

"But you're the bond guy, right? Oliver? You're pretty much how she described. Tall, dark and scowly."

"Yeah," Oliver said. "That's…that's me."

Luna tried to check if he was offended. *Tall, dark and scowly* wasn't that bad, right? He'd heard way worse when he was eavesdropping on her phone call the other week. The bond in her chest fluttered. She couldn't get a sense of what Oliver was feeling, even when she secretly tried to reach him through the bond. It was like touching a brick wall. He'd closed himself off.

"Wow," Hector said. He punched Oliver's shoulder, a self-conscious grin widening when Oliver didn't even rock back with the motion. "Okay! Uh, there was an old lady following me, and I don't know where—" He jumped as Grandmother Musgrove appeared on the stairs. "Jesus!"

"Hello," said Grandmother Musgrove politely. "Would you like a tour?"

Before he could answer, Leo squeezed onto the stairs behind her and yelled, "Dinner's ready!"

Grandmother Musgrove's smile didn't falter as she corrected herself. "Would you like dinner?"

Hector stared at her, then at Leo, who was beaming at him with the excitement of a kid who had been watching a spark crawl up a line of dynamite for a long, *long* time, waiting for the fun to finally begin.

★ ★ ★

Luna had never heard the dinner table so silent. Even on that one night, when Sabine had bet the kids ten dollars they couldn't stay quiet for a full minute and everybody else joined in; there was still the ever-present snicker of Vida trying desperately not to laugh as Darren made faces at her across the table.

Leo kept looking at the other adults like he was waiting for someone to say something. Whenever he opened his mouth, Vida pinched his elbow and gave him a stare so pointed that Luna got the feeling she'd missed an important conversation.

"So," Hector said finally. "It's great to meet the family who's been taking care of Luna! You guys really own an inn, huh? Like, you *run* it. Fetch towels and man the front desk and all that jazz. That's adorable."

It *was* adorable. In theory. But Luna knew what went on behind the scenes now—the endless cleaning and admin. Fixing one thing only to have something else break. Even before the renovations, being in charge of anything was a lot to handle. If you were in charge, anyway. Not like her dad, who used his title to get everybody under him to do the real work.

"Uh-huh," said Oliver when the silence continued to stretch. He was sitting next to her, slowly and methodically sawing a rare steak to pieces. He held his arms tight against him, careful not to touch her. For once, Luna did the same. Their legs had brushed under the table a minute ago, and Luna had had to stop herself from jumping up out of her seat. It'd felt like a betrayal of the man sitting on the other side of her, even though she'd done so much worse with his express permission. The bond tugged at her ribs, wanting her to lean into Oliver. She told it to sit still and shut the hell up.

"Soooo," Hector said. "What do you do for fun around here? Go…sledding?"

He gave Luna a wide-eyed look. Luna couldn't figure out if it was because he'd run out of things to say or because he had a family of werewolves doing a very bad job of not staring at him. Uncle Roy was straight-up glaring, not even bothering to be subtle about it. Aunt Althea and Aunt Barney kept kicking him under the table—Luna could hear the impacts and see Uncle Roy's face crease up—but it didn't stop him. The kids were politer about it, except for Leo, who only stopped staring to look at the other adults pleadingly. The only ones who rarely looked were Grandmother Musgrove, who only glanced up at them a few times to give Luna a reassuring smile, and Oliver, who kept his gaze firmly on his steak.

Hector's wide-eyed look got even more panicked.

"There are some cute cafés we go to sometimes," Luna said. "They're thinking of opening more if tourism keeps increasing. And, um…"

Usually, when people asked what she did for fun, she started listing activities. Places with a high fee or a waitlist that would make whoever she was talking to jealous. Clubs or restaurants or classes for exotic new skills nobody needed. There was nothing like that here. Luna didn't know how to tell Hector that she spent most of her time emailing or talking to people; that she spent her time going for runs, playing board games, watching TV, going shopping, or holding tools while Oliver fixed up the inn. It wasn't glamorous, but it was somehow more fulfilling than every party or restaurant or experimental plunge she'd paid thousands of dollars to submerge herself in.

"There's this nice pottery place," Luna tried. "They're going to start offering classes on Saturdays. No, don't make that face, there's a lot to do! Especially with redoing the inn and setting up the fair—"

Grandmother Musgrove cut in. "Luna has been instrumental in getting the word out about Claw Haven. We never had this many visitors before she arrived."

Luna ducked her head. Grandmother Musgrove's compliments

always made her cheeks warm. Something about the *sincerity* in them, no joke or underlying irony to hide behind.

"Oh, yeah?" Hector reached over and touched her wrist. At first, Luna thought his hand was cooler than usual. Then she realized that she'd just gotten used to touching people who ran hot.

"What'd you do?" Hector asked. "Call your secret marketing team and beg for a...what do you call it?"

"Newsletter swap," Luna said quietly. "You promote them, they promote you. I had good luck with some sponsors today. Claw Haven is a good investment. I think we're really helping people find what they need here."

Hector nodded that empty nod he did when his dinner guests started talking business. "Sure! Yeah, it's cozy. The monster stuff is cute. Especially that fireplace. *Roar*, am I right?"

Uncle Roy grunted. It was obviously a lead-up to saying something—Luna could already hear it, *Yeah, 'cause cute is* definitely *what us monsters want to aim for*—but then his grunt went pained and Aunt Althea leaned forward with a strained smile, gold tooth glinting.

"It's been so lovely having Luna around. We're going to miss her. The inn has been a totally different place since she got here. And it's only going to get better! She's been showing Oliver how to man all the newfangled admin stuff—"

"And the ads," Aunt Barney added.

"—*and* the ads, yes, thank you. And we still have a lot left to do with her redesigns!"

Hector kept nodding. He was smirking now, stroking her wrist with his lukewarm thumb. "You must've had a *very* good time here to do all of that for free."

He said it like he said everything else: light, breezy, easygoing. It still made Luna stiffen, and she didn't have to look over to know that Oliver was rigid at her side.

Hector leaned around her to address him, still smirking.

"So, did you have to tag along to all those super-cool cafés, or did she leave you outside on a leash? Oh, man, she said she had to tag along when you went jogging. I'd pay to see that." He reached over and shook Oliver's arm. "You're strong, right? Ever just give up and carry her?"

Luna made the colossal mistake of glancing over. Oliver was staring. Not at the hand on his arm, like she'd expected. But at her. He looked away as soon as their eyes met, but it was too late. Luna knew what he was imagining: their trip down the mountain with Luna's legs around his waist and her chin nestled against his shoulder. After a while, it had become soothing. She'd almost fallen asleep against him as she had done the night before, her cheek pillowed against his warm skin, listening to him breathe.

"Well," Hector said, grabbing another bread roll from the dwindling bowl in the middle of the table. "Don't seem like much of a conversationalist. Guess you're fun in other ways."

"Hec," Luna said, stung.

Hector hesitated mid-bite, his grin faltering. He genuinely thought he was being funny, Luna realized. He even looked sorry that his "joke" hadn't landed.

"What? I'm glad you had fun. This—" he waved at the common room, meaning the inn "—the whole town, it seems like an adorable pet project. If it does well, who knows? Maybe your dad will let you do some actual work. Part-time or something."

"Part-time," Luna repeated.

"Yeah!" Hector bit another hunk off his bread roll, jaw slowing as he watched her.

Luna pulled up a hasty smile, but it was too late. He'd seen the look in her eyes. Haughty. Offended that he thought her work wasn't full-time material.

"We're not... Honey! You're not—" he spluttered, incredulous. He tossed down the bread roll and grabbed her hands—

not hard, *never* hard. Hector moved through life with a light touch and a wink. "Where's my fun little Luna? Huh?"

He laughed. She laughed with him, wondering why it felt so difficult. Things *weren't* difficult with Hector; that was the whole point of him. He made everything easy.

"I can't believe you stayed here," he admitted. "I expected you to bribe him to follow you to a resort. Somewhere that has room service. Someplace with stuff to do!"

"We have stuff," Luna argued. "We have a fair!"

"Yeah! Yes, great!" He clapped hard enough that Vida jumped, although that might have been from a loud song starting, headphones forgotten around her neck.

"Fair," Hector continued. "Awesome. So much hard work. Sucks you won't get to see it. You guys will send pics, right?"

Uncle Roy grunted again. For a good five seconds, it was the only sound at the table except for Vida's fork scraping a burned piece of skin off a baked potato.

Hector looked at Luna expectantly.

"Right," Luna said. She prepped her cutest smile. "About that!"

Hector chuckled uncertainly. "It's the day before the wedding, babe."

"I know! I just think it would be fun!" Luna batted her eyes at him and slid a finger under his watch strap. "Games, chocolates—"

"A day fair in the middle of Nowhere, Alaska," he said over her. Then he winced, eyebrows shooting up as he realized how that had sounded. He shot the table a reassuring grin. "I mean, hey, totally! I bet it will be super fun! I just— We have a lot of things booked."

Luna sighed, propping her chin up in her hand. "Like what?"

He stared at her. Trying to see if she was joking, she realized. Hazy memories swam back through the flood of admin she'd been doing for Claw Haven, but before she could say them, Hector was telling her instead.

"That hot stone spa," he reminded her. "With that state-of-the-art mud treatment? So we look peak hot for wedding pics. Their waitlist is a year, and you registered us the second we got engaged. It's one of the reasons we booked the wedding in Bali."

"Right," Luna said. "No, yeah, I remember."

She stared down at her plate, reeling. How could she have forgotten? She had that spa treatment circled on her calendar at home. Part of her—the part that had to discover a whole new range of skin products and subpar water pressure for her showers—longed for the glowing stress release that the pamphlet had promised. Then she thought back to Oliver's hands on her back, kneading the oil that Luna bought from the skincare shop in town, which worked shockingly well. His hot skin against her shoulders, working out her knots as the bond flared happily between them—

"I'm going to go to the bathroom," Luna said.

She looked cute, even when she was white-knuckling the sink. Luna tried to be gratified as she stared into her reflection, trying to dig up some semblance of relief. She was seeing her fiancé again! She should be over the moon! What was *wrong* with her?

Someone knocked on the bathroom door.

Luna's heart spasmed. It only took a moment to remind herself that the bond in her chest wasn't getting any warmer, so it couldn't be Oliver.

She opened the door. Hector stood there, hands in his pockets, oddly bashful. It didn't suit him.

"Hey," he said. "You feeling okay? That steak *was* pretty rare."

"They cook it more for us," Luna said faintly. She dragged

up a winning smile. "I'm fine! I'm good. I'm just—I'm crazy busy with the fair, and everything."

He nodded. He looked mystified, like he was still expecting her to throw up a pair of jazz hands and reveal it was all a joke. She could see how much he wanted her to go back to her regular self—careless and fun-seeking, always looking for the next party or spa treatment or adventure, as long as she got to go home with him at the end and laze around in their luxurious sheets. He'd come here expecting her to throw herself into his arms, and why shouldn't she? She should be clamoring to get out of here. To get back to her old life.

It was tempting. Luna could feel her old habits coming back: the urge to brush anything serious aside in favor of fun and excitement. Then she remembered Oliver, his voice low and true. *Nobody's fun all the time.*

"You were kind of weird back there," Luna said in a rush. "With Oliver."

He laughed again. It dimmed fast when she didn't join in. To his credit, he looked genuinely surprised. "What? It was a joke. Okay, probably not the best move to say it in front of his whole fam, that was my bad. I just…"

"Got jealous?" Luna asked. She tried to throw in a giggle, something cute and airy to break the tension. It came out more as a wheeze, and she had to cough to hide it.

He hesitated. "Babe. I don't care who you have sex with. As long as you come home to me."

Luna squinted at him. "Your tone's weird. What's with the weirdness?"

"Nothing! I just…" His whole face twisted, messing up the smile he was still desperately clinging to. "You *are* coming home to me, right? You haven't fallen for the guy with the one-ply shirt and the big, weird family who lives in a town that doesn't even have a subpar spa?"

"No," Luna blurted, face burning. "I— That's— Why would you..."

The bond in her chest flared. Luna looked up to see Oliver standing in the hallway behind Hector, his face unreadable.

Luna swallowed. She focused back on Hector, pulling up a playful smirk she wasn't feeling. "I've been here for two months. You think I'd throw away *us*, our whole *life*? I'm just going through a thing. I'll be back to normal soon."

She kissed him. She hadn't kissed him yet, she realized with a dim sense of unease. Who had their fiancé show up and didn't kiss him immediately?

Hector was frowning when he pulled back. But it was a Hector-frown, the faintest dent between his eyebrows.

"What?"

He shook his head. "You taste different."

Oliver cleared his throat.

Hector startled, jolting around. "Jesus."

Luna waved, trying to look like she didn't know he was there. She still felt guilty, and she didn't know what for anymore. For Hector, obviously. But also, for Oliver, his face stony and unrelenting. And the bond in their chests, the warmth fluttering in confusion. She couldn't help but feel bad for it, like a small golden butterfly they were seconds from stepping on.

"What is it?" she asked.

For a second, he just stood there, watching them. Then he blinked, and his face cleared.

"Ben and Sabine are back."

Chapter Twenty-Nine

"How's that?" Oliver asked stiffly.

Grandmother examined the glass silently. She hadn't said a word since they had retreated to her room to get the nectar ready, and Oliver was grateful. The last thing he wanted was to talk about this. He wanted to get the un-bonding over with, then hide in his room until his family learned to avoid the subject.

Not very alpha of him. But he wasn't alpha yet.

Grandmother hummed. "That will do. Only one more ingredient before you can drink."

Oliver nodded. He kept holding the glass out, hoping that she would take it from him. But she walked toward the door, her gait slower than usual but still steady. She looked back at him expectantly, then at the silver knife lying on the desk.

Heart thudding dully, Oliver picked it up and followed her out into the hallway.

Everyone was gathered in the lobby. Oliver had suggested the common room, but Ben had insisted it'd be nice to end the bond where it had started.

The chatter died down as Grandmother stepped in, Oliver on

her heels. Oliver took one look at his family gathered around the front desk and his stomach clenched.

"You don't need to be here," he snapped.

Ben groaned. "Oh, come on, Ollie."

"Yeah," Leo said, clinging to his dad's leg. "Come on, Uncle Ollie!"

Grandmother cleared her throat. "This works better with privacy."

Ben's smile faded. He picked up Leo, carrying him out despite the child's protests.

"Have a good divorce," he called back as he headed down the hall.

Grandmother looked at Hector. "Us too, I'm afraid."

Hector blinked at her in surprise. He had an arm around Luna, causing an unexpected wave of jealousy to rip through Oliver, cold and brutal. It had nothing to do with the bond; the bond didn't get jealous. It didn't care who else got close to Luna as long as he got to do it, too. That jealousy would still be there once the warm flutter in his chest was gone.

"Seriously? But I'm—"

"It's a wolf thing," Luna said, patting his chest. "See you in a minute?"

Grandmother gave Oliver a pointed look as she guided Hector down the hall. The ritual didn't need to happen in solitude, Oliver realized. She'd made that up so they could have a moment alone.

Luna's gaze dropped to the glass in his hands. Then to the silver knife.

"Whoa," she said with a nervous giggle. "What's *that* for?"

"We just need a few drops of blood," he explained. He placed the glass on the front desk. "Can I have your hand?"

She held it out. She was smiling, but he could see the reluctance behind it.

"Just a prick," he assured her. He pressed the knife tip into her finger.

She gasped. Three drops of blood fell into the nectar.

He turned the knife hilt toward her. "Now you do me."

Luna paused. Then she took the knife. "Wish the bonding ritual needed blood," she said as she held his finger above the glass. "Then we wouldn't be in this mess in the first place."

The blade pressed against his finger.

"Harder," he told her. "Come on, you have to actually cut me."

"I'm *trying*," she said, frustrated. "It's weird! I don't cut a lot of people! Especially not werewolves. What is your skin *made* of—leather?"

He was about to call Grandmother back and ask if he couldn't just do it himself when she changed tactics, dragging instead of shoving the blade. Blood welled up over the cut, dripping into the glass.

"Ow," Luna said with a wince.

"It's fine." Oliver picked up the glass, ignoring the smudge of blood he left on the side. The liquid had turned deep red despite the few drops of blood, with an almost wine-like consistency. He held it out to Luna.

"Cheers," she said quietly.

She didn't take it like he'd been expecting. She just leaned in, pressing her lips to the rim and waiting.

Oliver tipped the glass back. Her throat worked, nose wrinkling as some of the herbs slipped into her mouth.

"That was disgusting," she said as he pulled the glass back. "Un-bonding nectar. Two out of five— Oh."

She cut off as Oliver slammed back the rest of the glass in one gulp, grimacing at the admittedly disgusting taste. Gone was the sweetness from the first time. This tasted oily and dark, herbs crunching in his teeth.

"Well?" Luna asked as he set the empty glass down. "Does it just…"

She trailed off, eyes going wide. He didn't have to ask why, he felt it too. The warmth in his chest was getting colder. Burning down to nothing.

Luna sucked in a breath. She touched his wrist, and Oliver felt the faintest pang of heat sparking through his rib cage before it went out entirely.

Oliver reeled. He'd gotten so used to the sensor inside his chest telling him whenever Luna was near, pulling him toward her. It was strange to have her standing right in front of him, holding his wrist, and not have that spark in his heart leap in response.

A throat cleared behind them.

Oliver turned. A human man stood in the guest hallway, waving awkwardly.

"Excuse me," the man said, whose name Oliver couldn't remember despite signing him in yesterday. "What's the Wi-Fi password?"

"It's on the list above your bedside table," Luna and Oliver said in one.

"Thanks!" The man lingered in the hallway, scuffing his inn slippers. Thanks to Luna, they had little horns on them. "Also, I think there's a problem with my window."

Oliver turned to Luna. "I should go."

"Yeah." Luna stepped back, dropping his wrist. "I need to tell Hec it worked. He has the tab open on his phone, ready to book flights."

"Right." Oliver stood there, hands clenching around nothing, chest strangely empty. He wanted to ask something stupid—like *Will I ever see you again?*—but the window man was tapping his slippered foot on the new carpet and Luna had a fiancé to get to.

"Bye," he said stupidly and headed down the guest hall.

The problem with the window was simple: The guy wasn't pulling hard enough. After getting a sheepish thank-you and making a mental note to fix the stiff window later, Oliver slunk back to his room.

He didn't want to alert his family that he was around, so he employed an old trick that all wolves did when they didn't want anyone to hear them sneak down the hall: He went around the outside of the house and climbed through his own bedroom window. Thanks to the soundproof walls, nobody heard him come in. Now all he had to do was stay in his room for as long as he possibly could, or until his family stopped sitting around the common room, ears perked up, waiting to ambush and drag him into a board game or a movie or a jog like that would distract him from the great big *nothing* in his chest.

He was himself again, and he hated it. He'd spent weeks resenting the bond, wishing it would go away, and now it had finally gone, and he *hated* it. At some point, it had been comforting, the knowledge that Luna was nearby, the warmth getting bigger and bigger until they finally touched, and it flooded him. Like sinking into a warm bath at the end of a long day. Like coming in from the snow.

A knock on the door jolted him out of his thoughts. He rubbed his empty chest, then went to answer it.

"I don't want to—" He cut off as he saw Luna in the hallway, dressed in a hat and mittens. Her cheeks were flushed. She looked almost shy, something he still wasn't used to.

She bit her lip. "Want to see me off at the airport?"

Oliver pictured it: Hector waving a lighthearted goodbye, his arm slung over Luna's shoulder. Luna asking them to please send pictures of the fair, hugging everyone goodbye. Would she hug him? Would it be too weird? He didn't want to be the only one without a hug, but if she did hug him, that would somehow be worse. He'd have to hug her back like a normal person who didn't want to cling and ask her to stay.

"No," he said.

Luna ducked her head. "Oookay. Well, I have five minutes. Hec is in the car. What are you up to?"

Oliver tried to think of something that wasn't pathetic. "Going for a run."

"Oh yay, you can finally run as fast as you want. No human holding you back." Luna tugged at the fanged pom-pom at the top of her hat. It was, predictably, a werewolf. She'd bought it from the knitting shop after begging the owner to order it in for her. She'd picked it up this morning, spinning in the chilly street outside the shop. She wanted to wear it while she could, she'd said. Not much chance where she was going, all sun and sand.

"You should get going," Oliver said.

She paused. "I have fifteen minutes."

Oliver nodded down the hall. He was shocked the others hadn't burst out into the hallway yet. "Go say goodbye to the others."

"I have," she said quietly. "It's just you left."

Oliver was deeply relieved this hadn't happened at the airport. He'd hate for anyone else to witness this. It was bad enough that he was going through it, hands sweaty and throat dry as Luna stared up at him with those big blue eyes.

"I already said goodbye," he said. "You should—"

He stopped, stepping back automatically as Luna stepped forward. She closed the bedroom door behind her and took off her hat. Then her mittens, which were adorned with little knitted hedgehogs, courtesy of Beth.

"What…" Oliver swallowed as Luna moved closer, catching him by the front of his shirt so he couldn't move away. His breath caught as she leaned up, skimming their noses together.

"There's no bond," he reminded her. "There isn't— We don't need to."

"I know," she said. "I just…"

She hesitated. Then she slid her hands up his arms, skin on skin, fingers creeping up his sleeves to squeeze his shoulders.

Her touch still sent a fissure of heat through him, no bond required.

Luna shivered. Her lips parted with a gasp, pretty and pink and *warm*.

"Goddamnit," Oliver muttered and lurched down to crush their mouths together.

Luna groaned. Her hands knotted in his hair, urging him closer. She tasted like bond nectar and herbs and the hot chocolate she drank earlier. Oliver licked deeper into her mouth until it was pure Luna, nothing else.

"Gotta be fast," Oliver slurred against her lips. "Fiancé's waiting."

She nodded frantically, scrabbling at his clothes. Their hands kept tripping over each other, clumsy in their eagerness. Oliver couldn't believe how much he wanted her. He couldn't feel what she was feeling, but the want was just as bad as it'd been when the bond was yanking them together. The only difference was that now it was all his.

"I keep expecting—" Luna cut off with a moan as he bit gently at her neck. "I keep expecting it to kick in. You know? Like, to feel—"

"Please don't," Oliver said. He didn't want to hear her talk about the times they'd had together in this very bedroom, the shared sensations blurring until they couldn't tell which ecstasy belonged to whom.

She was still wearing her bra and he still had his boxers when he pushed her onto the bed and dropped to his knees. But before he could bury his face between her legs, Luna forced his chin up.

"Not this time," she said. "Get up here. I want you inside me."

The words set a fire in Oliver's stomach. He shot up onto the bed, grabbing a condom from the bedside drawer.

Luna rolled it onto his cock and then climbed on, both of

them moaning as she bottomed out. He caught her hips, trying to see if she was taking it too fast. But there was nothing but pleasure in her expression as she worked herself on him.

"Come on," she moaned. "Fuck me like you mean it."

She meant like the first time. Hard and primal, holding her bruisingly tight. He even considered it: pushing her into the mattress face-first, holding her there while he fucked her. The idea of it made his stomach twist. If this was the last time, he wanted it to be slower. Wanted to make it last.

He pressed her back into the sheets, twining their fingers together above her head. Something like surprise flickered over her face, but it was quickly lost as he started to thrust in earnest. She bit her lip, and Oliver waited to feel the echo in his own lip. It never came, and he buried his face in her neck so she wouldn't see whatever shitshow expression was happening on his face right now.

He missed her. He was inside of her, and he wanted to be closer. Wanted to feel what she was feeling, wanted to hear the tail-ends of her thoughts. He wanted deeper, wanted *more*, wanted everything they'd agreed they wouldn't have. Screw blocking each other out, screw not pushing deeper, he wanted all of Luna. And now he'd never get it.

Luna squeezed his fingers with a whimper. "Knot me. Fuck, Oliver, *please* knot me."

Oliver gritted his teeth. "Can't. No time."

"*Please*," she said, voice choked with tears. "I love it so much, please, I *love* it…"

For a moment, Oliver considered it: thrusting as deep as he could, locking them together. Teasing the knot gently back and forth, never quite pulling out, the way she liked. Sending her out to her fiancé forty minutes later than she'd promised, her hair a wreck, drenched in his scent.

"I love," she repeated. Then she cut off, her mouth falling open in a silent gasp as she came.

Maybe it was an echo. A phantom sensation from the bond. Maybe it was his own brain making things up. But a familiar warmth panged in his chest, his own orgasm chasing hers. He pulled out at the last moment, jerking himself around the condom. Watching the base of his cock swell around his fist.

Luna whimpered. He dropped his head on her shoulder in a silent apology. Then, against his own better judgment, he kissed the bandage on her thumb.

Neither of them spoke. Finally, Oliver sat up, wincing as he pulled the condom off his swollen knot.

"You should get going," he said as he tied it off. "Five minutes are up."

Luna nodded. She wiped her cheeks.

"Intense," she whispered. She gave him a brisk smile, as she always did when he was worried he'd hurt her. Then she pushed herself up, adjusting the bra strap they'd never gotten around to taking off.

He watched her get dressed. Watched her apply deodorant and finger-comb her hair until she looked totally normal. Even her smell was normal, the deodorant drowning him out.

She paused at the door. "Thank you. Not just for the sex. For...letting me stay, I guess? At the inn, obviously. But also, you know, with..." Her eyes were glossy, but only until she blinked. Then she was picture-perfect, ready to go back to her real life.

"I had such a *fun* time with you," she finished. She gave him one last smile, then flounced out.

Oliver lay there with his knot aching and his boxers around his ankles. He'd never felt emptier. He felt *cold*. It was so much worse like this. Holding her close, knowing he'd never do it again. He never should've let her back into his room.

Chapter Thirty

Fun, Luna reminded herself. *I am having fun.*

It *should* have been fun, was the thing. It should have at least been *relaxing*. The masseuse's hands had left her muscles loose and bendy. The aloe skin rub had left her shiny. Now they were reclining in the mud bath, which supposedly had healing properties from local mud pools. Luna used to go crazy for this type of thing. But she was sitting here in the pool, and she didn't feel revitalized. Didn't feel like she'd gotten a new lease on life like the brochure had promised. She felt like she was sitting in a hot tub full of mud. And she *still* wasn't warm enough. She sank lower into the mud, glad that she'd tied her hair up before she went in.

Hector plucked a cucumber slice off his eye and took a bite. He glanced over at Luna and laughed. "Having fun there?"

"You know it," Luna said, as chirpy as she could manage. Her cucumber slices were currently lost somewhere in the ooze.

Hector slipped the other cucumber slice into his mouth. "Really? 'Cause you kinda look like you're trying to drown yourself in mud."

"Just trying to get the full effects," Luna said, her mouth barely visible above the mud. It was making her sweat, sure.

But that was warming her from the outside in. Not from the inside out, like a certain werewolf had done, with his huge hands and deceptively soft eyes once he finally stopped scowling. Even that last time they were together, she'd felt it. An echo of it, anyway—small and golden, almost lost in the blur of sensation as he thrust into her.

She thumbed the almost healed cut on her finger where Oliver had pressed the knife. *I had such a fun time with you*, she'd told him. What kind of cop-out crap was that? It was what she said to people who came to her parties. Oliver deserved more than that.

Her phone vibrated on the tiles next to her head.

"Hey," Hector complained as she shot up and grabbed her towel to dry her hands off. "We're relaxing! Peak cute, remember?"

"I know," she said. "I'll be extra adorable on the day, I promise. I'm just going to answer this email."

It was Beth again. She was emailing to thank Luna for putting her in touch with a marketing expert, who had given Beth and many other shop owners a crash course on gift bags.

My to-do list is a million miles long, but I'm so excited, the email concluded. *Anyway, g2g, coffee with Sabine. She's so sweet!!! Hope you're having fun at the spa!!! I looked it up, and it seems so fancy. Does the mud seriously cleanse your spirit???*

Luna started typing out a reply about the dubious qualities of the mud, which she was less than hopeful for. She heard a wet squelch behind her as Hector sidled over.

"Don't," she warned as he hovered a muddy finger over her cheek.

"I won't if you put the phone down," he replied, turning his finger in a lazy circle.

Luna sent the reply—*proud of u, yay sabine hang!!!!*—and put the phone back on the gleaming tiles. "There! Try and mud me now. I dare you."

"Well, if you *dare* me…"

She ducked out of the way. He grabbed her, hauling her back and shoving his mud-wet chin into her cheek.

She screeched, grinning. "Come on! Stop it!"

"You dared me," he reminded her, rubbing mud into her face.

Luna giggled. It wasn't as loud as usual. She turned in his arms, bumping their noses together. Trying to drag back the girl who was wholly entertained by Hector's playful rough-housing. Part of her was. But mostly, it was like playing with dolls. After you hit a certain age, you couldn't see the Barbie battlefields anymore. It was just you in your bedroom, holding a doll over a makeshift spike pit made of hairbrushes.

At least he didn't notice. His grin was simple and easy as he asked, "Want to try flotation therapy next? They had a cancellation and can fit us in."

Luna thought about being alone in a tank with her own thoughts. The last time had been fun, it had been *relaxing*, but she hadn't had much on her mind back then except designing party invitations and planning their next trip to Paris and how she was going to remodel the kitchen. She'd lain there in that dark tank thinking happy thoughts about paint swatches. She didn't want to *know* what weird, tangled thought spirals she'd get in that tank now.

"Not today," she said.

Her phone rang. Luna lunged for it, elbowing Hector in the face when he tried to stop her.

He reeled back, blinking in shock and pain. He'd been teasing. Luna's elbow had *not* been teasing when it dug into his nose.

Luna tossed back a nervous giggle as she climbed out of the mud pool. "Sorry, babe!"

"Um," said Hector, muffled by the hand over his mouth. He dabbed at his nose, then checked his hand. "'S fine. Not bleeding."

"Great," Luna said, grabbing the phone. Sabine was Face-Timing her.

Luna clicked into the call to see Sabine's scarred face smiling at her, Beth crowding into the screen and waving. They were in the back room at Beth's store, Luna recognized from the wallpaper.

"Hey," Sabine said, the audio glitching slightly. "Look at you! You're so glamorous! Beth said you're at a luxury spa?"

"I *look* like I'm covered in mud," Luna said, wiping off her bikini with her spare hand.

"*Healing* mud," Beth added, nose twitching excitedly at the end of her muzzle.

Hector raised a muddy hand from the pool behind her. "Hi! Which ones are they?"

"Sabine and Beth," Luna said. "Uh, the sister-in-law and the chocolate girl."

"There's a chocolate girl?" Hector grinned. "Wow. Monsters come in all kinds nowadays."

"Shut up, she's a hedgehog." Luna turned back to the screen, gaze roving over the two friendly faces inside it. Beth didn't look wholly comfortable pressed against Sabine's side to fit in the screen, but she looked pleased to be included. It hadn't taken Luna long to figure out that while friendly touches bewildered her, she was almost always appreciative. Except when people tried touching her spikes. Luna had found that out the hard way, and Beth had spent the next half hour stammering apologies while they picked prickles out of Luna's hand.

"I found hedgehog-shaped soap to put in my gift bags," Beth started.

Sabine talked over her. "Hey! No shop talk, remember? Luna, how *are* you?"

"I'm good! How's Grandmother doing?"

"She's good," Sabine said. "Sleeping a lot more lately, and she won't be doing a lot of running this full moon. But her heart isn't getting any worse."

"Great! That's great." Luna wiped another slip of mud off her legs, mostly so she wouldn't have to look back at Hector in the pool. She hoped the bubbling mud was loud enough to obscure her as she continued, "And everybody else? How's Leo?"

"He still won't let go of those light-up shoes. We're stuck until he grows out of them. Uncle Roy started grumbling about the postman; I think having you here took all his ire away from being suspicious of the rest of the town. The aunts are making you a scarf—don't tell them I told you. You should get it after you get back from your honeymoon. Heath has Ben working the early morning shift at the bakery, which has been annoying, but we get the afternoons to ourselves. And Oliver's fine."

"Fine," Luna repeated. "Like…?"

She didn't get a chance to continue. The spa door flew open, and three familiar faces walked in wearing towels and shining smiles.

Luna gaped. "Oh my god."

Clancy Stack threw up a peace sign. His hair had grown a stupendous amount since she'd seen him last, and his goatee had finally grown in properly.

Behind him, their parents waved.

Beth asked, "What happened? Are you okay?"

"I gotta go," Luna said. She hung up, jogging toward her family. "You guys weren't supposed to get here until tomorrow!"

"Flight arrived early. Decided to come hang." Clancy let out an *oof* as she collided with him, shocked by the force of her hug. "Jesus, Lu, can you ease up? You're *muddy*."

"You're just about to get in!" Luna protested. But when she pulled back to hug her parents, she made sure to keep it light.

Hector whooped, muddy hands in the air. "Brother! How's college treating you?"

"Kicking my ass," Clancy declared. "Incoming."

"You probably—" Luna's warning was promptly disregarded as Clancy jumped into the mud pool with a yelp. Mud splashed over the tiles. Luna winced, glad she hadn't put her phone down until now, and laid it carefully out of the mud's reach.

"Did you break your ankles?" Dad asked as Clancy resurfaced. "No? Good."

Clancy shook his hair, mud splattering over Luna's torso as she climbed back into the pool with the others.

"You're disgusting," she told him. Then, overwhelmed with a weird fondness that made her think of watching the kids argue over the Musgrove dinner table, she leaned over and hugged him again.

Clancy paused in the middle of wiping mud off his face. "Double hugs. Alright. Didn't hug me like this when you didn't see me all freshman year, but okay."

"I missed you," she admitted.

He stared at her, obviously waiting for her to follow it up with a joke. When nothing came, her family traded surprised looks.

Hector slid over, tucking Luna into his muddy side. "We're spending our honeymoon at a luxury resort. All-hours room service and massages. She'll be back to normal after that."

Everyone laughed. Luna joined in, trying to ignore the irritation niggling in her gut. Room service and massages? Was that all they thought she was?

Mom sighed, sinking back against the edge of the pool. "You must be so relieved to be back. I can't imagine being stuck in a town *that* small for so long, nowhere to go, nothing to do."

"Almost nothing," Clancy muttered.

Hector snickered. There was an uncertain edge to it, but it was barely noticeable as he leaned up to take a drink off the waitress who had come in with a tray.

"Oh, that's awful," Mom said as she took a glass. "She didn't spend all that time having marathon sex with a werewolf; she's about to get *married*."

"Thanks," Luna said quietly to the waitress.

The waitress blinked. It took her a second to smile, and Luna wondered how many people were thanking her when she brought them their drinks.

Luna sipped her drink. It was cool and bubbly and had a strawberry floating at the bottom. It was the best thing she'd tasted in months. And yet she found herself longing for a mug of hot chocolate in the Musgrove common room while everybody crowded around to watch the TV.

"Exactly," Clancy said, saluting Luna with his newly acquired glass. "Going into married life with a bang."

Luna dug an elbow into his side. "Ew, shut *up*."

"Hear, hear," Dad agreed. "They didn't try to get you on the hook for any money, did they? It's such a mess trying to deal with those damn magical registries—"

"They didn't ask me for anything," Luna said hastily. "And I'm not on any magical registry anymore, I told you. We broke the bond."

"And good riddance!" Dad raised his glass. The others followed suit. Dad looked at her expectantly. "Honey?"

"What? Oh, right." Luna raised her glass. "Uh, good riddance."

Dad sat back, mud sludging over the side of the pool. "Then let's relax. God knows I need it after this week."

Luna clenched her teeth in a smile. "Yeah? What'd you do this week, Dad?"

"He was *so* busy," Mom sighed. "He went to work four times this week."

"Four times," Luna deadpanned. "Wow."

Hector tapped her collarbone. When she looked over, he was giving her that uncertain grin he'd been giving her a lot in the last several days. Like he was still hoping she was joking.

The room lapsed into silence, only broken by the soft bubbling of the mud and the occasional sip. Luna looked around at her family, all of them lying with their heads back on the cool tiles.

Luna sat up, twisting toward her phone. It was farther than she'd expected, out of range of the mud. The woman was mopping around it.

"Whoa," Hector said. "Where's that hand going? It'd better be signaling someone down for more drinks."

"I'm just answering some more emails," Luna replied. "They're really piling up."

Dad laughed. "What emails do you have to answer? *You're* not organizing the wedding."

Luna ignored him, grabbing her phone. Before she could even swipe into it, Hector grabbed it off her and tossed it in the air.

Luna made a noise like a broken ice dispenser as she watched it sink into the mud at the other corner of the pool. "Hec! Oh my god!"

"You need to chill out," he told her, his arm coming up to her shoulder.

She shrugged him off. "That's my phone!"

"We'll get you a new one! It's not a big deal, babe."

"I have so many emails," Luna said, already going through a mental list.

"You're getting married! Everyone will understand if you drop out of touch for a few weeks. Relax." He stroked her arm. It was meant to be soothing, but all she could think of was the heat of the mud, thick and suffocating and still somehow not warming her up where it counted.

She whirled on him, ripping his arm off her shoulders. "I've *been* relaxing! I've been relaxing all my life! I want to *do* something for a change! Not sit here in some useless mud, planning our next vacation! Our whole *life* is a vacation, one big party—it's *nothing*!"

She stopped. The spa was silent. The mud bubbled quietly between them.

Luna's cheeks burned. She hadn't yelled at her family since she was a teenager. If she ever got mad, she swallowed it and turned her mind to better things.

"Uhhh," Hector said. He laughed nervously. "Wow. I can't wait for you to go back to normal, babe."

"Hear, hear," Dad repeated, raising his glass a second time.

Mom made a noise into her glass. "I don't know if I'm a fan of these drinks. Could we get that girl back in here?"

Luna stared in disbelief as they lapsed back into their normal inane chatter. Of course, this wouldn't put a dent in their conversation. They were Stacks; they weren't about to let one outburst ruin their fun.

Hector sat back against the tiles, arm out in offering. He looked up at her, and his carefree smile wavered. His eyebrows raised in a silent plea. He wanted her to sit down. To let the moment of frustration pass. To come and laugh with them again. No worries, no consequences.

Luna climbed out of the mud. "I'm going to take a shower."

"What? Come on, babe. Babe!"

Her family's voices joined in as she strode toward the towel rack. She kept walking. She'd shower, get dressed, and go find somewhere that would sell her a phone.

Chapter Thirty-One

Grandmother leaned on the front desk and sighed. "You look worse than me."

Oliver scowled. He was bent over Beth's half-finished chocolate display, which was proving harder to put together than he anticipated. It was just a display, so why did it have so many slots and tabs?

"I look fine," he snapped.

"Your eye bags say otherwise," Grandmother replied. She reached out as if to touch his admittedly sweaty cheek. He'd been having trouble sleeping, racked with strange tremors and fluctuating body temperatures he was doing his best to ignore. It was the annoying aftermath of bond breaking and would go away eventually.

He ducked out of range with a growl. Both of them paused while Grandmother's eyebrows rose.

He averted his gaze back to the infuriating display. "How are you feeling?"

"Fine," she said.

He looked her over quickly. She was pale, but that had become pretty common in the past few months. No less than three shawls were draped around her shoulders despite how the heat was running at full blast.

"Today's a good day," she said, pulling the shawls tighter around her. She gave him a reassuring smile. "Are you excited for the fair yet? You promised Leo you would be. It's tomorrow; time's running out."

"He'll survive," Oliver said icily.

She gave him a knowing look. The fair marked the day before Luna's wedding. He couldn't pretend to be excited about a fair while Luna was about to marry some rich, useless jerk who had never held a hammer in his life.

Oliver went back to the display, trying yet again to slide the correct tab into the correct slot without bending anything. Why was it so *fragile*? This thing didn't look like it could hold up a piece of paper, much less bags full of chocolates.

"Oliver," Grandmother said.

He winced. The conversational tone was gone. Whatever was coming, he wasn't going to like it.

"I don't want you retreating back into yourself," she said. "You were getting better these past months. Back to your old self."

He glared at her. "For someone who's always telling me to be open about how I'm feeling, we didn't hear one word from you about feeling sick until you were passing out in my arms."

Oliver had never seen her look so caught off guard. He fought down the wave of shame that flooded him for speaking so rudely to his grandmother, let alone his alpha, and went back to the chocolate display.

"Well," Grandmother said. "I suppose you had to get it from somewhere."

Oliver focused on the cardboard. His hands were shaking. That had been happening on and off since Luna left. He clenched his hands into fists, feeling claws prick into his palms. He forced them back.

Grandmother cleared her throat. Oliver thought hard about telling her to leave him to his very important work. Then he looked up grudgingly, waiting.

She had her hands folded in front of her, chin held high. She looked even more regal than usual, and he straightened his spine reflexively.

"I want to make you the alpha during the next full moon," she announced.

There was a low *pop*. Oliver looked down to see his claws poking through the cardboard display.

"But that's tomorrow," he said, dazed. "And you said—"

"I have faith—" Grandmother paused, lips thinning. "I have *faith* that this is a minor setback. That what you experienced in the last few months will carry you forward, even if it's over now. Can I trust in that? Or should I wait a few months to see if you backslide entirely into that sullen, brooding man who doesn't let a handyman in to fix his roof? We already have one Roy in the family. We don't need two."

Oliver's hackles went up even as he tried to force them back down. The old paranoia rose—*it's not safe, gotta guard the family*—but along with it came a swarm of images. Luna grinning as she showed him how many orders Beth had gotten; Luna proudly displaying a whiteboard listing all the ways they could change the inn; Luna watching him fondly as he rubbed her feet. Luna stroking his hair, giggling at his dumb tattoo, and showing him her private sketchbook with that guarded look like she was afraid he'd laugh at her.

And of course, Uncle Roy. Standing in the corner with his back to the wall, glaring at anyone who dared to get too close. Oliver needed to wallow. But he wasn't going to let that be his future.

"I don't want to rush this," Grandmother continued. "But I don't know how much time we have left."

"You're fine," he argued weakly. "Right? You keep insisting."

"I do," she said. She paused. Then she reached out, ghosting her fingers over the dark bags under his eyes.

Oliver flinched. He couldn't help it. But he didn't move away this time.

Grandmother dropped her hand. "You really do look strange."

Oliver opened his mouth to insist he was fine. But he was exhausted and shaky, and he'd been lying through his teeth long enough.

"It's the bond," he said slowly. "Right? I remember you saying something about aftereffects."

She nodded. "Uncle Roy stayed in bed for days after. We had to force-feed him soup. Couldn't stop shaking long enough to hold a spoon."

"Seriously?" Oliver scrubbed a hand down his face. It came away damp with sweat. "That's so annoying. The bond is *over*."

"It is. But it was a big change. Your body has to adjust."

"Gotta scar over," came a voice from the hallway.

Oliver turned to see Uncle Roy, shoulders hunched. He sneered at them as he approached. "Can we quit talking about that woman? She's gone, and good riddance. She wasn't pack."

Grandmother sighed. "You know we can't subsist purely on pack, right? We have to let others in, or the Musgrove pack will get *very* small, *very* fast."

The lobby door banged open, letting in a gust of chilly air as Beth Haberdash stumbled in. She had a giant cardboard box in her arms and was teetering under the weight.

"Oof," she said as the door bounced off the wall. "Sorry! And on the new wallpaper, too!"

Oliver hurried out from behind the counter, steadying the package in her arms.

"Thanks," she said brightly. She'd started looking him in the face in the past few weeks, and Sabine said she'd been stammering less. "I came to drop off some chocolate."

"We'll need a new display," Oliver said, helping her heave the package down onto the floor. "I kind of, uh, punctured it."

"What?" Beth looked over at the front desk and blinked rapidly as she noticed the display banged up and torn. "Oh. That's fine, I'll bring something over tonight. Anyway, I dropped by and saw this outside! It arrived so fast!"

"What arrived?" Uncle Roy called from the front desk. He gave the air a suspicious sniff as if expecting to smell something dangerous emanating from the package.

"The sign!" Beth looked toward Grandmother Musgrove for confirmation. "At least, I hope so. It's sign-shaped. And Luna said she'd sent it express. Paid top dollar so it would get here fast!"

"It's about time," Uncle Roy grumbled. "Been sign-less for months now."

Oliver's grip tightened on the cardboard. He wanted to rip into it, but he didn't want to do it with anyone else around. He didn't know what his response to seeing Luna's work was going to be, but he didn't want to have it in front of these people.

Grandmother arrived next to him. "Don't keep us in suspense. Show us our new sign."

Oliver hesitated. Then he knelt and tore the cardboard off with careful claws. He'd be fine, he assured himself as he sliced through the layer of bubble wrap and yet another layer of cardboard. Whatever he felt, he'd just school his expression into anger. He'd gotten good at that in the past year.

The last of the packing fell away. Oliver held up the sign as the others crowded around it.

Grandmother hummed, squeezing the wood. "Sturdy."

"Won't hold up to another car," Uncle Roy said gruffly.

Beth made a small chirp. "That's so cute! Don't you guys think this is so cute? I'm going to take a photo. Is that okay?"

Grandmother said something. Oliver didn't hear it. Blood rushed through his ears.

It was a wolf sitting in an armchair. A fire roared behind him. The wolf had thick dark eyebrows standing out on his brown fur. His legs were crossed, a party-hat mug raised halfway to his muzzle.

Grandmother's hand on his arm brought him back to himself. "It's you," she said, pleased.

Oliver grunted. His vision was swimming, the roaring in his ears making his head spin. He let out a pained grunt as pressure built in his chest.

Grandmother's voice drifted over him, alarmed. "Oliver?"

Oliver opened his mouth to respond. But a wave of pain rushed through his chest, white-hot and overwhelming.

He fell forward and was unconscious by the time he hit the floor.

Chapter Thirty-Two

Warm sand between her toes. The sun shining on her bare stomach. Exotic food available at all hours, with drinks waiting at the bar.

It was the kind of day Luna would've given anything for two months ago. Now it felt…empty. Her old college friends were down below, playing volleyball on the long patch of sand that would host her wedding tomorrow afternoon. Luna had given her wedding planner a reasonably sized portfolio and told her to go nuts, but she'd still had to sign off on the final decisions. This time tomorrow, the sand would be filled with tasteful yet sturdy white chairs. There would be an archway covered in lace and real flowers, though Luna could no longer remember what kind. Nor could she remember what they were serving, since it had been such a hassle getting everyone's dietary requirements that she just told the chef to go nuts, too.

As long as everybody has a good time, Luna had said, *then I'm happy.*

It was still true. Sort of. But there was still that emptiness as she watched her old college friends giggle and throw a ball around, sleek and picture-perfect in their stylish bikinis.

Clancy fell into the deck chair beside her. "Loser sitting all by herself says what?"

"What? Oh, screw you." Luna leaned over and shoved him. Clancy snorted, feigning falling off the deck chair before settling back into place.

"Seriously," Clancy said, with the irony-soaked tone of a boy who had never been serious in his life. "What are you doing? Hec's over there. Your friends are down there. The bar's back there. And you're over here, all weird and sad. It's the night before your wedding, you should be doing... I don't know. Something. Not sitting on the balcony staring out at the ocean like you're waiting for your long-lost love."

Luna laughed. It came out much more bitter than she'd intended. She twisted her engagement ring, working it up and down over the cut Oliver had given her. She couldn't stop fidgeting with it. At this rate, she was going to open it back up.

Clancy looked nervous. He gave her a hopeful nudge. "Go on and play some volleyball. Everyone flew to Bali to see you."

"Everyone flew to Bali to have a party," Luna replied.

Clancy frowned. "What are you talking about?"

The old Luna would've pulled up a smile. Would've said *Sure, I'll play some volleyball.* Then she would've gotten a drink and made a game out of keeping it in her hand while she played until she inevitably dropped it or had it smacked out of her hand, and she would have made it *fun*. Even if she wasn't having fun when she started, she would've kept at it until it was. Fake it 'til you make it, right?

"I don't know those girls," she admitted. "I know a bookseller in Alaska more than I know any of them. I never asked about their lives, you know? All through college, even after college, I was just...fun times. Any hard topic was solved with a subject change and a Jell-O shot. Then with a margarita and—I don't know—flotation therapy or a seaweed mask."

She pointed at the girls piling on each other after too many dove for the ball at once. They were laughing, clinging to each other.

"*They're* close. I'm just the friend you heart-react to but never talk to. They only came here for a fun party with the fun party girl."

"And you paid for their flights," Clancy added.

Luna smacked him in the arm.

"Ow," Clancy said. "Um, wow. We were kinda hoping you'd go back to normal before the wedding."

"And what if I don't want to?"

"Uh..." Clancy twisted to look behind them. Their parents were sitting under a sun umbrella with Hector, who was holding up a strangely shaped olive for them to examine. Dad was nodding, scratching at his chest. He was still in his sleepshirt, a too-big T-shirt with the Stack's Appliances logo on the front.

"Then you're going to be a real bummer of a bride," Clancy said, turning back toward her. "Seriously, *what* was so good about Claw Haven that it's got you like this?"

Luna lay back in her chair. The evening sun was warm on her skin, her college friends shrieked with laughter down below, and her parents chuckled with her fiancé not far away. And she was longing for a tiny town in Nowhere, Alaska. A town with a terrible cell connection and spotty data service even after she changed providers—where everybody knew each other's business and there wasn't a single spa, frozen yogurt place, or even a mall.

She missed it. She ached for it down to her bones.

"It was...intimate," she said, grimacing even as she said it. "I don't know; don't make that face. People were so down-to-earth. They cared about stuff."

"We care about stuff," Clancy protested.

Luna ignored him. "And they talked about what was going on with them! Even if you had to pry it out of some of them first."

He made a face. "Since when do you *pry*?"

Luna didn't answer. She was too busy thinking about Oliver's scowl finally softening. Of him watching his family bicker at the dinner table, unable to hold back a fond smirk. He'd kissed her forehead sometimes when he thought she was asleep. He had such a big heart. She'd felt it pressed against hers, late at night. Beating in perfect unison with hers. Warming her up in ways she'd never felt before or since.

She sat up and rummaged underneath her deck chair.

Clancy groaned as she pulled out the laptop she had hidden in a blanket. "Come *on*, Lu."

"I'm just checking in," Luna said. "It's my wedding day tomorrow, so you have to let me do what I want."

She clicked on her emails. She had a few more from potential sponsors interested in the buzz she'd been making about the town, but she ignored them to click on the pottery store's latest email.

She beamed. "Oh yay, the plushies arrived! We were so worried. And they're going to do a face painting stall!"

A voice boomed across the deck: "There's that big smile!"

Luna looked up.

Hector was padding toward her, biting that weird olive and tossing the toothpick back into his drink. "What's my girl smiling about, huh?"

He leaned down, kissing her cheek. Luna tried and failed to not think about Oliver's hot arms wrapping around her, his nose brushing hers, and his eyes, which were so dark as he murmured, *You smell like mine.*

"Paint," Luna said, pushing the laptop screen down.

Too late. Hector zeroed in on it and sighed. "Okay. I see emails."

"Wait!" Luna grabbed for it, but Hector was too fast, tossing her laptop back onto the blanket under the chair. "Come on!

It's my prewedding day! You're supposed to let me do whatever I want!"

"And *you're* supposed to want to have fun," he said with an incredulous look. He turned toward the others, raising his arms. "Who wants the bride to put away the emails and have a good time tonight?"

Her friends jumped up and down on the sand, whooping. Her parents let out a half-hearted whoop from their table.

Hector dragged her arm over her head, pulling a twirl out of her. "Live a little, babe. You deserve some fun after the last few months of being stuck in that town."

Luna stilled. He tugged her arm, trying to get her to complete the twirl. He still had that hopeful smile, like he was waiting for her to giggle and pose. For her to roll her eyes fondly and kiss him and run into the sand, her worries forgotten. He still didn't fully believe that she'd had a good time in Claw Haven. He believed she'd had good sex, sure. But she could see the disbelief in his eyes every time she told him how nice it was to do something for the town, even with all the annoying admin work she'd had to learn on the fly. He couldn't believe the nosy townsfolk had grown on her. He nodded blankly and waited for her to bounce back to her old self, ready to party and go on vacations and remodel the house to her heart's content, never delving deeper.

She ripped her hand out of his grip. "I don't just want *fun*," she hissed. "I want to do something; I want to *do* something! Ideally, something that actually *matters*! I can't live like this, party after party and nothing under the surface!"

Hector wavered. Trying to smile, even as he shrank back against her vicious tone. She didn't *do* vicious with him. Just light, breezy fun. He'd only seen her like this a few times, and he'd retreated from her every time.

"I think someone needs a mai tai," he said, turning toward the bar.

She grabbed his shirt, jerking him back to face her. "I don't want a mai tai! And I—and I don't…" She lowered her voice. The others were staring, but they didn't need a full-volume blow-by-blow of what was about to happen. "I don't want to be with a guy who only wants fun and nothing else."

Hector stared at her. His smile shrank, ticking at the edges. Still hopeful that she was joking.

She slid her engagement ring off and pushed it into his hand. He took it, numb and automatic.

"I'm sorry," Luna whispered and stepped past him. She could hear the girls muttering down on the beach, her parents whispering at the table behind their drinks.

"Whoa," Hector said, shoving in front of her. He was still holding the ring. "Wait, you're *serious*?"

Luna badly wanted to shoot him a one-liner and flounce off. But she and Hector had been the perfect couple for a long time. She couldn't leave him like this.

"I'm sorry," she told him. "I just… I need to go."

"To Claw Haven," Hector said disbelievingly. "You seriously want to go *back* there?"

"I'm sorry," Luna repeated. "I wish I could go back to normal, but I can't. I *really* can't."

She stepped around him. There had been a second back at the mud pool that felt chillingly like closing a door, but she hadn't walked through it. Now she was full speed ahead.

"Hey," her dad called behind her. "Hey!"

Luna sighed. She paused and turned back to face her dad, who had gotten up from his seat to chase her.

"What are you doing?" Dad asked. "You can't— This isn't— Your wedding is *tomorrow*."

"Throw a party instead," Luna said icily. "We're good at that."

Dad scoffed. "You're actually leaving? Don't tell me you're going back to that nothing town; they're using you for your money! You won't see a cent from me if you leave, then where will you be?"

Luna laughed back at him so loud that he jumped. "I'm going to be fine, Dad! Wanna know a secret? I've been working for *years*! That logo on your shirt? *I* designed that, and everyone at work *loves* it. I'm good at what I do. And I want to do it there. In Claw Haven, where people care about each other! I don't know if the Musgroves—"

She stopped, pain fluttering through her chest as she thought about those last hugs in the common room. Then her goodbye to Oliver. The way he'd looked at her, right at the end. Like he'd been trying so hard to shut down, to not feel anything, and failing miserably.

"I don't know if they'll want me back," she managed. "But I have to try."

She swallowed and looked up at the deck. Mom gaping at the table, Clancy half risen from the deck chair and staring like she'd grown two heads. Her old college friends whispered behind them. Her dad's face contorted in disbelief, fingers twisting in his own shirt. Hector stood behind him, dazed, his eyes wet.

"I don't understand," Hector croaked. "We were—we were good!"

Luna sighed. Hector *did* have a heart, even if it was shallow.

"It's not you," she told him. "We really were a good match, once. I just… I want more than this."

"Him," Hector said weakly. "You want him."

"Yeah," Luna whispered. "Sorry, babe."

She looked back at her dumbstruck family and fluttered her fingers. "Toodles."

Then she ran out.

Chapter Thirty-Three

The moon was full.

Oliver could feel it pulling at his bones. Wanting him to change. And yet every time he tried, his wolf retreated. It still didn't trust him after what he'd almost let happen to his family back in Arizona. It was closer than it had been in a year, but that didn't stop it from lingering just out of reach.

He groaned, eyes fluttering open. He was lying on his back in the moss, a sleeping bag draped haphazardly over him. It was crumpled from him constantly pulling it on, then shoving it back off as he alternated between blazing hot and icy cold. There was a water bottle balanced on a stump next to him, which got refilled every hour by his helpful, deeply annoying family. Sabine, Leo, Grandmother and Uncle Roy were taking up the night watch, no matter how many times Oliver insisted he was fine and they should go back to the inn.

"So much for being made the alpha tonight," Oliver gritted as he shivered on the ground.

Sabine peered down at him, one hand stroking Leo's hair absently. "Shouldn't he be in bed?"

"No," Grandmother replied from her place on the stump,

right next to the water bottle. "He needs to get in touch with his wolf. Being in the forest will help."

"I don't know," Sabine said in that dubious tone that made Oliver remember she'd grown up in a human family. "He looks pretty sick. This seems like a blankets-and-cocoa situation."

Grandmother shook her head. "Embracing the wolf will help him cure the bond sickness faster."

Oliver shuddered as another icy spasm racked his body. He pulled the sleeping bag tighter over him. Werewolves ran hot. Before the bond, he'd never felt cold so deeply in his life. But he'd never felt so warm either. Lit up from the inside out. He'd probably never feel it again.

A shaft of moonlight fell through the trees and onto his face. The wolf inside him rumbled, trying to rise to the surface. But the moment Oliver tried to reach back, it shrunk away. He could feel its hot breath. It was so *close*.

"It doesn't trust me," he gritted. "I can feel it, goddamnit—it's *right* there. Little bastard."

"Don't call your wolf a bastard," Grandmother said. She offered him the water bottle. He knocked it away, striking out harder than he'd meant to.

Uncle Roy growled, fur sprouting along his neck. "This is a waste of time. Just let him sweat it out, and we can get to running."

"We're not gonna leave him here while we *run*," Leo said, small face twisting in disgust at the concept. "Not 'til later, anyway. It's barely dark!"

"It's the full moon. If he's going to reclaim his wolf, it will be tonight." Grandmother placed the water bottle back beside her on the stump and looked over at Uncle Roy. "Just because *your* wolf didn't return for years doesn't mean your nephew should suffer that same fate."

Uncle Roy growled again, and more fur prickled up his arms. If he ever had a problem summoning his wolf, it was long gone now. If anything, he was having trouble keeping his wolf contained.

Leo squirmed out of his mother's arms and got on the ground next to Oliver, taking a deep breath to scream in his ear, "Go toward the wolf, Uncle Ollie!"

"I'm *trying*," Oliver snapped. He looked up at Sabine pleadingly. "Can we get the kids out of here at least?"

The crack of twigs made him look over. It was Ben, striding through the trees with a wrapped bag of sweet, oily food in one hand and a hedgehog plushie tucked under his arm.

"You heard him," Ben told Leo, nudging him gently with his shoe. "Move it."

Leo pouted but scrambled up. He did a half-hearted jump to try to reach the bag of food, but Ben held it out of reach before relenting and breaking off a piece. Leo took it and scurried into the trees, waving goodbye to his mom as he went.

"Hey bro," Ben said, sitting down on the space Grandmother had cleared for him on the stump. "How's it going?"

"A-awesome," Oliver replied, teeth chattering. He nodded at the oily bag dusted with sugar. "What's that?"

"Churro," Ben said, mouth full. He held up the plushie next, dangling it in Oliver's face. "Hedgehog. Beth's handing them out. Want me to grab you one?"

Oliver batted it away. "No. Is the fair still going?"

"Uh-huh." Ben bent down, wedging the plushie under the blankets with him. "There we go. Have a little buddy."

Oliver thought about throwing the plushie in his face. But Grandmother was right there. Also, he couldn't be bothered lifting his arms.

Ben opened the water bottle meant for Oliver and took a sip. "We should get Luna to come back."

"Go to hell," Oliver croaked.

Ben ignored him and looked over at Grandmother. "It helps when they stick around after, right?"

"She's busy," Sabine said gently, her face so full of sympathy Oliver had to avert his eyes. Everybody had been handling him with kid gloves since Luna left. He'd been getting better at not snapping at them, but it was more difficult when he was weak and shivering on the forest floor.

Ben grunted into the water bottle. "I don't know. I kind of expected her to show up anyway. She could still make the wedding."

Sabine's eyes went wide, gaze darting pointedly to Oliver. He almost wanted to laugh at the ridiculousness of it. He'd been counting down the days with increasing dread. He knew it was the day before the wedding. It had been impossible to think about anything else. He thought about it while he was brushing his teeth, while he was doing paperwork, while he was out for a run or changing guests' beds—Luna in another man's arms, giggling at his jokes, partying up a storm. She was never going to stay. They both knew that. So why did Oliver feel like he'd lost something?

Something flared deep in his chest. An echo, he told himself as the wolf's ears perked up inside him.

"What?" Ben asked as Sabine stared. "He *knows*. Hey Ollie, your ex-bondmate is getting married tomorrow."

"Ben!" Sabine whispered.

Uncle Roy grunted. "No, 's good. He needs to get over it."

"He needs to stop having a fever," Ben corrected. "She could drop by before her honeymoon. Wait, would that make things better or worse? Is it better to go cold turkey?"

"Everybody shut up about Luna!" Oliver shouted.

The forest went silent. Oliver squeezed his eyes shut, trying to focus on anything that wasn't the ghost of warmth in his chest. He'd never feel it again.

"Oliver," Grandmother said.

"Nope," he snapped. He struggled to a sitting position, pushing the sleeping bag and the hedgehog plushie off him. The hot flashes were back, chasing out the chill. They were even more powerful than usual, the heat curling through his chest in a way that was so similar to the bond that Oliver ached.

He gritted his teeth. "Seriously, if one more of you say—"

"Oliver," Grandmother said, voice so tense and urgent that he stopped.

She was staring out into the trees, face slack with shock.

Oliver froze as a familiar scent hit him: jasmine and sage.

Heat pulsed through Oliver's chest, a faint echo that died as soon as it arrived.

He turned.

Luna stood behind him, her blond hair frizzing around her shoulders. She wore a puffer jacket and smelled like sweat and airports, but mostly, she smelled like the flowers he'd come to associate with her.

Another echo of warmth pulsed through his chest before dying. The bond was gone. But Luna was here. She was *here*, staring at him with the smallest smile on her pink lips. She looked uncertain. Like she wasn't sure if he wanted her there.

"Luna," Oliver breathed.

Luna's smile grew. "Hi."

A growl ripped through the forest, making everyone jolt. Uncle Roy was curled over, shaking hard. His teeth formed into huge fangs, fur rushing out to cover every inch of his face except the old burn scar. That stayed bare and gnarled, every single time.

"Sh-she can't," he choked, slurring through his half-transformed mouth. "I won't—won't let—"

"Hey, whoa," Ben said, surging up with his hands raised peacefully. "Cool down, Uncle. Nobody wants to hurt us."

Uncle Roy shook his head. It twitched, ears shooting up toward his scalp, bones shifting under his skin. He let loose another growl and fell to his hands and knees, which were growing longer and hairier.

"He's losing control," Sabine warned. She started growing fangs, fur sprouting over her cheeks. Ben started shifting with her, but Oliver barely noticed. Everything in him screamed to get between Luna and the threat.

He shoved himself up on shaky arms. "Uncle, don't."

"Roy," Grandmother said, sharper than Oliver had ever heard it. A tail sprouted from underneath her skirt. "Stand *down*."

Uncle Roy arched, his fingers turning into paws. The transformation was complete. His head snapped up, eyes flashing on Luna. There was no human left in them. Just wolf. Primal and snarling and scared, ready to pounce.

"Uncle," Oliver yelled. "Don't!"

Uncle Roy leaped.

Oliver surged up. The only sound that existed was Luna's yelp.

There was no slow change, like with Ben and Sabine, and even Grandmother, stumbling after them on half-formed paws. The wolf burst out of Oliver as if it had never left, the world coming alive around him in a way it hadn't in over a year. Oliver didn't see anything but Luna, who had her feet planted even as she trembled.

He raced forward, barreling into Uncle Roy and shoving him into a tree. Uncle Roy snarled and snapped, but Oliver was already climbing off him. He darted to Luna and curled around her, baring his teeth.

"*Safe*," he rumbled, slurring around his fangs. "Don't hurt pack. Safe. *Mine*."

Uncle Roy snarled. But Ben and Sabine were there, and Grandmother, who limped up to fix him with a stare that made Oliver's tail twitch.

Uncle Roy's ears flattened against his head. He gave another weak growl, but Grandmother nipped his flattened ear, and the growl turned into a whine.

Luna's breath hitched. She'd never seen him like this, Oliver remembered as he twisted to look at her.

For a second, Luna looked uncertain. Then her face split into a wondrous smile.

"Hi," she whispered. Her hand sank into Oliver's fur, right at the back of his neck.

Oliver shuddered as the rightness of it filled him up. His wolf was back, Luna was back—he felt complete. Like a puzzle piece finally clicking into place.

Luna yanked her hand back. "Oh no, sorry!"

"No," Oliver replied, still slurring through a mouth not made for speech. "'S good."

He nosed at her wrist, licking the warm skin. Then he paused. There was no wedding ring on her finger. Not even an engagement ring.

He couldn't think properly like this. He closed his eyes and reached down inside him, pulling the human back. When he opened his eyes, he was looking down at Luna, his clothes in tatters.

Oliver swallowed. "Don't you have somewhere to be?"

"I do." Luna hesitated. Then she laid a hand over his chest, skin exposed by his ripped shirt. "Here. With you."

Behind them, his family was nudging Uncle Roy farther into the woods. Uncle Roy let out an irritated yip but let it happen.

"How long?" Oliver asked.

"Um," Luna said, cheeks flushed. "As long as you let me?"

A howl echoed through the trees, loud and joyous. Another one joined it. All over town, the pack would know. The aunts would head back, kids in tow. Time to run.

Luna laughed, startled. "Do you want to go with them? It's been a while."

She started to drop her hand. He caught it, pressing it back to his chest. Her hand was cool, but it was warming up fast.

"Later," he said. "I need to get changed. There's a fair in town. Want to come with me?"

Luna grinned. "Love to."

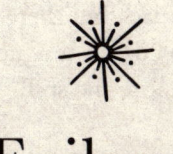

Epilogue

One Year Later

Luna sprawled back on the bed, fingers drumming on the fine beading of her wedding dress.

"Almond," she instructed.

Sabine leaned over and dropped a chocolate-covered almond into her open mouth. They'd started this when Luna's nails were wet. They were desert dry now, but Sabine kept offering, and who was Luna to turn down hand-fed almonds?

"Thanks." Luna crunched the almond, letting out a happy sigh. "God, Beth cracked the jackpot with these. I want to eat nothing but Prickles chocolate almonds for the rest of my life."

"I'm sure Beth can arrange something," Sabine said.

The bathroom door opened and Luna twisted to watch Vi Harper walk out, brushing down her dress. The wine spill from the prewedding appetizers hadn't come out, but they had found a cute bow to pin in front of the stain.

"Thank you again," Vi told Luna. "I shouldn't have even asked, it's your *wedding* day. You have bigger things to deal with than Nick Wicker being his usual oafish self."

Luna giggled and traded a look with Sabine, who looked

just as amused as she did. For all Vi's book smarts, she was still oblivious to Nick being completely gone on her.

"Anyway, I should get back out there before Chester insults someone else," Vi continued, her tongue looser from the wine she had been drinking before the spill. "Thanks again, Luna. You look incredible."

"Thank youuu," Luna drawled, waving her next chocolate almond until the door closed behind her. She sighed, crunching the chocolate almond and looking back over at Sabine. "She *has* to figure it out sometime. Right?"

"I don't want to be there when she does," Sabine admitted. "Nick's a good guy, but he puts his foot in his mouth every time he sees her. I don't blame her for hating him."

"I just want him to *admit* it," Luna said. "*And* I want him to admit what the hell was going on with the flour. You know he still won't tell me? And on my *wedding* day."

The door creaked open, and Luna's dad poked his head in, clearing his throat.

"It's time," he said. "I'm supposed to, uh…"

He motioned stiffly with his elbow.

"Showtime," Luna said and beamed. She kissed Sabine on the cheek, still chewing. Then she heaved herself up, wedding dress clouding around her heels, and twined her arm in her dad's.

"I still think you could've done this somewhere fancier," he told her as they headed into the woods, Sabine scouting ahead. "A *forest* wedding? Seriously?"

"It's romantic," she insisted. "And it's a werewolf tradition!"

"It's right next to the inn! It's practically a backyard wedding," he replied, face twisting. Then he looked over at her, and his expression smoothed out. He'd been making an effort to be more openly supportive since they reconciled.

"But I'm glad you could finally fit this into your schedule.

You've been working so hard on this town, it's about time you get something to yourself."

"Thanks, Dad," Luna said, touched.

She didn't mention the bigger reason why it had taken a year to get married. Work was one reason. But the main reason was so she and Oliver could be together without the bond influencing them. One year later, they were more in love than ever, no bond required. But they were relieved to be finally getting it back. Luna couldn't wait to feel Oliver's relief for herself. She missed his emotions flooding over her, and they would be much more powerful now neither of them were holding back.

He squeezed her arm. "You look beautiful."

Luna preened. "I know."

For a moment, the only noise was Luna's heels clicking against the wheelchair route into the forest. The wedding path was for the mer guests and of course for Grandmother Musgrove, who had been primarily using a wheelchair for eight months now, just a few days after she passed the mantle of alpha over to Oliver.

Chatter drifted through the trees. The quiet tune of a harp played over Bluetooth speakers. Luna's dad blew out a panicked breath as the chairs came into view.

"You're not going to turn," he said, rushed. "Right?"

Luna laughed. "Dad! I *told* you, just because I'm getting bonded-slash-married to a werewolf doesn't mean I'm going to take the bite. I like being human."

"Okay," her dad said, relieved. "Good."

She nudged him. "Don't say that in front of them, alright?"

He frowned. "Why? What'd I say?"

The chatter died as they emerged through the trees, everyone turning to watch Luna walk down the aisle. It was a long walk—half of Claw Haven had shown up. Vi waved with one hand, straightening her hair ribbon with the other. Beth was openly sobbing, tears rolling into her fur. Jackson rubbed one of her arms, wings tucked tight behind him. Rubbing Beth's other arm was Joshua the minotaur, a bright red rose in his lap and fur hanging over his eyes as always. Next to him was Nick Wicker, wearing a bulging button-down that for once wasn't smudged with engine oil, looking deeply awkward as Beth sobbed with joy. The Musgroves were crammed into the front row, the younger kids shoving and hissing for each other to be quiet. Uncle Roy sent them a steely stare, which grudgingly softened as he looked back at Luna. He gave her an awkward nod, and she returned it gladly. That fateful full moon had been a turning point for Uncle Roy, who had been shaken that he'd almost harmed someone in his wolf form. It led to a grudging apology, which—after a lot of coaxing and well-meaning threatening from Oliver—involved telling Luna all about his ex-wife, Georgia. Things had improved from there. Nowadays they could even have a conversation without Uncle Roy rolling his eyes.

A flash of movement caught her eye, and Luna turned to see Hector squeezing into a row on the other side of the aisle. He grinned when she met his eyes. He doffed an imaginary hat, and she doffed one back. The Musgroves had been confused by her decision to invite him, but Luna had felt it was only right. It was surprisingly good to see him. Like meeting a friend you knew back when you were a very different person.

Luna's side of the aisle would have been emptier—Hector, her mother, brother, and three of her college friends who had shown up on their own dime and were giggling excitedly in their seats—but they'd run out of room on the Musgrove side, so they'd packed more of Claw Haven behind Luna's gang.

Luna gave her family a fond look. They had come around quickly after seeing how stupidly happy she was in the new and improved Claw Haven. It helped that when the Stacks came to visit, everyone in town said hello as they passed. Her dad had even grudgingly admitted he was proud of her on her last birthday, which had made Luna duck out of her own party and cry in Oliver's arms before fixing her makeup and striding coolly back inside.

Clancy was currently flirting with a blushing orc, only stopping when their mother grabbed his chin and forced him to look in Luna's direction.

Clancy grinned sheepishly, then mouthed *Eaten in monster country*, something he'd never let go of since she'd announced she was moving to Claw Haven for good.

Luna rolled her eyes. Then she turned to look down the path.

Grandmother Musgrove waited at the end, smiling proudly from her wheelchair. The bond nectar sat in her lap, the blue bottle draped in bright wildflowers and drizzled in sweet oils. Sabine stood to her right, looking like it took physical effort not to close the distance and nuzzle Ben, who stood to Grandmother Musgrove's left.

And in the middle of all of them, grinning in a way she'd once thought him incapable of, was Oliver.

Luna's dad squeezed her arm again, then went to take his seat. Luna hardly noticed. Her gaze was locked on her future husband.

"Hi," Oliver whispered as she took her place beside him. "You look good."

She giggled. "Just *good*? That's all you got?"

"There's more," he reassured her. "Just not in front of my family."

Grandmother Musgrove held up the bond nectar. "Officially, the bonding ceremony is officiated by the alpha. But you two have done things unconventionally so far; why not keep it going?"

She held the bottle out. Luna took it, her fingers overlapping with Oliver's. Oil dripped down her wrist.

"The bonded pair will pour the nectar into each other's

mouths," Grandmother Musgrove recited. "Solidifying their bond. Do you have anything to say before you are bonded?"

Oliver tugged on the bottle, bringing Luna closer. For a moment, she forgot about everyone watching them, only able to focus on those big dark eyes staring at her so tenderly.

"I was in a bad place when I met you," Oliver began. "My family tried to pull me out. Everybody did. Nothing worked. Then you showed up. I thought getting stuck with you was the worst thing that could've happened. But I needed it. I needed *you*. I've been looking for you forever, and I'm never going to let you go."

Luna sniffed. Oliver raised his dark brows as if to say, *top that*.

Luna laughed wetly. "My life has been so different since I met you. *I'm* different. I'm so glad I got stuck with you. I want to be stuck with you for the rest of my life."

She raised the bottle to Oliver's lips. He drank deeply, then lifted it to hers.

Warm liquid poured down Luna's throat. She pulled the bottle back, gasping as the warmth collected in a tiny coil in her chest. There was no gradual trickle like last time. Oliver's feelings flooded into her, disbelief and delight and relief and *love*, so overwhelming that Luna's eyes pricked.

"I now pronounce you bondmates," Grandmother Musgrove said.

Luna barely heard it. She was surrounded by Oliver's love, cradled and held by it, a hot rush she was feeding right back to him.

He nosed at her cheek. "I missed you."

"I've been right here," she whispered.

He brushed a petal off her chin. "I missed you, anyway."

"Well. You'll never have to miss me again." Luna flung her arms around his neck, kissing the nectar off his lips. She was crying when she pulled back, grinning so hard her mouth hurt.

She turned to the crowd. "Let's get this party *started*!"

The crowd cheered. Luna dragged Oliver in close again, sinking into his arms with a grateful sigh.

Finally warm.

★ ★ ★ ★ ★

Special Thanks

Thank you for reading *Accidentally Wedded to a Werewolf*! If you loved Claw Haven, be sure to pick up *Christmas with a Chimera*, a Claw Haven novella!

Get exciting author updates on new releases, freebies and sales by signing up to my newsletter at isabelletaylorauthor.com.

You can find me on TikTok and Instagram: @isabelletaylorauthor.

Acknowledgments

First off, I'd like to give a big wet cheek kiss to all of my amazing Kickstarter backers who funded the indie release of this book before Harlequin picked it up—you guys are the OGs! Let's go down the list:

Heidi Havelin, Sabrina Nguyen, Cat Langford, Rachael Herron, Zelda Hartland Author, John Callahan, Kenzie, Jenny Y., Phoenix, A. Martinez, Cristal and Flavio Juarez Lopez, Franchesca Caram, Caitlin Millsaps, EJ McFadden, Dina, Marie Cardno, Lisa Millraney, Nikki T., Elisha Padilla, Sadie, Faith Dam, Cristen, Serena Sharber, Eriko, Michael Anthony, Zee Smith, Angel G., Samantha Newberry, Honour, GrammaToni McConnell, Melanie Rios, PunkARTchick "Ruthenia", Valerie Laing, Christina Logan, Natasha Tucker, Holta, Giuliana M., Chanel Holm, JabberwockyStories/Kristina, Hannah S., Kari Parks, Shauna Hadinger, Tessa Barnes, Stephanie Burgis, Kali D., Isis Q., Julie, Monica Kim, Xan Dawson, Anonymous.

And now let's hear it for the Harlequin publishing team!

The editorial team, Stephanie Doig and Eugénie Szwalek. The marketing team, Maya Price-Baker and Shana Mongroo.

PR/publicity, Shannon Dales. And of course our cover artist, Magen McCallum. And a shout-out to the production team! You guys rock!